OF TRUTHS & BONDS

HIS ONLY OPTION WAS SUCCESS

ZAVI JAMES

This is a work of fiction. Names, characters, places and incidents either are a product of the author's imagination or are used fictitiously. Any resemblance to actual persons, living or dead, events or locales is entirely coincidental.

Copyright © 2022 by Zavi James

All rights reserved. No part of this book may be reproduced or used in any manner without written permission of the copyright owner except for the use of quotations in reviews.

Cover design by Books and Moods
Interior formatting by Books and Moods
Editing by Heart Full of Reads Editing Services

ISBN 978-1-9169030-6-7 (paperback)
ISBN 978-1-9169030-5-0 (ebook)

Published by Zavi James
www.zavijames.com

Trigger Warnings

This series contains topics that some may find triggering. These include but are not limited to sexually explicit scenes, graphic violence, infidelity, death, discussion of suicide and sexual assault.

If you are uncomfortable with reading these situations, then the Elysian Gods series may not be for you.

Reader discretion is advised.

To those who feel like they are judged because they can't keep their head above water—they do not know your story or what you battle every day. Your strength knows no bounds. Keep fighting. This is for you.

A LIST OF NOTABLE GODS FEATURED IN OF TRUTHS & BONDS

ELITE GODS

Hunter – God of protection and forgiveness

Larkin – Goddess of strength

Grayson – God of chaos and destruction

Erik – God of love and desire

Sloan – Goddess of fertility

Ignacio – God of luck and opportunity

Elva – Goddess of death

Bexley – Goddess of knowledge

Malachi – God of patience

Waverly – Goddess of rest

Flynn – God of travels

Aria – Goddess of health

MINOR GODS

Archer – God of secrets and deception

Dionne – Goddess of dreams

Tobias – God of agriculture

Marcel – God of stars

Andreas – God of war

Mabel – Goddess of vanity

ONE

GRAYSON

One side of my face was pressed against the plush carpet of Erik's living room, the fibres grating against my skin, while the sole of Ignacio's shoe crushed my exposed cheek. Vibrant auras expanded in the space, illuminating it as they ensnared my body, keeping me pinned to the ground as I struggled.

"You'll make it worse, brother. You need to calm down," Erik pleaded.

He sat on his knees beside me, his bright blue eyes wide, saying a thousand things that he refused to vocalise. I would have dared him, any of them, to say what they were truly thinking. To face the truths that I accepted the moment they ripped Quentin from me.

"I don't trust him," I gritted out through my teeth. Any more pressure and they'd be at risk of shattering. "I should have stopped him!"

Ig's shoe pressed harder against my cheek until the pain blossomed across my cheekbone and up to my temple, adding to the thrum that already pulsated there. His body loomed over mine, casting a long shadow as I writhed against the floor. My aura was useless against

the four others in the room that bound me in position. The slightest leverage was easily overturned, causing my blood to boil until I was certain it would burst from my veins, spilling pure, unadulterated chaos through the house and beyond. There would be no survivors and no mercy.

"But you didn't," Ig informed me bluntly, leaning in closer. "Because you knew what it would do. For once, we're not doing as you say. For once, we need to use some logic because otherwise she's going to wind up dead."

Logic was a fine thing if you possessed it.

Rationale was wondrous if you had the control to apply it.

But how could they expect those from me when my soulbound had been forced away with my psychotic brother who made it clear he wanted her dead?

A heavy knock on the door forced heads to look up, but Ig refused to relent. We'd known each other for too long and fought each other too often for him to give me an advantage by turning his attention away from me. The usual admiration I would have at facing a worthy adversary withered into irritation under the circumstances.

"I don't trust him not to go against the vote," I spat, wanting them to understand my concerns.

"He won't—" Sloan started.

"You can't guarantee that!" I shouted, cutting her off. My disrespect caused Erik to tense beside me.

"No, but I can," a silky female voice cut through the argument.

This time, Ig's foot faltered, and I twisted my head, tipping it back to see Bexley standing in the doorway. Beckett, Erik's eldest son, stood next to her, gaze bouncing along each face in the room.

"Beckett," Sloan said softly, maternal instinct dripping from her son's name. "Go look after your brothers and sister. We'll explain later."

He looked from his mother to me, and I swallowed hard. My godchildren had never been on the receiving end of my wrath, and I refused to start now.

"Do as your mother says," I told him, pushing down on the tornado of emotions that raged in my chest.

Beckett nodded before disappearing soundlessly.

"An entire planet, and you find the only demigoddess that survives," Bexley stated, folding her arms across her chest and leaning casually against the doorframe.

She had the same bone structure and blonde locks as her older sister, but unlike Larkin, Bexley possessed a friendlier disposition. I was yet to discover whether she was born with it or if it was acquired after years of watching her ice queen sibling and the tactics she deployed. Correcting herself to appear more palatable after witnessing the reception Larkin received. No one could blame her for wanting to craft herself in anything other than her sister's image.

"I didn't exactly go looking for her, Bexley," I said, words sharp and failing to match her teasing tone.

She remained unaffected by my attitude as she continued, "No. Chaos just seems to find you, doesn't it?"

"Why are you here?" I asked, narrowing my eyes and trying to ignore the block of lead that settled in my stomach.

Bexley never sought us out unless it was a family function. She kept to herself, preferring to descend into lower Elysia and spend her days with minor Gods. If Bexley turned up here, she must have been sent, and that meant news. It was pathetic how even a crumb of knowledge about Quentin felt capable of dousing some of the rage that roared through my body.

"Curiosity." She pushed herself away from the door and stepped towards us. "I tried your place first, but there was no answer. Now I see why." Her arms swept out, signalling the display on the floor. "But I don't understand it."

"There's nothing to understand," Ig replied with an indignant sniff.

That fucker may have had his foot against my face for the last thirty minutes, but his loyalty ran deep.

"Grayson's pinned to the floor, and none of you have eased this bizarre hostage situation to display good old-fashioned Elysian hospitality," Bexley commented, tucking a strand of her bob behind her ear. "Why are you so desperate to see her, Grayson? Why didn't you report her?"

My fingers flexed at my sides. I'd never really been able to decipher where things stood between me and Bexley. Sometimes she fell into step easily with me and Erik, just as irritated by Hunter and his antics. But it was clear to see that her true alliance stood with her sister and that made her something dangerous in my eyes.

"I couldn't," I snapped, unwilling to give her anymore.

Auras might have been able to restrain me, but my temper continued to flare, pushing wildly against my form and spilling words that should have been locked away.

"Why not?" she asked, cocking her head.

Bexley's responsibility was knowledge. She was like a dog with a fucking bone. It irritated her not to know the answers to questions.

In another universe, she would have been a good friend to Quentin. As it stood, I'd never allow Bexley to come near her. No one would be allowed to touch her or even look at her when she was back by my side.

"Trust her," Erik muttered, unwinding his aura from my body.

"Are you insane?" I asked, finally sitting up.

"Maybe we should leave," Elva muttered, looking at Ig.

He glanced at me. "Do you need backup?"

I shook my head, appreciating the support, but knowing that I'd be capable of handling Bexley. Ig would want to take Elva away from the uncomfortable situation. As difficult as it was for me knowing that my soulbound's life was on the line, Elva struggled with the harsh reality that someone could rip away her flesh and blood without ever having the chance to know her beyond a single dinner together.

"If you need anything, you know where to find us," Ignacio said.

A warm orange glow filled the room as he wrapped his aura around Elva and they both left us.

"What are you planning, Grayson?" Bexley's curiosity echoed in the room. "I thought you both hated each other, but you're voting to keep her alive."

"So did you," I reminded her, rising to my feet.

It was the first time I'd seen Bexley and Larkin falling on opposite sides of an argument. Where one went, the other followed. That was their dynamic. In the chambers, I'd barely given it a thought, but now I wondered why Bexley opted to save Quen.

"I'm curious." She brushed her palms down her skirt. "Do you know how long it's been since we've had a demigod?"

There was more to it than that. Her links to lower Elysia drove her inquisitive nature.

My jaw tightened. "She's not a test subject."

"Enlighten me, Grayson. What is she?"

"Trust her," Erik repeated from over my shoulder.

"And if she betrays us?" I snapped.

"What other option do we have? She voted to keep Quentin alive, and we need someone who can tell us what Hunter is doing."

It was a risk to tell Bexley the truth, but I was struggling to find a way out of our predicament. She wouldn't leave it alone and I didn't need to keep shaking her off when my efforts were better put towards bringing Quen back home where she belonged.

I stared at Bexley for a few moments. "There will be nowhere in Elysia that you can hide if I find out that this went further than these four walls."

"This better be good. The way you're all talking—"

"She's my soulbound. If I hadn't brought her here to be gifted, she would have died. I wanted to save her, Bexley. I had to save her."

Her mouth opened, features warping from shock to composure. "Wow. Well…"

"If you all don't mind, I'm going to make sure my idiot brother and your psychotic sister don't murder her in her sleep."

The last crumb of calmness that resided in the recesses of my being finally evaporated, and I leant into the darkness that pooled inside me until it became impossible to ignore.

I went to push past, but Bexley caught my arm, fingers gripping tightly. I barely registered the pressure.

"You go in there with this attitude and they'll realise something isn't right. If they find out she means anything to you, you know they won't hesitate to use it. Let me go. I'll say I'm there for Larkin if I have to, and I can make sure she's okay."

"Why?" Suspicion crept through my veins as I stared down at her. "Why would you do this?"

Her brown eyes met mine, hardened and flickering towards the coral colour of her aura. Something was unsettling her.

"I have never liked Hunter," Bexley said, voice low and deadly. "He's always treated my sister like shit and she's put up with more than she needs to or deserved. I won't let him destroy someone else."

Whether she meant me or Quentin, I wasn't certain, but despite my mistrust, I nodded.

Bexley released my arm. "Do you want me to tell Quentin anything?"

"Tell her—" I started, but caught Erik looking at me and changed my mind. "Tell her not to worry."

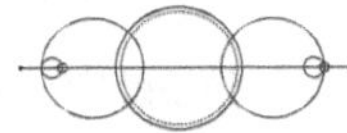

"It was a mistake to trust her." I seethed, dragging a brush through Tenley's pale blonde hair.

Erik and Sloan found my only other weakness and weaponised it. The moment Bexley left us, my godchildren descended on me, uninhibited with the weight of politics and unencumbered by life and death decisions. The sharp edge of my temper dulled in order to keep them entertained.

"You don't know that," Sloan replied, ever the diplomat.

"It's been hours."

My niece turned around and frowned at me. "Pigtails," she demanded.

"Manners, Tenley," I replied curtly. They could get away with murder in my eyes, but Sloan and Erik had certain things they wanted to enforce, and manners were one of them.

"Pigtails, *please*, Uncle Gray."

I gently directed her away from me again and parted the hair down the middle of her head. Tenley was still tiny and under her parents' watchful eyes. I was forced to be softer than my soul desired, pulling her hair up and wrapping a hair tie around the strands.

As the clock ticked through the minutes steadily, the sense of dread continued to grow until I felt I'd made the biggest mistake of listening to those around me. Erik sensed a degree of fondness from Bexley towards us, leading to his request for trust. I should have gone with my usual cynical view of beings and relied only on myself.

I shot to my feet with Tenley in my arms when there was a knock at the door. Erik was already pulling it open when I reached the entrance hall and Bexley stepped over the threshold.

"What took you so long?" I barked. "What have they been doing?"

"I didn't see her," Bexley told me. "Larkin was suspicious. I didn't want to push my luck."

A worried-looking Sloan took Tenley out of my arms. Without the calming influence that my godchildren bestowed on me, I finally unleashed my chaotic nature. Smoky tendrils shot towards Bexley at an alarming rate, wrapping around her waist and pulling her to me. One gripped her jaw and another lifted her from the ground, forcing her to look me in the eye.

"Grayson," Erik warned me quietly. "My household is not one for force. Especially not in front of my children."

In the distance, I heard Sloan's footsteps retreating as she muttered softly to Tenley. I would need to apologise to my niece later for being the big, wicked uncle.

"I trusted you because Erik told me to," I hissed. "Don't make me regret it, Bexley, because I will make your existence a nightmare."

"I pity her," Bexley spat back. "Imagine being bound to the likes of you."

"Enough!" Erik shouted. "Put her down and let's hear what she has to say."

Grudgingly, I lowered her to the ground, but refused to remove my aura from around her.

"Talk!" I commanded.

"Larkin didn't want her at the house," Bexley explained. "You know what she's like."

"Less than accommodating unless it benefits her," I replied. "Tough shit because they're stuck with her."

"They aren't."

My blood ran cold. I could already sense where the conversation was going, but I didn't want confirmation. There were few places Quentin could be if she was no longer with Hunter and not with one of us. He wouldn't return her back to Earth when she couldn't control herself. That left one other place…

"She isn't with Hunter and Larkin?" Erik asked.

"Not anymore," Bexley said, turning her head to look at my brother.

"Then where the fuck is she?" I asked calmly, but the entrance hall grew darker as my aura spanned out around us, engulfing any light.

"Archer took her to lower Elysia," Bexley answered quickly.

"*Have you lost your mind?*" I roared.

"I told Dionne to keep an eye on her." She choked on the words as my grip on her tightened.

"You think I'd trust your girlfriend? You think she'll be of any use against Archer?"

"What other choice do we have?" Erik said. "We can't go down there and force her back to us."

"Why not?" I snapped, already planning a way to bring her back.

"You're not that stupid. It's one thing to fight Hunter. Archer will figure it out quicker. Secrets are his territory. Be grateful he won't be able to read her without consent."

"Her gift—"

"I told Dionne to get to her before she can tell him," Bexley croaked.

"If anything happens to her, I will hold you and your girlfriend personally responsible," I hissed, releasing Bexley from my grip forcefully so that she landed in a heap on the floor. "Now, get out."

TWO

QUENTIN

Deep green so thick I felt like I was suffocating, dissipated away, revealing a beautiful and sprawling garden hosting rows upon rows of yellow tulips. If I wasn't concerned about how my life laid in the hands of volatile and vicious Gods, I might have asked to walk between them and brush my fingers along the petals. I craved an act so frivolous and mindless.

"Welcome home," Archer said, voice close to my ear.

It was a phrase laced with so much affection that it dripped from him with saccharine sweetness. But the words were abrasive, travelling down my ear canal and violently crashing against my eardrum. They burrowed under my skin, leaving me with an uncomfortable sensation that made me want to claw into my dermis and release them back into the wild.

Home.

It was a place I registered with safety and family. It was where I returned after a long day in the lab to shut the world out and recover.

Archer's fingers were still wrapped around my forearm, brushing against one of the copper cuffs he placed on me as I swayed, bones

suddenly becoming jelly. His grip tightened to keep me steady, and I took a deep breath through my nose.

Freshly cut grass. The scent should have been comforting and brought to mind well spent summers, but it was wrong. I wanted something earthier. Something more familiar and chaotic.

"I thought you might prefer it out here," he said, cautiously letting go of my arm. "I don't want you to feel you're trapped."

"But I am," I said, finding my voice. It was still hoarse from crying.

"Would you like to walk?" Archer offered brightly, falling back on how we used to spend time together.

"No."

He cast me a look before nodding and guiding me towards a swinging bench that was placed near the back of his home. Holding it still, Archer allowed me to settle first before taking a seat beside me. He sat a fraction too close, the heat of his body radiating next to mine, and the smallest twitch of his fingers causing our skin to meet.

"I understand this must be overwhelming for you," he said, looking out ahead at the rows of flowers. Their heads swayed in the breeze, giving the appearance of a dance. "You are surrounded by those you thought you could trust and they've led you into a potentially fatal situation."

Saliva filled my mouth as sourness puckered my tastebuds. There was still too much to process. Too much to understand, and I didn't know where to start. My body had triggered every mechanism that warranted me to flee, but there was nowhere to go.

So, I panicked. My lungs burnt as I tried to take in enough air. Each breath was shallow despite how much effort I placed behind it. My mouth grew numb and my body trembled with the adrenaline that shot through my vessels. A pain radiated in my chest and a pathetic whimper escaped my lips.

Archer moved, kneeling in front of me. "You need to breathe."

"I can't," I rasped.

"You can. You're capable of more than you know." His hands squeezed mine, and I returned it, digging my nails into his flesh just to feel something. "In through your nose and out through your mouth."

As Archer exaggerated his breathing, I copied the best I could. I wasn't sure how long we sat like that, me clinging to him as he calmed me down. When my breathing evened and he tried to move, I gripped onto him tightly, terrified that the moment I let go of him, I would spiral again.

"Quentin," he said, an essence of amusement in his tone that I didn't appreciate. "I'm just coming to sit next to you."

I was too exhausted to feel embarrassed and hesitantly loosened my hold on his hands. Archer rose in one fluid movement and sat beside me again. His weight pushed the bench, causing it to swing. The repetitive motion brought a sense of calm, forcing my heart to mimic the rhythm.

"What happens next?" I asked quietly, needing answers.

"You'll stay here with me. I'll teach you how to control your aura."

"What about my brother? My job?"

"We'll deal with it, but going back to Earth isn't an option until you know how to keep your powers under control. It poses too great a risk."

"He's going to kill me before I get the chance to go back down there," I whispered, finally admitting the truth out loud.

"I won't allow it," Archer replied, a steely edge in his voice. "The council voted, and he doesn't have a majority."

"Does it matter?"

Voicing my concerns brought another dimension to my panic. Since being pulled from the pool, I'd seen a different side to Hunter. The calm and collected God that stood in my kitchen and healed the damage Grayson inflicted had been replaced with an icy deity that needed everything to run the way he saw fit. Protecting himself, what he'd built and what he stood for, outweighed anything else.

I would do anything to go back to being an inconsequential speck instead of a glaring error in his master plan.

"Try not to worry about him," Archer said, turning his head towards me. A smile stretched across his features, dimples forming in his cheeks and making him look younger. "You should celebrate, Quentin. A demigoddess."

He said it with such reverie that I wanted to shake him. Did he understand the magnitude of my situation? It was fine for Archer to romanticise what I was and behave like I was some lost princess being brought home, but the reality was far from the fairy-tale he appeared to be concocting.

His fingers brushed across my hairline, and I pulled away. There was nothing to celebrate. No reason to be overjoyed by the news.

"I wish I'd been there," he continued, oblivious to my discomfort. Or maybe he didn't care. "What was it you were gif—"

"Archer!" A voice rang clear from inside his home.

Archer's face fell before he fixed the smile back in place. It was forced, dimples hidden away and masking his irritation at the interruption.

"Archer," the voice called again, closer this time.

I craned my neck towards the doors that led back into the house to see a tall woman scanning the grounds. Her skin was dark and her raven hair was twisted into dozens of thin braids that hung down to her waist.

"There you are," she said, spotting us and flashing perfect white teeth.

"Dionne," Archer gritted out, refusing to move from his position. "It's polite to knock."

"When have I ever needed to be polite with you?" Dionne quipped before setting her dark gaze on me. "You must be our latest addition."

Archer rose from his seat, stepping in front of me so that he hid me from view.

"I see Bexley couldn't keep her mouth shut," he commented tightly.

"There are no secrets between us," Dionne replied.

Archer clucked his tongue knowingly. "We both know that's not true."

The comment hung in the air, wiping away the ease both of them held and leaving me curious to what Archer was alluding to.

"I thought it would be good for her," Dionne said eventually, jerking her chin towards me, "to have a female contact down here. I bought her some clothes and other things she might need."

"How kind." Archer's words were anything but grateful.

"Thank you," I said, struggling to get up from the bench while my hands were cuffed in front of me. "I think I'd appreciate a shower and a change of clothes."

Anything to cut the tension. I'd caused so many arguments that my stomach soured at the thought of causing another.

A shower always calmed me, and as ridiculous as it seemed, I wanted to employ the tactic and have a sliver of normality.

Archer looked at me over his shoulder. "Of course. I'll show you to your room."

The three of us walked into the manor. Archer's home was vast, just like the others I'd visited in Elysia. The accent colour was the same forest green as his aura, but there were touches of blush pink that made me curious about who else lived there. Delicate touches to the decor made it hard to believe this was solely Archer's abode.

We climbed two flights of stairs; Archer leading the way and Dionne behind me. The formation did nothing to ease my concerns about being imprisoned here. He stopped in front of a door and pushed it open before walking inside. Turning to face me, he spread out his arms.

"I hope it'll suffice," he said, playing the role of humble host.

The room was larger than my living room—a beautiful mixture of green and white. A four-poster bed stood by the wall along with a dresser and vanity.

Archer stepped towards me, pulling a key out of his pocket. I jerked my hands back, and he frowned.

"I didn't think you'd appreciate me helping you shower," he commented, arching an eyebrow.

"I can help her," Dionne snapped. "Get out and give us some privacy."

Archer's eye twitched, but he pocketed the key and shrugged. "I'll be downstairs when you're done. Don't dawdle, Dionne. I have matters that need to be discussed with Quentin. I'd appreciate some privacy in my home."

He brushed past us as he left the room, and Dionne ushered me inside before shutting the door. I opened my mouth to talk, but she put a slender black finger against her lips and pointed to another door in the room.

My shoes sunk into the plush carpet with every step I took. Dionne reached around me and opened the door to reveal a bathroom, and we stepped inside. She immediately turned on the shower, water hitting the tiles so violently that it bounced away from the floor and filled the room with noise as steam flooded the space.

"Does he know what your gift is?" Dionne asked, rounding on me.

The move was so sudden that I stepped back, bumping into the sink and wishing I'd let Archer undo the cuffs so I could protect myself. My eyes widened as I shook my head. "No. I don't think so. He was about to ask me about it when you arrived."

She let out a shuddering breath, straightening her spine and towering over me. "Don't tell him. Keep it a well-guarded secret."

"He'll know I'm lying. It's his responsibility."

"You're not fully mortal anymore. His intuition might lead him, but he won't be able to read you. If he asks, you need to lie and say they never told you what it is."

"Who are you?" I asked, narrowing my eyes. "Why should I listen to you?"

"Because if you don't, you might end up in a worse position."

The statement was ridiculous, and delirious laughter left my lips. "I have twelve Gods currently deciding if I should live or not. How the fuck could it get any worse?"

"I'm dating one of those Gods. I have an idea of what's going on because she trusts me and asked me to tell you this."

"Who?"

"Bexley."

"Larkin's sister?" I asked. The information was a vague wisp in my mind.

"Yes."

"And you want me to trust her? Larkin hates me, and Hunter is counting the days until he can get rid of me."

"You should trust her because Grayson does," Dionne said viciously.

All my arguments died in my throat at the mention of Grayson's name. The last image I had of him was ingrained in my brain—furious, but stoic. Gray had stared after me as I'd left the room, and it'd taken everything in me not to scream out to him and ask him not to let them take me away.

"Gifts are powerful," Dionne told me. "But they can be used against you. If a God asks another directly for the use of their gift, they can't refuse. It's taboo to ask, but some of us are more shameless than others."

"You think Archer would use my gift?"

"I've known him longer than you. With a gift like yours—" Dionne stared down at me so hard, I wondered if she could see my soul. "I have no doubt he would."

"There are a dozen other Gods that know the truth," I pointed out. "How do you know they won't use it?"

"I don't. The elites operate by their own rules. I can't make any promises, but I'm trying to minimise the damage."

There was no reason to trust Dionne. I knew nothing about her other than she was dating Bexley. But if Gray was connected to her, if there was a single thread that wound back to him, then I would grasp it with both hands.

"What am I meant to do here?" I asked Dionne, deciding that I needed to arm myself with as much information as I could pry from her during this short meeting.

"Keep your head down, learn to control your aura, and do not draw any unnecessary attention to yourself."

THREE

QUENTIN

A savage rush of voices filled my head, pressing against my skull and begging for it to be split open. So many desperate pleas that made my insides twist until nausea shoved away my organs so only it fit inside the cavity. Intimate prayers that deserved privacy and to be handled delicately were delivered directly to me with so much clarity and anguish that my eyes shed tears without hesitation.

Dissociation was an experience I was familiar with, thanks to years of being unable to manage my anxiety and panic, but this was another level. The moment the cuffs came off my wrists, I struggled to ground myself in reality. The true extent of what I was made me feel like I was no longer tethered to my body.

"Come on, angel," Archer's voice coaxed, sounding vague and distant. He was a whisper swimming upstream in a torrent of prayers.

People prayed with such intensity and faith that it made me quiver. Why would they put belief in a system that gave them no guarantees? In a person who was nothing more than a fraud when it came to her gift? I wanted to scream that they needed to get off their knees and

find another solution. I couldn't save them.

What hope did they have when I couldn't save myself?

"You can do this," Archer said. "You've done it before."

Three days. I'd spent three days with Archer in a thick fog of voices. Regardless of whether I wanted to, he removed the cuffs periodically. The weightlessness around my wrists was a short-lived reprieve. The first few times, Archer merely cocked his head to the side and watched as I fell to my knees under the weight of devotion. He made no offer of empathy or comfort. Tear tracks carved their way down my cheeks and left salty residues at the corners of my mouth, reminding me that there was nothing sweet to be found in the heavens.

When it became apparent that I would not find the answers on my own, Archer coached me through it, trying to help me find my control.

Nothing worked. Deep breathing. Counting. My divinity rendered all the usual methods I employed to keep me balanced on the knife's edge, useless. Two halves of me fought against each other until death looked like an attractive option. How was I meant to contemplate a lifetime of this when seconds of it made me weaker than I'd ever been?

"You're above them," Archer had whispered to me as he'd helped me up from the floor. *"You're divine, Quentin. Embrace it and ignore them. You have control over this."*

The words buried themselves under my skin, registering uncomfortably in the folds of my brain. I didn't want to rely on them. Didn't want to become what I raged against so vehemently.

Stubbornness will only sign your death warrant. Archer's voice sliced through the countless others when I tried to ignore him. *You're giving*

Hunter what he wants and sentencing yourself.

That was what forced me to listen.

After spending almost three decades rejecting deities, I had submitted to them. Resigned myself to their will. The council would cast their votes, and if it swung in my favour, I'd be grateful. And if it didn't, then I would meet my end.

I would not reduce myself for them. Would not fold at their mercy and implore them for my life or be painted as the disastrous soul they claimed I was. I needed to succeed because I refused to beg.

Swallowing back the nausea, I *embraced* my divinity. A swell of self-importance blossomed in my chest and reverberated along my spine as I reminded myself confidently that I was a demigoddess. I crushed the fear that the statement brought with it to dust. Any doubt diminished my hold over the situation.

Who were these people? Why should I care for what they requested? If they wanted me to answer, they needed to prove how badly they wanted it, and then I might grant them their desire. Allow them some ease from their burdens.

The voices died away and my chin rose until I met Archer's gaze. Bright green eyes stared back at me with pride glinting in the irises.

"There she is," he said, taking my face in his hands, thumbs gliding along my cheekbones.

Lips brushed against my forehead, and I pulled away from his hold, stumbling backwards. Exhaustion set in fast after training, like I'd been underwater for hours, and finally broke the surface to take a breath. Archer caught my arm and steadied me, clucking his tongue as the world finally stopped swimming before my eyes.

"I'm done," I spat. "I don't want to practise anymore."

The sun was disappearing, drowning lower Elysia in soft orange and pink hues that seeped through the windows and cast long, menacing shadows across the walls. It was the perfect combination that summed up the heavens. Soft and scary—a dichotomy that felt impossible to exist under the pure weight of believers who deemed it as perfection.

"It's important for you to learn how to manage it," Archer replied patiently.

"I know and I can, but it's easier with the cuffs in place."

The disgust caused his lip to curl. "They taint what you truly are."

"I don't know what I truly am!"

"Yes, you do. And we'll help you transition."

"We?"

"Lower Elysia," he said, spreading his arms out. "Everyone will want to help you settle into your new home."

"This isn't my home." The words came out through clenched teeth.

In moments of clarity, over the past few days, I'd learned that Archer and I had differences of opinions that led to heated arguments. He was insistent that this ordeal was a gift and that I'd returned home. No importance or value was given to the fact that I had a life before this—family, friends, a career.

He released a laborious sigh. "The attitude is getting tiresome, Quentin."

"Then send me back to Hunter."

That was the last place I wanted to be, but I couldn't think of another way of seeing Grayson. With every passing day, I grew anxious about his absence in my life. Divinity brought with it a lack of sleep that left me staring at walls and overthinking until I wore a hole in Archer's lavish green carpet.

Had Hunter got to him? Had he realised how much trouble this all was and stopped caring?

"You don't belong up there," Archer said. There was an eeriness to the calm. His smile looked too pinned in place to pass as natural. "This is your home. This is where you'll be appreciated."

The doorbell chimed loudly throughout the house and Archer closed his eyes for a moment before ignoring it.

"My home is on Earth," I argued back just as calmly.

"You're not giving us a chance, Quentin. Nearly three decades rotting away on that planet without knowing what you truly are. You owe it to yourself to learn about your divinity. Unlock the potential you were created for."

"Are any of you going to appreciate my existence as a whole? I'm not two people. I'm not a goddess and I'm not mortal. I'm a mixture of both. One doesn't come without the other."

People continued to take a swipe at my existence without considering the bigger picture. My divinity wasn't worth it, and neither was my mortality.

As a child, I don't think I ever truly valued myself. Never knowing my biological parents left deeper scars than I wished to admit, and I struggled to accept who I was. That changed when I was adopted. Mum and Dad helped me work through the anger and sadness, and I realised I needed to see and appreciate my worth. If I could do that, then fuck everyone else and what they thought. I'd forgotten that.

Yellow, the bright shade of buttercups, illuminated the room and cleared away to reveal a God. He bore a nervous expression and his soft blonde curls fell just above his shoulders.

"I hope I'm not interrupting," he said, staring at me from behind circular wire-rimmed glasses.

"Tobias," Archer hissed, stepping in front of me. "I didn't answer the door. Did you not take that as a sign that I'm busy?"

Tobias tore his gaze away from me and blinked at Archer. "We're all busy, Archer. You told me this was of utmost importance and I cleared —"

"Go to your room," Archer said, looking over his shoulder at me.

"I'm not a child," I hissed through my teeth, unhappy with his tone.

Something inside me stirred. Something I hadn't felt since I was on the floor in Hunter's house. A warmth that flooded my chest with such intensity that it blurred my vision. It spread down my limbs before I refused to let it go any further.

My aura was the one thing I'd come to terms with because I'd mastered my emotions. Or so I thought.

"You could have fooled me," he replied, arching a perfectly groomed brow.

"There's no need to leave on my account." Tobias' curious gaze flicked between me and Archer. "She's not going to be a secret for much longer. We've been waiting for this since you said the pool held her secrets. People are already asking questions, and here I am, getting a private audience."

My mind had been too preoccupied to worry about the rest of Elysia and if they knew about my existence. The fact that I wasn't a secret unsettled me. Dionne advised me to keep my head down and to avoid drawing attention to myself. I thought that was the easiest request, considering Archer never suggested venturing outside the house, and I never asked.

My fingers wrapped around Archer's elbow. "What does he mean about the pool? How do people know about me?"

Hunter wouldn't have told anyone. I'd disgraced the perfection of his Elysia. Nothing more than a pest that needed to be exterminated.

"I'm not going to tell you again," he barked, looking down at me.

It was the sternest he had been with me. A reminder that there were no friendships in the heavens. Whatever alliances I thought I had were steeped in an agenda that suited each individual.

My grasp slipped from his arm, and I stalked past the pair with my chin held up. Resenting the dismissal, I walked upstairs. There was no use in me hiding away to try and listen. Archer would sense me there and further embarrass me. I might have been young compared to the majority of Gods that roamed Elysia, but I didn't appreciate being treated like a child.

The anger bubbled wildly in my chest. Emotions were something I felt in control of but since awakening in the pool, everything coursed through me so brutally that I no longer understood how to suppress them properly.

A few faint wisps materialised in the surrounding space. If they didn't horrify me, I would be fascinated by them, but all I wanted to do was step out of my skin and get away from all the unanswered questions.

I needed answers. It was what I strived for. I was sick of letting everyone else dictate what I did while I was in Elysia. The only way to gain a better understanding was to take advantage of the situation I found myself in.

With Archer occupied, I could venture through the house and

see if there was anything useful that could help me figure out what he was planning. Tobias' talk of introductions had left me suspicious that Archer had ideas he was yet to share.

The first place to start was Archer's domain. I stood at the door, hand wrapped around the handle and took in a deep breath. Before I could talk myself out of it, I pushed down and let myself into his bedroom.

The space was nothing like I imagined. I assumed Archer's signature deep forest green would cover every surface, in the same way Gray's house was decorated in black, but instead the room was a beautiful blush pink that made it appear larger than it was. It was feminine and soft—qualities I didn't associate with my host. My gaze bounced from the walls to the bed and surfaces. The pink remained a mystery to me. In the days I'd lived with Archer, I hadn't come across another being who inhabited the house.

Hesitantly, my fingers trailed along the surface of the dresser as I noted colourful ornate perfume bottles and delicate jewellery draped on stands. Evidence that Archer shared his life with someone, but no answer as to who. The entire house lacked a single photograph or any distinctive identifier. Perhaps he kept a mistress and the visits had waned under my appearance. I wasn't exactly house trained by the standards of the Gods.

"You have your own secrets," I muttered to myself as I padded through the room.

From the moment I'd met him, I was acutely aware that there were plenty of truths that Archer hid. Keeping secrets was his territory, a game he played and was champion at. Archer knew how to extract things from others while keeping everything about himself under lock and key.

It would have been stupid of me to trust him implicitly. The hospitality he extended came at a cost, and I wasn't sure what the price was yet. All I knew was that I needed to keep my gift a secret because Dionne and the others were sure Archer would use it.

A large metal planter graced the windowsill, and I approached it, drawn in by the pale pink flowers that sprouted from the sickly bush that was rooted in the dirt. An unfamiliar ripple passed through me, making me shudder. Ignoring it, I reached out and brushed the petals as my brow furrowed.

"I wouldn't do that again, Quentin." Archer's soft voice sounded directly behind me, as smooth as velvet.

I jumped, spinning around and knocking the planter. Pain shot through the back of my hand for a few moments and the room was illuminated in gold. Any strong emotion pulled my aura to the surface, unleashing it from the restraints I placed it under. Archer's unexpected appearance set my heart racing, and with each beat, my aura flickered around us.

Anger warped his features as he hissed, his aura shooting out from his body and catching the plant before it hit the floor.

"Careful!" he barked, delicately setting it back on the windowsill. "What are you doing in here? I don't remember extending an invite."

"Took a wrong turn," I lied as he brought his face close to mine.

I'd only encountered the charming side of Archer, but the sudden aggressive facade reminded me that even the most charming Gods were still deities that regarded themselves above all other beings.

"This is not the time to play cute," he crooned. "What were you doing in here?"

"Trying to understand you better."

"Then ask questions like a normal person." I wanted to laugh at the sentiment. "You don't invade someone's personal space."

"Like you did? Filling my house with tulips whenever you got the chance."

"That's hardly the same."

"Fine," I bit back. "Who lives here with you?"

"No one," he replied, staring me straight in the eye.

"Then whose flower is this?"

"No one's."

"Why are you growing it here?"

"It's a project."

"You have a whole garden."

"I only grow tulips out there."

"What kind of project?" I asked, narrowing my eyes.

"Now, angel, you know I don't give my secrets away for free. Are you willing to partake in an exchange? Something tells me you're not being honest. Let's call it intuition." He chuckled at his own joke. "If you tell me what your gift is, I'll tell you what I'm growing."

I tried to keep my face calm but felt the vague twitch of my left eye as I stared up at Archer. "I don't know what it is. They never told me," I said as steadily as I could.

"Even if they didn't, you're a smart woman, you can figure it out." Long fingers gripped my jaw. "What do the mortals beg you for, Quentin Scott? What are they praying for?"

"I don't know," I gritted out. "There are too many voices."

Archer held my gaze for a moment. Time stretched between us and I worried that he was going to burrow into my brain and pull the truth out from me. However, he stepped back and straightened up, calmness washing over his features.

"No worries," he said smoothly, brushing his knuckles against my cheek. The gesture was tender compared to the way he pinched my chin seconds ago. "We'll figure it out together, but you should get some rest. It'll be busy this week."

"More training," I said, stepping away from him.

"No. I've decided to host your gifting ball."

FOUR

GRAYSON

Chaos and destruction were my tools. I'd mastered them and learned to wield them to do my bidding. People called on me when they were at their lowest point, with nowhere else to turn. When they were finally ready to give into their darkest desires. And I was happy to indulge them.

But for the first time in my existence, my powers did not bring the unparalleled rage that I was used to. Instead, it cocooned around me, caressing every nerve in a lethal manner, putting me in a strange state of calm.

There was too much at risk for me to head to lower Elysia and drag Quentin back home, no matter how strongly that need pulsed through me. If I gave in, there would be too many questions to answer that would only serve to further Hunter's agenda.

Ego was my big brother's driving force. Millenia of going up against him had taught me he wouldn't listen if I used my limited charm to get to him. If I wanted success, I had to change the way I played the game.

With each passing day, I grew unbearable until Sloan asked me

to stop visiting the house. Solace was better to stew in. To plot and to plan. Without Dionne or Bexley's appearance at my door or whispers from the lower heavens, I resigned myself reluctantly to the fact that Quen was safe. Archer was cherishing the time she spent under his roof and in his care.

And then came the invitation, just like I knew it would. Hunter wanted a family dinner. All of us sitting around a table pretending we were a functional unit, when it couldn't be further from the truth. That had always been the case, but the vote in the council had aired it for the rest of Elysia. Not exactly the united front he wanted to show. Cracks appearing in the carefully crafted image and crumbling before the audience he manipulated respect from.

"I don't like it when you're quiet," Elva said, her delicate fingers digging into my forearm.

My invitation had come with the usual caveat. It was a wonder Erik still possessed his gift with the way Hunter believed himself to be a matchmaker.

"I'm always quiet," I said, staring ahead as I walked.

True tunnel vision. There was no space for distractions when Quentin was the goal.

"Not like this. This is unnatural."

The corner of my mouth tugged, but I bit back on any remark.

"She's safe," Elva continued, jogging to keep up with my steps.

"She's smart," I corrected her.

Quen's untrusting nature would work in our favour. Archer may have tried to weasel his way into her life, but she trusted no one at their word. She would much rather drive you insane and force you to prove your loyalty, and that was exactly what would keep her alive.

While she was untrusting, she was alert and aware and brilliant.

"What are you planning?" Elva pleaded as we reached the door to my big brother's home.

"Unfortunately, I don't trust you enough to disclose that."

Her face crumpled. "We're friends."

"You are not my priority."

"Then I'll leave," she retorted. Her sadness morphed into anger easily but was unmatched to mine. "If you're about to drag me into a war, I want to know."

The term collateral damage came to mind. The talk of wars was still a distant notion, but not an impossible one. I would spill blood for Quentin if it came to that, but there were other avenues to explore first. Avenues that wouldn't see Quentin tear me apart when she saw sense.

"You're hysterical," I said, placing a hand over hers.

She snatched it away, unlinking our arms. "Don't you dare. You're not the only one who's worried about her."

I agreed with the sentiment, but I was the only one willing to do anything about it. The others were too eager to sit back and let things play out, but I craved control over the situation. Quentin needed to be where I could see and guide her. Next to me so I could soothe her worries and praise every minor success until she was comfortable in her skin again. Just because she was forced to cope alone didn't mean she should have to.

"I never said I was," I responded coldly.

"You behave like it."

"I'm sorry I can't bury my head in my relationship and trust the only family I have left will navigate through whatever trials a devious minor God sets before her. I'm sure she'll appreciate the deep care you've shown."

Elva looked like I'd slapped her across the face, but I was tired of the lack of initiative from my kin. Did they believe a simple split vote in the council chambers kept her safe? Even if it did, how long before another vote was called? Had they forgotten the way Gods could be? Vindictive, fickle, selfish, and with a blatant disregard for everyone but themselves.

The tendrils of deep purple unfurled from Elva's body, wrapping around my wrist and stopping me from knocking on the door.

"Let go," I said through my teeth.

"Take back what you said."

"Truth hurts, Elva. I expected more from you."

There was more I could say. More I wanted to say. It was part of my nature to be destructive, and it was difficult to rein it in, but there was a bigger picture, as everyone kept reminding me.

"Lovers' tiff?" Larkin asked, opening the door. Her fair eyebrow arched as her gaze flitted from my face to Elva's and finally landed on my wrist bound by her purple aura.

Elva released me immediately, the fight flooding out of her and her usual calm demeanour cascading around us. It was a mask. I sensed the chaos that still simmered beneath the surface. A few more moments and she'd have made me taste death.

"Of course not," she replied, stepping over the threshold as Larkin moved back. Elva threw a glance at me over her shoulder before walking with Larkin.

I pushed the door shut behind me and steeled myself for what would be a long night before following both further into the house.

Despite the lack of necessity for food, Hunter insisted on family dinners. Far removed from the friendly, familial catch-up they were disguised as, it was a way for him to keep a close eye on us while projecting the image of a family man. I hoped Larkin would grace him with children soon, so his focus would be diverted.

I sat beside Elva at the dinner table and sank into my role. Alcohol flowed freely, and I cut across conversation with the odd biting remark that would be expected. I kept myself close to Elva, attracting a few curious looks from Erik. It was better to balance irritating my big brother with giving him a glimpse of what he wanted in order to keep him sweet.

"What are you doing?" Erik muttered under his breath, rising from the table as we finished dinner.

I didn't trust that Hunter wasn't paying close attention, so I turned my head away from Erik. "I need to talk to Hunter."

Although I couldn't see his face, I imagined the vague sense of panic that ran through him as Sloan pulled him away.

"Grayson," Elva said.

"I have business," I told her abruptly.

She sucked in her cheeks, and I knew I would be hearing from Ignacio later.

When the room cleared, I echoed Hunter's footsteps towards the study without invitation.

"What do you want, Grayson?" he asked, taking a seat behind his desk. "I've had enough of you for one night."

Even with minimal participation at the table, I was still deemed the biggest problem in his life, second only to Quentin and her partial divinity.

"I wanted to talk to you about Quentin and your plans for leaving her in lower Elysia," I said, dropping into the chair opposite.

"It's not your problem. It's a temporary arrangement and once the council sees sense, she'll be back here for a hearing."

"You're going to risk leaving her there? The minor Gods aren't exactly willing to fall in line with our desires."

"The vote isn't extended to them," he snapped. "Larkin didn't want her here, so I got rid of the problem."

"And potentially created a larger one in doing so. You've entrusted her with Archer. Have you forgotten what he's been like over the last few centuries?"

"Are you fond of her?" Hunter asked, voice smooth like silk as he glanced up from his seat. "Are you after a little half-breed whore? I'm not convinced by the little display you tried to put on with Elva tonight."

Brutal images flashed before my eyes. I wanted to spill his blood and paint the walls with it. There would be no need for my aura. I'd dig my fingers beneath his flesh and rip it away from his bones, savouring every scream, and when his body repaired the damage, I'd inflicted, I would do it again until there was a blue and gold river flowing through Elysia. When he'd beg, only then, would I show him mercy by ending his pathetic life.

Hunter leaned back in his chair, lounging in it as he took me in. "You've spent a lot of your time with her, Gray. It didn't catch my attention until Larkin pointed it out."

How fitting that two snakes should find themselves together, bound by marriage? I would have been impressed by their cunning if they didn't act as if they were above it. Paint me as a villain, but at least I owned it. I wasn't ashamed of who or what I was.

"She's my host. You told me to make this initiative work. Told me my very existence was on the line if I didn't comply," I pointed out.

"That didn't mean jumping into bed with her."

"What proof do you have?" I asked, pushing my luck. "Or is it merely speculation of your wife?"

"Archer is insistent that you're hiding something."

Tipping back my head, I let out a hollow laugh. It was a tough decision on who to murder first. Hunter or Archer? Which one would bring me the most satisfaction?

"We all have secrets, brother," I said, lowering my gaze to him once more. "Be worried about the ones that Archer is keeping."

Hunter straightened, narrowing his eyes. "When I gave you the position on the council, I thought you might grow up. Learn to rise above the hatred you receive. I don't expect him to forgive you for what you did, even if it has been a lifetime."

He was trying everything in the book to get a reaction out of me. It would have worked if I didn't have Quentin to think about. If I launched myself across the desk and beat my brother's skull against the wall, it would lengthen her time in limbo. She needed certainty to feel comfortable, and I needed to deliver that to her.

"I doubt he's forgiven you," I quipped in return. "Or perhaps he no longer cares about Larkin, since he has a new obsession."

The only way to throw Hunter off the scent was to place distractions before him.

"I told you about the tulips he floods her home with," I continued. "How he follows her around like a lapdog when he can. And you just handed her over to him."

"He's not that stupid. She might be pretty, but she's not worth losing your life over," Hunter told me unequivocally.

"You don't know that. She should be here where we can make sure nothing more comes of this."

"Her divinity or their so-called relationship?"

It would have been easy to stride over and smack the smug look from his face. He wanted the admission from me, concrete evidence so that he could play the next cards in his deck. And if there was no one else involved, I would have given it to him.

We'd played the long game, and I'd grown tired of it. The bloodlust simmered so close to the surface. I wanted to rid the heavens of my brother and take my place. I wanted to watch it all burn and rebuild it from the ashes in my image.

But that was impossible without scorching Quentin. I refused to risk her, no matter how much my ambition pushed against my skull and sparked hot in my veins.

"Careful, brother," I said, letting the anger shift from red-hot to silent and black. "It's sounding like lower Elysia has more say in affairs than those on the council. We wouldn't want them getting any ideas."

His lip twitched at the comment. Attacking his ego always worked.

"She can rot for all I care," he spat.

"Then why let her be trained at all? If you're so determined for her to fail, why hand her to a God who would be desperate for her to succeed?"

"Because this time when she fails, which she will, Archer will have no one to blame but himself."

I knew I needed to leave before it escalated into a fight where I lost control. The way he disregarded the prospect of her succeeding when it was her gift made me furious.

"Mark my words, Hunter, you'll regret this decision," I said, rising from the chair. "He can't be trusted."

"And neither can you."

FIVE

QUENTIN

When Archer said that lower Elysia was less refined than its counterpart, he wasn't joking.

The few memories I had of upper Elysia were bright and beautiful. Lush green grass, cobbled streets, white stone buildings. It was the picture of perfection that made something deep within me ache, like it was a missing piece I hadn't realised was gone. A familiarity that I craved for my entire life.

Although lower Elysia was beautiful, it didn't carry the same charm as the higher heavens. The residents were less composed and debauchery awaited around every corner. Casinos. Bars. Brothels.

Classical sins were only punishable if you were mortal. The Gods indulged with no concern for the consequences.

Over the course of the week, Archer escorted me through the streets of lower Elysia as he prepared for my gifting ball. No amount of reluctance from me got him to change his mind. Archer was planning to celebrate with me as the unwilling guest of honour.

The few trips we'd taken resulted in curious stares and whispers behind hands. For the first time in my life, I walked with my head

down to avoid the crushing judgement that crowded in from every angle. It had worn me down and I decided it was better to pick my battles than be brash towards every single being I crossed.

When Gods were brave enough to approach, Archer became a physical barrier, telling them they would all be properly introduced at the ball. It begged the question of why he brought me out in the first place. He was a child, dragging me along like some prize that he coveted but refused to share.

"This is hardly keeping a low profile," I said to Dionne as we walked to a boutique to pick up the dress for the evening.

Archer relinquished his duties to ensure the last of the party plans were on point for the evening. This was his gesture, and it needed to be perfect in the eyes of everyone he invited.

"I didn't think he planned on introducing you to everyone in such a grandiose way," she grumbled.

"Do any of you understand the term low-key?" I muttered under my breath. The only gifting ball I'd experienced was baby Cato's, and if that was anything to go by, then this would be a lavish affair. "You've told Bexley about this?"

"As soon as I found out. She said she would pass on the information."

I left the questions at that, unwilling to implicate the others by asking after them. The disappointment continued to swell at the thought of being rejected by Gods who had posed as my friends. A deep sense of abandonment accompanied me throughout the days. Dionne only ever mentioned Bexley, a Goddess I'd never spoken to. The rest of the elite remained silent spectres.

We avoided all the dens of sin and temptations, stepping into the glossy boutique. The stares I attracted on the streets were intensified in the small space. Dionne handled the talk and took the garment bag that held my dress for the evening's festivities, before we returned to Archer's home.

My steps were hurried, as I avoided the curious glances that were shot in my direction. Perhaps immortality didn't require manners. Or maybe it was divinity. After all, who did the Gods answer to?

The outside of Archer's grand house was elaborately decorated in shimmering streamers of deep green that fluttered in the gentle breeze. I lifted my hands, unbound by the cuffs, and tugged at one of the satin ribbons, ripping it down and then dropping it to the floor. It curled up on the ground like a snake and I pushed away the urge to continue tearing down the decorations, satisfied with crushing it under the sole of my shoe. The minor act of vandalism made me feel like I was fighting back, even if it was a completely ineffective gesture.

Dionne hurried me up the stairs to my room. The distinctive hum of chatter followed us as the ground floor filled with guests, but the host of the evening remained out of sight.

"What am I meant to expect from tonight?" I asked as she pulled the dress out and motioned for me to get out of my clothes.

Things had been frosty between me and Archer in the morning. He continued to slather on the charm, but there was a tension behind his words, and his smile was tighter than usual. At least he tried, which was more than I could say for myself. My politeness had withered away, replaced with abrasive irritation.

"A lot of peacocking." Dionne shrugged. "Everything up here is a dick measuring contest."

I huffed a breath out of my nostrils. "That's not exclusive to Elysia."

She shook her head with a wry smile, braids whipping around her waist. "I like you, Quentin. I hope they don't kill you."

My smile fell at the blunt reminder. "At least I get a party before I die."

The conversation sunk away under the weight of reality. It was laughable that while a death sentence hung over me, I was the guest of honour at the most extravagant party I would ever attend.

How did Archer expect me to enjoy this?

The simplest answer and the only one I could deduce was that he didn't. This wasn't entirely for my benefit, but something that aided him in whatever secrets he was keeping.

I slipped into a pair of gold heels with Dionne's help, wobbling slightly as I towered beyond what was comfortable. As I stepped into the dress, she pulled it up around my body.

"I look ridiculous," I said, staring at my reflection in the full-length mirror.

The bodice of the dress hugged my torso, slimming my waist, while my legs were hidden beneath layers of tulle. Colour of choice for the evening was gold, but vines of forest green crept along the corset—a nod to the host.

But it looked wrong.

A colour shouldn't have unsettled me so deeply, but a faint voice rang through my mind.

I wanted them to know you belonged to me.

"He's going for a *lost princess returning home* vibe," Dionne said, barely containing her laughter.

"I'm not a doll," I snapped. "He doesn't get to play dress up with me."

A soft knock on the door forced me to turn my head, and I scowled at Archer as he leant against the frame. His slender figure was draped in my colour. A gold shirt and tie were hidden beneath the golden suit. I peeked at his shoes and even his loafers honoured my aura. Archer could have been placed in a cabinet amongst other trophies for how good he looked in gold.

"Dionne, get ready and join the party," he told her, eyes never leaving me.

"I haven't started on her hair," Dionne argued.

"She's perfect as she is." His gaze travelled down my body, and my arms wrapped around my middle.

"I'll see you down there," she said to me, squeezing my bicep.

Dionne slipped past him out of the room, and Archer sloped in, walking up to me.

"If you dislike the dress so much," he said, "you could always turn up to the party naked." When I didn't laugh or comment, he sighed. "Come on, Quentin. This is a celebration. You haven't even said thank you. This ball is to honour you."

"Thanks for finding a sure-fire way to get me killed," I said, stilted and cold.

"Angel," he murmured. "We're friends, but you're behaving as if we're strangers."

"I don't trust you."

"But you trust the elite?"

"No."

"Grayson?"

"No."

"Sweet, innocent Erik?"

"I don't trust any of you."

There was some truth behind those words. It was difficult to trust them when I didn't know what they were doing. And yet, I still trusted them more than I did Archer.

"That's probably for the best," he said. "But you're not exactly proving yourself to be trustworthy."

"I haven't—"

"I was around you before you were gifted, Quentin. You hold a lot of secrets. So many of them are bubbling under the surface. You could ease the burden if you shared them."

I had never been an open book. Trust and vulnerability weren't appealing to me. There was too much fallout if it went wrong. That was my opinion before Gray and all the secrets we'd woven together. There was no way I could let any of that slip, because the consequences would be greater than a broken heart and bruised pride.

"Why don't I start?" Archer suggested. "A little while ago, when you first visited Elysia, I saw you all gathered near the pool. I stepped into it and asked it to give me its secrets and then I saw you. I knew then that there was something special about you."

Yet another person who'd failed to tell me anything that might have seen me prepare better for the situation I was in. Steeling myself, I responded flippantly, "I cheated on a spelling test when I was eight."

He pressed a hand to his chest and feigned shock. "They should strip you of your degrees."

"I'm sure you'll keep my secret."

"Every single one of them," he said seriously. "All you need to do is trust me."

"We're not at the stage where we get wine drunk and I spill my guts."

"Not yet." He fixed his smile back in place, dimples hidden, so I knew it wasn't genuine. "What happened, Quentin? You used to let me into your dreams and walk through Elysia with me. You used to seek me out when you were afraid in those moments."

"You infiltrated my dreams and brought me to the heavens, where I shouldn't be. You were the only one I could find. I had to rely on you."

"You make it sound so sinister."

"You're proving to be Jekyll and Hyde." I'd probably regret calling him out on his behaviour, but I couldn't swallow it back any longer.

"I'll strike a deal with you," I said confidently, although I felt anything but. "Tell me your secrets and I'll tell you mine. What's all this for? And spare me the bullshit about kindness. What are you gaining out of this?"

"So cynical for someone who's yet to gain an understanding of the world."

He clucked his tongue and pulled the cuffs from his trouser pocket and looked at me expectantly. Usually, I was happy to use them, but this didn't feel like it was for my benefit, so I stood rooted to the spot. There was a waver in his patient demeanour as he sighed and moved towards me.

"You won't be in them for long," Archer assured me, grabbing my wrist roughly and trapping it in the cuff. "But you've been a little volatile lately. I expected you to be a star student with all that education behind you, but it's my fault for making assumptions."

I bristled at his attack on my intelligence. This wasn't the lab or something I could learn from a book. He expected me to rein in my emotions when there were so many reasons that amplified them beyond my control.

"We don't want to unnecessarily scare any of them," Archer finished.

"Why not? What does it matter?"

He clipped the cuff around my other wrist and dropped my hands so they were bound and rested against the lower part of my abdomen.

"They'll be your family," Archer said. "And you only get one chance at a first impression."

"I have my family," I gritted out between clenched teeth.

"If you're talking about Elva—"

The events after I walked out of the pool hit me, and I remembered Elva explaining that my mother—biological mother—was her cousin. But she wasn't the person who instantly crossed my mind the moment someone mentioned family.

"Cassidy," I said forcefully, cutting across him. "I have a brother who's probably wondering where I am."

It was a concern that clawed at my brain, but I'd yet to find the courage to voice it. Anger was the driving force behind me finally being able to ask about my true family.

"You don't have to worry about that," he replied, guiding me out of the room. I tried to move away, feeling uncomfortable with his hand at my lower back, but the heels hampered my escape attempt. "I'm sure Hunter will have explained the situation."

The blood drained from my face. "He told Cass?"

I didn't want my brother to know about this. Not yet. Never if I could help it. Cass and I had a good relationship and telling him I was part Goddess was bound to change the way he viewed me, and

I wasn't prepared to lose him. Wasn't ready for the cavernous chasm that would erupt between us and separate us further than the Atlantic currently did.

Archer snorted. "No. He won't want anyone finding out about you. But he will have made a valid excuse to halt the project for the time being and to come up with a reason you're not in touch with your brother."

No loose ends. Hunter would want this swept under the rug. The last thing he wanted was for there to be an unexplainable blip in his neatly planned project. A project that was meant to restore faith in the Gods rather than having mortals question how they didn't even know what was going on in the heavens.

"He's still planning to finish the project?" I asked.

E.L.I. had slipped to the bottom of my priority list. For once, there were more pressing matters in my life than work.

Archer's hand pressed against my back, forcing me to keep walking. "He spent years devising it and setting everything up. Hunter won't abandon it for something he deems an inconvenience."

The insult washed over me as I processed his words, formulating a plan that could buy me some more time.

E.L.I. was my bargaining chip. Hunter wanted to continue the project, and I was the scientist who could help move it along at a faster pace. Without the real need for sleep, I could give all my hours to the lab. It bought me time, took me back to Earth and proved my worth to the council.

All I needed to do was get to Hunter and convince him I wasn't an inconvenience, but his most valuable asset.

SIX

GRAYSON

Bexley had told me about the gifting ball days ago. My entire estate was shrouded in black for the rest of the afternoon. Erik stopped me from descending to the lower heavens and ripping Quen away from Archer. Several fissures appeared in the flooring, and the surrounding walls crumbled as the rubble hit the floor. My vision blurred while an obsidian rage pulsed through me.

Archer was hosting her gifting ball? What right did he have to organise one of the greatest honours a God had? He was nothing to her. Those plans should have fallen into our hands—*my* hands—once we knew she was safe from death. Quentin wouldn't want to celebrate when the guillotine hung inches from her neck. The sheer tactlessness of the move sparked further fury in my chest.

In the hours as the anger dissipated, I made a decision. I wouldn't tell Hunter just yet. There was a chance that he would find out before the ball happened. Our benevolent leader paraded as omniscient, but ignorance clouded his vision more often than not. If that was the case, then I would deliver the news on the night. To do so beforehand would allow Hunter to calmly descend to lower Elysia, and Archer to

expertly craft a lie. If I wanted to sever whatever deal they'd struck and bring Quentin home for good, the party needed to be in full swing.

Erik's eyes followed me as I paced the room. "I've never known you to be so patient."

"I am exercising a lot of self-control."

"You would know if she's in any distress," he said. "Your bond would allow you to feel it."

I grunted in response.

"You're not feeling pain. You aren't feeling affliction. She's okay," Erik continued.

"She's good at hiding things," I snapped.

Erik snorted, and I glared at him.

"She's not exactly the most agreeable person," he pointed out. "As a mortal, she's prone to indignation. As a demigoddess, those feelings would be amplified."

I chewed on his words. There were times throughout the day where a sudden wave of unparalleled rage hit me, but I thought nothing of it. After all, that pure sense of chaos was what I was built on. Now I wondered if it was Quentin who added to the blinding fury. The thought both satisfied and aggravated my soul. What was getting under her skin enough to spark that delicious temper of hers?

"You can't guarantee he'll bring her back here before the vote," Erik said from my sofa. "Your time might be better spent trying to convince the others that she won't be a threat."

"And Archer—"

"Will play his games, but you need to trust her."

"I trust her. It's him I don't trust. His fascination with her is to get back at me."

"Gray," Sloan called.

I turned my head to see my sister-in-law in the room's doorway. Dionne stood behind her draped in a gold dress that shimmered under the lights. Lower Elysia would be a sea of gold tonight, and it seemed fitting that Quentin would herald the colour of our blood. She was what beat through my veins from the moment I laid eyes on her and would continue to do so until fate saw fit that I no longer existed.

The only issue was that the wrong section of Elysia was celebrating tonight. She didn't belong to them. She didn't belong to upper Elysia. Quentin was solely mine, and it should have been my right to welcome her into my world.

"She just got dressed," Dionne said, gaze darting around the room. "He won't want to wait to introduce her so I would go now."

"You've left her alone?" I asked through gritted teeth.

"You were going to leave your entrance to luck?" Dionne asked.

"There's no pleasing you," Bexley hissed before turning to her girlfriend. "Go join the celebrations. You've done more than you should have."

Dionne's gaze flitted to me before she kissed Bexley and disappeared from the house.

"You can leave as well," I told Bexley.

"What are you planning on doing?"

"That's none of your concern."

"Yes, it is," she argued. "My sister is married to your brother. If you piss him off, she's the one who has to endure it."

"Larkin's a big girl. She doesn't need anyone to save her."

"The same could be said about Quentin."

A wall of black rushed towards Bexley, but Sloan stepped in front of her, and it took all of my restraint to stop it.

"Enough!" Sloan ordered. "Fighting amongst ourselves won't help anything. Bexley and Dionne have done us a favour by telling us what's going on down there. Whatever you have planned, you need to act on it now, Gray."

Tendrils of my aura wound themselves back towards me, bringing light back into the room.

The situation was a delicate one. Archer had overstepped a mark and potentially inched the knife further into Quentin's back by trying to play the perfect host. But informing Hunter was a guaranteed way of taking Quen out of Archer's clutches and back to upper Elysia, where I could keep a closer eye on her.

"I need to visit my brother," I said, cracking my neck.

"I'll come with you," Erik said.

"No."

"Gray—"

"What?" I turned on him. "What help do you think you could possibly be?"

"Referee."

"I'm not stupid. I know what's on the line."

I didn't waste another breath on the trio before wrapping my aura around me and taking myself to Hunter's estate.

My fist banged on the door, and moments later, Hunter pulled it open. His face fell when he saw me, and he turned away without greeting. Following him into his home, I began, "I assume you know what's happening."

I couldn't help but take a swipe at him. Old habits die hard.

"You're bothering me after a long day," he said, running a hand through his hair.

"Oh, please accept my humblest apologies. I didn't mean to make your life difficult," I shot back sarcastically.

"What do you want, Grayson?" Hunter had moved back into his office, and I stepped inside, ready for round two.

"Quentin—" I started.

"You're like a broken record. This obsession you have is disgusting."

Shaking off the insult, I said, "She's having a gifting ball."

Hunter's face contorted with anger. "No. She is not."

How cute that he thought it was a request. "Oh, but she is. Courtesy of Archer."

"What?"

The unstable flicker of his aura joined us in the room. Hunter was the most composed out of the three of us. He didn't possess the same lack of control as me, and there was never a gentle glow in the style of Erik.

"This is exactly why you shouldn't have trusted Archer with Scott." I seethed.

"I told him to be discreet until we've decided."

"When have you known him to listen? He's throwing her a gifting ball. Plans to show her off to lower Elysia. No doubt he'll fill their heads with ideas. Who's saying he hasn't done it to her already? He has a fondness for half-breeds, if I remember correctly."

The words tasted bitter on my tongue. Referring to Quentin as if she was something beneath me was wrong, and if she ever found out, she'd make me pay.

"He wouldn't dare," Hunter said. His tone brought a chill to the air.

"You have no guarantee other than his word, and he's already broken it by hosting a ball. Do you truly believe it'll be a small affair?"

There was a beat of silence while Hunter weighed up my words. Methodical and calculated, I would have loved to see what ran through his mind. In his eyes, regardless of the fact I was his blood, he didn't trust me any more than he did Archer. However he chose to deal with this information meant he gave in to one of us. I needed to make sure this fell in my favour.

"The longer she remains down there in his care, the more we risk her finding out what happened to her kin," I pointed out.

"Archer knows that conversation is off limits."

I secretly hoped that would be the case, but had no guarantee that Archer had kept all the secrets the heavens held.

"Are you prepared to take that risk? He's about to introduce her to the rest of them. The minor Gods have looked for an excuse to rebel for centuries. We've just handed them the perfect reason. Reopened old wounds."

Hunter turned away from me, walking to his desk. The tension caused his shoulders to rise as he took in my words. The stance flooded me with memories that were becoming more difficult to escape.

"He's going to use her," I pressed on, "to gain an advantage over the elite. If that advantage belongs anywhere, it's with us."

Ego had always been the way to win Hunter over. He believed he was the most powerful and most important. If he saw value in you, he would keep you close. What else was the council, but those Hunter deemed too valuable to have their own thoughts and opinions? Humans relied on them and he collected them.

It took me an embarrassingly long time to realise that my brother didn't place me on the council to help me like he originally claimed. The closer he kept me to him, the tighter the hold he had on me. During those years where I was naïve enough to believe the words that fell from his mouth, Hunter controlled the narrative that surrounded my life, and I did nothing about it because I wanted to stay in his graces.

Never again.

I would never allow it to happen again.

The narrative was mine to control. I just needed to twist the strings until he danced to my tune.

I opened my mouth, prepared to continue fighting my case, but it wasn't necessary. Hunter had arrived at his decision.

"We'll need to retrieve her."

He moved from his desk to a small cabinet and pulled the doors open. A gentle metal clanging filled the room as he picked up an item, but with his back to me, I couldn't see what it was.

"I requested for this to be made," he explained. "Mortals were only too willing to help. I brought it back up here today but didn't expect to use it so quickly." Hunter turned to face me again. "You'll need to fix it to her. She has too much bark for my liking. She'll be your responsibility. If I so much as find out that she's caused an issue up here, there will be consequences. Understood?"

He tossed the copper collar onto the table between us with a long chain link lead.

"Unless," Hunter said, locking eyes with me, "this would prove to be a problem for you?"

Underestimating Hunter would be fatal. Despite what I thought of him most days, he wasn't as stupid as he looked. As tired as I was of playing the long game with him, I still had to pick my battles. The option of going rogue, albeit an attractive one, would only give me temporary bliss, and I was chasing after eternal.

I picked the collar up from the table, growing accustomed to the weight of it in my hands. "Why would it cause me problems?"

Quentin was going to murder me.

SEVEN

QUENTIN

I navigated the stairs with some difficulty, taking each step slower than usual, thanks to the ridiculous heels. It was unfair to blame my footwear entirely. There was a healthy dose of stubborn reluctance that forced me to make my gait unnaturally slow. Archer matched my pace patiently until we hit the ground floor of the house.

Muted music drifted through the space, growing louder as we headed towards the source. Large wooden double doors separated us from the party where chatter and laughter joined the notes. Even behind a barrier, it was easy to tell there was a sizeable crowd.

"What did you tell them?" I asked him. "That this would be the party of the century?"

"Millenia," he corrected.

Archer straightened his tie and shot me a look. Slender fingers rose between us until a yellow tulip materialised between them.

"We'll find your flower soon," he assured me. "Until then, you can borrow mine." He placed the bloom in my hair behind my ear, and I shook my head, in an attempt to dislodge it. Archer let out a

deep laugh. "What did I just tell you? First impressions are important. I've fixed it in place for you, but you're messing up your hair." He smoothed the wild strands back into place, one finger winding around a lock and tugging gently. "You really are perfect," he whispered.

It was a sentiment that I was sure he wanted to come across as sweet and sincere, but dressed up in the way he wanted and cuffed like a criminal, it lost all meaning.

I imagined lifting my hands and bludgeoning his temple with the heavy copper cuffs. The bruising of his skin and fracturing of his skull would offer some compensation for being his personal Barbie doll.

And then the sobering thought that he wouldn't feel a thing and I would sign my death warrant washed over me.

'Well behaved women seldom make history.' Wasn't that how the quote went?

I'd spent my life speaking up when I was expected to be quiet. My work required me to challenge what people knew, prove what they didn't believe, and constantly question everything around me. Censoring myself chipped away at my soul.

The deafening sound of the double doors flying open and hitting the walls drowned my careful response out. They bounced, shuddering with the effort, and revealed a room full of Gods who no longer laughed and gossiped without a care.

Front and centre of the crowd was a figure I hadn't expected to see.

"Don't keep us all waiting," Gray said.

A torrent of emotions swirled in my chest and almost brought me to my knees. Seven days without him would have been my idea of bliss a few months ago, but things had changed and the relief that flooded me made me lightheaded. The ache that resonated at the centre of my chest and made it difficult to breathe finally eased.

It was short-lived. The expression on Gray's face, teamed with the black tendrils and scandalised minor Gods in the room behind him, made a weight settle in the pit of my stomach.

Archer's fingers sunk into the flesh of my upper arm as he pulled me behind him.

"It's invitation only," he spat at Gray.

"You really think I'd listen to instructions from you? You think I care?" Gray replied. "I've come to collect her and bring her back to the upper quarters."

Archer scoffed. "Under whose authority? Or did I miss the part where you were put in charge of Elysia?"

A deep voice sounded from behind me. "Under my authority."

Turning on my heel so quickly I almost tripped, I found Hunter stood tall with a vicious look carved into his features. Archer pulled me aside as Hunter glided through the hallway towards us. He stopped in front of Archer so that they were toe to toe.

"You better have a good explanation of what is going on here," Hunter whispered menacingly. "Because this is not what we agreed on."

A dark chuckle that belonged to Gray rang through the house and made my blood run cold. It was a hollow sound that reminded me of when we first met. When I believed he didn't have the capacity to care for anything or anyone but himself.

"Whatever deal you've made with my brother seems to have reached its end," Gray pointed out, stepping into the hallway with us.

"There's nothing wrong with welcoming her to Elysia," Archer gritted out. "She's doing no harm."

"Not yet," Hunter hissed. "But this cements that I shouldn't have trusted you. You have most of lower Elysia here. She was meant to be kept a secret."

"Maybe you should have expressed that specific desire," Archer pointed out. "A direct request. That was an oversight on your part."

An electric blue tendril knocked Archer out of the way, slamming him into a wall and damaging the plaster work. He sank to the floor in a cloud of dust and debris.

"Larkin won't accept her back in the house," Archer yelled. "What are you planning to do with her?"

"My wife's desires have not been your concern for years," Hunter replied, walking towards him. "I have placed Scott in Grayson's care."

"You can't be serious!" Archer rose to his feet. "After everything I've told you?"

"I have much better things to concern myself with than a half-breed," Gray drawled.

The comment was a punch to the gut. I thought abomination was bad, but the pure vitriol behind the words 'half-breed' knocked the air out of me.

I fought through memories, trying to understand what was going on. Gray professed to love me. He tried to fight for me in the council chambers. But that Gray wasn't here. Had our time apart warped his thinking? Was I truly that repulsive to the elite Gods?

Words travelled up my throat and lodged there in a painful lump. I found comfort in the worst of the Gods and now I didn't even have that. I knew I shouldn't have relied on anyone but myself.

"You don't care for anything but yourself," Archer spat at him.

Gray shrugged. "True enough."

Archer's aura sparked to life and crept towards us, but Hunter struck out. Blue wound itself around Archer's body, holding him in place while he struggled.

"Uh, uh," Gray said, wagging his finger. "We don't want to cause a scene in front of your guests."

The crowd behind him had not left, but they didn't make a move to save Archer. They watched with vested interest, a gentle hum of whispers starting again. Selfish. Unequivocally selfish. Gods looked after themselves above all else. No one would step into the fray.

My gaze slid to Gray. All the relief had morphed into anger.

"What are you doing?" I asked Gray spitefully, as if I hadn't been hoping for his presence at every waking moment.

"There she is," he said, turning his focus on me. "I was wondering if you'd lost the ability to speak." The words were just as clipped as my own. "Hope you've enjoyed your little stay here, but you'll be coming back with me."

I bit the insides of my cheeks so hard that I could taste the ferric tang of blood as it coated my tongue and teeth.

"Grayson," Hunter barked. "You're forgetting something."

My gaze flicked between the pair, heart hammering so aggressively against my chest that I worried it might actually punch a hole through my body and land on the floor as an offering in return for safety.

Reaching into the inner pocket of his jacket, Gray pulled out a single halo of copper that split open in his hands.

A short burst of laughter escaped my lips out of relief. "I'm already cuffed," I bit, holding up my hands to show him the blatant evidence.

For the briefest moment, I was grateful that Archer had fixed them on me and hadn't had the chance to remove them yet. I posed no threat, so the hole I was in grew no deeper.

"It's not for your wrists," Hunter informed me.

With a small tug, a chain leash fell from Gray's jacket, and I shook my head as I realised what he held in his hands.

"No," I snapped, taking a horrified step back. "You've got to be fucking joking."

Gray clucked his tongue. "Language, Scott."

My brain quickly stacked up the odds, firing up the sympathetic nervous system. A fight was out of the question. There was no way I could win. That left me with one other option.

I turned quickly, ignoring the three Gods that surrounded me, and ran. It was a week late, but my survival instinct had finally showed up instead of hovering like a vague idea in the background.

I'd barely made it a few metres down the hall, towards the front door and away from the Gods, when my heel got stuck in the tulle skirt and the floor rushed to greet my face. Squeezing my eyes shut, I waited for the pain, but it never arrived.

Something solid wound around my waist, dragging me backwards, and turning my body until I was nose to nose with Grayson.

"Don't you dare," I hissed through my teeth.

His eyes were stormy, tumbling between deep blue and grey. Somewhere in their depths, I tried to find the man I'd grown to know.

"What are you going to do about it?" he asked, cocking his head to the side and staring straight back at me.

"Stop playing with her, Grayson. I don't have time for this," Hunter called.

Gray's hands reached up, and I tried to pull away from him, but his aura was too strong. The copper was cold as he clipped it into place, resting heavily on my collarbones as goosebumps cascaded over the bare skin of my shoulders and arms. The vision of his face became blurry as tears of frustration filled my eyes.

His aura released me so that my feet hit the floor and he held the lead in his hand, turning back towards the packed room of minor Gods.

"Let this serve as a reminder," Hunter said smoothly. "Do not forget your place here. We voted on decrees to keep *all* of Elysia safe."

Dozens of gazes landed on me, pitying and potent. I was completely humiliated and powerless to do anything to help myself, but blinked back the tears, refusing to crumble in front of them.

"Grayson," Hunter said, addressing his brother. "Take her back to upper Elysia. You have no other business here."

"And you?" Gray asked in return.

"I have matters to resolve with Archer." Hunter's attention turned to the full room of glittering party guests. "You're all dismissed."

The order set about a chain reaction of bright flashing colours as minor Gods and Goddesses took their leave.

Dionne caught my eye, and she mouthed the words, *Trust him*, at me before she also left the room.

Gray tugged on the lead, forcing me to stumble towards his body. He gripped my elbow, and I tried to pull it away, refusing to look at him.

The last thing I saw before Gray wrapped us in black was Archer, aura pulsing around him, as he screamed, "If anything happens to her, I will kill you!"

EIGHT

GRAYSON

My feet hit the plush carpet of my bedroom as we materialised in the space. The chain lead bit into the flesh of my palm as Quentin did her best to pull away from me.

"You're going to hurt yourself," I warned her. The skin around her neck was already red from her efforts.

"I'm going to hurt you as soon as I'm out of this thing," she spat.

I couldn't help the laugh that spilled out of me. There she was. My soulbound was as feisty as ever, even when she faced an abyss of uncertainty.

Fear was not an emotion I was accustomed to. There was no need for me to be fearful until Quen walked into my life. I worried about the state I'd find her in at Archer's abode. But dressed in finery was not a scenario I imagined.

The relief and humour were flushed from my system and replaced by the familiar sensation of chaotic anger as I took her in.

"You're wearing his colour. Parading on his arm," I commented, voice dangerously low.

My fingers plucked the tulip from her hair. Archer must have fixed it in place for it to have survived her escape attempts.

"Is that the issue you see here?" she screamed as I decimated the flower, crumbling the ashes onto the carpet. "You called me a half-breed and stuck me in a collar. You humiliated me in front of lower Elysia."

"And you survived. You'll continue to survive because of it."

"You left me for days without a word. I didn't know what was happening up here."

"Did you expect me to play knight and rescue you?" I asked, dropping the lead from my hand. "I didn't think of you as the damsel in distress type."

"I'm anything but myself up here," Quentin said, vitriol still wrapped around the words, even though she'd lowered the volume. "A half-breed. An abomination. A date."

My aura darkened the room, and Quen took a few unsteady steps backwards.

"Date?" I asked darkly.

"You think I'd opt to dress like this?" She fanned out the ridiculous tulle skirt. "It's part of the fucking charade."

"Did he touch you?" The anger amplified and my blood pulsed in my ears.

There was a beat of silence before she looked straight at me. "Days of pure bliss, rolling in the sheets with him. The best I've ever had."

"Petty, insolent woman."

Quentin's body tensed, eyes tracking the single strand of my aura that trailed across the floor and crept towards her. It snaked up her body and landed on the fabric of her dress that laid between her breasts.

"Ignorant, egotistical God," she shot back, but some of the fire had gone out and was replaced with wariness.

"You will never wear his colour again."

"Says who?"

The confession was on the tip of my tongue, but I swallowed it back. This was not how I planned to tell her. I'd already fucked up my declaration of love. I wasn't about to admit to our binding when she looked ready to murder me.

The single strand of aura that rested on her dress dragged downwards again, splitting the fabric until it pooled around her feet. Beneath the hideous amounts of gold and green, Quen donned black lace.

My colour.

My bound.

"If you touch me, I'll scream murder," Quen snapped.

The goosebumps cascaded along her flesh as I drank her in, my aura unbinding itself from me and growing larger in the space. Whenever she was in front of me, I couldn't help but lose control.

"You belong to me," I reminded her.

"Is that what the show was? Crashing a party, putting me in a collar—you're taking me to Hunter yourself?"

"Who said anything about taking you to Hunter? I will let no one else have you."

I took a few steps towards her, and she held her spot, steady on her feet. The moment the pool gifted her, I'd lost my ability to read her thoughts. Her divinity had locked me out and although the copper around her wrists and neck dampened it, she couldn't deny what she was.

"*You* don't get to have me," she pointed out.

"You don't get to tell me what to do when it comes to you."

The tips of my shoes hit the point of her heels. She moved quicker than I expected without my advantage of reading her mind. Quentin raised her hands and swung them hard, hitting me across the side of the face with the cuffs that bound her. The impact was enough to make me hiss and sway on the spot.

When I straightened up, Quen had turned and was making a break for the bedroom door. The heels hampered her speed, and she appeared to forget that she was only in her underwear and some metal.

"Where do you think you're going?" I asked, striding after her.

She barely made it out of the room before I grabbed her around the waist, hauling her back inside. Quen fought against me, trying to get free. The feel of her body against mine brought unparalleled comfort after days without her.

"Let me go!" she screamed.

"Where do you plan to go?" I asked, kicking the door shut. "There's nowhere to run. I am the safest space you have here."

"Then I may as well walk into Hunter's place and beg for death!"

I dropped her from my grasp and shoved her back against the wall. I needed to rein in my anger before I did irreparable damage. She couldn't fight back in the cuffs, but I wasn't keen to let her out of them just yet. Not when I had one shot of total submission from her.

"Do you really think I'd let anything happen to you?" I asked, pressing my forehead against hers.

The hypnotic notes of honey, orange blossom, and peach ensnared me again. My hands cupped her face, grip tightening to hold her in place when she tried to pull away.

"Do you?" I pressed.

Erik informed me I'd be able to feel her emotions. The rage was evident but there was no fear. Comfort, relief, and need swirled through our bond. She wanted to lean into my touch, collapse against my body, but she wouldn't allow herself.

"You tell me," she said through clenched teeth. "You left me for days without a word, and when you turn up, you're an asshole."

Every word she spoke forced her lips to brush against mine until I couldn't help but kiss her properly. A week of barely there patience had driven me mad. If I had it my way, she wouldn't spend another second away from me.

A sharp pain radiated through my bottom lip as Quen bit down on it. I grunted and pulled back.

"You always did like it rough," I said, chuckling.

With zero conviction and her gaze on my mouth, she muttered, "Stay away from me."

"Is that really what you want?" I asked, cocking my head to the side and forcing an arm around the back of her.

She tried to press herself against the wall, but my fingers unclasped her strapless bra so that it fell between us. Quen raised her hands again, aiming a blow to my chest, but I gripped her wrists and pinned them above her head, feeling the cold metal against my palm.

"I want you as far away from me as possible," she said, but the words were a breathy command that lacked punch. Her pulse thundered beneath her skin and her pupils dilated with the lusty haze I was used to.

Brushing a lock of hair away from her face, I rested my forehead against hers again. She wanted space, but I refused to give it to her. We'd had too much of it. Too much wasted time because I couldn't resolve the unexpected issues that had arisen.

"Do you trust me?" I asked her, burying my face in the crook of her neck and breathing deeply.

Without her, my world lost vibrancy. There were days I would throw her from the cliffs at the back of my estate without hesitation for the way she spoke and behaved, but I'd always rescue her before she hit the abyss. I depended on Quentin's existence to bring a semblance of sanity to my own.

My tongue ran over her pulse point, and her body shuddered, relaxing against my touch. She'd always been responsive in the most beautiful way.

"You told me I couldn't," she whispered. The words were strained as she fought against her waning resolve.

One of my hands trailed along her shoulder, across her collarbone, and rested on her breast. Her nipple pebbled beneath my touch.

"Forget what I said," I told her. The pad of my thumb brushed against her nipple. "Do you trust me?"

"I shouldn't."

"But you do." I smirked against her skin and bit down on her neck, forcing a gasp out of her. "You were waiting for me because you trusted me to come to you. And I did."

"You haven't explained anything to me."

I pulled my face away from her neck and stared at her. Reflected in her eyes, I could see my own were fully black and the veins along my face and neck were the same onyx shade.

"You're a smart woman," I said, tapping her temple with my index finger softly. "You'll figure it out."

"I'm not playing games with you, Gray," Quen snapped, looking like she was ready to bite my finger off. "Get me out of all of this and tell me what's going on."

"Not until you've calmed down," I replied with a smirk.

I sank to my knees, her eyes following me as I settled on the floor in front of her. Gently, I pulled the heels from her feet, tossing them away, and Quentin shrunk to her true size. I dragged my nose along her leg, kissing and nipping the bare skin as I moved upwards. The sounds of her quiet gasps mixed with the scent of her arousal made it difficult to take my time.

"The easiest way to calm me down is to be honest with me," she protested weakly.

"Not necessarily the best way." Pulling the lace down her legs, I bared my goal. "Step out," I ordered her. She didn't move. "Quentin, I'm not in the habit of asking twice. Step. Out."

This time she moved her feet, and I picked up the damp scrap of fabric.

"Now what?" she asked, looking down at me.

Two simple words filled with so much attitude. It was impossible for me to believe that they could kill her. Quentin had too much spirit, had survived through so many trials—so how could this be her ending?

A shrill squeak escaped Quen's lips when I roughly lifted one of her legs over my shoulder, quickly followed by the other.

"Gray!" she called my name as I rose from my knees.

Quen's arms came around my neck, the cuffs cutting into the nape and pulling me close as she tried to find stability. I was happy to oblige, pressing my face into her pussy. Her back was flat against the wall as my tongue eagerly lapped at her. All the patience I'd conveyed had been wiped away the moment I had her alone. While her body writhed against the wall, grinding her pussy against my face, Quen let out strangled whimpers.

Pulling away, I looked up at her, feeling her wetness around my mouth. "I want to hear you, Quentin."

"Then you'll need to work harder," she bit back in response.

Her temper was still too close to the surface. Of all the things she was good at, holding a grudge could have topped the list. Stubborn even in the face of pleasure; Quen refused to let it go. She wouldn't get her way. Not yet. Not until I figured out how much to tell her without making her situation worse.

"I'm not afraid of a little hard work," I replied.

Even in a collar and cuffs, she was trying to run the show. Submission wasn't something that came easily to her when it fought against her stubborn nature and search for answers.

"Not when it suits you!"

Her voice rose an octave on the word 'you' as I sucked on her clit. My cock strained painfully against my trousers at the taste of her. Seven days may have been a drop in the ocean in the millennia I'd existed, but without Quentin, without her body in my hands, it felt like an eternity.

My teeth nipped at the bud of nerves before my tongue soothed the rough play. Sweet, salacious moans filled the room. It was the melody that played through dark nights when she was away from me. Nothing compared to the knowledge that I elicited those noises from her. Coaxed this beautiful and strong woman into a quivering mess under my ministrations.

Reaching up, I pushed a finger into her slick heat, pumping it before adding another. Quen bucked her hips, grinding against my face, attempting to use me to find the high she craved.

"Please," she moaned, "don't stop."

I would have loved to oblige. Watching her come undone at my hands was something that gave me immense pride—greater than any of my other work. But she wasn't getting rewarded when she'd given nothing but attitude since the moment we arrived home.

As I pulled away from her again, she whimpered, and I almost caved. That fucking sound… the one she made because she depended on me to bring her pleasure no one else could, would be my downfall.

I removed my fingers just as her walls started to tighten around them and ducked out of the chokehold she had me in.

"Gray?"

The look on her face was vulnerable. Beautifully reliant. That was how it should be. The way I relied on her, craved her presence in my life, should be reciprocated. There was a bond between us that proclaimed it to be the case.

Carefully, I unhooked her legs from my shoulders and slid her down the wall until her feet touched the ground. Quen kept her focus on me, waiting and wondering what the next step was. When I turned her around, she placed her bound hands against the wall to stop from being pressed against it.

"Tell me again," I said, undoing my trousers and pushing them down so my dick was finally free. "Did he touch you?"

Silence.

Stubborn woman.

Quentin tried to turn around, but I caught the lead on her collar and tugged hard to keep her facing the wall.

I began the question again. "Did he—"

"I've already answered you, haven't I?" The fire had reignited, and the fight flooded her body again.

"You did," I replied, running the tip of my dick along her pussy.

It was pure torture not to drive right into her, but Quen mirrored the agony I felt. She pushed her hips back, desperate to fill herself.

"Pure bliss," I repeated her words. "Best you've ever had."

More silence.

"Which means you don't need me or my subpar cock," I continued through gritted teeth.

My free hand replaced my dick, running along her pussy, dripping wet with her arousal, until I pinched her clit between my thumb and forefinger. Quen yelped and rested her head against the wall.

"I should just tie you up and leave you here," I considered.

"No!"

"No?" The amusement laced the single word. "There's no point in me being here."

"I lied," she said to the wall, breathing heavily. "He never touched me."

Enough games. I kicked her legs apart wider and tugged at the chain, forcing her to arch her back before pushing my cock into her warm, wet heat without warning.

"Fuck," I groaned, finally coming home after days. Leaning forward, I whispered in her ear, "I know he didn't touch you because otherwise he wouldn't be alive right now."

My fingers continued to rub her clit as I thrust into her.

"I hate you," Quen managed between laboured breaths.

"That means you care," I told her.

If she was trying to hurt me, she'd have to try harder. Love and hate were two sides of the same coin. She hated me when we first met. She professed to hate me now because I won our little argument. But if that's what she felt, I would take it because I'd seen Scott when she was indifferent and that was a far worse outcome.

"I don't care," she moaned, pushing back to meet my hips. "You're the worst of them."

"Keep talking dirty to me, Scott."

But her words were stolen from her as I thrust harder. Her elbows buckled and her body slammed against the wall. I let go of the lead and braced my arm near her face to stop myself from crushing her. She turned her head and bit down on my forearm.

"You can say you hate me," I grunted, trying to keep a steady rhythm. "But you still can't stay away."

Quen's walls started to tighten around me again, squeezing my cock, and her teeth sank further into my flesh. I slowed down, barely moving, and she whimpered again. I would never tire of that sound.

"Please," she begged. "Please, Gray."

"Tell me I'm the best you've ever had."

"I'm going to kill you."

"I'm sure you will, darling." Bending down slightly, I licked up the length of her spine, and she shuddered. "Tell me I'm the best you've ever had and I'll let you finish."

Her breath was ragged, and I thought she would let her pride take over, elongating our game. But then she dropped her head and said, "You're the best I've ever had."

Happy with her confession, I picked up the pace, kissing along the side of her face, and Quen bit down on my arm again. She'd given me enough. She wasn't willing to scream for me.

"See how much easier it is when you tell the truth," I said between thrusts. "Such a good girl."

It didn't take long for Quen to reach the edge. Her walls spasmed around me, pulling me in deep and keeping me there. Her teeth broke through the flesh of my arm, further proving the divinity in her blood, albeit dampened by the copper monstrosities. I followed soon after, filling her so much that it leaked from where we were joined and dripped messily down her thighs.

Quen's legs buckled as she lost my support when I pulled out, but I kept her upright, turning her around to face me. My arm had already healed, but the evidence of her assault was smeared across her lips. Gold blood decorated her bottom lip, and my cum dripped down her legs.

Collar. Cuffs. Cum and blood. This was an image of my soulbound that would stay with me for the rest of my life.

Did she really think I'd let anyone survive if they took her from me? Did she believe I wouldn't tear them all apart even if they tried?

Wrapping an arm around her waist, I pulled her flush against my body. "I don't think I'm done with you yet."

NINE

QUENTIN

The familiar scent of bonfire, leather, and books tickled my nose. I turned my head into the soft pillow, begging the scent to stay and comfort me until I realised who the heady mixture belonged to.

My eyes snapped open, and I groaned as I rolled onto my back. A dull ache resonated between my legs, across my chest, and at various other points of my body.

Memories flooded back, and I closed my eyes again, squeezing them tight. Gray, dominating and all-consuming as he pushed me to the brink all night. If there was ever a way to welcome someone home, that was it.

Somewhere in the depths of my brain, I should have pushed him away and left the house. But the way it felt to be in his arms again, the way every touch, kiss and bite filled me with a desire to survive, had me pressing my body against him as if we could really become one entity.

Pushing myself up, I swung my legs over the side of the bed and stretched before catching sight of the mirror. The image drew me

towards it and I stood in front of my reflection, taking it in.

No new bruises from our night together. No visible marks, courtesy of Gray. But my stretch marks remained forked like lightning across my skin. White tracks against brown skin that made them impossible to hide. My fingers brushed against my thighs, hips, and ass trailing along the marks, pissed that they still existed. The least my divinity could have done was gift me the same exquisiteness the Gods exuded along with the shit storm.

"You are still a highly flawed individual."

I whirled around to be greeted by Gray. He lounged against the doorframe, shirtless and in sweatpants. In his hands, he held a pile of clothes and his eyes were trained on me, flickering between blue and black.

He pushed away from the door and dropped the clothes on the bed before joining me at the mirror. I turned away from him and stared at our reflections. Absolute perfection and a highly flawed individual. It seemed stupid to be fixated on something so small, and yet my brain latched on to the thought until I wanted to reach inside my skull and claw it out.

Strong arms snaked around my waist, pulling my back flush against a warm, chiselled chest. When Gray spoke, his breath tickled my ear. "I wouldn't want you any other way."

Ignoring him, I replied, "I see you took the restraints off me."

"I have no intention of keeping you tied up, Quen."

"Could have fooled me," I grumbled.

When I tried to break free of his hold, Gray swept me up in his arms and strode into his bathroom.

"What are you doing?" I asked, clinging to him.

Mind melting sex hadn't erased the fact that there were things that needed to be discussed.

"I ran you a bath," he answered. "I thought it might help while we talk."

The freestanding tub, black like everything else in the house, was filled with a ridiculous number of bubbles topping the water.

"I didn't have you down as someone who enjoyed bubble baths," I muttered, not wanting to feel grateful for the gesture.

"I don't," he said, kissing my temple.

Gray placed my naked body into the tub, and I sank into the water, allowing the warmth to cocoon me. I leaned back and slid down a little further until only my head was visible above the bubbles.

He leaned against the counter, crossing his legs at the ankle and folding his arms across his bare chest. "I'm sure you have plenty to say. Where would you like to start?"

Straight to the point. There was no reason to beat around the bush. He got what he wanted—what *we* wanted—last night. This morning was solely for me.

"You knew," I said. It wasn't a question. There was no doubt in my mind.

In the council chambers, Grayson had expertly taken control of the situation. I know he had a stroke of brilliance in him being a God, but it was suspiciously smooth how he'd been able to stand in front of the rest of the Gods and plead my case with no preparation.

He took in a deep breath through his nose. "I did."

"Erik? Sloan? Ignacio?" With each name, my temper rose.

"If you want to pick a fight, then you pick it with me, Quentin. Erik wanted to tell you, but I refused."

"You refused?"

"I was trying to protect you."

I pushed myself up, water sloshing over the edge of the bath.

"You're pissed, but you're showing considerable control right now," Gray commented, pushing himself away from the counter and stalking towards me. "I keep expecting your aura to appear."

"This isn't a zoo or a circus. I'm not on show. Why should I trust you, Grayson?"

"I'm sorry, but did you expect me to sit and have a conversation with you about how you're a demigoddess?" He made it sound like an unreasonable request.

"Yes!"

I locked eyes with him and the anger in me swelled. A warmth grew in my chest, and I pushed back on it, refusing to give him what he wanted.

"You know now," he said, shrugging his broad shoulders. "You're asking why you should trust me, but you already do. You were waiting for me in lower Elysia. While in a collar and cuffs, you allowed me to fuck you. You sit naked in a tub in *our* home. These are not actions from a woman who distrusts me."

Swiping my arm through the tub, I aimed the water at him, but it fell short, only soaking his feet.

"Ouch," he deadpanned, looking from his feet back to me. "I'm melting."

"I hate you."

"Have you convinced yourself of that yet? Or are you hoping that I'll change my mind and decide to stop loving you because you keep declaring such nonsense?"

My cheeks heated as I remembered the last conversation before coming up to Elysia. Gray admitted he loved me before Ethan turned up.

"We really should discuss why you were running through the streets in the middle of an earthquake." He looked livid. "Do you have any regard for your safety?"

"I was coming to find you."

"And why was that?" he asked, coming to the tub and kneeling beside it. "Soak your hair."

Slipping under the water, I re-emerged with droplets running down my face and hanging off my eyelashes. "I made a mistake leaving with Ethan. I went home to find you, but you weren't there. I was heading to Erik's."

I couldn't bring myself to admit that I was going to confess that I loved him. Too much had happened, and the icy fortress was resurrected around my heart. I needed to protect myself while I figured out what was happening around me. Whether I would survive this long enough to make the confession worth it.

Gray snapped open a bottle and deposited a dollop of shampoo into his palm. My brow furrowed at the familiar scent.

"That's the one I use at home," I pointed out.

"You're very observant this morning."

Leaning over the tub, I looked at the bottle. It bore a dent on the left side. "That's the exact one I use at home. You've been back down to Earth." My focus snapped to him. "You went home. You could take me home."

"No," he said calmly. "I took an unauthorised visit to bring you back some comfort. Shampoo. Clothes. I'm not about to risk taking you back to Earth."

"You risked it."

A muscle in his jaw jumped, and Gray brought his face close to mine. "My priority list comprises two people. You and myself. You're a smart woman to figure out the order. Now, turn around."

Slowly, I put my back to him and Gray inched closer, lathering the shampoo into my hair. A lump materialised in my throat, making it hard to swallow. It'd been so long since someone had looked after me like this. Gentle touches that were wrapped in concern and care… It made me feel like a child.

"You need to be honest with me," I said, tipping my head back as his fingers massaged my scalp. "If you love someone, you don't keep secrets."

"You'll have to excuse the *faux pas*," he said. His fingers stopped, and I twisted around to face him again. Gray locked eyes with me as he spoke. "Someone did not exactly design me for love. This is my first experience of it outside of family and even that's only with selected members."

The admission sent a thunderous crack through the ice palace that guarded my heart.

"You've been in love before," I argued.

"I can assure you, I have not."

"You've been alive for centuries."

The corner of his mouth twitched. "Millenia, Quentin. But I appreciate the compliment." When he was met with silence, Gray twirled his index finger in the air. "Turn."

I obeyed his command, facing away from him again, and he resumed washing my hair.

"We were only ever meant to be on Earth temporarily," he explained. "I knew the repercussions of knowing what you were. There was no need to tell you when you would not be around us forever."

The words felt like a stab in the heart. We were still going to separate after all this. 'Til death do us part was never going to be an option.

"But when I saw you on the road, when I thought I might lose you… I did what I had to," Gray said.

"It was a wasted effort if Hunter and the others are planning to kill me. Am I that much of a problem, Gray?"

"We've had issues before," he said, words clipped. "Some things are harder to forgive than others. But I won't let it happen, Quen. We can win this."

"How?" I asked. I swallowed the nervous laughter that threatened to spill from me. "I want to go home. My brother and lab are what I want. Am I ever going to be allowed that?"

He sucked in a deep breath, rinsing my hair and slathering conditioner along the length.

"Quentin," Gray muttered. "What I'm about to tell you goes no further than these walls. Do you understand?"

The anxiety flourished in the pit of my stomach, and I gave a small, uncertain nod of my head.

"I have spent centuries trying to take Hunter's position. It's partially the reason for my reluctance with the project. If he makes a success of it, then it makes it more difficult for me to usurp him."

My heart beat so wildly in my chest that I could hear it thumping in my ears. A steady, thunderous noise that made my words sound distant. "I thought you didn't want the throne."

"We never discussed my intentions," Gray corrected me. "Just that Hunter was losing favour and would prefer an heir. You're the first to remind me of my ego. Do you really think I'd pass up on the opportunity to have everyone dance to my tune?"

"But you aren't in charge. Hunter calls the shots, Gray. How is you wanting to take over going to make a difference?" I asked, failing to see his logic.

"We need to prove that there's value in keeping you alive. That you aren't a threat."

It appeared we were on the same wavelength about proving my worth.

"And then?" I pressed.

"Your allegiance is with me. Correct?"

I stiffened as the pieces snapped into place. "You want me to play a game to help you get what you want?"

A large hand wrapped around my throat from behind, lacking pressure but guiding my head back. Gray's lips brushed against my temple.

"What I want," he whispered, "is for you to survive this. It just so happens we're able to kill two birds with one stone."

"No," I argued. "You could still win that coveted seat if they kill me."

Fingers pressed against the sides of my throat and I tried to ignore the gentle throb that occurred between my legs.

"If all I wanted was the seat," Gray said, "I could have let you die when that car hit you. You have been an unnecessary complication from the moment you stepped into my life. I am selfish. I am vile. I am all those things you believe me to be and worse. But you are my priority now. Before anything else, you and your survival matter the most to me. I need you to trust me."

Trust was something that I gave so sparingly. No one deserved it and I wasn't entirely sure that Gray was worth it, but I knew my soul had trusted him from the moment I woke up in the pool. It believed that he had my best interests at heart.

Plus, Elysia had layers of politics and customs that were a minefield to navigate, and if my goal was to survive and return to Earth, I needed someone to watch my steps. Gray wasn't keeping secrets the way Archer was. He'd been honest about his plans.

My hand ran along his forearm, fingers finding the space between his. Gray released his grip on my throat, and I held his hand, bringing his wrist to my lips.

"We have one shot at this," I mumbled against his skin. "If anything goes wrong—"

"It won't." He said it with such conviction it was difficult not to believe him. His warm breath fanned across my ear, causing goosebumps to appear. "I'll tear Elysia in half if it means I get to keep you."

I wanted to take those words with a pinch of salt. Everything needed to be approached with caution, but the small sliver of me that contained a crumb of hope released a fresh flood of adrenaline at the base of my stomach, unfurling it with alarming urgency. Even if he didn't mean it, I took some comfort in the gesture.

"Did Archer treat you well?" Gray asked, tension seeping into the words.

"Mostly," I replied, squeezing his hand. "He was determined to find out my gift."

"You didn't tell him, did you?"

"No. Dionne told me not to, so I lied and said I didn't know."

"And he believed you?"

"Not at all, but I kept lying. He has his own secrets. The stupid gifting ball came out of nowhere and he was going to introduce me like a prize pig."

"Did he say anything to you? Tell you anything?"

"Nothing. He just kept telling me lower Elysia is my home. It's where I belong. Barely answered any of my questions. The prick." I bit my bottom lip gently. "Who shares his home, Gray? The place isn't just green. There are touches of pink."

"I try not to concern myself too much with Archer's personal life."

Realising I wouldn't get an answer from him, I let go of Gray's hand and dipped under the water again to rid myself of the conditioner. When I resurfaced, Gray had a fluffy black towel in his hands. I stepped out of the tub and let him wrap me in it.

"Do you own anything that isn't black?" I asked.

"No, and I don't plan on redecorating," he replied proudly. "What would you prefer? Gold?"

Pulling a face, I tightened the towel around my body and turned away from him, heading towards the door.

"Such a shame," Gray called after me, sounding smug. I ignored him and kept going. "The colour really landed itself to the fact you'd be the most perfect trophy wife."

It happened quicker than I could react to it. The insinuation that I'd be some pretty, decorative element for any man set my blood on fire and the warmth exploded in my chest. It burned straight through my skin as I turned on my heel to face Gray and watched him knocked clean off his feet before smashing into the mirror above the counter.

My hands flew to my mouth while the room glowed in golden hues. "Shit," I whispered.

Gray looked up from the floor, surrounded by shattered glass. There was a moment of silence before he tipped his head back and laughed so loud that I jumped. When he calmed down, he looked at me again, blue irises robbed by the black of his aura.

"Of all the things that have happened recently that could make you lose your shit, it's me calling you a trophy wife," he said, picking himself up from the floor. "You truly are a marvel, Quentin Scott."

We were never going to be that picture perfect couple who coveted a soft love. There were moments we shared, and I appreciated, but Gray and I were destined to be chaotic and messy. It might not have been perfect, but it was all I wanted.

"You are the worst person in my life," I told him, struggling to keep the smile at bay.

"I'm banking on it, golden girl."

TEN

GRAYSON

"You're making coffee." Erik's voice sounded from behind me. "She's home."

Leaving the pot on the counter, I faced my brother. "I thought you would have been here yesterday."

"Sloan made me wait," he muttered sullenly. "Thought you would appreciate time alone together."

I chuckled under my breath. A day of peace was exactly what Quentin needed. Physically, she was okay, but my golden girl had retreated. She was lost inside her head as she sat out on the cliffs that backed the manor. She was glued to my side, constantly in contact as she asked questions and carefully shared her thoughts until she was ready to retire to bed.

Throughout the night, I watched her. She was as restless in her sleep as she was in consciousness, and I knew she would have more to discuss. Hence the pot of coffee to ease us into things this morning.

"Where is she?" Erik asked.

"Still in bed. It's been a long few days and there are plenty more ahead of us. She needs to rest."

"Have you figured out what happens next?"

"She wants to go home, Erik."

My brother's face fell, and I hated the fact I'd delivered the news that disappointed him.

"She is home," he whined. "This is her home."

"Not to her."

Quen didn't accept Elysia. Her home was what she grew up with. Her lab. Her brother. Kin meant little without loyalty. And the Gods had given her nothing.

"And you're happy to watch her go?" Erik asked briskly.

My aura flared out around me. "I didn't see you banging on Hunter's door to bring her back home."

Erik had the decency to look embarrassed. But I understood. This wasn't his fight. He might have been fond of Quentin, but he had a family to protect, and the way to minimise collateral damage was to step back. I might have been pissed at him for the decision, but I respected that he chose to protect what mattered to him most. I would have done—was doing—the same.

A wave of uneasiness rushed through me and my aura faltered.

Erik looked up. "I truly am sor—"

"Gray?" Quen's voice rang through the house, laced with panic. "Bubba!"

She ran into the kitchen and came to an abrupt halt, and it was clear to see why. The tile on which her bare feet touched had changed from my signature black to glittering gold.

"It keeps happening," she whispered, looking up at me with wide eyes. "I don't know how to stop it."

I beckoned Quen with my index finger. "Come here."

"You come here," she replied. "I'm not sure what else I'm going to do."

"Come here," I repeated. "Or I'll bring you here myself."

When a tendril of my aura reached towards her, she let out a frustrated sigh and walked towards me. Each step she took changed the black tiles beneath her feet into a glorious rippling gold. I bit the insides of my cheeks to stop myself from grinning as she walked cautiously into my arms.

When I enveloped her into a hug, she buried her face into my chest, and I dropped a kiss on her head. I was the comfort she sought.

A faint red glow emitted from my brother as he joined my side. "You won't be able to stop it," he said, glee clear in his words. "The house recognises you. It's wonderful."

She turned her head so that she looked at Erik, but still rested it against my chest.

"Quentin," he said warmly, but the smile soon dropped.

She didn't move towards him or beam at him the way she usually did when she saw my baby brother. Instead, Quen stared at him like he was a stranger.

"Did you need something?" she asked, tone icy and detached.

I suppressed the smirk that tugged at my lips. My soulbound knew how to hold a grudge. She wasn't happy, and she wasn't about to bullshit Erik into thinking things between them remained the same. The lack of contact was taken as a personal affront, and it wasn't my job to patch things up between the pair.

Erik rubbed the back of his neck, gaze flicking to me and back to her before he answered. "I wanted to come and check on you. See if you are okay."

"Well—"

Her rebuttal was cut short as a trickle of electric blue appeared beside the coffee pot and disappeared, leaving a scrap of paper in its place.

"Fucking fantastic," I mumbled as Erik grabbed it off the counter.

His eyes skimmed along the paper. "Hunter's expecting you to see him at your earliest convenience."

"He wasn't that polite," I stated.

"No."

I rolled my eyes. "A solo visit, I assume."

"No," Quentin said, looking up at me. "I'll come with you. I want to speak to him."

"Quen—" Erik started hesitantly.

"You said I needed to prove my worth, and I thought the same thing. Let me talk to him. He wants the project to be a success, but that means he needs me on Earth. He needs to let me go home."

"That doesn't align with what we were discussing yesterday," I reminded her. "And it's a temporary solution. What happens after you conclude E.L.I.?"

"We'll have time to figure it out."

"Let me see what he wants first. I'll ask him to see you."

Erik smiled at her. "I'm happy to stay while you—"

"I don't need a babysitter, Erik," Quen cut across him. "I'll be fine on my own."

She detached herself from me and went to the counter. As her palms touched the surface, it turned to a shimmering gold.

"For fuck's sake," she hissed the curse. "Gray, can you fix this, please?"

Walking up behind her, I placed my hand on the countertop but the black marbled with the gold in a tangle of swirls.

"Sorry, darling." I kissed the back of her head. "It looks like your changes have some permanence here."

"How long will you be with Hunter?" she asked, grabbing the coffee pot and pouring a mug with a little more vigour than necessary.

"I'll keep it brief. I don't want to be around him any longer than I have to be."

"What do you think he wants?"

We both looked at Erik, who shrugged and said, "Your guess is as good as mine. Progress update? Lay down the law?"

"Don't worry," I told Quen, rubbing her hip with my palm.

"Easier said than done," she mumbled, sipping from the mug. "I'll be on the grounds. Come back in one piece."

She reached up on her toes and kissed me. My arm wrapped around her waist, pulling her flush against me as I deepened the embrace, tasting bitter notes of coffee. Quen hummed into the kiss before pushing me away with some help from her aura.

"Go," she ordered, waving me off as she slipped past Erik. "Figure out the best way for us to play our first move."

Once she disappeared from the room, Erik's shoulders sagged and he directed his attention towards me.

"What's that look for?" I asked. He looked utterly pathetic, as if he was a puppy who'd been kicked.

"I'm not used to people being so cold with me," he mumbled. "She forgave you for being stuck with Archer."

"I'm her favourite," I reminded him smugly.

"And I'm meant to be universally loved."

"You look a moment away from stomping your foot and having a tantrum, Erik."

He blew out a breath and ran a hand through his hair. "I don't like people being upset with me."

"She's not exactly known for her cool temper. Even you're not naïve enough to believe she'd be okay with the way we left her to fend for herself down there, with no help. The fact we hid things from her."

Nodding, he asked, "Would you like me to stay while you deal with Hunter?"

"Yes. But for your own safety, stay out of her way."

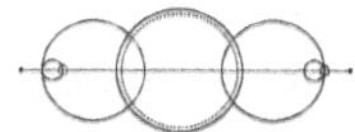

I'd spent more time in Hunter's home than I would have liked over the past few days. We didn't maintain a relationship that saw us visit each other often the way me and Erik did. I only stepped over Hunter and Larkin's threshold if it was a necessity.

When I walked into his living room, I saw him lounging, arms spread across the back of the sofa and ankle crossed over his knee. He truly was the king of his castle.

"What do you want?" I asked, pulling him from his thoughts.

His movements were predatory. The slow turn of his head as he fixed his gaze on me, rolling his shoulders back, would have unnerved most people. It only served to aggravate me. I'd wasted enough time away from Quen and wanted to return home.

"Has she ruffled your feathers already?" he asked, picking a piece of lint from his trousers and letting it flutter to the floor.

"Not as badly as Archer did yours. Did you offer to repair his wall?"

"He's lucky it was just the wall." There was a ripple in his calm demeanour. "How is she without them?"

"What do you mean?"

Hunter gestured to the chair opposite him. I didn't want to take the seat but needed to continue to show my willingness.

"You were never one to follow the rules, Grayson. And I'm not stupid. You'd have taken her out of the binds the first moment you could just to see what she could do. So, share with the class."

I rolled my neck, the cracking sound filling the room. I had two choices: lie and irritate Hunter, falling out of his favour, or tell him the truth and try to paint it in a light that might win us some points.

"She displays a surprising amount of control for someone who's just been gifted," I explained casually. "There's been the odd hiccup, but nothing too damaging."

No need to tell him about the mirror incident. It was a quick fix, and I had no lasting injuries from it.

"We can't afford the odd hiccup," Hunter replied.

Despite his calm facade, a muscle jumped near his jaw and there was a ripple in the air that belonged to me. Quentin made him angry. Her existence went against everything he stood for. The fact she hid in plain sight for so long must have driven him mad. Confirmed what I had known all along—he was unfit for the position he held.

Hunter uncrossed his legs and leaned forwards. He rested his elbows on his knees and looked at me. For a moment, I was transported back to centuries ago when I looked at my brother, longing for his approval. There was nothing more I wanted than for Hunter to see me as worthy of being his second-in-command.

But I had grown up since then. Why settle for second when you could be first? Approval was highly overrated. Especially coming from this clown.

"There are questions about the study and why it's been paused." Hunter ran a hand down his face. "The problem with turning to someone devout and using them as a vessel means they will not leave you alone when something goes slightly off course."

"This could have been entirely avoided if you'd listened to me and abandoned this ridiculous plan in the first place," I said, checking my nails.

There was a flash of blue that forced me to look up. Hunter's face contorted with rage, tired of being questioned by me once again on the need for E.L.I.

"This project needs to be a success—"

"If you say so." I leaned back in my chair and sniffed.

"And you will help make it a success."

"And how am I meant to do that? I've played along and offered myself as the perfect test subject, but everything is on hold."

"You're going to teach her to control herself so we can descend and finish the business I started."

It felt too perfect, the hand I'd drawn against my brother. He was giving us exactly what we wanted, but I needed to keep calm.

"You're prepared to release her back to Earth?" I asked smoothly.

"Temporarily. Once the project is done, we can convene for a council meeting and make a decision about what to do with her."

"We don't know how long that might take."

"Uncertainty breeds fear and fear breeds compliance. I want her to be compliant, Grayson. If you don't think you're up to handling a half-breed, I'll ask Aria."

"Yes, because I'm sure Aria would strike fear into Scott's heart," I said, rolling my eyes.

Aria was the Goddess of health. She had a bite and a self-importance that made her walk with her chin tipped a few degrees higher than the rest of us. Not that she could face off against Quentin. My woman was in a league of her own.

"You'll do as I've ordered."

"How long do I have to train her?"

Hunter narrowed his eyes. "I'll give you a week. I don't particularly care what methods you use. You have a lead for the bitch. Use it at your discretion."

The pain shot through my jaw as I nodded. "I'm sure it won't come to that."

"No. I'm certain you have more creative ways to make her listen to you. Share some of your stories. I'm sure that would keep her in line."

He was baiting me. Hunter didn't want her to know the truth any more than I did.

"Anything else?" I gritted out.

"No. You can leave."

I wasted no time pushing myself out of the seat and stalking out of the room. Larkin's slim frame hid just outside the doorway and she watched me curiously.

"Is this what you've resorted to?" My voice was nothing more than a whisper. "Sleuthing for information. I expected more from you, Larkin."

I didn't wait for a response as I brushed past her. To my surprise, she followed me and my dismal mood grew more grim.

"What?" I hissed over my shoulder.

"Why were you so desperate to bring her back up here?" Larkin asked, keeping her voice down.

"She's a liability, Larkin."

"Then why is Bexley running errands for you? Getting Dionne to keep an eye on her?"

I should have known Bexley would talk to her sister, but it didn't sound like Larkin knew any more than she had to. If I had the vaguest sense that she knew about the bond, then all my plans were about to be thrown out.

I stopped in my tracks and Larkin appeared in front of me. Her blonde hair fell in straight sheets around her long face.

"I don't know what it is, and I don't want to know, but you're playing a dangerous game," she warned me. "Hunter and Archer and you. You're all after something. I suggest you drop it, Grayson. That poor girl doesn't deserve to be dragged through the mess happening up here."

I scoffed. "Am I meant to believe you care about her wellbeing?"

"When she's landed herself in the middle of three psychopaths? Yes."

"The only psychopath you can talk about with any sort of confidence is your darling husband." I cocked my head to the side. "That's not quite right, is it? I guess you might know a thing or two about Archer, although times might have changed."

The slap didn't even sting. My sister-in-law stood before me with a furious expression. I cut deep today and I had no regrets. Bringing up her past relationship was a definite way to get a rise out of her.

"Hunter won't let this go," Larkin told me. "Don't be an idiot. We don't need a war, Grayson. The kindest thing you can do for her is to prepare her for the inevitable. Death is a better option than dragging her through all of this. For what? Ego? Pride?"

"Should I help her pick out her coffin? Or would you like to come around and do that with her? Will you offer your flowers or are my lilies more appropriate for the occasion?"

"Stop being so flippant!"

"Larkin, I don't need your concern. And I'm sure Scott wouldn't appreciate it either. Focus on yourself and your marriage."

"We split the vote, Grayson. All it would take is for one person to change their mind and she won't exist any longer. Why put her through months of uncertainty just so you can all play mind games with each other?"

My aura flexed around me and I wrapped it around myself, leaving before we drew Hunter's attention.

Larkin's words echoed in my head as I left, but she was wrong.

All it took was for one person to change their mind and Quentin could exist for eternity.

ELEVEN

QUENTIN

The grounds of Gray's home were exactly how you would expect them—dark and foreboding. There was a gentle rolling fog that made it difficult to see too far ahead. After three laps of the vast estate, I settled down amongst the Odessa calla lilies that grew in clusters along the path.

It didn't take long before a strange tension crackled through the air. It forced me to sit up straight, and when I looked over my shoulder, Erik was walking towards me with an umbrella in hand.

"It looks like it's about to rain," he said, and I bit back on the response that it always looked ready to rain here.

I turned away and focused my attention on my mug. My silence didn't deter him. Erik folded himself on the ground beside me and opened up the umbrella, holding it above us as the first drops fell.

"I'm sorry," he said without prompt. "Please don't be mad at me."

"It's not just you," I told him.

"We never meant for you to feel like we'd abandoned you."

The word 'abandoned' was like a bucket of icy water being tossed over me. I was used to the feeling, but it had been years since anyone

had a chance to commit the act again.

"It's my fault. I shouldn't have trusted so many of you in such a short space of time," I said, picking at blades of grass.

Erik's hand landed on mine, stopping my assault on the ground. "You guard your heart fiercely, Quentin, and I understand why."

I'd always hated that Erik knew more about me than the others. He accessed my vulnerabilities before I could offer them to him.

"But you have so much love to give. You didn't make a mistake." He squeezed my hand. "Matters are complicated and—"

"You did what you thought was best," I finished shortly.

"There's so much you don't understand. Gray has plans—"

"I know about his plans, Erik," I said, finally looking up at him.

"He told you?" Erik's eyebrows disappeared into his hairline.

Being mad at Erik was a difficult task. He was the only God who had no agenda or malicious intent. He didn't quite understand my boundaries, but he tried harder than any of the others. Untangling my hand from his, I brushed some of the white blonde hair out of his eyes. There were moments where he reminded me of Cass—always spreading himself thin, trying to keep things afloat.

"He told me," I confirmed.

"He adores you."

"He loves me."

Erik's face broke out into a grin and there was a faint red glow that surrounded him. "If you matter to him, you matter to us. But we need to tread carefully."

"I understand," I said, letting go of my anger towards him. "You have a lot more to lose than I do."

His expression crumpled, and I looked away. Erik grabbed my

hand again and said, "Please don't say it like that."

"You have a wife and children. Gray is yours. You need to protect them." My voice was thick with emotion.

The truth was a painful pill to swallow. We all had people we cared about. People who we placed importance on in our lives. I didn't expect to have even made a dent in that list to the Gods when they'd known me for a few months and I'd hardly set the best impression.

"You have—"

"Why am I not surprised that you're both out here in the rain?" Gray's voice boomed across the grounds.

I crawled out from under the umbrella and looked at him as he strode towards me. No cuts. No bruises. No blood. I could breathe easier again.

"What did Hunter want?" I asked Gray.

Gray picked me up off the ground, my legs wrapping around his waist and arms around his neck, and he carried us back towards the manor.

"Your services are no longer required, Erik," Gray called out.

Looking over Gray's shoulder, I watched Erik chuckle to himself and then he disappeared in a flash of red, leaving my coffee mug and the umbrella surrounded by lilies.

"Tell me what Hunter said," I demanded.

"We can take you home."

"What?"

I didn't want to believe it. Hope blossomed so rapidly in my chest that I felt lightheaded and my mouth grew numb. I tried to school my emotions, knowing that there would be a catch.

"In a week," Gray continued. "I need to make sure you can control your aura. He wants to go back and finish the project, and once it's complete, he'll call a council meeting to decide what to do with you."

"That seems a little too… simple."

This had been my plan, but it felt too serendipitous that Hunter had the same thoughts with no prompting.

"Agreed," he said, walking through the house and up the stairs. "I don't know what he's thinking other than proving he can still make this a success through any obstacle."

"What does that mean for me?"

"We do what he wants. I'll teach you what I have to and we get you back on Earth. There's something else I need you to do."

"What?"

Gray placed me on the bed in his room, and I looked up at him, waiting for the stipulation.

He pressed his knuckles into the mattress on either side of me and leaned in. His forehead rested against mine as he spoke. "I need you to be a social butterfly. You need to win over the rest of the Gods, golden girl."

It was worse than I imagined. Gray wanted me to play nice and convince the Gods that my life was worth living.

"Would you like me to don a pageant dress and crown as well? Should I bake and ask them all around for tea?" I retorted.

"Is it really that difficult for you to be pleasant?"

"Do you ever ask yourself the same question?"

Gray laughed, forcing me back on the bed and climbing onto it with me. One arm tucked under my waist while the other rested on my thigh, and despite the situation I was caught in, I traced one, four, three across his chest.

"I don't know if I can lie that well," I admitted to him. "I don't know if I can play nice with people who voted to end my life."

"You sound so much like Mallory," he said, squeezing my thigh.

"My mother?" There's a small tremble as I said the word. It didn't feel right on my tongue. "Did you know her?"

Gray nodded, and I followed the motion.

"Can you…" I stumbled. "Will you tell me about her?"

"I can show you," Gray answered.

I blinked at him as he lifted a hand from my thigh and held it out to me. Hesitantly, I placed my hand in his and watched the scene unfold in front of me.

The weather in Elysia was warm and a gentle breeze rustled the grass as a group of Gods lounged around, enjoying the day.

A woman with olive skin and long dark hair laid back on the ground and spread her arms out wide. "Hunter needs to calm his shit. Why is he so desperate to get you two together? It's like it's his secret kink or something."

Elva flushed bright red while Erik and Gray laughed.

"It won't happen," Erik said confidently. "Not that he'll listen to me."

Mallory rolled over, lying on her stomach and looked at Erik, flipping her hair to one side. "What about me, Erik?" she questioned. "Who am I destined to fall in love with?"

"I'm not a crystal ball, Mal. You'd have to let me read you if you want me to know that."

She pulled a face and rolled onto her back again, staring up at the sky. Elva's fingers gently combed through her cousin's long locks.

"I don't think I'll ever be in love," Mallory declared.

"Join the club," Gray chimed in.

Mal laughed. "It's a little different, Gray."

"How do you work that out?"

"You won't fall in love because no one will have you. You're a handful and you're picky as fuck. Gods help the woman who catches your eye."

The group fell apart with laughter except for Gray, who maintained a stony expression.

"For me," Mallory continued. "Greed and selfishness are in my blood. I'm too selfish to share my time with anyone or… well, I'm going to want to love someone with everything I have and demand the same from them." She pushed herself up onto her elbows, enjoying the attention from the group. "Do you think our gifts are more of a curse? Sometimes I wonder what it would be like to forget all of this and live amongst the mortals—"

"Mallory!" Elva scolded. "You can't say that."

"Why not?"

"If Hunter hears you, he'll pull you in front of the council."

Mallory shrugged her shoulders.

"You've got some balls, Mal," Gray commented.

"Bigger than yours," she shot back.

The memory faded away, but the room remained out of focus as tears blurred my vision.

"She seemed…" I struggled, trying to get the words out around the lump in my throat.

"A lot to handle? You had to get it from somewhere."

"Did you know about me, Gray? Why she didn't want me?"

"First, she wanted you, Quentin. Mallory couldn't bring you back here and your father died, so that left you in the care system. Mal saw that to be better than death. But she couldn't live without you, either.

She didn't want to see anyone else raise you, so she asked Elva..." Gray paused. "She asked Elva to use her gift."

I sucked in a breath, knowing that Elva was responsible for death.

"I didn't know about you," Gray admitted. "None of us did. That was one of the last memories I have of Mallory. I guess after that was when she visited Earth more often and found someone."

Nodding slowly, I said, "I don't think I want to talk about this anymore. Not right now."

That simple memory had stirred up more than I thought it would and more than I could process healthily.

"That's fine." Gray brought my hand to his lips and kissed it gently. "You can ask anything you want, whenever you want, and I'll try my best to answer."

"Thank you."

"Quentin, I will say that Elva would love to spend time with you. She's your blood, and it would mean a lot to her."

"Not yet."

Gray didn't press the matter any further. His hand moved back to my thigh, tracing circles along the fabric that covered them.

"May I ask you something?" Gray said.

"Sure."

"Is Ethan planning to hang around?"

A weird stabbing pain occurred in my chest, and I took in a deep breath, trying to recover from it.

"I'm not sure," I replied once the pain passed. "I didn't stick around long enough to find out. I assume he'll be gone. It was so strange that he turned up after I got rid of the ring."

"You got rid of that hideous piece of shit?"

I slapped his chest hard. "Yes. I pawned it before I came to the pub."

The grin that Gray wore looked wide enough to split his face as he grabbed mine and kissed me passionately. I moved to straddle his lap and gave in to every ounce of want for him that coursed through me. I knew my life was complicated and that this thing with him wasn't needed because it would make things worse, but when had we ever chosen logic?

Gray's hands gripped my ass with bruising force, and I buried my fingers into his hair as our tongues fought against each other. The draw towards him would forever be indescribable. All I knew was when I was with him, my soul was at ease. Beside Gray, life felt manageable and the exhaustion I carried through my life was shared, making it easier to breathe.

We broke apart and the grin still graced his face, but his eyes were turning from blue to black.

"You need to keep some control," I said, kissing the tip of his nose.

Gray snorted a laugh and picked me up in one swift motion. He walked us over to the full-length mirror in his room, setting me down in front of it.

"Try again, love," he said, voice low and husky.

His hand guided my head until I looked at myself and gasped. My eyes, that were usually a deep brown shade, were gloriously golden. The image made me seem otherworldly.

Divine.

"There's no more hiding it now, Quentin."

TWELVE

GRAYSON

Gathered down by the waterfalls behind Ig's estate, I watched closely as he worked with Quentin. That had been Erik's idea since Quen and Ignacio were likely to be teamed when she was accepted by the Gods. An idea I wasn't best pleased with as it made the jealousy boil deep in my soul.

But we needed to get out of the heavens and away from the prying eyes of my kin. In order to do that, Quen had to control her aura better, which meant I accepted the need for reinforcements.

"You need to reach it when you aren't feeling powerful emotions," Ignacio said, crossing his arms over his chest.

"Well, that's easier said than done, Ig," Quen snapped as they worked for the second day in a row.

"You're a pain in the ass. You know that?"

Erik and I were perched on the grass watching them argue and trying to work through the lesson.

"Try. Again," Ig gritted out. "Are you sure your gift is success because—"

Quentin knocked him off his feet in a wave of gold. Orange

sparked up around Ig before I projected my aura out in front of her.

"Ignacio!" I barked, livid with his response. "Teach her or give up and I'll do it myself!"

Quentin looked over, frustrated at her situation. "I don't need you protecting me."

"Quentin." There was a slight warning in my tone.

"I am perfectly capable of doing this on my own."

"I never said you weren't."

I would protect her because I loved her, but she needed to allow me that courtesy. Needed to place her pride aside. That was a big ask.

"I'm fine," she told me, and I pulled my aura away.

"Try again, Scott," Ig said, picking himself off the ground.

She stood there and after a few more tries, for the first time in two days, Quen summoned her aura without being provoked.

"Finally," Ig exclaimed, throwing his hands in the air. "Now, you need to keep it under control when you get provoked."

Erik sat up straight and pushed himself to his feet. "I'm not sure that's the best idea."

"And if we don't teach her and she loses it back down there?" Ig asked. "Hunter's going to be thorough in making sure she isn't a threat to our security. You put me in charge, so let me do my job."

I leaned back against a tree and put my hands behind my head, keeping my eyes on Quen. She glanced over at me and her eyes lightened as I gave her a wink.

"Oi!" Ig yelled. "If you two can't keep it in your trousers, then you can get your ass out of here."

Quen flushed pink. She was still getting used to people calling her out, and I would be lying if I said I wasn't smug as fuck to know that I had that effect on her.

"Scott!" Ig barked. "Focus!"

She turned back to Ignacio.

Erik shifted his weight between his feet. "I really don't think—"

But his words were lost as Ignacio sparked his aura to life. He looked me in the eye and I narrowed mine in response. He had never given me a reason to distrust him, but I'd never handed him the most treasured possession in my existence. If Ignacio stepped one foot out of line, I wouldn't hesitate to watch that bridge go up in flames and there would be no repairing it.

"I'm trying to help her," Ig warned me. "So stay out of it."

I ran my tongue over my teeth, uncomfortable with what he was planning, but I nodded, allowing him to proceed.

The bright orange aura struck out towards her. Quentin called on her own but not quick enough, taking the blow and landing on her ass in the grass. I controlled my anger, reminding myself that she needed to do this on her own. Ig was capable of more damage than what he'd just dealt.

"Rein it in, Scott," Ig warned her.

"You just put me on my ass!" she shouted.

"It wasn't hard, sweetheart."

Her aura pulsed around her and she glared at him as she got back to her feet. A wall of gold rushed in Ig's direction, but he stopped it.

"You have one hell of a temper, Scott," he commented. "Almost as bad as your boyfriend over there."

That caught my attention. To be referred to so openly as her boyfriend was something new. Apparently, it wasn't just my attention that was piqued because Erik began to glow and Quen's aura faltered.

Ig pulled a contemplative face. "But still not as bad as him. Gray… well, he's the worst of us."

What was he doing? This wouldn't provoke her.

"You really know how to pick them," Ig continued. "I'm not sure why you're wasting your time with him."

Quentin's aura stopped flickering and grew solid, pulsating around her frame menacingly.

"Control it, Quentin," Erik said, bouncing on the balls of his feet.

Was she actually getting angry at what Ignacio was saying about me?

"Chaos and destruction all teamed with death." He almost looked like he was enjoying goading her. "There's not a decent bone in his body and yet you think what exactly, Scott? That you're going to be the one to change him?"

Ignacio threw his head back and laughed. Quentin strode towards him with such purpose that I got up on my feet.

"Quen!" I called. "Don't. Control it. Just like Sal taught you in the ring."

She halted in front of Ignacio, silence engulfing us as she took in my words. Her aura slowly faded and eventually dissipated away. Ig banished his, and I let out a breath. Quentin turned around to address me, but for some reason, Ignacio opened his big mouth.

"Surprise, surprise," he said. "He's the only one who can keep you under control."

It happened before any of us could stop her. Quen's hand turned into a fist, wrapped with her aura. She turned around and pulled her arm back before punching Ignacio straight in the jaw and Ig went flying before he slid across the ground and came to a stop.

"I am not controlled by anyone," she said, pointing her index finger at him.

Ig sat up, a small cut marring his lip, and Erik hurried over to help him up.

"Crazy bitch," Ignacio muttered.

He barely got to his feet when my aura pinned him against a nearby tree. He had my blessing to train her. He was allowed to use his aura to prove a point. But I didn't appreciate him running his mouth because she fought back.

"Gray!" Erik yelled. "Let him go."

I dropped Ig as he hissed and left in a flash of orange without another word.

Erik sighed. "You two need to work on your people skills. We're getting people on side, not pushing them away. I'm going to check on him. Join me when you both calm down."

He left us, and I rolled my eyes, but beside me, Quentin looked worried.

"I'm sorry," she muttered. "I just—"

"It's fine."

"It's not. I hate people thinking they control me or that I can be controlled."

"Trust me, darling, I know."

"And I hate what he was saying about you." Her aura flickered back into life around her.

A smirk graced my lips. "Aww, you care about my reputation. I am touched, Scott."

"Fuck off, Gray." But there was a smile on her lips as she walked away.

"You want to watch yourself, golden girl," I called after her. "You keep defending my honour like that and I might just think you love me."

She looked over her shoulder at me and, for a split second, I thought she might just say it. But she flashed me a grin, and I was knocked off my feet and straight into the river behind me. The ice-cold water soaked through to my bones, and when I resurfaced, Quentin was staring at me from the bank.

"We wouldn't want you getting any ideas now, would we, bubba?" she said.

It was way too late for that.

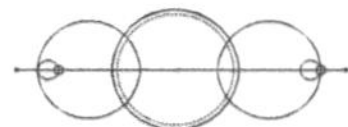

The temperature dropped as evening crept in. I'd smoothed things over with Ignacio. He had never been one to hold a grudge and Quentin felt awful for hitting him so hard. She'd promised to take him to Sal's as recompense, and Ig swallowed her in a hug that lasted a fraction too long for my liking.

However, the guilt still consumed her and the melancholy lingered until I couldn't stand it.

"Where are we going?" she asked.

It was late as I guided us along the back streets of Elysia, away from prying eyes. Quen wrapped her arms around herself and I longed to pull her against me, but it wasn't safe yet.

As we passed the park, a vast row of greenhouses came into view. They stretched beyond the horizon, glass misty from the humidity they held.

"Gray, what is this?" Quen asked, jogging to keep up with me as I strode ahead.

"You'll see," I replied.

Reaching the glass structures, I glanced around before opening the door and leading her inside.

"We shouldn't be here," she deduced.

Once Quen crossed the threshold, I closed the door behind us and wrapped my arms around her from behind.

"Probably not, but you've looked miserable," I whispered into her ear. "You need to choose your flower."

"I can't." She wriggled against my hold.

"Yes, you can," I argued. Quen tried to turn in my arms, but I kept her facing the myriad of blooms. "It's your right."

I was desperate for her to accept her divinity and stop running from it. Fancy balls were only one facet of this life. Quen should enjoy every custom we offered her, and whereas Erik and Archer wanted to throw her in at the deep end and have her accept this was home, my golden girl needed gentle persuasion. Quen worked best when she believed she was in control.

"Gray," she said, hesitation lacing her words before she sighed. "How am I meant to pick one?"

I knew part of her wanted to give in. Quentin's ego wouldn't allow her to completely shun the fact she was a Goddess. It just needed to outshine her fear.

Unwrapping her from my embrace, I took her hand and walked down the aisle.

"You'll sense it," I explained. "Trust your instincts."

Her head turned left and right, taking in the blossoming blooms surrounding us. I pointed out Ig's sunflowers and Sloan's peonies, but she made us stop at my flowers.

"I still think these are my favourite," Quen muttered, brushing her fingers against the black petals of the Odessa calla lily.

"You can have a never-ending supply of them, if you wish."

I'd produce them for her every day. Vases of them until she had no space left. Whatever she wanted, I would strive to deliver. The desire to satisfy her every need grew stronger with each passing day until I was sure it would consume me entirely.

We walked through changing flora and fauna, with Quentin asking questions before she tensed.

"What is it?" I asked, becoming alert.

"Come with me."

Quen walked with more confidence. She'd sensed it. Sensed the flower that called to her and would represent her. We weaved through the others before she stopped in front of it.

Orchids.

Her flowers were orchids.

"They're beautiful," she breathed, staring at the delicate petals that came in a range of colours.

"You wouldn't have been capable of being associated with anything less."

The pink coloured her cheeks as she looked at me. I gently broke off a flower from the plant and tucked it into her hair behind her ear.

"I love you, Quentin," I told her softly.

More and more, I found myself saying the words. It was as if I couldn't contain them within me anymore.

She glanced up at me from under her lashes. "I love you too, Gray."

My eyes snapped to her face, and for once I was unsure if I heard her correctly. "Quen," I said, cupping her face in my hands.

"I love you," she repeated, almost making it sound like a question.

Something bloomed in my chest until I thought it might cause me to burst. Three simple words were enough to tear me apart at the seams and offer her my heart. I pressed my lips hard against hers and Quen fisted my shirt before I pulled away.

"You're sure?" I asked, suddenly wary.

I searched her eyes, wanting to know this wasn't another game of ours or a passing whim. I needed to know that she truly meant it. Love wasn't something I craved until I came across her. Quentin was the only being in existence that I longed to impress and win affection from. Everyone else could burn and I wouldn't blink, but she needed to love me with as much depth as I offered her.

Her expression softened, and she rose on her toes, trying to meet my eye. I leaned down slightly to meet her, hands sliding to her hips. The dark irises that I was accustomed to were flecked with gold.

"I don't know what's going to happen," she whispered. "But I wish every day that I could have told my parents how much I loved them before I lost them. I don't want to regret not telling you. So, yes. I'm sure. I love you, Gray."

THIRTEEN

QUENTIN

I'd finally found the courage to admit it. Living on borrowed time was pulling me apart. The declaration seemed worthless if I couldn't guarantee that I'd be around for much longer. But the thought of my parents, of how I would have given anything to hear them say it one last time, let those three little words slip past my lips. We were never guaranteed tomorrow and I refused to waste another second.

Ignacio's estate was blindingly bright after the comforting darkness of Gray's manor. Even with my golden touches, the house remained shrouded in fog and an ominous sensation that I associated with the man I loved.

Ig's manor was an open space. He preferred a minimalist approach to decoration, making every room seem cavernous. Sunflowers featured in varying sizes along the hallways. It was a house that radiated warmth, but it wasn't quite home.

Not that Gray's was home.

"You've improved," Ig said, winding his aura back towards himself and walking up to me.

Gray had left me with Ignacio to train again. It was probably for the best. My emotions were never under control when Gray was around. They bubbled just under the surface as he pulled the best and worst out of me. Without my favourite distraction, I could focus better and Ig's drills felt less draining.

A heavy hand clapped down on my shoulder and I gave him a weak smile. "I really want to return to Earth."

He grimaced. "What's so great down there? Don't you want to be a part of Elysia?"

"What's so great about this place?"

Ignacio laughed, a sound so deep and warm that my smile grew. "We're meant to work together. That should have been enough of an argument to convince you to survive and join our ranks," he explained.

"You're not selling it," I teased, and he showed me his middle finger. "Ig, can I ask you something?"

"Depends on what it is."

"It's about our gifts. You can't deny a God a direct request, but you all seem hesitant to ask."

Ignacio jerked his head at the sofa, a lock of his dark hair falling out of place. We sank onto the orange monstrosity, my body almost disappearing in the soft cushions that were backed there.

"It used to be normal for us to request favours from each other. A way to be a cohesive unit and aid our kin. But there are always those who take it too far. Your gift is exactly that. It's the essence of you. When someone requests use of it, they are taking something that belongs to you. Something sacred." Ignacio took in a deep breath and had a far-off look in his eye. "You can't say no and people abused that. Kieran, Gray's father, forbade Gods from asking."

"But they still do."

"We are selfish beings, Quentin. We will not stop at getting what we want."

The hairs on my arms and at the back of my neck rose to attention. I reached out and placed a hand on his arm gently.

"People have used you to get what they want," I breathed, but the words seemed loud in the room.

Ig's hand reached up, resting over mine. His fingers drummed against my skin gently. "Gifts like yours and mine are beautiful. I'd argue that they're the most valuable. But they are dangerous in the wrong hands. I learned the hard way to keep your circle tight, Scott."

"I'm sorry."

"It might not be my place to advise you because you have Gray, but his gift isn't like ours. It's rare that someone would ask Gray directly for the use of his gift. The consequences are too grand. Plus, he's not the most personable God," Ig told me with a sheepish grin. "Question everyone's motive for wanting to know you, Scott. Be selective with the Gods you let near you."

"You don't have to worry, Ig. I've always been cautious."

"Ig, sweetheart, is she still here?" Elva's voice rang through the house.

The haunted look disappeared from his eye, replaced by the light I was accustomed to. Elva's voice was enough to remedy the past betrayals Ig relived.

"Where else would she be?" he called back. "She's got the happiest slice of Elysia with her."

Elva's slender figure appeared in the doorway, draped in deep purple. Her gaze momentarily landed on him before flicking to me.

"I'll get out of your hair," I said, jumping to my feet. "Get myself back to Gray."

"He can wait a few minutes," Elva replied.

She entered the room, making a beeline for me and it took all my control not to step back and away from her. Elva's hands were icy as they cupped my face, thumbs running along my cheekbones before she pressed a kiss against one cheek and then the other.

"It's good to have you back with us, where you belong," she said, beaming.

Her hands trailed down my face, to my arms, until she laced our fingers together. Stepping back, she took me in, eyes growing glassy.

"Elva," Ignacio said quietly. "Let her go."

Her gaze travelled to her boyfriend. "Could you leave us alone to talk?"

My head whipped around to look at Ignacio, pleading with my eyes not to be left in this situation. But he was completely besotted with Elva, and what she desired was what he strived to accomplish.

"Of course. Be gentle with her." Ignacio planted a tender kiss against her lips before leaving the room.

"How was training?" Elva asked. "Better than last time?"

"You heard about last time?" I mumbled.

"You're like your mother. Quick to react and worry about the consequences after. The more I look at you, the more I can see Mal. She would have been so proud to see what you've become and—"

I ripped my hands out of Elva's and took a step back, suddenly feeling like the walls were closing in.

"What's wrong?" she asked, echoing my footsteps. I held out my hands to keep some space between us. "Quentin —"

"I'm not Mallory," I told her, lowering my arms.

"I know that." Elva bit her bottom lip and dropped her gaze to the floor. "I'm sorry if I made you uncomfortable. That wasn't my intention. It's been a very long time since I've had any family around me."

When I was younger, before I was adopted, I often wondered what it would be like to meet my biological family. I imagined it would be overwhelming and beautiful. *Cinematic.* That I would finally feel like I belonged and this strange sense of being alone would permanently disappear. In truth, it left me confused and with a knot of anxiety deep in the pit of my stomach.

"I'm not trying to replace anyone," Elva assured me. "Gray told me you have an older brother. Cassidy? Correct?"

I tensed, hearing her mention Cass' name. "Yes."

"Perhaps we can all meet?" Elva suggested. "Family. He has a wife?"

"Fiancée."

"I'm sure Gray will want to be there. And Ignacio will join us if you'll allow it—"

"Elva," I said, voice rising. "Wait."

"What's wrong?"

Gods were selfish. Sometimes that selfishness was not wrapped in malice. It was cocooned in a deep desire to fulfil whatever need they had. Elva's was to surround herself with family again and she ran with her plans without considering if it was something I wanted. Why wouldn't it be? Blood family and divinity; I'd apparently hit the jackpot. No one, aside from Gray, understood that this was my version of a nightmare.

"I don't want you bringing Cassidy into this," I told her. "Or Sophie. The less my brother has to do with the Gods, the better."

"He'll still deal with you." Elva read my face and her eyebrows rose. "Oh! You don't plan to tell him."

"There's nothing to tell."

"You'd hide your divinity from him?"

"Isn't that the whole point of this? No one down there knows I'm part God."

"What about when you ascend?"

"Ascend?"

"When you come home to us. Live in Elysia permanently."

"I wish people would stop saying that. Half of you want me dead and the other half of you think I'm going to move here as if I don't already have a life." I ran my hands through my hair and tugged at it.

Her next sentence was muttered quietly with a furrowed brow, as if she was struggling to process my logic against hers. "We assumed because of Grayson that you'd want to be here with him."

The anxiety blossomed so viciously that my aura unfurled itself around me. I was so focused on the life I knew and what was familiar to me; I didn't factor in how Gray and I would continue our relationship if I survived this. E.L.I. couldn't last forever and Gray hardly seemed the type to relocate to Earth.

Elva didn't flinch as gold fluttered around us. She stepped up to me and pulled me into a hug. I battled with the desire to push her away, but eventually relaxed in her arms.

"I'm sorry," she whispered into my hair. "You have a lot to think about and decide. I shouldn't have assumed."

My arms went around her willowy frame. It was strange to hug the woman who essentially murdered my biological mother. From what I understood, Elva had no choice. Not really. She couldn't have taken any solace in the fact when her hand was forced and it felt pointless to punish her. The way she tried to induct me into her family and make herself a part of mine told me she was still deeply hurt by the loss and trying to make amends in her own way.

"If you'd like, we can spend time together," I said, fighting against the sudden rush of tears. "Get to know each other. But please, leave Cassidy out of this for now."

Dad used to tell me I was awful at compromise. That I was bull-headed and wanted things my way. I couldn't disagree with him and it had served me well throughout my life, but there were moments where it exhausted me.

"I would like that," Elva said, releasing me. "We should get you back to Gray's."

Smoky purple wisps appeared around us. Elva's control over her aura was beautiful. It danced around her delicately, waiting for her command.

"Could we walk there?" I asked as it crept around me. "I don't want him to see me in this state and worry."

Gray's attentiveness was something I was growing used to, but he had enough to deal with. My minor panic about belonging and family and him did not need to be added to his overflowing plate.

"Of course," she said, offering me her arm.

Tentatively, I looped mine through it and Elva guided me through Ig's home until we walked outside.

"Do you live with Ignacio?" I asked, unable to curb my curiosity.

"Not yet. Hunter hasn't learned of our relationship. You know he's been trying to pair me and Gray together."

"So I've heard," I muttered through gritted teeth.

"We planned to tell him, but with everything that unfolded, we decided to wait."

"I'm sorry. I've put your plans on hold."

Elva's hand covered mine in the crook of her elbow and she clucked her tongue. "Don't apologise. Things happen for a reason. We will get there eventually."

"Are you a fan of Hunter?"

Elva laughed under her breath. "You are trouble," she muttered before answering my question, "No."

"Why not remove him from his council seat?"

"If it were only that simple. Some of the elite adore him. Same with lower Elysians. If we remove him, we'd have to replace him, and right now, there isn't a viable option. No one that we all respect and agree on. Instability here leads to instability on Earth. If we're focused on fighting each other, then we aren't focused on prayers. Most of the wars, famines, and epidemics can be traced back to problems in Elysia. There are a lot of factors to weigh up."

"It's a delicate balance."

As we came up to Hunter's estate, the door slammed shut and Archer rushed down the path. His hair was stuck up in odd angles as if he'd pulled at it and deep cuts split the skin along the left side of his face, weeping gold blood with green flecks. Larkin followed him out the door before stopping abruptly when she saw us.

Archer's gaze landed on me and a sinister smile came to his face. "Enjoying family time? I'm surprised he let you off the leash."

My face burnt with embarrassment as I remembered the state I was in when I left Archer's home a few days ago.

"Take her back to Gray's," Larkin said to Elva before turning to Archer. "That's enough from you. Are you a glutton for punishment? Hunter's already dealt with you this evening."

"Don't act like you care." Archer seethed. "See, Quentin. They'll pull you into a web and make you do their bidding. Or is he trying to convince you he cares by giving you an ounce of freedom? Ask yourself if he'd have valued you if you were still completely mortal."

"Archer!" Larkin snapped, shoving him roughly. "I suggest you go home before I get Hunter myself."

His eyes narrowed before he swept into a low bow. "Whatever you say, Your Highness."

As he straightened up, a swirl of green surrounded him before he disappeared from sight.

"Larkin," Elva started.

But Larkin didn't even spare us a glance before storming back up to the house.

"Are you okay?" Elva asked, turning her attention to me.

I nodded. "I didn't expect to see him up here."

"Archer's a law unto himself."

That was something I was well aware of.

"I think it's best we cut this walk short and take you back to Gray's. If Hunter's in a bad mood, the last thing we need is for you to be walking around Elysia," Elva commented. She cloaked us in her aura before we appeared in the entrance hall of Gray's home.

"You're back, Miss," a woman said, striding up to me. I blinked a few times wondering who she was.

"Um, yes," I replied.

"Is he ready for her, Poppy?" Elva asked.

"Everything's in place," she answered.

Elva looked at me, a grin plastered on her face. "I'll leave you to it."

"Wait." I grabbed her hand. "What's going on?"

"Don't worry, Quentin. Just enjoy the evening."

FOURTEEN

QUENTIN

Twenty minutes later, I walked through Gray's home towards the grounds. My jeans and t-shirt had been swapped for a golden dress that only he could have chosen. The satin material didn't allow me to hide any flaw, and teamed with the cowl neck and the split that ran up to my hip, there was plenty of flesh on display.

Poppy, a minor Goddess with freckles splashed across her nose, had refused to tell me what was happening, and my breath grew shallow as we stepped outside. The chill in the air rose the hairs on my arms and my nipples grew tight under the silken fabric of the dress.

Grayson appeared almost instantly. His suit was tailored to perfection for his body, pitch black and moulded against his frame. I noticed the dark embroidery on the lapels and nestled in his hair was his crown. The sharp black points rose from his head and the dark gems glittered in the night.

"Thank you, Poppy," he dismissed her, and the minor Goddess walked back inside.

My eyes followed Gray's movements as he bowed deeply. Still

bent at the waist, his gaze flicked up at me and he extended a hand.

"What are you doing?" I asked. When I placed my hand in his, he brushed his lips against my knuckles and straightened up.

"If you come with me, I'll explain."

"It's not like I can run."

"I'd catch you even if you tried."

"Creep."

Our fingers laced together as we walked along the paths that carved through lilies. The fog still rolled across the ground and the sky looked angry, but despite the chill in the air, an odd warmth ran through me that could only be attributed to Gray by my side.

"I was robbed of the chance to host a gifting ball for you," he explained. "So I thought a private one for us might make up for the occasion."

"Just the two of us?" I asked as we climbed to the top of the cliff.

"I thought you would prefer it this way. No pressure. No stress. After all, this is not a zoo or a circus."

I bumped my shoulder against his arm as he used my words against me.

The wind whipped my hair around my face as we reached the top and Gray's arm came around my shoulder, pulling me tight against his body.

"There's something I want you to see," he said, steering me to the left.

He pointed to a row of lilies that swayed in the breeze and dotted in between them were orchids, petals valiantly fighting to hang on against the assault of the weather.

"Terrestrial orchids," Gray said. "I'm not sure if they'll survive here, but it felt right that they grow beside mine."

"I trained, and you spent the day gardening?" The laughter was threatening to trickle into the sentence. I couldn't imagine Gray doing something as trivial as tending to the garden.

"Not quite," he admitted. "I invited Tobias to plant them. He's the best in the business. Can get practically anything to grow."

"Tobias," I repeated the name. "He's a minor God?"

"Yes. Why?"

"He came to visit Archer."

"What for?"

"I don't know. Archer wouldn't let me stay for the conversation. He's growing something in his bedroom."

Gray's mood darkened. "Why were you in his bedroom?"

"I was trying to find something to use against him," I answered sharply.

"And did you find anything?"

"No. Not that it matters anymore."

"No," he agreed, tucking a loose lock of hair behind my ear. "It doesn't."

Melodic notes filled the air around us, but there were no speakers or musicians. Elysia held its own magic, and I was still learning its secrets.

"Will you dance with me, Quentin?"

"How could I say no?"

Gray's arms circled around my waist as mine looped around his neck. In moments like this, it was easy to block out everything else that was happening in my life. Death was not imminent. I had no responsibilities weighing on my shoulders. There was nothing except me and the God I loved.

"You know," I said as he pressed his forehead against mine. "If you keep being this sweet, you'll lose your well-earned reputation."

"I highly doubt it. This is just for you." One of Gray's hands left my waist and his fingers splayed around my throat. "And I know you won't tell anyone about this newly acquired facet of my personality."

I had no intention of sharing this version of Gray with anyone. This strange God who made people tremble in his presence, who destroyed anything that displeased him, softened only for me. He tried things and pushed himself out of his comfort zone for me.

A thought bubbled in my head and I tried to push it away, but it took root and forced me to tear my gaze away from Gray's face.

"What's going on in that brilliant mind?" he asked, removing his hand from my throat and brushing his fingers against my temple.

"It's stupid," I admitted.

"Almost certainly, but I still want to hear it."

I swatted his chest, but his silence made me continue. "We bumped into Archer on the way home."

Gray tensed under my touch, and I looked up at him. His jaw was set, a vein throbbing along his neck. Reaching up, I placed a hand on his cheek, and he relaxed a fraction.

"He said something—"

"What?" Gray asked, eyes boring down on me.

This was a mistake. I regretted the fact I'd let my insecurities take hold, but I couldn't back out of it now. "He said that you wouldn't have cared about me if I was still mortal. Implied that you were only taking an interest because of my divinity."

"Is that what you think?"

My chest caved as I traced the embroidery on his suit. I swallowed the lump in my throat, trying to remind myself that Archer was trying to cause trouble.

"I love you, Quentin." Gray said it with such force that it caused me to look up at him again. "I have loved you long before I knew any part of you was divine. I'm not telling you this so I can hear it back. I'm telling you so you might realise what a ridiculous being you are."

The words continuously echoed in my mind and made my chest feel like it could burst open, unable to contain the pure joy.

"Don't be mistaken. I do not see you as my equal," he said, staring down at me.

Emotional whiplash.

Anger replaced the joy so quickly that wisps of gold surrounded us. Dread and disappointment accompanied it. A crack of thunder from above mirrored my mood as rain fell. Gray drew me closer to his body, towering over me in an effort to keep me dry.

His knuckles brushed against my cheek, brows pulling together. "I see you as so much better than I am."

Shock forced away all other emotions and stilled my thundering heart. "What?"

"Do you know I asked Elva to bring you back to me? I got on my knees and I begged for you. I am a God and you were nothing more than a mortal at that point, but I begged for your life."

The enormity of the words hit me and I inhaled deeply, trying to calm my heart down.

"Archer speaks of what he sees. I have never been the most affectionate God." Gray sniffed indignantly. "I do not feel the need to justify my love for you to someone that means nothing to me. But those who matter understand the lengths I would go to for you."

Gray rarely explained himself to anyone. Of course, he wouldn't lay everything on the line with Archer. There was palpable tension between them both, and Gray would rather sever an arm off than try to gain Archer's favour.

"I know you are better than me and I also know that in no way do I deserve you. So no, Quentin, I do not see us as equal."

"Grayson—"

"Would you like me to prove it to you?" Gray sank down to his knees before me, gripping my hips.

"Get up," I told him. "It's raining."

"I'll be the first to worship you," he whispered before another crack of thunder sounded. The lightning that followed illuminated his face, and the vulnerability knocked the breath out of my lungs. "No mortal. No other God. Me, Grayson, Lord of chaos and King of destruction, an elite God will worship at your feet."

He bowed his head until it rested gently against the softness of my stomach, and he muttered quietly. I couldn't make out the words over the rain that fell relentlessly around us and the thundering of my blood in my ears.

Just as I was about to tell him to stop the madness, something inside me shook, forcing me to tremble. I held onto Gray's arms, nails digging into the fabric of his suit as he continued, and the feeling became unbearable. A strange snapping sensation occurred in the depths of my being, as if I was being set free. I let out a moan, feeling undeniable pleasure ignite every nerve in my body.

Slowly, Gray lifted his head and looked at me before rising to his feet. The rain slid down his nose and flattened his hair. He lifted the crown off his head and placed it gently on mine. The heavy metal slipped, not quite fitting, and sat crookedly in its new place.

"Look at yourself," he said.

When I glanced down at my body, it glowed gold and the veins visible beneath my skin took on the same hue.

"Gray," I whispered, panic filling my chest.

He shook his head, spraying droplets of water like a dog. "This will happen from time to time when you are worshipped. You'll learn to suppress it."

"You glowed like this on your birthday," I replied, remembering that morning.

"Because people were focused on praying and worshipping me. I worshipped you, Quentin. As Gods, we do not do this for each other, but this should show you, *prove* to you, how much I do not believe you're beneath me."

Reaching up on my toes, I pressed my lips to his, kissing him deeply. Customs amongst the Gods were new to me, but I knew this meant a lot. They valued their traditions more than anyone I'd met.

"I would like to spend the rest of my night worshipping you," he muttered against my lips. "Would you allow me to, Goddess?"

I nodded my head, feeling incapable of vocalising anything after the display he'd put on.

The expectation of his aura, of the warmth and dryness of the bedroom, disappeared when Gray kissed me, pushing his tongue into my mouth. I clung to him, my body already yearning for more. The simplest touch from him always drove me wild, extinguishing any sense or logic I maintained.

My back hit the muddy grass of the cliff as Gray took us to the ground. His crown dislodged from its resting place, rolling across the grass.

"Here?" I asked breathlessly, breaking away from the kiss and looking at him.

Gray's lips had moved to my neck, teeth grazing along my pulse point while his hand went to the slit in my dress, pushing it wide and cupping my bare pussy.

"There's a fine line between worship and defile, as far as I'm concerned," he said before nipping at my skin and making me groan.

Both his hands ran up my body, palming my breasts through the dress that was soaked and stuck to me. My nipples hardened, forming peaks beneath the fabric, and Gray tore through the material between them, exposing them to the elements.

While he rolled one of my nipples between his fingers, his mouth descended on the other. His tongue swirled around it before biting down and eliciting a yelp from me. He hummed, the vibration spreading across my skin and making me throb between my legs.

"Mortals will want to herald you," he said. His free hand went to the apex of my thighs, fingers brushing lightly against me and making me tremble. "All this light you'll bring to them. All the prayers you'll answer."

Gray pushed a finger inside me, and I whimpered, grinding against his hand. His thumb rubbed my clit as the glow of gold pulsed out from around me and brightened the cliff space.

"If only they knew how you yielded to the darkness. What would they say?"

He removed his finger and held it to my lips. I didn't need prompting to suck on the digit and taste myself from him. Gray was my ultimate weakness, and when he had me like this, I would give him anything he wanted.

"Tell me what you want," he said, pulling his finger from my mouth.

"You know what I want," I whined.

"You're a Goddess, Quentin. Tell me what you want. Demand it from me." Gray's eyes had long lost their blue and his veins ran black under his skin.

Demand.

I pushed myself up from the ground so I was sitting, staring at the God before me. I never understood when to stop. If I had an idea, I ran with it.

"I want you in the collar," I told him. "Naked."

Gray's face remained impassive for a moment. Then he moved, shedding his wet clothes in the rain, revealing the perfectly sculpted body that laid beneath it. He disappeared in clouds of black before returning with the copper collar in his hands.

"As you wish, Goddess," he said, holding it out to me.

With trembling hands, I took it from him. Gray and I played games in the bedroom. I wouldn't submit with ease, but I enjoyed the moment I gave in to him. There were times when I chased after what I wanted, fought him for control, but I always relented in the end. It felt good to hand him my trust and my body, but he told me to demand and I was curious to see if he would listen.

"Come here," I said, still unsure of myself.

Gray looked sinful, standing naked in the rain. Droplets ran along his broad shoulders and down his abs. They cut a course down the V and dripped down his muscular thighs that usually pinned me in place. His cock was hard and ready and my pussy ached, longing to have him inside of me again.

He came to me and lowered himself to the ground. When I clipped the collar around his neck, it sat snugly, instantly dissipating his aura and bringing his eyes back to blue. The traits that marked him as divine were suddenly gone.

"Lie back," I ordered.

There was a spark of amusement in his eyes as he laid back in the mud. I shed the remnants of my dress, leaving the tattered fabric on the ground beside the key before looking at him.

"What next?" he asked curiously.

I rose from the ground and walked over to him. Standing over Gray, I turned around and lowered myself so that my pussy was at his mouth. My head dipped between his legs and my tongue came out to drag along his dick. He groaned before his hands came around my thighs possessively, and Gray pushed his face into my core.

My tongue traced the veins on his dick twice before I took him into my mouth, hollowing my cheeks and joining him in delivering pleasure. It was hard to focus on the task in hand when his tongue expertly lapped at my pussy.

Gray might have declared me better than him, but in my eyes, we were equal. A partnership. I trusted him more than anyone else. And it was that trust that drove me into his arms and let me be myself around him. It was that trust that sparked my desire to survive and figure out a way to keep him in my life.

His hips jerked and bucked, forcing his cock to hit the back of my throat, and I relaxed, allowing him to slide deeper. I breathed through my nose, struggling to keep any steady rhythm while I ground my hips against his face.

One of my hands gripped his thigh, nails leaving marks on his skin, while the other played with his balls. He grunted from beneath me, licking from front to back before pressing his tongue inside my pussy and fucking me. All the sounds and words were muffled by his dick down my throat.

I let him out of my mouth with a wet pop as the pressure built in my lower abdomen.

"Stop!" I cried, not wanting to finish yet.

Gray sucked at my clit, ignoring my command. His teeth grazed against it before he bit gently and tugged. My body bucked wildly, and I screamed his name as the orgasm hit me so hard that my vision blurred. His tongue continued, lapping up every drop that I offered. Wave after wave of pleasure pulled me under, forcing my muscles to shake.

He finally moved his head away and after a few moments to compose myself, I rose on weak legs, positioning in a way so that I faced him. His mouth glistened in the storm's darkness and Gray's tongue swiped across his lips before he shot me a depraved smile. Even without his aura, without the black that usually took over, he looked unhinged. It was impossible to remove the raw essence of chaos from this man.

My fingers closed around the chain leash, and I pulled, forcing him to sit up slightly, resting on his elbows. "I thought I was in charge."

"You'll have to forgive me," he said, looking anything but remorseful. "I thought I made it clear you were my favourite meal."

I let go of the lead so he fell back and closed my hand around his cock, pumping slowly. He hissed and closed his eyes, pushing his head back into the dirt.

"Apologise," I told him.

He opened his eyes and stared up at me. His face was flushed, and the rain collected on long, dark lashes.

"Apologise and I'll let you into my pussy. Otherwise, you can just sleep out here tonight."

"All this power is going to your head."

"If you think I'm joking…" I let go of his cock and went to stand, but Gray's hands gripped my hips with bruising force.

"I'm sorry," he said through gritted teeth.

"That wasn't so hard, was it?" I asked, grinning.

Leaning down, I kissed him, tasting myself on his lips. Carefully, I moved back and guided his thick cock into me. The head slipped in and I eased myself down his length, savouring the way he filled me. There would never be a time where the stretch wasn't satisfying. I picked myself up and then slid back down, angling my body so that he hit the perfect spot. My hands landed on his shoulders as I ground and worked, focusing on my pleasure.

Gray's hands closed around my hips, uttering curses, and I tipped my head back as the storm continued to rage above us. The closer I climbed to my high, the brighter the gold grew around us. My aura was an extension of my emotions and it perfectly displayed the pure bliss that ran through my body.

"My golden girl," Gray grunted, bucking his hips, abs rippling, and thrusting his dick further into me. If he continued, I was certain he'd split me in two. "So fucking filthy and so fucking perfect."

Moving one hand from his shoulder, I rubbed at my clit in rough circles, desperate to find my release as fatigue set into my legs. Gray sensed my urgency and lifted me, helping me to keep my pace.

He worshipped my body just like he said he would. His hands, his mouth, his cock. Everything was focused on me until I couldn't see straight.

The orgasm crashed over me, extracting a strangled scream from my lips in the form of his name. Pleasure licked at every nerve, making me feel everything and nothing simultaneously. As I collapsed on his chest, breathing deeply, Gray continued to pump his hips. The muscles he possessed even with the collar, remained powerful as he gripped me. His teeth sank into my shoulder as he came, filling me with hot spurts of his cum deep inside. Even when he'd finished, I felt the twitching of his dick and wondered if it was viable to stay like this in the storm for the rest of the night. I didn't have the energy to move.

He nudged my head with his own so that I looked at him through the lusty haze.

"That's my girl. Take what you want with no apologies," he told me. "And never let anyone make you believe you are less than perfection."

FIFTEEN

GRAYSON

Quentin sat by the banks of the reflecting pool, listening to Ig who held court with her, Sloan, and Elva. The tension she carried since arriving here had disappeared as she tipped her head back, eyes closed, enjoying the sun. A true inhabitant of Elysia.

I shouldn't have kept her in the storm last night, but my need for her was great and I didn't want to waste a single moment. My concern came afterwards as I watched her sleep. What if she became sick? She was still partially mortal. Immortality may have been granted and she would heal quickly, but that didn't mean I wanted to see her suffer in any capacity. But when she awoke, there was a distinct spring in her step and she seemed content to spend the day with the others.

"Please bring her home," Erik said, joining my side and following my gaze. "She belongs here with you. With us. Look at her."

"All I do is look at her," I muttered. "What do you think I'm trying to do?"

"Have you thought about telling her?"

"Do you only ever have love on the brain?"

"And sex."

I snorted. "That is something I can relate to." I heaved a sigh. "I was thinking about telling her about the bond when we're back on Earth. She'll feel comfortable being back in her environment and I can break it to her. I don't want to startle her. Quen's slowly coming around to the idea of what she is. It needs to be handled delicately."

I'd cook us dinner and let her complain about the lab and the work she had to put in to get things running again. She'd curl up against me on the sofa, head in my lap, and I'd tell her softly this time about my love for her and how it ran deeper than any mortal could comprehend. That her soul was crafted from mine the way mine was from hers. There was no other being that would fit together so perfectly because they designed us as a pair.

Erik hugged me with such force that I stumbled. "I'm so excited for you!"

The attention of the group shifted towards us, and Quentin's gaze instantly found mine. She cocked her head to the side, hair falling over her shoulder and giving her an air of innocence. It was laughable that she could possess that look when I was privy to her darkest fantasies.

Shoving Erik off me, I walked over to them, settling down beside Quen. Our pinky fingers brushed as I set my palm down beside hers and she didn't move. This was the most I could offer her in public. Other Gods sat scattered around the pool, having visited from lower Elysia to enjoy the sunshine.

"Ig was just telling us stories about Phillipe," Quentin said, leaning her body towards mine. "You don't have funerals here."

"We cease to exist," I replied. "And life moves on. There is no use in mourning when we have to continue to run things. Prayers will be divided between those who shared Phillipe's gift."

"Is that what will happen to me if the decision goes against me? You'll all move on and others will take on my prayers?"

"You need to stop thinking you're going to die," I hissed through my teeth. She raised the issue so casually, but the prospect of that reality left me hollow. "Plus, you're an anomaly. We haven't had someone in charge of success for just over a century."

"I thought there were multiple Gods that shared the same gift."

"There are, but Liesl was the last."

"Her existence..."

"Mortals are fickle. They stop believing. Stop being grateful. Many of them started to fade away from existence. She couldn't fight against it in the end."

"And the pool hasn't gifted success to anyone else since? Why?"

"Perhaps it hasn't deemed mortals worthy of a God with such a gift. Or perhaps it was waiting for the right one to come along."

"There's that golden tongue of yours."

"It has many talents," I whispered knowingly.

She flushed and knocked her shoulder against mine before I caught movement from the corner of my eye. Ig had left the group and was walking away to meet Archer, who was striding towards us.

"We're leaving," I said without hesitation, pulling Quentin to her feet.

Archer truly was proving to be the most difficult obstacle that I couldn't remove. His infatuation with Quentin ran deeper than I originally assumed, and I couldn't decipher the reasoning behind it, and I didn't care. He needed to stay away from her.

Unfurling my aura, I cloaked it around Quentin, but wisps of green infiltrated it before the three of us landed back in the living room of our home.

"Get out!" I barked at Archer, pushing Quentin behind me.

"What are you doing here?" Quentin asked, moving next to me again.

Archer focused on her. "I wanted to see if you'd like to join me in lower Elysia again. Spend some time with your kin since we were so rudely interrupted. So many of them are still waiting for an introduction, but it appears I've walked in on a cosy afternoon. Please, correct me if I'm wrong."

"What exactly do you think you saw?" I asked him, keeping my aura around.

"You both seem very close," Archer answered. "And don't brush me off, saying you're just friends. I don't look at mine like that. Then again, if that friend were Quentin…"

A muscle in my jaw twitched as he took her in from head to toe.

"Maybe it's a friends-with-benefits scenario," he continued. "I don't blame you there, Grayson. There were plenty of eyes on her at the gifting ball." He sighed, focusing on her. "I'm trying to figure out what's going on here, Quentin. Though I would have hoped you would be a little more intelligent than to be seduced by him."

She narrowed her eyes, upset with the swipe at her intelligence.

"Get out of my house," I demanded.

Archer took a step towards her, but I let my aura build a wall between them.

"Always so protective of her. If she's a quick fuck, why go to all this effort? And if she's a quick fuck, you won't mind sharing."

Logic and sense had never prevailed where I was concerned. Not when anger and chaos simmered close to the surface. And they didn't just simmer but scorched through my veins as my aura slammed him against the wall with such impact that the plaster fractured. Quentin grabbed my arm just as Archer unleashed his aura.

"Don't you dare speak about her like that!" I thundered.

"Why not?" Archer asked, picking himself up from the floor. "Just another conquest in your long line, right?"

I struck out again, but Archer blocked the attack.

"I only came to offer her my company," Archer mused.

"It's not happening, Archer," Quen spat.

"And why not, angel?"

Quentin moved towards him with defiant purpose, but a tendril of my aura wrapped around her waist, pulling her back. She lost her balance, arms flailing and hand dragging across the table in the room as she tried to stabilise herself. Quen crashed into my chest as the table transformed from black to gold.

Archer's face contorted. "Are you serious?"

"I asked you to leave," I told him darkly.

"She loves you? You! After everything you've done?"

I turned away from Archer, Quentin still pressed against my chest as I shielded her. "Go to Erik's," I instructed.

"Gray—"

"Just go!" I roared, releasing her from my aura.

Archer tutted behind us, his footsteps growing closer. "You just can't help yourself, can you? All the chaos you cause."

"Archer, I am warning you—"

He raised his voice so Quentin could hear him clearly. "Do you want to know something about the God you love?"

Quentin looked up at me, curiosity colouring her features. She was always after answers. Always wanting to know more. He appealed to that and even if Archer didn't spill the secrets now, she would never let this go.

"Quen, listen to me," I pleaded, but got no further.

With my back to Archer, I hadn't seen the wisps of his aura that shot around me and grabbed her. It dragged her away from me and she yelped before coming to a stop against his body.

"You're really pissing me off," she told Archer, balling her fist and smacking his chest. Gold fluttered around her frame, ready to fight for her.

If I struck him, I struck Quentin, and I wasn't willing to do that. Archer had an advantage here.

"You love him?" Archer scoffed. "You know nothing about him."

"I know what I need to know."

Gold flared wider, filling the space to join my black, but it barely had a chance to exist because his next words made it falter until it flickered into nothingness again.

"Do you know he murdered my wife?"

Quentin grew rigid in his arms.

"Archer—" I began, but he continued.

"Killed her without a second thought, and do you want to know why?"

She hadn't relaxed at all and I knew the next words would shatter everything that had built between us over the last few months.

Archer's gaze flicked to me, and he smiled. "Because she was a demigoddess."

"Quentin, please listen to me," I said, desperate to salvage what we had.

"Are you going to deny it, Grayson?"

"Quen…"

"Let me show you."

"No!"

My aura wound towards him, trying to pry him away from her. He cupped her face in both of his hands and let the memory unfurl around us.

"Grayson," Archer said, tears coursing down his face. "I'm begging you. I'm begging." He dropped to his knees before me. "Please don't do this."

I turned to look at him. "It's the law."

"Even you know that's bullshit. You're tarring them all with the same brush. They aren't all like that. They aren't all causing problems. Elara has never, would never—"

"We can't take that risk."

"Keep her alive," Archer said, rising to his feet again. "I'll be held accountable for any mistakes she might make. You can have us both if she ever betrays us. Please!"

"That's not how this is done."

The council chamber came into focus and a blonde woman, wrapped in multiple auras, looked up at me. Everything about her, from her features to her movements, was soft. She turned her head towards her husband. "I love you," she told him. "Forgive me."

She turned her attention back to me and nodded her head. My aura wrapped around her ponytail and pulled her head back, forcing her mouth open.

"Stop wasting our time, Grayson," Hunter barked from behind me.

There was the sound of glass tinkling against the stone of the council chamber as the top of the vial popped off and fell to the ground.

"No! No!" Archer roared while multiple auras kept him held in place. Elite and minor Gods who understood the cause we fought for.

Carefully, I dripped a mixture into Elara's mouth, not wasting a drop. A mixture that would taint her divinity.

When my aura fell away from around her, she swayed, and Elva's aura replaced mine. It constricted Elara's lithe form until it crumbled to dust in the centre of the room.

Archer fled from the chambers onto the streets of upper Elysia, promptly vomiting onto the grass. The pure chaos that unfolded had been my element, and it continued to rage on the outside.

The memory faltered as my living room came back into focus around us. Archer's eyes were glassy from emotion and his aura slowly unwrapped itself from around Quentin.

I'd been running from that memory from the moment I'd found out about Quen's divinity. The moment she left my side, it plagued me. How was I meant to tell her about my past without destroying our future?

"That," Archer said, voice thick with emotion, "is what the God you love does to people like you. Repulsed him so much that he murdered them."

SIXTEEN

QUENTIN

Something warm and wet ran down my face as I stumbled away from Archer. Gray's hand reached out to steady me, but I recoiled from his touch.

"Quentin," he breathed.

"Is that true?" I asked. "Did you kill her?"

"You need to listen to me."

"Did you?"

My aura burst into life around me, flexing and pulsing as it radiated my anger and pain. I needed answers from him. I needed him to tell me that Archer had manipulated a memory. Falsified it.

But the look on Gray's face told me there was no mistake.

"You," I said, feeling my chest tighten. "Just because she was half mortal?"

"It was a different time back then, Quentin. I'd never let anything happen to you."

"What? Because it's me? Because you love me?" I raged. My throat was raw from the effort of screaming the words. "He loved someone, Gray!" I pointed at Archer, finger trembling. "He loved someone, and

you saw fit to take that away from him!"

Gray flinched but straightened his spine, staring down at me. "You have no idea what was happening back then," he repeated. "You didn't exist. There are politics here that—"

"Maybe I should leave you both to have this discussion alone," Archer said, stepping away from behind me.

Gray's gaze followed him, irises turning dark.

"Don't even think about it, Grayson!" I warned him.

He turned his attention to me. "Quentin, do not judge me on my past."

"A past you conveniently forgot to tell me about."

"I would have told you."

"You lied to me. Again."

"I omitted the truth."

"Are you really trying to argue a technicality?"

A scream ripped out of my throat. I wished more than anything that I wasn't standing in front of him. I needed somewhere safe. Somewhere I could process what Archer had shown me. The gold grew so blindingly bright that it forced me to squeeze my eyes shut.

When I opened them again, I was no longer in Gray's home. I stood precariously at the edge of a pond and almost lost my balance until a mustard-coloured aura grabbed my wrist and pulled me away from it.

"You certainly know how to make an entrance," the man who possessed the aura said.

He stood beside Dionne, sharing the same skin colour, bone structure and hair, although his braids ended just past the nape of his neck.

"Marcel, go home," Dionne muttered, striding towards me.

"And miss out on this," Marcel replied. "Not a chance."

I straightened up and pinned my gaze on her. "This is your home?"

"Yes," she said, stopping in front of me, with Marcel behind her.

"I need to stay with you for a few days."

"Quentin, I'm—"

"I need a place to stay, Dionne. Can you help me or not?"

"Does Hunter know?"

"I don't give a flying fuck if he knows," I said, aura reappearing. "Please don't make me go back up there."

"Okay," she said, putting her hands up between us. "You can stay the night."

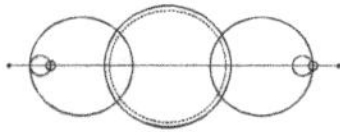

I wanted sleep to be part of the equation. A distant part of my brain tried to convince me that this was all a bad dream. That if I slept and woke up, I would regain consciousness on the canvas at Sal's after taking a rough hit. There would be no Gods. No job. No lies.

But the excruciating pain that burnt in my chest and knotted in the depths of my stomach demanded to be felt. Pain didn't belong in the beautiful land of dreams. Emotions this strong only existed in the dismal dread of real life.

A knock on the door made me wipe the tears roughly from my face before Marcel walked in. "You have a visitor," he said, leaning against the door.

"I'm not in the mood to see anyone."

"Archer's refusing to leave until he's seen you."

I jammed the heels of my palms into my eyes and took in three deep breaths. If I could go back in time, I would tell Gareth exactly where he could stuff his job. It led to more trouble than it was worth.

"Dionne's my twin. This is her home. She's my family."

"I get it," I snapped, moving my hands away from my eyes.

Everyone had family. Everyone had someone they wanted to protect the best they could. Put it all on the line for. I didn't fall into those circles, which meant that I once again needed to rely on the only person I could. Me.

Pushing myself off the bed, I brushed past Marcel and went downstairs. The sound of Dionne and Archer arguing cut clear through the house, but I didn't bother to knock on the door before I walked into the room.

"You're taking stalking to a whole new level," I told Archer. If Gray managed to harm him, he bore no marks from the assault.

"Would you like me to stay?" Dionne asked.

"I think your brother might put my head on a pike if I asked you to do that. I can deal with this," I answered sharply.

Dionne sucked in a breath and muttered, "Marcel."

She didn't hang around, marching out of the room and closing the door roughly behind her. The space filled with a thick silence that I refused to break. If Archer was so desperate to see me, he could tell me why.

"Dionne's home?" he said eventually. "I thought you might have ended up at mine."

"I think I was trying to escape the psychopaths and liars in my life."

"I can't be classified as either."

Out of control.

That was the only way to describe what I was feeling.

I was surrounded by Gods who I should never have trusted. Sweet talk and empty promises had turned my head. How naïve to forget myself and give them what I swore I never would?

More than anything, I wished to be on Earth. To call Cass and laugh about the stupid Netflix series we were trying to watch together and lead a monotonous life. Tedious but controlled. I knew what to expect, unlike now.

"Do you think you did something here, Archer?" I asked, trying to put a lid on the wild chaos that banged against my breastbone. "Do you think you helped me?"

"I think I opened your eyes before it got too far. I want what's best for you."

"What's best for me?" I repeated.

When I was younger, Alice in Wonderland was one of my favourite tales. I was obsessed with the Mad Hatter and wondered how he felt when he lost his mind and succumbed to the madness. Now I knew it was because there was no other choice. Sometimes, the only option was to let your mind snap and let others deal with the consequences.

"You have hounded me for months," I said, taking measured steps towards him. "You have plagued my dreams and watched my moves so you can turn up when I least expect you, God of secrets and deception. For months, you've been certain I've hidden things from you. I've watched you try to pry it from my lips and break Gray, to force a confession out of him. And for that whole time, you knew what he'd done and what I was, and you never uttered a word. Don't you dare make out like you gave a shit about me or my wellbeing."

"That was when I thought he was playing a stupid game I could use against him. I didn't expect him to manipulate you into falling for him. Even then, he wouldn't have killed you as a mortal; just got himself in trouble with the council. Now that you're a demigoddess, I don't trust him or his brothers. They're already plotting your death."

Manipulate me? That didn't sit right. Gray might have lied, but he didn't manipulate me into loving him. Neither of us wanted anything more than sex, but a deep connection formed between us that I struggled to explain. I'd loved no one the way I loved Gray, and that was what made this whole situation worse. Not only had I opened myself to getting hurt again, but it felt like it was destroying me this time. Ripping apart my soul and taking away my ability to do anything other than succumb to misery.

Curbing some of my anger, I looked him in the eye. "I am sorry for what happened to your wife."

"Elara. Her name is Elara."

"But I am not a replacement and I don't wish to be a pawn in your vendetta against Grayson or anyone else. You want to fight him? Knock yourself out. But I have a life, Archer. I have feelings and I am tired. I'm so fucking tired of all of you."

My voice wobbled as the lump grew in my throat and tears blurred my vision. I blinked them away quickly, refusing to wear my vulnerability in front of him. This was my fault. I trusted the Gods when I knew they never pulled through for me.

He narrowed his eyes. "How do you expect not to be a pawn when you don't even understand the game? Don't know all the players."

"If you're talking about Hunter, I've guessed that he's not the perfect protector he wants people to believe he is."

"Took you long enough to figure that out," Archer said. "But it's interesting that you came to Dionne's. If you're going to be untrusting, then you need to be like that with everyone."

"Stop talking in riddles."

"Did you ever wonder how I got into that pretty little head of yours? All the dreams you had."

"You're a God."

"You're still a partially naïve mortal."

The gold spiralled out around me, and Archer laughed under his breath. The moment he marbled his green aura with mine, I retracted it. The mixture of colours made me even more uncomfortable than I already was.

"I'm a God who's in charge of deception. I have nothing to do with dreams. But Dionne, well, it's a beautiful gift, and it did the job."

Another heavy weight settled in my stomach. Elysia was hailed as a paradise. A residence for the Gods that was perceived with awe amongst mortals. But all I saw was a nightmare that I couldn't escape.

The anger transformed from white-hot into something icier. As tired as I was, I refused to let people continue to take swipes at me for free. If Gods were uncaring, if they were above each other, then why shouldn't I give in to part of my heritage?

"I hope you're content, Archer," I said, schooling my features and straightening my spine. "And I hope Elara would be proud of you."

There was a sick sense of joy that flooded through me when Archer's smug expression warped into something uglier.

"About that game," I said as he seethed. "I may not know how to play it, but I'm a quick learner."

"I'm not your enemy here. There's a whole host of Gods up there who want you dead. Don't think just because you've fucked one of them, they'll see you as an equal. I told you we are your family. This is where you belong."

"I think I'll decide who I take on as family, Archer."

"All that time in the lab should help you make an intelligent and informed decision, I hope."

"Oh, didn't you know? There's this thing that happens to women when they get some decent dick. Our brains melt and drip out of our ears, so I can't guarantee anything."

"You're a very difficult being to help," he said through his teeth.

"Then don't. I never asked you and it isn't appreciated."

"You don't even know what you're capable of yet."

"I know I don't want you as my mentor."

"You'll change your mind."

"I highly doubt it."

He cracked his neck and sniffed indignantly. "You should take some time to process everything before you make any rash decisions. Impulsivity seems to be a key flaw of yours."

"I'll add it to the list. It's a mile long, by all accounts."

"See you soon, angel. Maybe in your dreams."

If I had something in hand, I would have thrown it at him, but he disappeared in wisps of green, and I bit the insides of my cheeks to stop myself from screaming. I forced my muscles to move, walking myself out of the room, and jumped when Dionne pushed herself away from the opposite wall.

"You heard everything." My words were a statement, not a question.

"I wanted to make sure he wouldn't hurt you."

"Where's Marcel?"

"I sent him home. Quentin, what Archer said—"

"Is it true? Did you help him?"

She looked at her shoes. "Yes, but only because he asked me directly. I couldn't refuse him and I didn't know who you were then." Dionne's dark eyes met mine again. "When I saw you at his estate after Bexley sent me, I was shocked to see it was you."

It was difficult to be angry at the woman when she'd had no choice. Archer was trying his best to make me dependent on him. To prove that he was the only option around, but I'd grown wary of the manipulative fucker.

Critical thinking was a key component in my life. Troubleshooting was a daily occurrence. This didn't differ from something going wrong in the lab. Only, in the lab, if something went wrong, you potentially risked other people's lives. Here, it was only truly mine that was on the line.

Hunter wanted me to prove I had control, and as long as Archer and Gray stayed out of my way, I could guarantee we'd be back on Earth. That left the council vote, and I needed to figure out a way to turn it to my favour.

"I'm sorry that it aided in causing this mess," Dionne continued. "It's not a gift that's meant to be used like that. It's usually creatives I help. The ones who rely on their dreams for their next projects."

I looked at Dionne as she explained her job, but my mind wandered. She was in a relationship with Bexley. There were ties to upper Elysia down here. Archer continued to refer to lower Elysia as my home. This was where my 'family' were supposed to be. The two strands of thoughts wound themselves together until they cemented themselves into a decision.

"Dionne," I said, cutting across her monologue. "I need to get out of here."

"Sorry?"

"I need to leave. I want to explore lower Elysia."

"I don't think that's the best idea."

What Dionne thought didn't bother me. She owed me. I might not have been angry at her for what happened, but it was still a violation and I would use it to get what I needed to survive.

"I'm not asking you to come with me. You need to tell me about the most populated areas."

Dionne looked unsure, but it was about time I took matters into my own hands. It was time to form alliances of my own.

SEVENTEEN

QUENTIN

It would be a lie to say I had two days of bliss.

I was acutely aware of the clock ticking down towards meeting with Hunter, where I would need to prove I had control over my aura. The first few hours in the streets of lower Elysia saw them highlighted ferociously as if Midas were striding through the heavens. The sudden attack of memories brought on emotions that I couldn't control, but it benefited me.

Minor Gods and Goddesses approached with caution as my hue dimmed to something less terrifying. My brain was filled with names and faces of so many people that nothing clearly matched up. They shook my hand and bolder residents pulled me into crushing hugs. I swallowed my aversion to physical contact with strangers to play the perfect, docile newcomer. Curiosity had them ask after my gift, but I refused to share it, sticking to the lie I'd been taught.

When I was exhausted by the interactions, I followed Dionne home, but there was no escape. I'd opened a can of worms and her house filled with visitors. Voices scrambled over each other, worse than the prayers that infiltrated my mind. Everyone wanted to display

their importance, tell me their stories, and get me on side. I was the shiny new attraction that broke through the monotony of immortality.

A common thread weaved itself through every conversation—the elite could not be trusted. Especially Grayson. Every time he was mentioned, their eyes flicked to my throat, and it reminded me they'd seen me dragged away in a collar.

They subjected me to the most vivid tales of the Elysian cull that wiped out demigods, reliving the trauma with those who'd lost their husbands, wives, and children simply because of who they were. None of these gruesome tales had filtered down to the mortals. If they had, I was sure the world would become godless. The more I learned, the more certain I became that I wouldn't survive to see Earth again. It was only the thought of Cass that gave me the strength to push on with my plan.

Others shared stories of Mallory, who left a lasting impact on those she was close to. A big personality with no filter between her mouth and brain—she seemed a world away from my mum. Vanessa Scott was stern, loving, and soft-spoken. She had a quiet determination that I admired. There were slivers of guilt that I couldn't shake off. I didn't feel a connection with my biological mother the way I did with Mum.

By the end of the second day, I was exhausted and wanted to shed the weight that had crushed me in moments of silence. Instead of being able to ignore what was going on around me, I threw myself further into the fire.

I'd never gambled in my life. Never felt the temptation to put money on a chance with no kind of guarantee. And I'd certainly never stepped into a casino, but Dionne assured me that The Vermillion Lady was the most popular spot in lower Elysia once the sun disappeared.

We stepped into the building, and I tugged at the hem of my dress. Despite my protests, Dionne insisted I would look out of place if I turned up in jeans. I eventually relented and shoved on the sky blue dress that belonged to her.

"I'm really not sure about doing this," she muttered.

"You don't have to be here, Dionne."

"I'm not going to leave you here alone."

She followed me like a shadow throughout the days, watching from a distance. There were moments Bexley joined her, but Dionne never left with her girlfriend. Whether it was out of guilt or morbid curiosity at my next move, I wasn't certain.

"Stay close," Dionne instructed.

There was no worry about me running off. The space was packed with tables. There were no automated machines or uncomfortable ringing like I'd seen in films. The Gods favoured cards, and the noise was a din of voices, all vying to be heard. For those who needed a break from the tables, a large bar was situated at the far end of the room and various minor Gods and Goddesses dressed in practically nothing, swayed hypnotically and seductively to music.

A few eyes landed on me and I raised a coy hand to Gods that I was vaguely familiar with now. They shot me smiles and asked me to join them for a drink, but I shook my head.

"What is it you're planning to do here?" Dionne asked as we pushed through the crowds.

"I'm trying to get to know people."

"There were a million other options. You've been meeting them on the streets."

"You said that most of the Gods would be here at some point."

Pleasant. Pliable. Performative.

A strong will was useful if it didn't land my head on the chopping block. Not all the Gods were going to visit the house or come and find me as I walked the streets, and sitting there waiting for them only fed into the narrative that a demigoddess was trouble. That I believed myself to be better than them. I needed to head out and put myself amongst them, regardless of my anxiety.

Dionne shook her head and found a table with space. We slid into seats, watching the end of a poker game. Eyes looked up from the cards in hands and fell on me. My throat grew tight with nerves, but I brought a smile to my face.

"Don't stop on my account," I said. They returned to the game, and I looked at Dionne. "What kind of money do you use here?"

At the centre of the table, there was a stunning lack of chips, coins, or notes. Instead, on the surface, sat different coloured wisps of auras. They behaved, shimmering along the table as if waiting patiently to return to their owners.

Dionne leaned in close and whispered, "We don't bet money here. It's all about what's useful. Favours. Sex. That sort of thing."

My cheeks warmed at the information. Before we arrived, I'd toyed with the idea of joining a game or two. I needed all the luck I could get with Hunter's test on the horizon, but there was nothing I was willing to put on the table.

I drew my attention back to the game and the players. There was only one face I recognised, and it belonged to Tobias. His gaze continued to flit between the cards and my face as they wrapped up the game with a Goddess winning the pot. There was a break from the gambling as they swept away auras and cards were collected again.

Slowly but surely, curious glances turned into conversations as I brushed shoulders with lower Elysians I hadn't met yet. They ranged from highly inquisitive to suffocatingly welcoming. I was hugged more times than I cared to admit. Each interaction forced the fear and anxiety away and filled me with a sense of belonging. It was a dangerous emotion that I squashed. This was a means to an end. Once I was told I could survive, I would never set foot in the heavens again.

Tobias rose from his seat and took the space beside me that had just been vacated. "So glad to see you back here, Quentin," he said. "Will you be joining us in a game?"

"I'm not sure what I could offer."

"Your gift," a tinkling voice came from across the table. It belonged to the woman who'd just won the previous pot. Something about her rang familiar, but I struggled to place where I'd seen her before. "Mabel," she introduced herself.

Mabel's silky brunette hair fell over her shoulders and her curvy figure was perfectly on display in a near sheer dress that moulded against her body. I felt mildly conservative in my clothing in comparison.

"Quentin. And I don't know what my gift is," I lied.

"Doesn't mean you can't offer it."

"Mabel," Dionne cut in, sounding sterner than I'd witnessed. "That's hardly fair. She hasn't had the chance to acquaint herself with it yet."

Mabel shrugged her shoulders and pinned me to the spot with her hazel eyes. "We can figure it out together. Or."

A slender wisp of neon pink came towards me and wrapped around my wrist, pulling me across the table violently. I gasped as the pain blossomed across my hip bones. It would have been easy for me to call on my aura and shove Mabel away, but I didn't want to look like a troublemaker, so I squirmed in her grasp, trying to get out of it.

"You could offer me your body instead," Mabel said, bringing her face close to mine. The suggestive proposition made my cheeks heat as I continued to struggle.

"Let her go!" Dionne demanded.

Something wrapped around my waist and tugged, but Mabel's aura held strong.

"I'm just providing her with options," Mabel argued.

"I appreciate it," I replied tightly. "But I think I'll keep my gift and my body off the table."

"You're going to get us all kicked out," Tobias told her.

An unfamiliar voice joined the fray, deep and booming. "That's exactly what's going to happen."

Mabel released me, shoving me away from her. The pressure around my waist disappeared, and I flew backwards. Tobias caught me before I hit the floor. His arms gripped my forearms, and I glanced down at the strange sensation against my skin.

Gods were flawless beings that basked in perfection, but three of Tobias' fingers were deeply injured and almost skeletal. He'd kept it beneath the table during play and I thought nothing of it. Quickly, he pulled his hands away from me, stuffing the injured one into the depths of his pocket.

"The three of you can leave," the new voice said.

I turned back to look at him. He towered over all of us, reaching seven feet and his build was strong and wide. His dark hair was a distant memory, overridden with grey on his head and beard, and deep scars decorated his face and forearms. Not the type of God I wanted to be left alone with.

"Andreas," Mabel crooned sweetly.

"Out!"

She scarpered, muttering to herself, and Tobias scowled before following her. Dionne caught my arm, ready to drag me out of the building, but Andreas shook his head.

"Leave her," he ordered.

"Andreas, she didn't do anything."

"I'm not going to repeat myself, Dionne."

She flashed me a worried look before letting go of my arm and leaving. I swallowed hard when I met Andreas' eye. There was nothing forgiving about this God.

"Follow me," he said, turning away.

Straightening out my dress, I did as he said. A myriad of whispers reached my ears as we walked across the floor and took the stairs. I wanted to ask him what I'd done wrong, but my tongue was stuck to the roof of my mouth. Why hadn't I been kicked out with the others?

Andreas opened a door in the hallway and we stepped inside. Something familiar pulsed through me. A sense of comfort and rage that I couldn't describe but filled the empty sensation that plagued me for hours.

"Thank you for the help, Andreas," Gray's voice emanated from the corner of the room, and my head snapped in his direction. He stepped out of the darkness, and I scowled at him.

"No problem, Grayson. I'll give you both some privacy."

Andreas left the room, shutting the door behind him, and Gray wasted no time in crowding my space.

"How did you know I was here?" It was the first question that spilled from my lips.

"You're not exactly keeping a low profile."

My back hit the wall, and I called on my aura so it drifted around us, lighting up the space. Gray's didn't join it. He'd caged me in between his arms. An easy prison to break out of if I wanted to.

I didn't need to justify myself to him but the words flew from my mouth. "Hiding away won't help me. I'm finding Gods to trust."

"And you thought this shit hole was the best place?"

"It was the most populated place. Plus, I'm not sure Andreas will appreciate you calling his business a shit hole."

"He won't care. We're family, after all. Andreas is Sloan's father and a God of war. He's heard much worse over the course of his existence."

That explained his imposing and intimidating nature. A shudder ran through me at being ordered about by a God of war. I couldn't believe that he had raised someone as gentle and positive as Sloan and had a son-in-law like Erik.

"I gave you space so that you could calm down, and you dressed up and walked into the lion's den?" Gray asked, eyes slowly turning black. "Any other day I would encourage all the chaos, but this is reckless."

"You want to act like you care now?"

Gray pressed his body against mine and I forced myself to stare straight back into his eyes. "I saved your life once and I'm trying to do it again. Don't you dare question whether or not I care about you."

His chest heaved with the effort behind his words, and I dropped my gaze to his collarbones. Dealing with Gray was like dealing with two completely distinct entities. He was the embodiment of destruction whose past made me question everything. But he was also the man who got on his knees and begged for my life. It shouldn't have been possible for both versions of him to exist, but they did, and I struggled to untangle my feelings.

"Come home," he whispered against my skin. "Let me explain."

My resolve wavered. Any time I was away from Grayson, the seconds stretched into eternity. The idiot girl in me wanted to forgive him. To collapse in his arms and allow him to take the weight of everything I carried. He would tell me his side of the story and I'd forgive him and everything would be fixed.

But that level of naivety would get me killed. I needed to listen to my head instead of my heart. My brain had never steered me wrong. It'd got me a well-respected job. It led me away from trouble. All my heart had ever done was left me broken after convincing me to make stupid decisions.

"These things are always done on your terms, Grayson," I muttered in response. "You withhold information and expect me to go along with it. This wasn't a small thing."

"I understand that. I told you this is new to me. What Archer showed you… I knew you would never take it lightly, but you've only seen his memory of it."

"I've heard what the others down here have to say. It was a massacre."

"If you let me explain—"

"Gray," I said, finally looking up at him.

Electric blue materialised behind him, and I shoved Gray hard to put some distance between us before Hunter appeared in the room.

"Why is it you can't handle the simplest tasks?" Hunter asked, looking at his brother with disdain. "When I told you to teach her control, what made you think I wanted her to be paraded down here again?"

"I needed to see Andreas," Gray replied smoothly.

"You couldn't go alone?"

"And let her roam around the house without supervision? I'd rather not take that chance."

"And you felt the need to dress up for the occasion?" Hunter asked, gaze sliding over to me.

"There's a strict dress code, or so I'm told," I replied, fighting the urge to tug on the hem of the dress.

"Quentin, when I put rules in place, I expect them to be followed," Hunter said. "And you keep defying them."

"I came here with Gray and I haven't caused any harm."

"Your very existence means harm." A wicked smile stretched his lips. "I thought you would know better than to lie to a God. Mabel was quick to let me know you were roaming down here alone."

Gray huffed. "I wouldn't trust a word that comes out of Mabel's mouth. She only knows how to cause trouble."

"But she's proven to be more trustworthy than you, Grayson. I gave you a leash for this bitch and you're letting her roam free."

I bristled at the words, forcing my aura to pulse in the space.

"Since you seem so comfortable in your skin," Hunter continued, fingers cutting through my aura, "we'll set the time for your test. Tomorrow. Eleven o'clock sharp, at the council chambers."

"Chambers?" Gray asked. "I thought you'd want us to stop by the house."

"This isn't a private matter. The entire council deserves to see proof she won't be an issue when she's returned home. I will inform them about this little unsanctioned trip." Hunter looked directly at me. "Do not be late, Quentin. I hope that's an order you can both follow."

EIGHTEEN

GRAYSON

I fought against every instinct to follow her when she left our home. Our bond conveyed she was in no more pain than what I'd inflicted with my lies and I knew her well enough to understand that she wouldn't want to be backed into a corner. She needed time to process before allowing me into her circle again. This woman would be driven mad if she didn't have answers, and I was the only being who could give her the ones she wanted. Fill in the blanks that allowed her the entire picture.

I could allow her that space, knowing she was safe, but the moment Bexley turned up to inform me she was planning a trip to The Vermillion Lady, I was ready to retrieve her and force the conversation to happen.

Impulsive and reckless was my domain. It was my comfort zone. She was the logical one who could work through her mist, not give in to it. And the moment she did, we found ourselves in a predicament.

Quentin returned home with me after Hunter gave his order, but she requested Ignacio. Despite the late hour, he arrived without complaint and worked her through drills. My eyes never left her as

she faltered through the first few hours, hair pulled back tight as she focused.

I imagined her younger, preparing for the exams that would lead her to her PhD and the life she had before I crashed into it. Alone and focused. Quen didn't need anyone to flourish. Given adequate time, she could master her feelings and her aura in the way she had everything else.

The brilliance she showed as a mortal would only be amplified with divinity. It was the idea I floated in front of Hunter, wording it as using her to our advantage, but my brother was never great at picking up on subtle hints. Perhaps another shove into my line of thinking might help move things along quicker.

The guilt washed over me as she struggled through yet another drill. There was no doubt in my mind that this was down to me and what she'd seen through Archer's memories.

"Again," Quentin said, coiling her aura back in towards her and picking herself up from the floor.

Ignacio shot me a concerned look, and I rose from my seat to join them.

"You need to rest," I said, coming to a stop next to her.

The sun streamed weakly through the fog that surrounded our property and bathed the room in a soft light. It highlighted the dark shadows under her eyes and the tightness in her jaw.

"I need to survive," Quen snapped without looking at me.

"You need to see your brother," Ignacio chipped in. "Which will happen if you can unwind yourself. Grab a shower. Eat a meal."

She buried her head in her hands and took a deep breath, shoulders rising and falling with the motion. "Okay. Will you be here when I get back?"

Quen was grasping for a buffer between us.

"No," I told her, cutting in. "He'll need to prepare for the meeting."

Quentin frowned, but nodded her head. "I guess I'll see you there."

Ignacio closed the distance between them and pulled her into a hug. The jealousy scorched through my veins at how easily she wrapped her arms around him, taking comfort from my friend that she couldn't find in me.

"You can ask," he said, not quite letting go of her. "I would give you all my luck, but you have to ask me for it."

Yet another thing he could do for her that I couldn't. Ig's gift lent itself to being something useful in this situation. All I could offer was a way to make it worse.

Quentin blanched, fingers digging into his sides. "I can't do that to you. I won't be that person."

"Quentin," I said, but she ignored me.

Ignacio was giving her a lifeline, but there was a look that passed between them that I didn't quite understand. There was a bond between them that didn't require words to convey their thoughts.

"I'll see you in the chambers," Quentin told him, stepping away.

The house grew quiet after Ignacio left. Any attempts at conversation were thwarted, and I begrudgingly understood that she needed to focus. The tatters of our relationship sank down the priority list while Quentin dealt with the matter at hand.

With five minutes left until eleven o'clock, I adjusted the crown on my head in the bedroom mirror and found her staring at me in the reflection. Turning slowly on my heel, I met her gaze.

"I can almost hear the way your mind is ticking," I said. "Ask me whatever it is you're thinking."

"What's he going to do?" she asked, with no further prompting. "Hunter. How will he test my control?"

"We've never had to do this before. I imagine it'd be in a similar fashion to how Ignacio has trained you."

She stared at her lap, hands balling into fists. Her wrists were bound in the cuffs, forcing her to look submissive. "I hate going into things unprepared."

"You are not unprepared."

"What happens if I fail?" Quentin looked up at me again. "I don't get to go home and he just kills me there and then?"

It was impossible. He would have to taint her blood first and that would take some time while he gathered what was needed.

"I'd murder him before he has the chance."

Her eyes hardened at my words. It was something that I was capable of, and she'd witnessed that fact. I prepared myself for the argument, but her shoulders sagged.

Quentin was a strong woman. A bull-headed battle axe may have been a better way to describe her. But everything in Elysia over the past few weeks had taken their toll on my golden girl. There was too much uncertainty that drained her. Too much chaos that she couldn't break through the surface in order to take a breath.

Extending a hand out to her, I said, "It's time to go. I will be there, and even though I cannot offer you luck, I promise I won't let anything happen to you." She would hate me more than she already did for saying it, but I needed her to know. "I love you."

Slowly, she lifted her hands and placed them in mine before I helped her to her feet. Her words were almost inaudible, swallowed by the depths of our bedroom. "I love you too."

The black of my aura swirled out and consumed us before it cleared away, leaving us standing in the council chambers. My hand slipped from Quen's to around her wrists, pulling her gently to the centre of the room. I cast her one more look before climbing the steps towards my throne.

"Now that we're all here," Hunter said once Aria had taken her seat. "We shouldn't waste any time."

He left his throne and walked down to Quentin. Her anxiety rose, the bond allowing me to feel the nervous energy that pitted in her stomach until it gave way to nausea. My fingers gripped the arms of my throne. I felt Erik's stare boring into me, but I refused to look away from Quen.

"This is simply to test your control, Quentin," Hunter continued. He unlocked the cuffs with the key I handed him earlier and they fell to the floor with a clanging that echoed around the chambers and made Quentin wince. "I've invited the others because I felt it was their right to attend and witness what you are capable of. It may help their decision when we vote again."

She gave him a definite nod, lips clamped tight.

"Call on it," Hunter demanded. "Show us the essence of your gift."

The fatigue she'd displayed earlier when her shoulders slumped had vanished. Quentin straightened her spine, giving her short frame an inch or so, and gentle wisps of gold materialised around her, curling and uncurling around her body.

"Amplify it," he ordered.

This was a strange route to take. He wanted her to control it, but I'd expected him to ask her to hide it, not showcase it.

The chaotic energy Quen exuded trickled to nothing as she grew her aura around her. She was a beautiful sight to behold, illuminated in golden light so bright that it made the elite shield their eyes.

"Enough!" Hunter barked. "Get rid of it."

The room dimmed as Quen pulled her aura back into her. The last wisps disappeared, and her gaze flicked to me briefly before returning to Hunter.

"She's done well," Erik said, leaning towards me.

"I never had a doubt."

"You've shown considerable control," Hunter announced. "For a half-breed."

I sucked in a breath while a titter of giggles came from some of the elite. He was baiting her. Quentin was a prideful creature. She took everything as a personal slight and struggled to remain calm. Her instinct was to snap and defend herself.

"You'll need to use whatever limited intelligence you have to maintain this ruse while we finish the project," Hunter goaded her. "Or it'll be more than your life on the line. That man you refer to as your brother and the pretty blonde he plans to make a wife will also pay for any mistake you make."

"It's my *limited intelligence* that is going to help complete it," she informed him.

"There's an entire team of scientists working on my project. You think too highly of yourself."

"I'm a demigoddess. The ego comes with the territory from what I've witnessed."

I stifled a laugh, biting down on the insides of my cheeks. That sharp wit was always ready to deliver a comeback.

Hunter turned away from her, walking back towards the steps that would lead him to his throne. "We'll prepare to return this afternoon."

Quen's lips twitched as she suppressed a smile. First hurdle conquered—the relief was palpable through our bond, and I itched to go to her. Express the immense amount of pride that ran through me as she took on my brother.

"But for all our peace of mind," Hunter said, diverting my attention away from Quentin. "I want to make sure that she won't put us in any uncomfortable situations. You all know that my priority is Elysia and this council."

I stood from my seat. "She's just proven—"

But my sentence was cut short when Hunter turned away, a solid wall of blue rushing towards Quentin. It slammed into her with force, picking her off her feet and landing her across the council chamber.

"Hunter!" I yelled, aura flaring out around me. It faltered as a deep pain coursed through my chest.

My brother sauntered down the stairs, back towards Quentin. Erik's aura wrapped strongly around my wrist and forced me back into my seat.

"If you get involved, he'll make it worse," he muttered.

This was true. My sadistic big brother had interesting ways to prove he protected us all. If anyone went up against him, he'd figure out how to make them pay. He'd make me pay for embarrassing him in front of the council, and I couldn't risk her by stepping in. Bruised pride was curable, a corpse was not.

"I've heard a lot about you at the institute," Hunter continued as he approached her. His aura picked her up and set her on her feet.

"That you have a foul temper. That you can be difficult to work with. That you believe yourself to be better than everyone else."

Her aura pulsed to life, and Hunter clucked his tongue.

"Are you losing control?" he asked. "Because it would be a shame if the first thing I need to do when I return is to kill your pathetic excuse for a family. Leave you abandoned and alone again, and this time it would be all your own doing."

Pain rippled through my chest before Quen's aura disappeared from view.

"You have no right to talk about my brother," she spat. "Look at how you treat your own. Blood means nothing over a genuine bond."

This time, when his aura struck her, it was directly to her abdomen, throwing her back into a pillar in the chamber. She hit the stone, folding in on herself before collapsing to the floor like a rag doll. Pain blossomed in my torso and along my spine so wildly violent that it pulled me out of my seat and to my knees. My howl was only drowned out by the crumbling of the pillar. As the stone fell on top of her, an unbearable ache ran through my chest and hips.

"Hunter, stop!" Erik called, falling beside me.

But my big brother was in his element. Through hazy vision, I saw her body lifted through the rubble, blood staining her skin. Why wasn't she defending herself?

I called on my aura, summoning it around me before she was plunged into the stone floor. Quen's screams ripped through the room, echoing mine as my body writhed with the fresh wave of pain down my back. It was so powerful that tears sprung to my eyes and nausea rolled in my stomach.

"Stop!" Erik yelled.

Hunter ignored his cries, and I tried to pull myself to my feet to do something. Through blurred vision, I watched as another load of rubble cascaded from the ceiling and landed on top of her body, driving my head to the ground and robbing my aura from around me.

"Stop this!" Erik's voice drifted away from me. "They're bound!"

Silence fell over the chamber and the pain subsided before I pushed myself up to my knees properly. Chest heaving from the exertion of the assault, I looked up to find Hunter staring back at me.

"Repeat that again," Hunter said, voice quiet and laced with danger.

Erik looked back at me apologetically. "They're bound."

"He'd have to possess a soul to be bound," Waverly remarked.

"Bound to a half-breed." Aria chuckled. "Only suited to something useless."

"Enough!" Hunter yelled. "You're all dismissed except for Grayson and Erik."

The chamber filled with movement as Gods left us in a flurry of whispers and auras. Rising to my feet, I pushed past Hunter and dropped beside Quentin. Calling on my aura again, I searched through the debris before finding her. Quen's body lay curled on the ground, looking worse than when I'd found her on the road a few weeks ago. This time death would not come to claim her, but the pain she'd felt and the damage Hunter had caused brought a lethal and quiet rage to my soul.

"Are they truly bound?" Hunter asked.

"I've read Gray. There's no mistake. Quentin is his soulbound," Erik said.

As I brushed the hair out of Quentin's face, she didn't stir. Her breathing was shallow, and I picked her body up from the fractured floor. She laid limp in my arms, blood smeared across her skin. The red liquid was flecked with gold, conveying her divinity.

"You knew," Hunter said, striding over to me. "I thought you were just using her, but you knew you were bound."

My aura formed a solid wall between us, protecting her like I should have when he started the whole fucking interrogation. I shouldn't have let her stand there alone to take him on. I'd let her down. Failed at keeping her safe.

"If you *ever* think about touching her again…" I paused, gritting through clenched teeth. "… I will not hesitate to call on my gifts with everything I have and destroy anything you hold dear."

Hunter looked amused as he observed us through a veil of black. "I wouldn't be so brave to throw around threats if I were you, Grayson."

"Hunter, you know what would happen—" Erik tried to reason.

"I don't want to hear a word from you. I can't trust a single thing that comes from your mouth." Hunter turned on him. "You've both embarrassed me in front of the council again. I've told you we're meant to show a united front, but you both continue to betray me."

"We didn't know until recently," Erik lied.

"And now the entire council knows about this affliction."

"Hunter—"

"We descend again this afternoon," he said, cutting across Erik. "Since she's so certain of herself, she can heal in her own time. I will know if you've helped her, and I will make sure that she'll be in a worse state if that happens."

He flicked his gaze to Quen, and I curled her tight against my body, cradling her close.

"This changes nothing." Hunter stared at her limp form. "The council decides her fate."

He left the chamber, and Erik took two steps towards me, but my aura grew in size.

"Gray," he said sadly. "I would never hurt her."

"I don't trust anyone anymore."

NINETEEN

GRAYSON

Every whimper I'd ever extracted from Quentin coaxed a carnal desire from deep within me, but the sounds she made from pain as she laid in our bed ignited a bloodlust that felt unfamiliar. It was a raw emotion that burnt every nerve, demanding to seek revenge. The strength of the emotion forced my body to tremble and it only temporarily subsided when I looked at her.

The dark bruises across her cheekbones faded and gave rise to flawless brown skin again. Damaged capillaries were an easy fix—it was the shattered bones and punctured organs she'd suffered through for hours. Partial divinity was being heralded as a gift, but I could only see it as a curse while it struggled to heal her instantly.

I wiped the last of the blood away from her lip and threw the towel into the bowl of water on the bedside table. She groaned, a weak sound that splintered my heart. Her brows pulled in as she writhed on the sheets. Reaching out, I gingerly ran my thumb along the space between her eyebrows, gently straightening the crease.

"You can do this, Quen," I whispered.

The fear of touching her right at that moment ran rampant. I was not known for being gentle. Destruction was my forte, and I didn't trust myself with the swirl of psychosis that was trying to drag me under that Quentin wouldn't end up as collateral.

When I moved my hand away from her, she sank back against the pillows, finding temporary respite.

"I promise you, golden girl," I said, gaze transfixed on her face, "I will never let anyone touch you again."

A heavy knock sounded on the bedroom door and I scowled at the wood.

"Brother," came Erik's timid voice from the other side.

Of course, it would be him, and I had no doubt he'd brought the cavalry with him. There was a deep pang of regret that I'd extended an open door policy. It was a small compensation that they couldn't enter the bedroom directly with their auras.

"Go away!" I barked and then winced when Quen whimpered. My gaze snapped back to her. "I'm sorry, darling."

There was scuffling outside the door that made me narrow my eyes.

"Move," Ignacio's voice came clear. "Fuck manners. Use force."

I shot to my feet as my aura expanded, filling the room. Carefully, I controlled the dark shadows to cloak the bed. A privacy screen for Quentin. She would never forgive me if I allowed them to see her weak and vulnerable. If I gave them more ammunition to use against her when they saw fit. The rest of my aura pushed against the door as I strode towards it.

"There's no reason for any of you to be here," I told them darkly, unable to rein in my temper. "Leave us alone."

"You can't keep her hidden for the rest of her days," Ig replied, voice coming through the wood. "We're going back down there. What do you plan to do? Keep her locked up in her home?"

"If I have to."

"I'm sure she'll love you for that."

"Grayson, please." It was Sloan's turn to try. "We want to make sure she's okay."

"She's not," I bit, leaning my back against the door to glance back at the bed, where she was obscured from view.

"We would never hurt her, Gray," Sloan continued. "I want to help you, just like you helped me."

I closed my eyes for a split second before pushing myself off the door. "Only you. I mean it, Sloan."

"Only me," she repeated.

Moving away from the door properly, the doorknob turned and Sloan slipped into the room. My aura slammed it shut behind her to ensure we were left alone.

Her gaze slid from my face to the bed and back again. "May I see her?"

"No."

Sloan nodded slowly. Getting up on her toes, my sister-in-law rested a hand against my cheek, and I tensed beneath her touch. "I can't imagine what you're going through right now," she said, eyes growing glassy with tears. "But don't shut us out."

"This has already got out of hand. I refuse to risk her, Sloan. I can't…" Something painful lodged in my throat. "There will be no point in my existence without her."

"Grayson, I am forever indebted to you for helping me with my bond. I promise I will do everything in my power to help you with yours."

It was difficult to think of Sloan and Erik as anything other than the sickeningly perfect couple they were. But when Erik first found her, Sloan refused to have anything to do with him. Why would she risk her heart for a God who was known for salacious sex parties and a lack of commitment? Then there was Andreas to contend with. Even now, Erik wasn't good enough for the war God's only daughter.

"And the rest of them?" I asked, deciding Sloan was a safe bet.

"Erik is your brother."

"Hunter is my brother."

"Don't you dare compare them," she snapped, a flicker of her aura lighting up the room as she dropped her hand from my face. "He would never pull a stunt like this. Erik adores you. Has always adored you. Quentin is an extension of you and Erik doesn't have the capacity—"

"I get it," I cut across her speech. "Erik is fine."

"And so are the rest. We've spent millennia together. Don't let Hunter win because he will if he divides us."

"You really are your daddy's daughter, aren't you? Already plotting out how to win a war."

A soft smile came to her face. "I only fight for what I believe in."

Taking in a deep breath, I let a tendril of my aura snake past her and pull open the door. Ignacio almost fell to the floor, only saved by Erik, who kept him from the humiliation.

But it wasn't my brother or friend that I focused on. It wasn't even Elva who slinked past us to stand next to my aura that shrouded her family, trying to find her way through it.

Instead, my gaze landed on the hulking form of another elite God. Malachi lifted his hands in a placating gesture, white palms in stark contrast to his dark skin.

"Grayson," Sloan said, holding on to my arm. "Malachi came to talk to you. He's not here to cause—"

"You voted to put her to death," I said steadily, ripping my arm from Sloan's hold. "And now you have the audacity to walk into our home!"

The top floor of the manor grew dark as my aura expanded out to cover it, engulfing us all in the abyss.

Malachi stood calmly in a shimmering dome of ivory, protecting himself, which only further pissed me off.

"I understand your animosity towards me, Grayson," Malachi said. His voice, as always, kept a level and soothing tone. "I won't insult you by trying to rationalise my vote, but I came to tell you that my decision is not final."

"And you expect me to believe you?"

"Not at all. I wouldn't if the roles were reversed, but it is my prerogative to change my mind and I could be swayed."

My eye twitched. "Why?"

"If we're to believe the display in the chambers and what Erik said, you're bound to her, no?"

"Why is that of any importance to you?"

"Because I still believe in some traditions here. I don't believe in touting them only for my benefit or to gain favour. Soulbinding is a sacred gift from fate. It should never come down to us to sever that bond."

There were scores of customs and traditions that Elysians learned and followed. Some were fading from existence while others remained strong. Soulbound couples were a rarity, a gift of fate, but I didn't think anyone would care for the customs surrounding them.

"That would be enough to sway the vote in our favour," Elva said, still facing the black void where the bed should be. "It'd save her." Her fingers brushed against my aura before she sighed and dropped her hand.

"If he changes his mind? I don't trust that Hunter won't try to remove him from the council if he finds out. He'll replace Malachi with someone else who wants her gone," I argued.

Ig huffed. "I never had you down for one with paranoia."

"Grayson," Malachi called my name, redirecting my attention to him.

"You've delivered your news. You can take your intentions and leave now." I turned away, ready to tell the others that they were free to go.

"Ask," Malachi said. The room stilled and my nostrils flared as I took in a shaky breath. "You know of my gift. Ask," he repeated.

"No."

Of all the terrible things I'd done throughout my existence, I could say I'd never asked another God to use their gift to help me. I steered clear of that taboo, rather unwilling to be indebted to someone in that way.

"Ask me to give the rest of the council patience and I will do it, Grayson. It may give you more time," he pressed.

"No!" I said, turning back around. "No."

Malachi bowed his head. "If that's what you want. In which case,

I'll do my best to convince the others, so there's a strong majority behind you." He lifted his head so his dark eyes met mine. "It would be nice to meet her properly once she's healed."

"Don't push your luck."

Fuck trying to get everyone on our side by playing nice. They all sat back and watched the spectacle unfold like some theatrical piece in the chambers. It had been a stupid idea for me to ask her to parade herself to the whim of people who wanted her dead.

"You are pushing yours. She'll need to integrate herself if you have any hopes of swaying a vote. I include myself in that. Your bond is enough to pique my curiosity, but I still want assurance that she will not be an issue." Malachi left no room for discussion, leaving in wisps of ivory.

"Why wouldn't you use his gift?" Elva asked, ignoring the pointed look from Ignacio. "He gave you permission."

I ground my teeth together so forcefully that a vague ache ran through my jaw.

"Because," Ignacio said. I could feel his stare on my skin, but refused to meet his eyes. "Quentin knows it's taboo and she would never forgive him. Not even if it helps her. She wants her survival to be based on her own merit."

"This is not the time for stubbornness and morals."

"You need to leave," I announced, straightening up. "All of you."

"I haven't seen Quentin," Elva argued.

"Schedule an appointment with her when we're back on Earth," I snapped.

Frustration ran through her features. "You don't get to monopolise her, Gray."

"I do, when she can't make a damn decision on her own."

"We'll see her tomorrow," Sloan said and then faltered when she saw my expression. "Or whenever she'd like to see us."

"We'll see you soon, Gray. Give Quentin our love," Erik said, whisking himself and Sloan away.

Ig's orange aura grabbed Elva around the waist, drawing her into him. "Don't be a prick," he told me. "If you don't invite us to see her, we'll arrive unannounced."

Any retort was useless as he left my home with Elva in tow.

With our home empty of threat, I recalled my aura. The floor slowly became lighter as the windows were revealed and dim sunlight shone through again. It dissipated from around the bed, bringing Quentin into sight. She was still pale, but as the light hit her, her eyelids fluttered. When she opened her eyes, I rushed to the bedside.

"There you are," I whispered.

She looked at me, eyes unfocused and heavy from fatigue. A pain-induced haze. If she had her wits about her, I doubted she would have spoken to me with such softness and vulnerability.

"Did I do it?" she asked. "Did we win?"

"Round one to us, golden girl."

TWENTY

QUENTIN

Descending to Earth was meant to solve all my problems. Not really, but I'd hoped it would lessen the heavy pressure that sat on my chest. Instead, everything was amplified. Without the imminent threat of Hunter ripping my life away, I was forced to address all the other issues that were plaguing me.

Once my body healed, the awkward iciness settled between me and Grayson again. There were so many questions I wanted to ask him, but I couldn't trust myself to. Not yet. The sting of being lied to was still fresh, but I needed to understand his actions so I could find some peace again. A large part of me mourned our relationship. It felt unsalvageable after Archer's revelation. And if that was the truth, then all of this, the last few weeks of stress in the heavens, had been for nothing.

I wasted no time in running to the lab and seeking sanctuary. Gray hadn't followed me and I was grateful that my colleagues were only dipping in to get experiments up and running again before returning home.

It had been a shit show of a day from the moment I opened my eyes.

Before stepping into the lab, I phoned Cass, who picked up on the third ring. Cassidy rarely, if ever, sounded disappointed in me, but there was a first time for everything. I didn't blame him. We were weeks away from his wedding and I'd gone radio silent. It was Sophie who suggested that it might be work related, which was the only reason he hadn't booked a flight home. With a lump in my throat, I apologised profusely to my brother before telling him it wouldn't happen again. He sighed irritably before thawing, but as I got off the phone, all I wanted was a hug from Grayson. Without that comfort, a lead weight settled in my stomach and refused to leave me all day.

Cass was the reason I kept control of my aura in the chambers. If it came down to it, Hunter could kill me. But the moment he mentioned my brother, I knew I couldn't lose control. With Cass' image firmly in my mind, I took every blow Hunter offered because for once, someone needed to look after Cass.

Charlie hovered around the lab as I pulled cryovials of cells from liquid nitrogen and revived them. Every time she got close, I inched away, feigning illness and cursing the fact I hadn't slapped a cuff on my wrist that morning.

"This is an unusually late hour to still be at work."

I'd sensed another God before he spoke. When I looked up from my laptop, he was standing by the door, watching me with his dark eyes.

"Gods don't take holidays. Or I'm sure that's what I'm meant to believe," I replied, and then clamped my mouth shut. The filter between my brain and mouth had yet to reappear since Hunter dislodged it in the chambers.

He took measured steps towards me, but I didn't feel threatened. There was something calming about his presence. Like a teacher or a parent who wanted to have a gentle word.

"I'm not sure you should talk to me," I said when he pulled up a seat opposite me and sat down.

"Why not, Quentin Scott?"

"Hunter wouldn't be happy about it."

After his display in the council chambers, I didn't want to come up against Hunter again. I was used to being alert, walking with my keys between my knuckles when it got dark. But Hunter's attack was in broad daylight. It was also difficult to swallow that not a single one of the Gods had asked him to stop the brutal attack. They were all happy to sit and watch. I wouldn't risk his temper again.

"How else do you expect me to make an informed decision?" he asked.

I closed the laptop and looked at him properly. "You should introduce yourself if you're going to discuss such sensitive topics with me."

A smile tugged at his lips. "Malachi. God of patience."

He stretched his large hand out across the table. Multiple silver rings decorated his fingers, and I regarded it for a moment before shaking it.

"What is it you want to know?" I asked, taking my hand back.

"Do you understand why you're in this predicament?"

"Mallory didn't follow the rules."

He hummed. "She did not. But I meant more specifically."

"Some of the minor Gods explained it to me," I said, dropping my gaze to the table. "Demigods were trouble. They were convincing mortals to stop praying and threatened your existence. But it wouldn't affect them because they were part mortal. They'd lose their divinity but continue without it."

"Precisely. So we got rid of them."

"I'm one being." I looked up at him. "How much harm am I capable of?"

"You're a scientist, Quentin. One microlitre. One milligram. One decimal point. The smallest fraction can change the course of your work and endanger lives, no?" When I didn't reply, he continued. "What guarantee can you give that you wouldn't turn your back on us? You were never a believer. You didn't care about our existence before. Why would you bother to protect it now?"

I bit my tongue from offering the first crumb of truth that popped into my head. Grayson was always going to be the reason, but I couldn't tell him that, so I went for the next thing.

"I've made friends with some of the elite. Erik and Sloan. Ig. Elva is my family."

"Blood doesn't always mean loyalty. I'm sure you're aware of that."

"I feel you're playing a game, Malachi," I said, leaning back slightly. "Like you know more about me than you're letting on."

"I know that you rarely prayed and that you're rather impatient."

My confidence wavered. "Not exactly the best qualities to be highlighted."

"Would you like to tell me some of the better ones?"

It was like an interview. Malachi was asking me to sell myself. All of my usual qualities fell flat. Efficiency, team work, critical thinking— all great for a lab environment but utterly useless for keeping me alive in the eyes of a God.

"I don't let people close to me, but when I do, I give them everything," I admitted quietly, unable to look him in the eye. "I want to protect them. Malachi, I don't wish to ascend. I don't want a place in Elysia. I want to live my life and watch my brother get married and maybe become an aunt one day."

"And when they're gone?"

My throat closed up, and I blinked at him. Immortality hadn't quite sunk in. I was in my late twenties and the gift of divinity meant that I'd have a million lifetimes ahead of me. While Cass grew old with Sophie, I would be stuck as I was. My heart clenched painfully in my chest.

"You don't appear to be a threat," Malachi said, standing up, completely oblivious or maybe uncaring to the tailspin he'd sent me into. "But you should discuss options other than a funeral with Grayson. I have a feeling you won't be needing such dire plans."

I opened my mouth to respond, but he left my lab and I dropped my head onto the desk.

Every time I felt like I might get through this, every time I jumped over a hurdle, something else happened that pulled me under.

Shoving my laptop into my bag, I grabbed my things and finally left the building. It was pointless frustrating myself by staring at data points when my brain refused to process them. The better plan would be to head home, crawl into bed, and hope I could switch off from everything for a few hours.

As I made my way towards the tube, the car long damaged and abandoned after the earthquake, something caught my eye. Further up the road was a white brick building. A small group of people spilled out onto the streets, and I held back, letting them disappear around the corner before stepping up to the entrance.

The last time I'd stepped foot into a temple was for my parents' funeral. My memories of that day were hazy, but I remembered swearing I would never visit a temple again. I officially washed my hands of the Gods that day and never doubted my decision.

Until now.

Stepping over the threshold of the building, I toed off my shoes and placed them in a holder in the entrance hall. The nerves coursed through me until I shook and the numbness trickled through my body. I pressed my tongue to the roof of my mouth and took a slow and measured pace into the main hall.

The room was empty, smoky trails of incense wafting lazily through the air and making the room somewhat inviting. The lighting was dim, and I walked up the central aisle until I reached the front and lowered myself to the floor, legs curled beneath me.

When I was younger, I used to sit beside Dad and fidget. I couldn't bow my head long enough, couldn't focus on begging for what I desired. Cass had always been better with his religious intention and rather than being the black sheep of the family I pretended. But the older I got, the more questions I had until I couldn't contain them. Dad answered as openly and honestly as he could, and I loved him even more for never forcing the matter on me. He never questioned when I stopped attending temple as frequently.

What would he think of me now?

"This was the last place I expected to find you."

I jumped at the voice, too caught up in nostalgia to hear the steps or follow intuition.

"Larkin," I said, tipping my head back to look up at her. "What are you doing here? Are you following me?"

"Yes."

I blinked at the blatant honesty that flowed from her. Larkin threw her sheet of blonde hair over her shoulder and joined me on the floor, gracefully folding her legs and staring ahead at the bare white wall. No distractions were permitted while the faithful sought guidance.

"Why?" I asked eventually, unable to tear my eyes away from her flawless face.

"Because you might actually listen to me. Hunter, Grayson, and Archer won't. Men." She spat out that single word. "Always thinking they know best."

"Fatal flaw," I agreed.

Larkin turned her head, meeting my eye, and I swallowed hard. She didn't instil a sense of comfort or trust in me. Even before I discovered my divinity, Larkin made me feel unworthy, and a vote against me in the chambers crushed any crumbs of hope that I'd misread the situation.

"Quentin," she said, expelling a breath. "I want you to consider what you're trying to do."

"I'm not sure I understand."

"You've seen what Elysia holds. How the council was split over the decision. I know Gray might have promised you the heavens because you're soulbound but—"

The word shoved my neat thought process off track, and I stuttered, "W-we're not… Why would you…"

Larkin's brows drew together. "He didn't tell you."

The world around me felt unsteady. No one knew we were a couple, and Larkin just said we were soulbound.

Gray had given me a vague description of soulbinding. It was a bond stronger than soulmates. How would Gray know if we were soulbound when he admitted to not knowing too much about it? Erik was the expert.

"I'm not surprised. Don't bother lying about what's gone on between you. The entire council knows," she grumbled, shaking her head and pulling me away from my spiral. "They have a way of working things in their favour."

"They?"

"A particular trio of brothers." Larkin looked ahead again. "I know the heavens might seem wondrous after a life on Earth. You worship us. Well, not *you*. We're held in high esteem, but we have our own issues. I tried to tell Gray, but he won't listen to me. Quentin, sometimes death is not an option to be disregarded so quickly."

My walls went up, and I leaned away from her. "If you're here to do Hunter's dirty work, then it's a waste of your time and mine."

"I'm not here for him. He'd lose his shit if he knew where I was. If he cared enough to wonder where I was. I came here for you."

"Larkin, I want to survive," I stressed. "I won't ask the council for death."

Her head turned back to me, hair fanning with the motion. "Because Gray said he loves you? Did he promise you'd sit beside him? Did he make you believe you were his equal?"

I hated the way she made it all sound so trivial. Those moments when Gray had worshipped me were sacred. Seared into my memory.

"I've heard all those promises," she continued. "I believed every single one of them and I don't want someone else to fall into the same trap." Her eyes grew glassy with unshed tears.

"You said the trio of brothers," I replied eventually. "But Erik is besotted with Sloan."

"You didn't know him before he met her. Sloan didn't trust him easily."

"But she did eventually. Gray isn't like Hunter."

"Gray is destructive and chaotic, Quentin." Her tone left no room for argument. "Since you've met him, has anything gone smoothly for you? Or do you wonder why everything feels completely out of your control? I know you are bound, but in the simplest terms, if you accept him, then that is what you can expect for the rest of your life. You will never have peace. We bring elements of our gift with us into everything we do. This whole mess you've found yourself in is likely because of Gray's chaotic nature."

So much made sense if that was true. The lack of cooperation from him. The way Matthew discovered us. Ethan showing up at the door. Gray's brand of chaos wasn't something you couldn't escape. It rained down relentlessly and sanctuary wasn't granted.

"Even if that's the case," I mused quietly, "that wouldn't make me choose death. That's an extreme, Larkin."

"What do you think will happen if you survive? That you'll live happily ever after in Elysia?"

"No one has asked what I want. You've all made assumptions about my desires and intentions. I have a family here. A job. My life was perfectly fine before you all descended into it. I don't want to be in Elysia. I don't want to be a God."

"But you are part divine and Gray will never let you go that easily.

I've known him for a long time and I've never seen him risk as much as he has for you. Never known him to have an obsession like this."

"Then I should be pretty safe."

"You will never be safe with the Gods," she whispered, dropping her gaze. "You're an intelligent woman, Quentin. I wouldn't be here trying to convince you if there was another way."

"I think you've wasted your time." I pushed myself off the floor.

"I was like you," she said, making me freeze. "Not bound, but ambitious and conceited."

"I'm not conceited," I replied, sitting back down.

Larkin offered me a weak smile. "We are women who know our worth and people hate that, but we refuse to yield. That lends itself to ego, and there is nothing wrong with that."

In that small phrase, I felt closer to Larkin than I ever had before. A few months ago, she would have had me believe that there was no common thread between us. This was a strange crumb of progress, but I'd take it.

"I had dreams of doing great things in Elysia and cementing myself in legend," Larkin admitted. "When Hunter took an interest in me, I didn't hesitate, but I should have. Everyone knew his position and he could be charming. He praised all the strength I showed. Told me I was the type of woman he envisioned by his side to rule the heavens. The rush of power and sweet words, Quentin—sometimes you believe that's all you need to keep your world spinning."

I hugged my knees to my chest, listening to her. I'd encountered Hunter's charming side. He had a way of making you feel small and safe. It was his job to make you feel protected, and he carried it out easily.

"That changed after we were married. He adored my strength, but not the way I used it. He took it whenever I challenged him."

"Strength is your gift," I said, once again remembering Charlie's uttered prayers.

"Yes. And he took it from me without permission." Her voice trembled. "And he didn't stop there."

My brow furrowed as an alarm bell blared in my skull. I pushed back on the panic, certain I was jumping to conclusions.

"If you repeat any of this, no one will believe you," Larkin told me as she stared at the wall. "They'll think you're a troublemaker. A whore trying to climb the ranks by spreading malicious gossip."

"I won't repeat anything you tell me," I said softly, ignoring the attack on my character.

"I will not give him children. I couldn't imagine a worse fate, but Hunter isn't used to being told no."

The insinuation was clear, and a tear rolled down her face. I felt sick at the revelation, frozen to the spot as Larkin continued.

"When it first happened, I didn't know what to think. He is my husband. He is a protector. I didn't believe that he would harm me. I thought maybe it was a power play. A kink?" There was a questioning tone in her voice. "It took me too long to admit to myself what was really happening. If I'm lucky, he cheats on me and I don't complain. I know some of the Gods pity me because he isn't discreet about it. He parades Mabel at the parties I refuse to attend, but it's an easier life. When Hunter's happy, carefree and his day is going well, he'll leave me alone and find someone willing. And then sometimes he wants his wife because he's had a bad day and he's angry and because it's behind closed doors where he can let the mask drop. There isn't much I can do when he uses my gift against me. He uses my strength to make sure he can win."

A sob ripped from her and I inched towards her, sitting up on my knees, but falling short of pulling her into a hug. I wasn't sure it was what she wanted.

"Leave him," I whispered. "Larkin, why are you still with him? Use his gift, protect yourself and leave."

"Sometimes I can't fight. And the times I do, it just ends up being worse."

"There has to be something you can do. Someone you can tell."

"Hunter is the head of the council. He is the only one who can grant marriage and divorce. Marriage is not taken lightly in Elysia, and I'm stuck." Larkin took in a deep breath through her nose. "I am trapped, Quentin. I'm not the most liked Goddess. Who would believe me if I told them? My husband. The protector by gift. Who would believe he rapes me after being married to him for centuries?"

I never thought that issues that arose on Earth would affect the Gods. Women who feared speaking their truth because they would be called liars.

"I believe you," I told her fiercely.

"You are a pariah," Larkin said, wiping her face. "I didn't tell you any of this for pity. I told you because I don't want you to succumb to a similar fate."

"You think Grayson could do something like that?"

Never once in our months together had Grayson forced me to have sex with him. Even with a collar wrapped around my neck and pressed against the wall, telling him I hated him, I was a willing participant. There was trust and respect between us in those moments.

She shrugged. "I never thought Hunter was capable of the things he's done, but his darkness is hidden under depths. Grayson doesn't even try to hide his. Think carefully. I couldn't save myself, but that doesn't mean I want anyone to suffer the same fate. Even if you are a traitorous demigoddess." Her attempt at humour fell flat.

"Larkin." I grabbed her hand that laid between us and she didn't pull away. "Can I do anything to help you? Please, let me help you."

"There isn't anything. I am trying to find a way. I will find a way."

I might have imagined it, but I thought there was a ghost of a squeeze against my hand.

"What if you fall pregnant?" I asked quietly. "He'll never let you leave then. Would he?"

"I won't fall pregnant," Larkin replied.

"How can you be so sure?"

Her blue eyes flicked down to our hands. "I used Sloan's gift. She made me infertile."

My heart shattered further in my chest until there was nothing left to beat in the cavity. There was a time in my life I imagined a home full of children, but had changed my mind since. Nothing stopped me from changing it back, but Larkin had taken the only route she could to protect herself.

"Why don't you tell Hunter you can't have children? He'd grant you a divorce if he's just looking for an heir," I suggested, trying to find a way for her to leave the nightmare she found herself in.

"It would put Sloan's life on the line and I refuse to do that. She is the only person aside from my sister to offer me kindness."

Elysian politics was a messy tangle of threads that connected everyone. There was no way to pull yourself out without cutting through someone else's or further embedding yourself into it.

"You didn't rely on us before," Larkin said, looking up at me. "You were right not to. Don't resort to becoming less than what you are for a shot at greatness, Quentin. It's not worth it."

TWENTY-ONE

QUENTIN

As I stepped onto the tube, the ripple of familiarity ran through me. Turning my head left and right, I spotted Ig sitting at the end of the carriage and observing me. I suppressed a sigh and trudged down the aisle towards him.

My head was still spinning after Larkin's confession and I wondered if the other Gods truly did not know what happened behind closed doors. I didn't trust that they wouldn't turn a blind eye if they thought it would save them. But Gods, like Ig, who seemed so deeply affected by those who stole his gift from him, seemed unlikely to let this pass so easily.

He scooted along the bench seat, allowing me to drop next to him, arms and thighs brushing against each other.

"Less man-spreading would help," I muttered, sitting my bag on my lap.

"I'm trying to blend in. Looks like I should take up as much space as possible."

"Did you need something?" I asked. "Or is this an unhealthy coincidence?"

"I wanted to talk to you about Grayson."

I sucked in a breath and dropped my head back. If I got off at the next stop, I would need to walk for some time before I got home. There was always the option of getting a cab.

"Quentin," Ig prompted.

"You knew what he did." I lowered my chin and turned my head to look at Ig. "You knew what he was capable of."

"We would never have left him with you if we thought he was a threat."

"Because it would have risked your existence."

Ig looked away, embarrassed. They had no loyalty to me and I was tired of trying to convince myself otherwise.

"Elva was involved," he admitted quietly. "They forced her against her will, but she still had blood on her hands."

My knuckles turned white as I gripped the strap of my bag, wringing it relentlessly. "Gray wasn't forced, was he?" The silence spoke volumes. "Did he send you here to do his dirty work?"

Ig snorted. "Do you think that's Gray's style?"

No. Grayson would crash into a situation and handle it himself, even if it meant making matters worse. He didn't delegate. That was something he would need to work on if he planned on taking over Elysia some day.

"Quentin, it's not something he's proud of. Surely you can understand why he didn't tell you."

"I had a right to know."

"Maybe you did, but it didn't unfold that way. Things between you both are messy. When was he meant to explain it to you?"

"Before he confessed he loved me?" I tucked my legs in as more people stepped onto the tube.

"He's been focused on keeping you alive." His voice lowered. "I've known him for a very long time and I can tell you I've never seen him so distraught over the prospect of losing something. Someone."

I fixed my gaze on my knees as they bounced with the movement of the tube down the tracks.

"How am I meant to love him when I know what he did?" I whispered.

Ig's weight pressed against my left side. "Have you heard his side of the story?"

"No."

"Maybe you should try that before you decide on what to do with him."

I turned my head to find whiskey brown eyes staring back at me. "Can't you just tell me?"

"He wouldn't appreciate that and you wouldn't be satisfied with it, either. You need him to talk to you. He's your bound."

Dropping my head into my hands, I blew out a breath and ignored the sting of tears. I hadn't been this exhausted in years.

"Just hear him out, Quen," Ig implored, rubbing my back. "And then if you want nothing more to do with him, I'll evict him from your house myself."

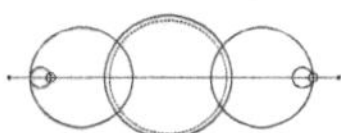

The heaviness that plagued me throughout the day amplified until I could barely lift my feet to walk to the door. Not a single cell in my body wanted to leave Larkin alone after her admission. She had carried so much on her shoulders and felt the need to share to save me from potentially making the same mistake. She wanted to help me escape, and I wanted the same for her.

The second unexpected conversation with Ignacio hadn't helped my mood. He declined the invitation to join me, unravelling the ruse and uncovering the truth that I didn't want to be left alone with Grayson.

I leaned against the front door after I stepped into the house. The lights were off and I closed my eyes, becoming part of the darkness that surrounded me. In the stillness of the house, something rippled through me. The sensation of relief washed over my body, causing my knees to buckle. Something solid held me in place, but I refused to open my eyes, and the warmth of Gray's body enveloped me as he stepped into my space.

"You're home later than I expected," he said, breath fanning across my face.

"I had a lot to do in the lab."

"Have you eaten?"

"I'm not hungry," I whispered, voice breaking.

A wave of sadness ran through me as my conversation with Larkin swirled in my mind. There was no chance of appetite when I was so full on the injustice of her situation. It pushed its way to the front of my mind, jumping to the top of my priority list. The mortal avenues of police were pointless. The council was the law and Hunter was the head. It made me want to scream.

Gray's hands cupped my face and my eyes snapped open to find him staring at me with concern written over his features.

"What's happened?" he demanded, gaze flicking over my body as he attempted to find the source of discomfort.

"Nothing."

"Do you think I can't sense everything running through you right now? Tell me. I knew I should have come to the lab with you."

That was the last thing I wanted. I was in a strange position where I needed space from him, even if my heart kept yearning for the opposite.

"We're soulbound," I blurted out into the darkness.

Grayson's hands dropped from my face. "How did you find out? Which one of them told you?"

"It's not important."

"Who told you?" His aura darkened the hallway until I couldn't see anything in front of me.

"Larkin," I admitted.

"I should have known."

The darkness faded as he controlled his aura and walked away into the living room. I kicked off my shoes, dropped my bag, and followed him.

"Is it true? Are we?" I asked.

"You need proof," he said, huffing a laugh. "You'll never be able to take anything at face value. Will you allow me to bring Erik here?"

I nodded and watched him disappear from my sight. The house felt empty without Gray's presence, and I wondered if this was how it would be. If Gray and I separated, I would live here in a silence that consumed every moment instead of the love and chaos I'd grown used to.

Dropping onto the sofa, I ran my hands over my face, trying to find something—anything—to anchor me in the madness that constituted my life. There was little to cling to when everything pushed against the boundaries of reality.

Before long, Gray returned with Erik by his side, lighting up the room in red.

"Quentin." Erik beamed, but I raised a hand to stop him.

"This isn't a social visit. I need you to tell me if Gray and I are soulbound."

Erik's smile faltered, but he kept it in place. "Would you like me to show you?"

"Please."

I worked best with solid facts presented to me. My brain thrived on logical solutions. I needed to be in control again and I didn't have the capacity to conform to social norms and niceties. What I needed was for Erik to do his job.

"Hold out your hands," he instructed.

Shuffling my butt to the edge of the couch, I did as he asked. Erik kneeled in front of me and took my hands in his own, ropes of red aura wrapping around my arms.

A strong lack of control took over me as memories ran through my mind. All of them contained Gray. The first time I saw him being dragged through the corridor. The way he leaned against the bar in Murphy's. Late nights where he held me tight against him as I fell asleep. The start of our relationship brought with it feelings of chaos and lust so strong that it was difficult to breathe.

Slowly, the memories morphed into more recent ones. The fireflies around the boat in Malaysia. Running through the streets in a storm to find him. Sex out on the cliffs as he worshipped me. The feelings were just as intense, but they transformed into love. Still just as chaotic, still fuelled by lust, but something more substantial laid behind every moment between us.

Erik slowly released my hands and I let out a shaky breath before opening my mouth to ask him a question. It died in my throat when my gaze went to my hands. The skin was jet black all over and it was creeping up my arms. I shot to my feet, panicked.

"What have you done?" I yelled.

"Quen, you're okay," Gray said, coming to join me. "Just wait."

He offered Erik his arms, and Erik took them. A gentle golden glow emitted from Gray's chest and engulfed his hands.

"This is your soul," Gray said, lifting his hand so I could see it properly. "And that"—he glanced at my hands—"is mine. We are bound, Quentin. Here is your proof."

"It's so beautiful," Erik whispered, looking on the verge of tears.

It was, but it was also terrifying. The inky blackness that crept up my arm looked like something out of a horror film. Of course, it would belong to Gray.

"A part of your soul resides with the other. It's a bond you'll have with no other being," Erik told us. "You'll feel each other's emotions. Pain, anger, joy. You'll learn to manage—"

"Erik," I cut across his words. "Can you leave, please? Gray and I need to talk."

He glanced between us before stepping towards me. Erik cupped my face in his hands gently and I forced my eyes to meet his. They held so much hope that my chest caved in, and I took a deep breath.

"You are truly blessed," he whispered with a smile. Erik pressed a kiss against my forehead before leaving my home in a glow of red.

"What is it you want to discuss?" Gray asked when we were alone.

He settled himself onto the sofa, and I took a moment before taking a seat beside him. I kept looking between my hands and his.

Black and gold.

Light and dark.

This was our twisted tango.

"How long have you known?" I asked, starting with something easy.

"I found out when you left for your conference in Malaysia. I felt immense pain in my chest and Erik asked to read me. My soul was missing yours. It was the first time we'd been separated since I'd descended." Gray's explanation was succinct.

"But you never told me."

"Things were complicated. You were still seeing that brainless oaf—"

"Don't use that as an excuse. It never stopped us from everything else." I wasn't proud, but it was a fact. "So why hide this from me?"

Gray looked at me and the intensity of the gesture made me shrink. "Because everything before that was sex. Or at least it was meant to be. I didn't want to tell you because I know you. I know the way you overthink a situation. You'd have seen it as an obligation. I'd bet my gift that you're thinking about it now. How you'll have to settle with me because you're bound and you'll have no other option. You have options, Quentin. I will not force you to stay. I didn't tell you because I wanted you to love me of your own volition. Although, I sense that's no longer the case."

"I never said I didn't love you."

"You've avoided me and refused to talk."

"Can you blame me after what I saw?"

"You saw one side of the story."

I folded my hands in my lap and stared down at them. The ticking from the clock in the room seemed thunderously loud, and I tried to compartmentalise each issue in my life. Running was only an option for so long. If today was anything to go by, burying myself in work wouldn't give me the temporary peace that it usually offered.

"There is a bias in the data you collected," Gray continued.

"Don't talk science to me."

"It's the only way to communicate with you sometimes."

A silence fell over the room again. It was lit by the glow that emanated from Gray. My fingers twitched in my lap as I tried to digest the information and a dull ache started in my head.

"Not all gifts are like yours, golden girl," Gray said, raising his hand and flexing his fingers. "Not all of us are blessed with the ability to bestow joy on others like you and Erik and Ignacio. Some of us were always destined to destroy. War and death and chaos—we didn't have a choice in what was given to us."

"But you have made choices since then."

"My apologies. I forgot I was speaking to someone who is the paragon of perfection," he snapped and then dropped his head. "I never claimed to be good." The statement was a whisper. "Quite the opposite, actually. I have always shown you exactly what I am and what I am capable of. I have never lied about that to you."

From the moment he stepped into the building, Gray had hidden no aspect of his personality. He was foul-tempered and vicious. He wore it like a badge of honour, which was one reason I fell for him.

No bullshit.

So then, hearing his side of the story should help with deciding what to do with the precarious ledge I stood on.

"Show me," I said to him. "Show me your point of view if you think it'll help."

Gray blew out a breath and held his hand out towards me. I cautiously placed mine in it, and he tugged me roughly, pulling me from my seat and into his lap. I wanted to push away, but the heaviness that pressed down on me soothed and I rested my face against the side of his, trying to keep myself together.

His arm wrapped around me, holding me close to his body. "Ready?"

I nodded, and Gray's fingers brushed softly against my temple.

It was a gloriously sunny day in Elysia. The reflecting pool glinted in the sunlight and laughter rang out across the space.

My eye was drawn to three young boys, who looked no older than their early teens, lounging by the pool. Gray, even as a child, wore a sullen expression, picking at the grass that surrounded him.

"Hunter, stop it," Erik pleaded, blonde hair falling into his eyes.

"I'm not doing anything," Hunter replied with a shrug. "Grayson already knows all of this. Don't you, Grayson?"

Gray didn't respond. He continued to pluck the blades of grass with more vicious intent.

"He's a complete liability. No one wants to be around him and I don't blame them. The literal black sheep of the family. Protection." Hunter gestured to himself. "Love." He waved a hand to Erik before looking at Gray. "And chaos. What use is that going to be? He probably won't exist for long."

The black smokiness surged out from around Gray like his own personal thunder cloud.

"Fuck you," he said to his big brother, enunciating each word and getting to his feet. "I hope you don't exist. I hope the mortals become so wickedly dependent on revenge that they never seek protection again."

"Temper, temper, Grayson," Hunter said smugly, walking up to his brother. "You're scaring people."

Gray looked past Hunter where the other residents of Elysia had begun to gather their things. He hung his head, balling his fists by his side.

"I'd be nice to me if I were you," Hunter warned him. "Everyone says I'm the one who'll take over after Dad. Mortals are fearful. They want to be protected. They'll rely on me until their dying days. Play nice and if for some reason they rely on you enough to keep you around, I'll spare your life."

Hunter knocked his shoulder against Grayson's roughly as he walked past, leaving his younger brothers behind.

Erik stepped up to Gray's side. "Ignore him. He doesn't know anything."

"I don't need your pity, Erik."

"It's not pity, Gray."

"Just leave me alone!" Gray raged, aura pulsing out uncontrollably and causing people to scatter. "I want to be alone."

The memory faded away, and I pressed my nose against Gray's cheek, processing what I'd seen.

"He's always wanted me gone," Gray said quietly. "The fact I still exist must truly be a thorn in his side."

"You were so young," I whispered.

"Age is nothing when you're immortal."

"He still shouldn't have spoken to you like that. He's your brother. Cass would never —"

"I didn't show you for pity," Grayson said sharply, but I didn't flinch. "I showed you, so what I show you next might have some context."

His palm rested against my face, and the room around us fell out of focus as another memory took over.

Gray walked hurriedly through the council chambers, descending some stairs down into the depths. He threw curious glances over his shoulder before heading down a hallway. His footsteps echoed around the space and eventually he came to a stop.

Sitting on the floor, back resting against the wall, was Elara. Her blonde hair was stuck to her face and dark circles coloured beneath her eyes.

Gray strode over to her, sinking to his knees. "Nothing I say will make him listen."

"You tried," Elara told him, tilting her head up to meet his eyes. "I know you did."

"He's forcing Elva to help. He's asked her directly for the use of her gift."

Elara nodded. "Grayson, please don't let Hunter do this. I don't want to die by his hands."

"I can't stop him. Elva will take control tomorrow. She won't be able to stop it."

"I need it to be you. I need it to be someone I trust. Who isn't being tricked into it and will need to live with that guilt."

"No." Gray went to get to his feet, but Elara reached out, grabbing his hand with a surprising strength for how weak she looked. "You can't ask me to do this."

"Grayson, how long have we known each other?" When he didn't answer, she continued, "Wherever you go, who cleans up after you?"

"Hope is always needed after chaos," he said tightly.

"And I have always done what is needed of me. I need this one thing from you."

"I won't do it. I spent years thinking he was looking after us all, but this is madness. He's tarring you all with the same brush without proof. Forcing the rest of us to do his dirty work."

"And you plan to challenge him?" Elara asked. The words seemed to be an effort, and she took a deep breath. "You see what lower Elysians see, Gray. Your brother has never been a leader. He's manipulated everything he could to work in his favour."

"I won't allow him to do it anymore."

"You get yourself thrown off the council or killed and he will do whatever he wants." Elara closed her eyes. "You're in a position most of us would have craved. You're right there to vote against him and to change the opinion of others. Offer them another option."

"It'll be too late by then."

"It's too late anyway, Gray." She opened her eyes, glassy with tears, and looked at him. "It's a long game if you plan to balance the heavens and Earth."

"And we lose our kin while that happens?"

"You've seen how many voted against us. If you go rogue, then you'll just join us in not existing and Hunter will continue to rule the way he wants."

"You said yourself that others see the truth."

"But we would need utter chaos when the time comes to remove him."

"Elara," Grayson said, balling his fists. "They'll never forgive me if I stand there and help take your life. I'll never forgive myself."

"You will forgive yourself. I forgive you. Archer will when the time is *right. When they are ready to listen and you show them this."*

"I don't want to do this." His voice broke, and he looked away from her.

"I know. That's why you have to."

The living room moved back into focus and Gray was tense beneath me. I moved my face away from his to look at him properly.

"You didn't do it because you wanted to. She asked you."

"Elara," Grayson whispered her name. "I'd known her for a long time. She was like a sister who brought her gift, her hope, everywhere. I spent less time with her after she met Archer. Our contact was non-existent by the time they got married."

"She was a friend, and you had your hand forced."

Not just by Hunter, but also Elara. She had asked him for a fatal favour, and how could Gray deny her a dying wish?

"It's not an excuse," he replied. "I made a decision and I am not proud of what I did, Quentin. There is not a day that goes by where I wish I had chosen another option. Elara was certain that I saw it clearest. Saw Hunter for what he truly was. She was adamant that I kept my position and tried to remove him from his seat. She forgot I am not the most congenial God in Elysia. I tried to be compliant, but it didn't last long. Some days it feels like it was all for nothing."

"Why haven't you shown Archer? Or any of the others?" I asked. "Why haven't you explained to them?"

"Do you think we have spent a single second in each other's company without vitriol flowing between us? Hunter took Larkin from him, and that was a blow. At least he can still see her in Elysia. I took Elara from him in the most permanent manner. I wouldn't forgive anyone if they took you from me, no matter what their reasons."

"But Gray—"

"When Archer showed you his memories, did you believe it straight away? You are a scientist, Quen. Tell me the marvels of the brain."

The brain was the organ I was fascinated with. If I didn't adore the mechanisms of development, I would have specialised in neurobiology.

The specific mechanism that Gray was alluding to was false memories. Manipulating them and showing others what you thought to be true. I didn't believe Gray was showing me anything fake, but neither had Archer. Both were genuine sides to a story, but in Archer's grief and anguish, it was unlikely he would believe Gray.

I believed what I saw. Teamed with what Larkin had told me, Hunter was a master manipulator. He found an individual's weaknesses and strengths and figured out how to use them to his advantage. Gray craved acceptance, and love and Hunter used him and gave him a position on the council to placate those emotions. The moment he took it too far, Gray could no longer deny what his brother was—a monster.

If I thought this was going to help me, I was mistaken. Getting a glimpse at Gray's past further complicated things.

He lifted me from his lap and set me on the sofa beside him. I instantly missed the warmth and comfort of his body.

"You are not obliged to stay with me," he said. "You have both sides of the story and you are more than capable of deciding what you feel is right for you."

"But we're bound," I pointed out.

The black from my hands was slowly fading to give rise to the usual brown of my skin.

"Bonds can be broken," he replied.

A sharp pain ran through my chest, making me gasp for air. Gray shifted next to me, his hand landing above my heart and the other on my back.

"Deep breath," he coaxed.

I did as he said, but felt unsteady.

"It will hurt to break the bond," he explained as another ripple of pain passed through me. "Erik told me as much."

I couldn't keep the shock from my face. "You already asked?"

"It would have put your life in danger if anyone else found out. I would have broken it to keep you alive."

"You make all these decisions without consulting me."

"I make decisions because I know Elysia. You rejected the world I lived in. I've been trying to keep you safe."

"That's not how things work."

"I am… sorry." The word was difficult for him to use. Apologies were not something that came lightly from Gray. "I am sorry that I wasn't honest with you. I'm sorry for my past and I am sorry that I have risked the best thing to happen to me in my entire existence."

The lump grew in my throat again.

"I need some time to think about all of this," I told him.

"Understandable. You have other priorities right now." He stood from the sofa, pulling my attention up to him. "Your research and family need to come first. Focus on those, Quentin. There will be time for us to decide what to do after."

Something about his words made my skin itch uncomfortably. Gray didn't see himself as a priority in my life. I'd never conveyed him to be one, and before, I would have shrugged it off. But after what we'd been through and what I'd seen tonight, I hated the fact that was the impression he had.

"Get some rest, Quentin," he said, and I stood from the sofa.

"Will you be here in the morning?" I asked, voice thick with emotion.

"I will never leave you."

TWENTY-TWO

GRAYSON

From the moment I met her, I'd wanted to crack into her skull and drink her thoughts. Dark and delicious. There wasn't a waking moment where Quentin wasn't thinking of something. There were times where people talked to her and she'd ask about something completely unrelated. It amused me to see how she continued to unravel her mind, even when she should be focused on the task at hand.

I stepped away from reading her thoughts as we grew closer. It was a choice I made to allow her some privacy and control. With her divinity no longer hidden, I had no choice, and it drove me insane.

The kitchen was deathly silent as she padded around the space. A thin tendril of my aura snaked past her and pulled a sleeve of coffee capsules from the top of the cupboard as she prepared to hoist herself onto the counter. She didn't say thank you, and my aura brushed against her waist as I recalled it.

"What do you think of women?" she asked when her mug was full and the bitter scent of coffee hung in the air.

Where had that come from? Of all the questions I expected her to

ask, my stance on women would have been at the bottom of the list. I was prepared for questions about last night and about my memories, but she was working on something else.

"Why are you asking me this?" I returned.

Quentin leaned back against the counter. She wore a pair of jeans and a hoodie that was two sizes too big and fell just above her knees. Comfort. She was seeking comfort in every form.

"When I first met you," she said, staring down into the depths of her coffee, "you said you weren't afraid to hurt women."

I pushed myself out of the chair and strode over to her. Quentin's head snapped up, watching me as I approached. Large brown eyes tracked each of my movements. My hands gripped the counter on either side of her, caging her into the small space. No fear resonated through our bond, nor panic, which left me even more confused. What was she trying to understand? Did she think I would kill her if it came down to it?

"If I dislike someone enough, I am destructive," I told her truthfully. "Gender is never a question."

"Would you hurt me?"

"No."

"What if..." she trailed off and focused her gaze on my Adam's apple. "What if I said I didn't want to do this anymore?"

Her knees buckled and my hands went to her waist to keep her upright.

"Is that what you want?" I asked, ignoring the splintering pain in my chest.

"No, I'm asking hypothetically." She continued to refuse to meet my eye. "If I didn't want this, would you force me?" Her grip on the cup tightened until her knuckles paled. "Would you force me to do anything with you?" she whispered.

The meaning of her question sunk in, and I attempted to keep as calm as I could.

"Quentin," I started, unable to unclench my jaw. "Has something happened? Did someone try to do something to you?"

I would have known. If something had happened while she was out of my sight, I would have felt it through our bond. But what if I hadn't? The murderous intent slammed violently through my veins and made my vision blurry.

"No, Gray," she answered, looking up at me with a flicker of panic in her irises.

My grip on her may have remained soft, but the room had become pitch black. Her hand came up to rest over my heart.

"I swear, nothing has happened to me."

"In lower Elysia?" I asked.

Archer had made comments about the heads that had turned. Of course she would garner attention, and Gods were not shy. She walked through the streets of that cesspit, sat at a table in The Vermillion Lady. Andreas mentioned nothing, but he would know I'd tear the building down if something had happened.

"No."

"Before I met you?"

Ethan was no man. He hadn't loved her the way she deserved, and the bile rose as I thought of Quentin accepting whatever he might deem as affection in order to keep her idea of the future alive.

"I promise you, nothing has happened to me, Gray. No one has hurt me."

It took a few minutes before the room was devoid of my aura. There were plenty of people I was prepared to destroy because of how they treated Quen, but if I ever found out someone had tried to force themselves on her, they would understand the true meaning of destruction.

"Why are you asking me this? Have I ever—"

There was a trickle of doubt that our bedroom games, the rough play we indulged in, might not have been reciprocated. I raked through memories of our time together, trying to pull any thread of discomfort she might have felt.

"Sometimes you think you know people and then you realise you didn't know them at all," she said.

"Where is this coming from?" I asked, cupping her face. "Quentin, I would never do that to you. To anyone."

"I just needed to know." She broke away from my hold, placing the full mug on the counter. "I don't need you in the lab today, so I'll see you when I get home."

She was already making her way to the door, ready to start her day now that she had answers to her questions, but she'd left me with many of my own.

As the front door closed, I allowed my aura to carry me up to her room. Sleep wasn't necessary for me and rather than encroach on her space, I spent my time wandering the house while she retired to her bedroom. If she needed me, she knew where to find me.

A small smile tugged at my lips to be standing in her version of chaos again. Our room in Elysia was a large space that was kept tidy. Her room on Earth was much smaller and Quentin crammed as much as possible into it. Papers and photographs. Fairy lights and blankets.

I peered at a fresh set of sticky notes that were stuck above her bed. A pros and cons list. It would have been too much to ask her to trust her heart with this decision. It was an organ she had little faith in.

The pros list remained empty, but the cons column had various notes stuck to it.

I'm going to die.

He isn't honest.

Bad temper.

Destructive.

The words expanded out until an oblivion of lime green notes took over one side of the wall. My fingers brushed along the empty side and I ground my teeth together. Not a single pro.

For years, I had people tell me I was impossible to be loved. I couldn't have cared less. I wasn't interested in such a frivolous emotion. My needs were met and then I continued to do my job. There was no need for love.

Until I met her.

When Erik found Sloan, when he worked to win her over, I was there. I remembered how he fell away from his playboy lifestyle and focused solely on the woman who had a part of his soul. It was ridiculous, the way he softened and folded for my sister-in-law. Changed into someone better because Sloan would accept no less.

I didn't understand it then, but I did now.

I couldn't change my nature or my gift, but I would do whatever else Quentin required of me. She asked if I would force her to stay and I hadn't lied. If she wanted to leave, she could, but I wouldn't give up on her.

I stared at the blank side of the wall for longer than I cared to admit. Was there really not a single reason she could find to give me a chance? Would it anger her if I added some helpful reasons to the wall?

As I turned to leave the room, something else caught my eye. At the corner of her desk laid a bouquet of stems and a few inches away rested the bright yellow tulip heads that had been sheared savagely from the body.

Thoughts of Archer infiltrated my brain and my aura unfurled as my intuition took me to where he was. People startled as I appeared in the lab, but Archer looked over at me with feigned surprise.

"Would you like me to bow?" he asked from the desk where he was lounging.

The scientist beside him was probably a decade older than Quentin and sported deep lines around his eyes and salt and pepper hair. He clapped a hand on Archer's shoulder in a friendly manner and turned his attention to me.

"Is there something I can help you with?" the man asked.

"He's here for me, Emmanuel," Archer said, unfolding himself from the chair. "Did Quentin send you?"

"You're making her uncomfortable." I seethed.

Was this what she was alluding to this morning? Archer was pressuring her in his own way and she felt uncomfortable with his gestures.

"Me?" He pressed a hand to his chest. "I'm not the one who's slaughtering her kin."

"Watch your mouth."

Mortals surrounded us and if any of them found out about what she was, then Hunter wouldn't wait for a vote.

"I gave her honesty. She'll thank me for it in the end," Archer said.

My aura shot out, wrapping around his ankle and pulling him sharply towards me. A sick sense of satisfaction rushed through my chest when his skull bounced off the floor and he cursed.

"Find Gareth," Emmanuel called, and from behind me, I heard the door opening and closing.

"Listen to me," I hissed, bearing down on Archer. "She has enough to deal with without unwanted advances from you."

"I'm offering her the hand of friendship," he replied. Archer kept his aura tightly coiled away. "She'll need people to rely on."

"She has me."

"A murderous psychopath. That must give her a deep sense of comfort and help her sleep at night."

"I did what I had to."

"You're defending it?" His irises flickered to forest green.

"You don't understand. Elara—"

"Don't you dare say her name."

"I knew her long before you bothered with her existence. You were too obsessed with Larkin to notice her."

The green flared out through the lab, and it cleared benches of glassware and paperwork.

"But I did notice her and then you saw fit to end her existence!" he yelled. "You'll do the same to Quentin. Destroy her the moment she's no use to you. Bonds can break, Grayson. I intend to shatter yours. Happiness is not something you deserve. You're only fit for an eternity of misery!"

"What is going on here?" Gareth's voice thundered through the room.

"Leave her alone," I warned Archer.

"I'm trying to save her."

"You're going to get her killed."

"Grayson!" Gareth called. "Let him go or I'll need to get Hunter."

"Gareth, don't do that." I turned around to see Quentin squeezing her way into the lab space. "Please," she said, looking at him. "I'll sort it."

She walked through the lab, and the green and black that swirled around us slowly disappeared.

"Morning, Quentin," Archer said from the floor, and I resisted the urge to kick him in the ribs for addressing her.

"I told you I didn't need you in the lab this morning. Did someone else in the facility need you?" she asked me, ignoring him.

"No. I had some business to resolve."

"You're making things worse."

"This isn't all on me."

"You didn't need to be here," she argued. "You came here to pick a fight. Please leave." Her cheeks were flushed red from embarrassment and her muscles were tense, making her look smaller than she was. "Go," she said, and I weighed up how much trouble I would be in if I threw her over my shoulder and marched out with her.

"If you can't handle your subject, then he shouldn't be out of cuffs." The attention of the room shifted towards Emmanuel, who'd spoken.

"For your information—" Quentin began.

"I run this programme, Emmanuel," Gareth cut in. "It falls to me to tell you how to conduct your work."

"Are you planning to tell her?" he responded. "Look at the state of my lab."

"It'll be cleaned. No actual damage has been done. I'm sure Archer will be happy to help."

Archer picked himself up from the floor gracefully and dusted himself off. "Of course. It shouldn't take us long and we'll be back on track," he assured Emmanuel. "Drop by any time," he said to Quentin.

Emmanuel scoffed. "I'd rather you not. Keep yourself and your subject off my floor."

"With pleasure," Quentin quipped. "Come on."

She marched past me towards the door, and I followed behind her. When the door swung shut, I opened my mouth, but she beat me to it.

"I don't want to hear it, Gray. You were the one who said I needed to be liked, but this isn't helping. Stay away from Archer. I'm begging you not to make this any more difficult than it needs to be."

She jabbed her finger against the button for the lift and turned around to look at me. The look in her eye told me that there were no reasons to stick on the other side of her bedroom wall.

And I couldn't blame her.

I was not built for love.

TWENTY-THREE

GRAYSON

"I want to say thank you to my sister, Quentin," Cass announced to the crowded room.

That Quentin had allowed me to attend her brother's wedding as her plus one was nothing short of a miracle.

After the incident with Archer, I kept myself away from the lab. During the day, if Charlotte didn't require my presence, I spent time with Malachi and Flynn.

Flynn was a young elite God, responsible for safe travel. He was also a gossip so my time with them benefitted me in two ways. I sang Quen's praises to them and answered their questions over our bond, and Flynn told me everything he knew about what was going on in lower Elysia. His overly friendly personality pulled people in and they trusted him without hesitation.

I made sure to be at the house the moment she stepped over the threshold, but she still called my name the moment she walked into her home as if she was terrified that I wouldn't be there. When I appeared in front of her, she calmed down enough to carry on with her evening.

"When Mum and Dad brought you home, I was so excited to have a little sister to look after and protect," Cassidy continued. "I didn't realise you wouldn't need any of that. You've been the one who's looked after and protected me most of my life.

"You were the first person I told about Sophie and you said, and I quote, 'Cass, if you don't marry that girl, I will. Who else is going to put up with you the way she does?'"

I let out a bark of laughter, and Quen grinned, dropping her gaze to the table for a moment.

"Well, I did it." Cass beamed, cheeks ruddy from all the champagne he'd thrown back. "Thank you for always being there and supporting me. You helped me with the ring, the planning, and the travel. You are the person I can depend on, no matter what."

He raised his hand slowly and flashed her the numbers one, four, and three with his fingers. She returned the symbol to him and my brow furrowed. As Cass finished his speech, Quentin doodled the numbers on my palm as a few stray tears fell down her face. Leaning over, I swiped them away with my thumb.

"He has no clue what I am or what might happen," she muttered as people raised their glasses. "But he has Sophie now. He's happy."

With the speeches over, Quentin vacated her seat. She'd stuck to my side, the cuff secured on her wrist, when she needed to, but the moment she could leave, she did. My frustration at the situation continued to grow. I'd hoped showing her my memories would help us, but she was still trying to work through this alone. Her stubbornness, which was usually amusing, grated on my nerves.

"Congratulations, Cassidy," I said, shaking his hand as he came over to me.

"Thanks, Gray." He grinned at me so openly I might have thought he liked me. "Gray, you make my sister happy and I have no idea how you plan to make it work, but please look after her. She called to say you two were having some issues." The alcohol was truly coursing through his system.

"Nothing we won't find our way through," I replied. "You have my word as a God, Cassidy, that I will take care of her."

He looked at me for a moment and only turned away when Sophie gently pulled his arm. She looked beautiful in her wedding dress and for two seconds I allowed myself to wonder what Quen might look like in something similar. Quentin head to toe in white, walking towards me as the greatest gift I could receive.

As quickly as the thought came, I pushed it away, feeling a faint blush on my cheeks.

Wife was another title she should add to her arsenal—if it cemented her to my side.

There was no doubt in my mind that I could win Quentin around. For all my talk of her having a choice, there was only one. Bond or not, that woman belonged to me, and deep inside, she knew it.

Even if she liked to push my buttons.

I shot up from my seat and strode across the floor to where she was currently being swung around by some man.

"My heart bleeds," she said as he set her down. "You chose trauma surgery, so you deal with the hours it brings."

Quen stepped back, her back bumping into my chest. A possessive arm snaked around her waist and pressed her tight against me.

"Care to introduce us?" I asked her.

"Gray, this is Wyatt—Cass' old roommate from uni and one of

his old friends."

Wyatt frowned. "Less of the old, Scotty."

She laughed and gave me her full attention, dark eyes pinning me to the spot. "Wyatt, this is my boyfriend, Grayson."

Just like that, every small piece of jealousy that was coiling in my chest disappeared.

Boyfriend.

She said it so casually.

Wyatt extended a hand, but I nodded in response. No cuff, no contact with new mortals. I was off the leash in case anything arose at the wedding. Quentin was cautious that Hunter would make good on his threats to come after her family.

"You look after Scotty or you'll have more than Cass to answer to," Wyatt warned. He nodded to a few men and women milling at the bar before looking at Quen. "Save me a dance, beautiful." He kissed her cheek and left.

"Ignore Wyatt," Quen said.

"I fully intend to," I replied, trying to calm myself down. "Boyfriend?"

"That's what you're meant to be today." Quentin broke free from my arms. "I need to mingle."

"If you want them to keep their hands, I suggest you make sure they don't land on you," I reminded her.

She muttered under her breath, "Possessive dickbag," before leaving.

Sitting down at an empty table, I watched her obsessively. The tension she'd carried with her since we descended hadn't left, but being around her family relaxed her.

This was how her life should be. Quentin was the embodiment of success. The golden girl who deserved to be worshipped. Instead, she'd withdrawn from Gods and mortals alike while she worked through issues alone, untangling them in her mind and trying to make sense of it all.

I would make it my life's work to ensure she never felt this way again—weighed down and alone in strife.

"Are you ready to leave?" I asked when we'd waved Cassidy and Sophie off from the venue.

Quen swallowed hard and nodded. I pulled her around the side of the building. Most of the guests would be too drunk to worry about where she had disappeared to. The black of my aura wrapped around us before taking us back to her home. We stood in her bedroom, and Quentin stepped away from me.

"Do you need help with your dress?" I asked.

The lilac number hung off her shoulders and draped down to the floor, hiding her figure. I couldn't decide if I was grateful or irritated by Sophie's choice in dress.

"I can manage," Quen said.

We'd moved back into the awkward space we once occupied where neither of us understood what laid between us. I wanted to respect her and the time she needed, but the frustration was growing.

"Okay. Well, night." There was nothing more to say and so I made a move towards the door.

"You are my priority," she whispered as I reached it. "I never told you because I didn't want to admit it. I didn't want to admit that you'd become so important in my life, but you, Grayson, you are my priority."

I dropped my hand from the doorknob and turned around to face her. How young she looked, hunched in on herself and gaze darting around the space.

"Is that all?" I asked.

"That's all you have to say to me?"

"Quentin, you know where I stand. You told me you needed time and I will give it to you. Telling me I am your priority is nice but nothing more than words that are thrown into an already complicated situation."

"Okay," she snapped, straightening up, unhappy that I hadn't bent to her whim. "Then yes. That's all."

With a frustrated sigh, I swallowed back a response and left the room to return to the guest bedroom I occupied when I first moved in with her. The vague sound of fabric tearing reached my ears, followed by Quen's frustrated scream. I huffed a laugh and walked into my room, stripping out of the suit I'd been confined in all day.

I loved her.

Adored her.

Worshipped her.

It amused me how her divinity shone through sometimes. Quen wanted to do the bare minimum, avoid the difficult conversations, and be given the fruit of it. I wouldn't allow that.

There was a rush of cold air as the door opened again, and I closed my eyes, waiting for Hurricane Quentin to be unleashed.

"Actually," she announced as I turned around. I bit the insides of my cheeks to find her clad only in her underwear. "No, that's not all." She stuck her hands on her hips, and the room darkened.

Grabbing my discarded shirt, I walked over to her. "If you're going to have an argument with me, I'd appreciate you do it while clothed."

Her cheeks flushed red as she took the shirt and shrugged it on, wrapping her arms around her waist.

"Please, continue," I said, sweeping my arm out as I took a seat on the edge of the bed.

A glimmer of uncertainty passed over her, and a tendril of my aura reached past her to shut the door.

"No more running, Quentin. You have something to say. Say it," I demanded.

She blinked, wrapping her arms tighter around her middle. Defensive. She was protecting herself.

"Don't make me do this," she whispered.

I raised my hands and sniffed indignantly. "I'm not forcing you to do anything."

"You can figure out what I want to say. I'll allow you to read me."

"No, I have no interest in rifling through your thoughts. If there is something you wish to tell me, you can stand there and say it."

Perhaps it was unfair to put her on the spot, but Quentin ran from her feelings, good and bad. It never truly bothered me, but we were precariously close to the edge and whatever had been brewing inside of her needed to come out, for both our sakes.

She stood rooted to the spot, hair half coiled up and half hanging loose around her shoulders. She'd wiped her face clean of makeup before storming in here, but a few streaks of mascara darkened the skin around her eyes. As usual, Quentin presented herself as a fucking mess and there had never been and would never be a more ethereal sight in the universe.

"I hate that I need you," she mumbled, staring at her toes. "I learned how to manage alone. I've never really needed anyone, but I need you."

"You need me," I repeated flatly.

"I don't enjoy doing this," she bit in return.

Her temper flared to life and sparked excitement in me. Since Hunter's trial in the council chamber, Quen had lost her fire. This was the first sign that my golden girl still possessed her fight.

"Why?" I pressed.

"Because people leave. What is the point in telling you all this? No one sticks around. They die or they move or they decide I'm not good enough."

Her parents. Her brother. Her ex-fiancé.

Breathing deeply, I wrapped my aura around her and pulled her body between my legs. "Golden girl," I crooned softly, settling her onto my thigh. "You remind me of a volcano. Everyone thinks you're dormant because you get on with your life, but there's so much beneath the surface. And then suddenly you explode."

She clung to the slight change in topic. "I want to be Vesuvius."

"Of course," I said before pulling us back onto the matter in hand. "You've been uncomfortably quiet, and I want to know what is going on."

She placed her hands in her lap and looked down at them. Huffing, I moved my fingers under her chin and tipped her head back up so she was looking at me.

"Less of that," I instructed firmly, irritated by the move. "You're a demigoddess. You rarely looked down when you were fully mortal. Why now?"

"Because I have no fucking clue how to control anything anymore."

The lack of control must have driven her mad. This wasn't how she walked through life. A little bit of chaos was what she thrived in, but she was fully immersed in my world now.

"You said that I had priorities, Grayson, like the lab and family, but the truth is, you are my priority. You have been for a long time even if I never admitted it."

One of her hands snaked around my neck, fingers playing with the short hair at the nape. The motion was enough to make me relax.

"Being a God is a complicated and complex job," she said quietly. "You've made decisions you thought were right. Had your hand forced by people who should have loved you and guided you. Would you do it again?"

"Quentin—"

"Would you?"

"I never did it out of joy," I reminded her. "If you expect me to tell you I would never do it again, I can't give you that guarantee. I will take a life if circumstances require it. If it's a choice between someone else and you, then I will always choose you."

She nodded slowly, falling silent again. I reached up, carefully untangling bobby pins from her hair and letting the strands fall loose around her shoulders.

Her fingers traced three numbers along the back of my neck.

"What does it mean?" I asked her. "One, four, three. You and Cassidy exchanged them at the wedding."

She stilled her movements and took in a deep breath. "It means I love you. It's the number of letters in each word of the phrase. Mum and Dad used it when they were in theatre and couldn't speak to each other. They taught me and Cass. I learned to use it when I was mad at them and didn't want to say the words out loud."

"You use it for your family."

"I use it for my family," she repeated quietly.

"You've been telling me you love me for a long time," I commented, thinking back through our time together.

"Longer than I care to admit. If we do this, you can't hide anything from me again," Quentin said.

I stopped undoing her hair. "If we do this—"

"*If* we do this, I need you to be honest with me. We make decisions together. You said I was your equal."

"I said you were better than me." The deep ache that felt like it would stop me from functioning instantly healed.

"I love you." Quentin put her hand on my cheek, and I leaned into the touch. "I don't think I'll ever be capable of stopping that."

"You are capable of stopping it."

"I don't want to."

"I noticed you couldn't find a reason to continue this," I said, referring to her wall. "So many reasons to abandon me. What changed your mind?"

"Grayson," she breathed. "That side of the wall is empty, not because I couldn't think of anything, but because there were too many things."

My brow furrowed as I processed her words. "Too many?"

She nodded in response. "And I don't know how to vocalise them. All my life I've had so many words, but I struggle when it comes down to how you make me feel."

"You understand I cannot change what I am. Destruction and vengeance and chaos. I work with death daily. I cannot give you some fairy-tale."

"I never expected you to."

"You have studied a tiny molecule that makes you who you are. You mastered it. But I tainted your DNA long before you even knew me. My name is graffitied across every cell in your body. You have a part of my soul and I have a part of yours, and I never want to lose it. I can't lose you."

Her cheeks flushed at my words before she muttered, "It will be a lifetime of disaster."

A smile tugged at my lips. "You will light up my darkest days, and I will corrupt you every chance I get."

"I will fight for every chance to spend the rest of my days with you, Grayson."

Pulling her against my body, I laid us down in bed. Quentin tucked herself into my chest before pulling my face towards hers and kissing me deeply. Her tongue probed against my lips until I granted her access. The warmth of her mouth on mine shot liquid heat through my body. My hand slid up the back of her neck and fisted in her hair, tugging on the strands while she cupped my jaw. When she pulled away, golden eyes stared back at me.

In that moment, I knew with renewed certainty that I could never lose the woman in my arms. The few days of distance were bad enough. Any permanence of her absence would see me at Elva's door with a very specific request.

"Quentin Scott, we will be together for eternity. I give you my word as a God."

TWENTY-FOUR

QUENTIN

I woke up before Gray in my bed. We moved back into my room after talking last night. Both of us were exhausted, and it was entirely my fault.

His face was pressed against the pillow, full lips parted, and looking peaceful. Gray laid on his front with an arm draped over me—possessive even when unconscious. I missed sleeping like this with him. The last few weeks had taken its toll, but I finally felt settled again.

For all his faults and mistakes, for all the dark and terrible things he'd done, Gray was mine. Reaching out, I brushed a few strands of hair away from his forehead.

Soulbound.

Gray was made for me.

This irritating, destructive, chaotic… sexy, caring, and thoughtful God was made for me. My breath caught in my throat as the enormity of the bond settled on me again.

Throughout my life, I lacked a sense of belonging. Even with Mum and Dad, there were moments where the lack of shared blood made

me feel like a puzzle piece drifting in the vast universe, completely untethered.

"What are you staring at?" If Gray meant for it to come out as threatening, he failed because it was a sleepy mumble as he opened his stormy blue eyes.

"At my—" I started to answer.

Boyfriend seemed like such an insignificant word. It didn't encompass everything Erik had unveiled, or that I felt.

A smile pulled at the corner of Gray's mouth. "Yes?"

More silence from me.

"Say it, Scott," he demanded.

"Soulbound."

Gray moved so quickly I didn't even register it. He sat up in bed, leaning against the headboard, and pulled me so that I straddled his lap. There wasn't a trace of sleep left in his expression. Without the blanket around me, the chill of the room hit my naked body and my hairs raised.

"Soulbound," Gray repeated.

The deep timbre of his voice and the way he looked at me made my stomach knot and my heart flip. A sudden burst of anxiety flushed through my body, and I tried to push away from him. His fingers curled into my hips, gripping tightly and keeping me firmly in place.

"What's wrong?" he asked.

"What if it's a mistake?"

He shot me a confused look as I rested my hands against his bare chest, trying to find the right words. Imposter syndrome clawed its way through my body and I couldn't look at him as intrusive thoughts filled my head.

"Quentin, what's going on up there?" Gray tapped my temple gently.

It'd been years since I'd felt so unsure of myself. Every layer of armour I donned had been stripped away until I was bare. The confidence I usually wore was worn down to nothing.

"I wasn't good enough for a mortal," I said eventually. "How am I meant to believe I'm good enough for a God?"

Taking my face in his hands, Gray stared at me. The fierce look in his eye made me swallow hard. "Listen here, Scott. You were too good for him. He never deserved you, and you weren't meant for him. Do you understand that? You're too good for me, but fate decided I deserved you and I won't fuck it up."

I nodded, and he let go of my face, arms slipping around my waist and moving down until his palms rested on the curve of my ass.

"Plus," Gray mused. "I'm not just any God. You're soulbound to an elite God."

I rolled my eyes.

"Lord of chaos. King of destruction. You were made for the best—"

I cut him off with a kiss. My arms wrapped around his neck and he squeezed my ass roughly before we broke apart.

"You play dirty, Scott."

"No. I just know how to get what I want."

"And so do I."

Gray shifted his hips so I could feel his arousal brush against my bare thighs. My cheeks heated and a gentle ache pulsed between my legs. Since claiming my divinity, I understood what Gray meant about Gods and stamina.

"Gray—"

"It's not a mistake, Quentin. You are mine for eternity."

Eternity.

Gods were immortal.

I was immortal.

If we convinced the council, then Gray and I would have an eternity together. The prospect both excited and terrified me.

He leant in and kissed me again, snaking his tongue into my mouth. Mine met his, but for the first time, there was no urgency in our movements. It was a gentle caress that made my toes curl. My fingers sank into his hair and his hands ran along my back, tickling the skin with the lightness of it. He shifted us carefully, so that I was under him, back pressed against the mattress.

"That is," he said, "if that's what you want."

"Yes," I replied, staring up at him. I placed my hand on his chest, above his heart. "I'm sorry it took me so long to realise it. To admit it."

"You don't need to apologise, Quen. My soulbound."

He brought his face down to the crook of my neck, kissing my pulse point and forcing me to tip my head back. A small moan escaped my lips as he nipped the juncture between my neck and shoulder. The room was chilly, but with Gray's body pressed against mine, there was more than enough heat.

My hands ran down his arms, skimming over the muscles, and the heat pooled between my legs. Gray's body was a work of art—tanned and toned and punishing. Something about the fact he could break me but never did thrilled me more than it should have.

He trailed lazy kisses along my collarbones, stopping to nip and suck at the skin until it bruised under his mouth. My mortality still aided in being marked, but it took less time to heal. I liked it this way, though. I liked that Gray could still mark me as his.

"Tell me you love me," he murmured, before swirling his tongue around my nipple.

I moaned, arching my back to his touch. "I love you."

Those words had rarely left my lips, cautious about who I gave them to. But I wanted to keep saying them to him until they lost all meaning and left my mouth numb.

Gray nudged my legs apart wider, the apex already sticky and wet with need. He settled between them and moved his mouth to the other nipple, catching it between his teeth and tugging gently. I whimpered as he ran a finger along my slit.

"Look how wet you are already, darling. Is this all for me?" he asked, chuckling under his breath.

My response was cut off when his lips met mine. Kissing Gray was like swallowing a thousand fireworks. Explosive and destructive. Any defences I had against him were useless the moment he put his lips on me.

The ache between my legs grew when I felt his cock rub against my centre. My hips bucked up, and I groaned into the kiss, feeling him smile against my lips.

"You're always so impatient, Quen."

"Can you blame me?" I breathed.

"You need to learn some restraint, love."

I had no intention of learning self-restraint around him. Why would I want to?

"So do you," I muttered. He was just as bad, if not worse, than I was.

"How can you expect that when I have a beautiful demigoddess around me at all times?"

The heat rose through my body, and I turned my head, but Gray's fingers caught my chin, forcing me to look at him.

"You are beautiful, Quentin. I have always thought that." His lips brushed along my hairline. "You believe I desire perfection. You fail to see that is exactly what I have. As a God, I've had so many things offered to me, but the only time I have held the universe is when you are in my arms."

My heart skipped several beats, and I writhed against the sheets as the pad of Gray's thumb pressed against my clit and moved in circular motions.

This side of Gray, soft and loving, was only ever shared with me. He made me feel like I was the only being in existence that mattered, and I'm sure if I asked him, he would tell me that was the case.

A single finger pushed into me, and I tipped my head back against the pillows, grinding against him.

"Did you miss me, Quen?" Gray asked, moving his mouth from my nipple. The amusement laced his words. "Your soul is mine, but so is your body. I own every inch of you."

I hummed in response, words lost in satisfaction. Did neural networks temporarily collapse under the weight of immense pleasure?

He added another finger, stretching me while he continued to play with my clit. "Does that bother you?"

My hips bucked against his hand, wanting more from him, but Gray took his time, curling his fingers in a way that made me grip the blankets beneath me.

"No," I breathed, but the word slipped into a moan.

"Are you sure? Because there will be no turning back."

"I'm yours," I said, looking up at him. "Only yours."

"Perfect girl," he praised, making me melt further into the sheets.

Gray kissed me deeply and removed his fingers. My hips lifted, following them, but his cock soon replaced them. My walls stretched to accommodate him and he angled me so he could push in deeper. Pulling back, he locked black eyes with mine. Gray braced himself on one arm as the other held my hip. He pulled out until just the tip of him remained inside me before pushing back in as deep as he could go. Each movement was slow and deliberate and the pleasure built as his hand moved to pinch and rub my clit. My eyes fluttered shut, giving in to the intense pleasure that he was building.

"Keep them open, golden girl," he demanded. "I want to see you come undone this time."

I did as he said, fighting against instinct. Pure gold was reflected in his deep black eyes. The wisps of our auras mingled around us as my hips bucked to meet his. My nails dug into his shoulders and ribs, and my toes curled as he hit the spot each time. His skin broke beneath the pressure of my touch, but he didn't complain, pressing his forehead against mine.

"Gray," I groaned.

The pleasure grew until it felt like I couldn't bear it. We were usually so caught up in lust, chasing the pleasure after pain, but this felt different. Every single movement, every single breath, was purposeful. Like Gray was trying to convey emotions he would never be able to put into words, but I understood. I knew what he wanted to say.

A tear escaped my eye, sliding down my cheek, and he kissed it away before his lips found mine again. I wanted to drink him in. The way we moved together—breaths and hearts in sync—I didn't want it to end.

I wrapped my legs around the back of his thighs, wanting him as physically close as possible. Was it possible to stay like this forever? Suspended in time with our only priorities being each other.

"Gray," I muttered against his lips. "I'm so close."

"Wait for me. Wait."

He picked up the pace, removing his hand from my clit and making me whimper. I didn't know if I could hold on, especially as I watched the way he was coming undone. His entire body was covered in a sheen that highlighted his muscles, and dark hair fell across his forehead. But it was the way he kept his gaze on me, hungry and loving and obsessed, that pushed me to the edge.

"I can't," I panted.

"Come for me, darling."

With his blessing, I let myself tip over the precipice into earth-shattering bliss. It ripped through my body in waves, making me arch off the bed, and Gray filled me until I couldn't hold anymore.

Slowly, we both drifted down from our high and I opened my eyes to look at him. He stared back with a lazy smile pasted across his face and his dick still pulsing inside of me.

"I love you, Quentin," he said.

"I love you too, Grayson." Then I noticed something between us that made me panic. "Gray, what is that?"

TWENTY-FIVE

GRAYSON

I'd yet to remove myself from her. It was safe to say Quen and I had fucked like rabbits since the first time we gave in, but this was different. I wanted her to know that she was safe with me. That I treasured her and that nothing could separate us.

Every time she admitted she loved me, a strange warmth ran through my body, resonating deep in my soul. After millennia of searching for a speck of clarity in all my chaos, she delivered it with her very existence.

"Gray, what is that?"

She looked at my chest, and I tucked my chin in, following her gaze. A mix of gold and black strung between our hearts, connecting us. I glanced back to her face, carefully sliding out of her and taking the space beside her on the bed. The connection didn't falter.

"I assume this is more of our bond," I told her.

Her fingers brushed against it, passing through with ease but refusing to break. Pulling her fingers away, she examined them to see they were clean. "It wasn't there before."

"No, it wasn't."

"Do you think it's okay?"

"Do you feel okay?"

She nodded, but the crease stayed between her brows. I wrapped an arm around her and pulled her close to my body.

This bond.

This woman.

I couldn't think straight around her. I'd never felt so desperately alone as when I almost lost her and I'd never felt as content as when she was with me.

I watched her quietly, the way her liquid gold eyes focused on the bond that was visible between our hearts. She was curious about the mechanics and I made a mental note to ask Erik so that she could have the answers that would settle her mind.

Her mind.

Fuck.

If her body was amazing, her mind was something else entirely. Quentin had always impressed me by how much she knew, how stoically she worked, and how curious she was.

This insufferable woman was mine for eternity. I'd make sure for the rest of our days that she was happy by my side. I'd start wars if it meant protecting her.

"Bubba?" Quen called softly.

I loved when she called me that. When she shook off the formalities and softened for me. Confirmation that I was part of the elusive inner circle that rarely took new applicants.

"What are you thinking?" she asked. Quen laid partially on top of me, chin resting on my chest and tipping her head to one side.

Curious. Always curious. Always looking for answers. If she

wanted to know what I was thinking, then I would tell her.

"Marry me."

Quentin froze. "I'm s-sorry," she stuttered, finally animating again. "What did you just say?"

"Marry me," I repeated the words for her.

I made no mistake the first time I said them. Marriage had been the odd fleeting thought since learning we were soulbound. It was never on the cards for me but the knowledge of our bond and looking at Erik and Sloan and then Sophie and Cassidy…

I wanted to make Quentin my wife.

She pushed herself up from me and got off the bed. I sensed it before she even opened her mouth. This was not what she wanted. Quentin had been stung before, whereas I'd never allowed anyone close enough. I prepared myself for her words.

"Have you lost your mind?" she asked. "Marry you? We don't need to get married."

She walked off into her bathroom; the sight making me want to take her all over again. The door slammed shut, separating us, and I rolled my eyes, getting out of bed and following her.

"And why not?" I asked through the piece of wood.

A few weeks of silence and distance cemented the fact that I no longer wanted my life to be empty. Knowing she was mine wasn't enough. She should bear my ring on her finger, and one day, Quentin would carry our children. A family of our own. We would strengthen the bond we shared.

She flushed the toilet and opened the door to let me in. Quentin knocked on the shower and said, "You said we have an eternity together, so why do we need to get married?"

She stepped into the water, done with the conversation.

Not a fucking chance.

I followed her into the space. She turned to face me and I couldn't help the way my gaze travelled down her body. The water fell off her curves with droplets clinging to her skin.

"Gray." She wanted to warn me, but I heard the underlying tone in her voice. Sensed the desire that mirrored mine.

"You haven't given me an answer," I told her.

We were both soaked by the spray of the shower and my hands trailed along her body, walking her back until she bumped into the wall. The cold made her arch away from it, breasts pressing into my chest and allowing my fresh erection to rub against her stomach.

"Aren't you happy as we are?" Quentin asked.

"I'm selfish and greedy," I countered.

Her hands ran down my body until I felt her fingers ghost along my cock. I half closed my eyes before I realised we both had the same plan.

"Quentin," I warned her. "Don't play this game."

She looked at me from under her lashes, doe-eyed and innocent. "What game?"

Her knees hit the tiles, hand working along my length in a rhythmic motion before taking me into her mouth. A guttural groan left me as I fisted her wet hair and pushed myself further into her mouth, hitting the back of her throat.

"You fucking know," I hissed.

This woman was a pain in my ass, but she knew how to work her mouth. Quen's tongue swirled around the head of my cock before taking me in again. Her head bobbed, inching me further down her throat while her hand reached up to play with my balls. I grunted and pushed, unable to help myself even if she was struggling against her gag reflex.

When she was like this, docile and submissive, I'd give her whatever she wanted, but not this time. I wasn't losing this one. Leaning down, I grabbed her arms and hauled her to her feet, earning a pout.

"You didn't like it?" she asked, still playing innocent.

"Are you fucking crazy?"

The act dropped, replaced with sass. "At least we'd both be in the same boat."

I kissed her roughly, pushing my tongue into her mouth and picking her up from the ground. Her legs wrapped around my waist as I pinned her against the wall.

"Marry me," I demanded.

"Gray, you are losing your mind."

I positioned myself, lining my cock up with her before entering her. Her pussy drank me in, welcoming me back, and Quen released a breathy moan.

"I'm not. I want you to be my wife."

Every few words were punctuated by my mouth on her neck, shoulders, breasts. Quen ground against me. She could never be patient, and I loved it about her.

"This isn't fair," she whined as I thrust deeper inside her.

"I don't play fair," I replied, licking her neck and then biting roughly at the skin. Her body curled against mine. "I get what I want."

Quen's muscles tensed as the conversation melted into pleasure. Her body was mine to do as I pleased and I wasn't above using it to get what I wanted.

Her walls clenched around me, keeping me in place and coaxing me to finish inside of her again. As her legs grew weak, I slid from her and helped steady her on the ground.

"You can't persuade me with sex," she said, resting her head against my chest and catching her breath.

"If you marry me, you'll get sex with me for eternity."

She lifted her head. "So, you're telling me you'll be celibate if I don't agree to marry you?"

I frowned. "No."

"It's a good thing you're sexy, bubba." She sighed, pushing a wet lock of hair out of my face.

Quentin turned away and reached for her shower gel. I took it out of her hand and grabbed her bath lily, washing her body.

"You won't even think about it?" I pressed.

Her shoulders dropped before turning to look at me. "Gray… we don't even know if I'll live to see tomorrow—"

"Don't say that," I snapped, tone sharp and harsh.

I couldn't imagine a world where Quentin Scott didn't exist. I'd come close to that reality and it was too much to bare. Now that she was immortal, I intended to keep her alive and by my side.

"Then there's the case of maybe telling everyone I love what I am. The project. Getting to know my family."

She gave me a list of every excuse in the book, but I knew the truth. Quen was scared. The biggest failure in her life had been a long-term relationship she believed would be her last. Being bound was a gift that was given to us, but somewhere in her mind, a marriage—an engagement—could still fail.

Usually, I would have teased her about being so worried over an issue, but held back this time. She needed to know I was serious about this.

"I'll ask again," I told her.

"Why?"

"Because I am a God and I'm used to getting what I want."

"Grayson—"

"I'll ask you every single day."

"You've got too much time on your hands."

In all the excuses she delivered, she'd never once said no. I clung to that thought and let the matter die as we finished showering.

Once we stepped out, Quen wrapped her hair in a towel and opened the bathroom door before letting out a scream.

"Oh!" Erik's voice sounded surprised and amused.

I strode past her to see my brother lounging in a chair. The urge to pluck his eyeballs out of his skull for witnessing her naked caught hold of me.

"I would have been here sooner," he explained, "but I sensed you were a little busy." A slender finger pointed to the sticky, rumpled sheets on the bed. "I assumed you were finished. I didn't expect you to both be naked."

"You're an idiot," I hissed.

Quentin had retreated into the depths of her bathroom in embarrassment, cursing under her breath. A golden glow filled the space. I walked into the bedroom and collected a towel and some clothes for her before handing them over and shutting the door.

"What do you want, Erik? Why couldn't you wait downstairs like a normal being?" I asked, towelling myself dry.

"Because I'm an extraordinary being," he countered innocently.

"Why are you here?" I snapped.

"Hunter called us for a meeting. I was wondering why you were taking your time, but it makes sense now."

"Why has he called a meeting this early?" I asked, pulling clothes on. "Does he expect her to be there?"

"No. Just the three of us. He hasn't said anything yet. Maybe he's let go of the ridiculous idea of wanting to get rid of her."

"Maybe he'll let me bash his brains out of his skull and offer me his throne."

Erik was an optimist but there were times it bordered on delusional.

"What have you done?" Erik asked suddenly, narrowing his eyes.

"Is something wrong?" I asked, brow furrowing.

"You're protective of her, but there's something else in the air… I can't put my finger on it. What have you done?" Erik was beaming at me.

Biting the insides of my cheeks, I cursed my brother before shrugging. "I asked her to marry me."

He jumped to his feet, crossing the space and hugging me. "When? When is it happening? Please, Gray, let me run the ceremony. I promise to be on my best behaviour."

"She didn't say yes."

Some of his spark dimmed. "She has reservations."

"Yes."

"You don't seem upset."

"I'll convince her, Erik. Don't worry." I wasn't sure how, but I would make Quentin my wife. "Do not breathe a word to anyone."

He mimicked crossing his heart, but the grin stayed firmly in place. By the end of the afternoon, I was sure Sloan, Ignacio, and Elva would know of my plans.

The bathroom door opened and Quentin stepped out, fully dressed. "I'm going to buy you a bell," she said to Erik. "And you better forget anything you saw."

"You're very—"

"Finish that sentence, brother." My aura filled the room. "I dare you."

He pressed his lips together.

"Hunter's called a meeting," I told Quentin, walking over to her. The colour drained from her face, and I continued, "I don't think it's to do with you, but I'm already late and considering we're trying not to piss him off any further, I should see what he wants."

"Gray," she said, looking up at me. "Whatever he says, keep a hold of your temper."

TWENTY-SIX

QUENTIN

Gray and Erik left, and the knot of anxiety in my stomach tightened. I would rather be at the meeting with both of them just to make sure it didn't get out of hand. Gray's temper often got the better of him, as evidenced by his run-in with Archer at the lab. Act now, think later should have been tattooed to my boyfriend's forehead.

I sat on the edge of the bed and pulled the pad of sticky notes and a pen from the bedside table.

Aria

Malachi

Waverly

Flynn

I made a list of the elite Gods that I needed to win over, sticking them to the wall near my bed. It was pointless adding Hunter to the list. After a few moments, I wrote Larkin's name with a question mark next to it.

Larkin.

In my spare moments, when I was too exhausted to worry about

my own troubles, my mind flickered to her. I wanted to talk to someone, anyone, who might help her, but she'd clarified that no one would believe me.

An idea had taken hold a few nights ago while I tediously worked through statistics, but it required me being able to talk to Larkin and engineering that wouldn't be easy. I couldn't walk into her lab without a valid reason, because scientists liked to gossip and that meant the word would get back to Gray and Hunter. I would dig myself an even bigger hole and Larkin wouldn't appreciate being pulled into a mess.

Without Gray as a distraction, a familiar sensation rippled through me and I tossed the stationery onto the bed.

"Gray?" I called, walking out of the room. "Erik?"

The ripple grew into a wave. Intuition that there were Gods nearby. More than one. Had all three brothers come back to the house?

Hurrying down the hallway, Archer met me at the top of the stairs.

"You have got to be kidding," I said, gripping the banister tightly. "I'm sure this classifies as breaking and entering."

"Do you plan to call the police?"

"I plan to tell Gray."

"But he's not here, is he? I sensed it."

"You need to leave because I have nothing to say to you."

"If I leave, I can't give you my gift."

"I don't want anything from you, Archer. Why don't you understand that?"

"Quentin?"

I looked past Archer to the bottom of the stairs. "Dionne? What are you doing here?"

Archer turned and leaned over the landing. "Apparently, she doesn't want this visit."

Ignoring him, I trotted down the stairs. When I reached the bottom, Dionne pulled me into a bone-crushing hug.

"You're okay," she breathed against my hair.

"Why wouldn't I be?"

She released me and looked me over. "Bexley told me about what happened in the chamber and Archer said you allowed Gray to move back in with you. We've been worried about you."

I glanced over my shoulder at Archer, who shrugged his shoulders. Then I realised what Dionne had said.

"We?" I asked, looking at her again.

Grabbing my hand, she pulled me into my living room where the space was full of minor Gods. They lounged on the sofa, perched on the coffee table, and stood by the bookcases.

"What are you all doing here?" I whispered, trying to decipher the strange overwhelming feeling that hampered my breathing. It wasn't panic or anxiety, but something lighter and more hopeful.

"We heard what Hunter did and wanted to check on you," Marcel told me. "You've recovered well."

"I'm perfectly fine." I stepped into the room properly.

Tobias rose from the arm of the sofa to offer me his seat, but I waved him off. I noticed his hand was healed and my brow furrowed. The skin looked perfect again, making me question if it had ever been injured in the first place.

"You're all going to get in trouble for being down here," I pointed out before turning to Archer. "I assume this is all unsanctioned."

"Are you worried about us, Quentin?" he asked me.

I bit my tongue, not wanting to tell him the truth and give him the satisfaction. I felt safer with the minor Gods than I did with the elite. They welcomed me into the fold and didn't hold the power to end my life.

"Is the other rumour true?" Andreas' deep voice asked from the corner of the room. "That you're bound to Grayson?"

My face flushed. How much had Bexley told them and how quick had the rumours spread?

"Is it?" Marcel pressed, looking at me curiously.

"Yes," I confirmed. "We're… he's…"

Archer tensed beside me and deadpanned, "They're bound."

"How is that possible?" Tobias asked. "He's part of the problem."

"Watch your mouth," Andreas warned him. "He's family."

"And look at what he did."

"Can we all calm down?" I cut across them, worried about an impending fight. "Binding is a gift."

"One that you can reject, breaking your bond," Archer pointed out. "I assume that'll be your plan once you've secured a position in Elysia. It's better to keep him on side until you can be with the rest of us again."

The room grew thick with tension as eyes fell on me. My skin prickled, and I swallowed the lump in my throat. Gray wasn't the easiest God to get along with, and he'd given himself a reputation that saw him shunned. Pinning my colours to him could tip the welcome committee into an angry mob, but I wasn't about to lie to placate them.

"I don't intend to break the bond," I explained.

"You can't be serious," Archer said. His aura crept out in wisps around his hands. "I've shown you what he's capable of."

"And Grayson showed me his memories."

Archer reached out towards me, but I took a step away. I didn't want to have an argument in front of the rest of the Gods. I'd made my decision and Archer wasn't going to persuade me otherwise.

"He's manipulating you." Archer caught my hand.

"I suggest you let her go." Andreas moved from the corner of the room until he was beside me. "It's their decision to make."

"You can't be that blind," Archer continued, and I winced when his fingers tightened around mine, pressing them together. "He's proven that all he'll do is lie."

"I said, let her go." A thick red tendril of aura appeared from behind me. It was darker—bloodier—than Erik's and perfect for a God of war.

When Archer didn't release me, Andreas' aura wrapped around his middle and picked him up before placing him on the other side of the room. A tame movement that caught me off guard, but I was grateful that the house didn't need repairs. Archer didn't say another word before he left the house, fury etched across his features.

I wiggled my fingers and cautiously turned on the spot to face Andreas. Tipping my head back, I met his eye. There was nothing gentle about his character.

"Thank you," I muttered. "I didn't mean to cause any trouble."

"I protect my family," he told me firmly.

"I'm not—"

"Sloan has spoken highly of you."

"She's been very welcoming."

Andreas smiled proudly. "She's very good at judging character. If you don't include her husband."

I raised an eyebrow at his comment. "They're bound."

"He's not good enough for her, and fate will not convince me otherwise."

Andreas had to be the only God who warmed to Gray over Erik, but I hoped that meant we would get on better than I imagined.

"So, you plan to honour your bond?" Marcel asked, lounging back in his seat. "I thought it was bad enough when Dionne started dating Bexley. Ow!"

Dionne slapped the back of his head and I stifled my laughter by biting the insides of my cheeks.

"I'm just asking," Marcel muttered, rubbing the spot. "Bound to an elite. There's no way they're going to kill you now."

"I wouldn't be so sure," I replied. "Hunter's not exactly the most trustworthy or merciful God."

Laughter broke out in the room, and I startled, realising I probably should have kept those thoughts to myself. A filter would aid in keeping me alive. And that was the plan.

"You really are one of us," Tobias said softly. "The less you trust the elite, the safer you will be."

Andreas grumbled behind me, "They're not all the same."

"Maybe this is the start of change," Dionne mused hopefully.

"What do you mean?" I asked.

"The elite have been known to choose their partners from families who were once part of the council."

Marcel straightened in his seat. "Dionne broke that trend."

"And you've joined the ranks," she finished.

Tobias scoffed and dropped his gaze to his thighs, shaking his head. "This won't change anything. They'll still look down on us."

"We have to start somewhere," Dionne argued.

"It should have started with removing them from their seats."

"What do you suggest? A conversation or a war?"

"Have a conversation and if nothing comes from it, then we prepare for war," he said, pushing his glasses up the bridge of his nose.

"And how do you intend to win such a war?" Andreas asked.

Tobias cocked his head to the side, blonde curls falling over his shoulder. "Surely, you'll lend us your skills."

"My daughter sits on that council. Do you really expect me to wage a war against her?"

"This has nothing to do with Sloan."

"You'll destabilise the heavens and Earth if you start a war," Dionne snapped. "There's too much to risk."

The surrounding voices became muffled as they descended into an argument.

War?

They couldn't seriously be discussing war in my living room.

A gentle hand landed on my shoulder and I looked up at Andreas.

"Are you okay?" he asked gruffly.

"Andreas, what is the likelihood of them starting a war?"

He shrugged. "We get a little restless in the lower heavens. The topic gets raised often. Your appearance, hearing what Hunter did to you and your bond with Grayson, has sent a seismic quake through lower Elysia."

"And I thought it would just be a little ripple," I muttered, trying to make a joke.

"It feels different," he stated. "Like something is brewing."

"Why?"

"You," he responded simply. "You're a symbol of what some of us lost and what some of us fear. Hunter is in a difficult position."

"How so?"

"He can't win. If he kills you, he sticks to his convictions about how demigods are a threat. If he lets you survive, then he's made an exception when he couldn't do that for the rest. I imagine that's why he's left it to the council. Don't be fooled by his version of democracy. He keeps them around for his own benefit. I've dealt with many people in my line of work, and Hunter is the definition of a coward."

He wouldn't find any argument from me. It made sense that Hunter was unwilling to pull rank and decide when it would further vilify him. If the council made the decision, he had multiple others he could blame.

"You think it might actually happen? A war?" I asked, worried about the repercussions.

"For everyone's sake, I hope not. But your existence has brought up some complicated politics and the answer won't be as straightforward as we'd like it to be. It may be my responsibility, but no one is truly victorious in the spoils of war."

"Can you stop it?" I asked, curious about the extent of his gift.

"I aid in it," he replied. "War makes my blood sing, but I won't be used as a pawn in a play that could potentially hurt my Sloan. I doubt it will come to a war. We have other issues to concern ourselves with."

Curiosity gripped me tight. "Such as?"

Andreas raised an eyebrow. "I shouldn't tell you anything when you aren't officially an Elysian."

"Gray will tell me if he knows," I pointed out.

"Already using what you have around you to your advantage? Sloan said you were smart."

My cheeks burnt at the comment. "I'm not using him."

"I know, but some may think you are. Thicken your skin, Quentin." He sighed and looked at the bickering minor Gods as he spoke. "Gods are ceasing to exist at an alarming rate. We've lost ten minor Gods since you've descended."

"That's unusual?"

"Highly. At worst, we've lost around two a month. Ten in a matter of weeks is making us question whether this project is really any help."

"People are losing faith."

"It would seem that way. Some of us wonder if it would be worth revealing ourselves to mortals again."

"But you can't because it might result in more demigods," I finished the sentence.

"Correct. We're in a strange state of limbo unless we get this project to work."

I nodded my head slowly. E.L.I. was the Gods' survival plan, and if I could get the results they needed, it would show them I was on their side. With matters resolved between me and Gray, I could busy myself in work properly again.

"Quentin," Marcel called, pulling me from my thoughts. "Do you have any whiskey? This conversation needs alcohol."

"It's not even midday," I said, laughing.

"We're Gods, Quentin." He leaned forward like he was letting me in on a secret. "The rules don't apply."

TWENTY-SEVEN

GRAYSON

Gareth's house was empty apart from the three of us. No audience for whatever matter had rankled my brother this time. As we joined Hunter, I wondered how the three of us ended up so different. Our gifts no doubt had a hand in the way we ended up. Mine made me a pariah, but Hunter and Erik had never been close. Love and protection. It should have been a match that allowed them to form a bond that excised me from their lives, and yet Erik trailed after me from the moment he was born.

"Punctuality is deeply appreciated, Grayson. How is it difficult to respond to a simple message?" Hunter drawled as I dropped into a chair. "Or were you too busy fucking your half-breed to care about the rest of Elysia?"

Yes. And it's the best fuck I've had. Why care about the heavens when I'm balls deep in my personal slice of it?

It would have been easy to let my mouth run, but that wouldn't have helped, and I was still unsure about what this meeting was called for.

"I'm here now," I replied tightly. "Is there a reason that the entire

council isn't here, or are you content with just making the family miserable?"

"This is a conversation to be kept between the three of us," he said, hands gripping the arms of the chair he was sitting in.

"Your trust in us is appreciated."

"And misplaced."

"Hunter." Erik moved, so he was standing between us. "What's the matter?"

He shifted in his chair and leaned forward, elbows on knees. Pressing two fingers together, he motioned for Erik to move aside, and Erik complied. Without the physical barrier, Hunter's icy blue eyes stared straight at me. When I was younger, this intimidation tactic worked. His gaze was enough to make me lower my head and listen. Now, it was a laughable move from a weak man.

"This conversation doesn't really concern Erik, but I brought him here so nothing can be misconstrued," Hunter explained. "And I have no doubt you would have told him the moment you left here."

I shrugged in response. It was pointless denying what he knew to be a fact. Unless it put Erik in danger, he would know what happened in my life.

"There have been a string of minor Gods that have ceased to exist. Ten since we descended from Elysia to return here."

My eyebrows raised in genuine shock. Ten Gods in the space of a few weeks was not something to joke about. Our kin were disappearing at a rate we weren't accustomed to, which begged the question of how long Elysia would continue to be inhabited by Gods.

"How do you know this?" Erik asked. "Have you been back up there?"

"He knows because I told him."

I inwardly winced at the saccharine voice that drifted from the doorway. Mabel leaned against the frame, arms folded across her chest, with a smug look across her face.

"So much for the conversation staying between the three of us," I grumbled.

My dislike for Larkin remained, but I preferred her to Mabel. Larkin fought back and never hid who she was. We were similar in that characteristic. Mabel was someone who built a castle of sugary words and fake smiles while holding a dagger. I wouldn't turn my back on Mabel—she didn't hold the same morals as Larkin.

"Some people understand what loyalty is," Hunter said, opening out an arm.

Mabel pushed herself away from the frame with feline agility and sauntered over to my brother like the perfect pet. It was a surprise that she didn't drop to the floor and purr.

"You clearly don't," Erik snapped as Hunter's arm wrapped around Mabel's thighs and pulled her into him. "You have a wife who deserves your loyalty."

"My relationship is none of your concern," he replied smoothly.

I sniffed and leaned back in my seat. "Remember, that applies to more than just you."

Hunter yanked Mabel down so that she sat in his lap, looking way too happy about what was unfolding in front of her. And people thought I revelled in others' misery. Mabel, Goddess of vanity, could give me a run for my money.

"This project needs to work," Hunter continued. "I suggest you tell Quentin that she needs to make good on those egotistical claims and start producing results."

"Why don't you just use her gift?" Mabel asked, running a hand up Hunter's chest.

His fingers curled into her waist until she let out a small gasp, and I narrowed my eyes.

"He wouldn't do that," I answered. "Because it's proving that she's worth something. Hunter, there's more than one scientist working on this. Quentin will do what she needs to, but you need to talk to Gareth so that he understands the importance of getting this done efficiently."

"She can do that."

Erik straightened. "You're trying to force Quentin to tell them what she is? If she speaks to Gareth he'll want to know how she knows so much about Elysia."

"What are you playing at?" I asked, suspicion prickling through my body.

Quentin refused to tell Cassidy about her divinity. There was no way she was about to tell Gareth before her brother.

"I'm trying to ensure that the rest of our kin remain in Elysia for as long as possible. If she wants to prove her worth, this is the chance for her to do it. I imagine there won't be many of the Gods who would deny her if she can save us."

I shot up from my seat. "You're setting her up to fail."

"Hunter, you're playing with more lives than just Quentin's," Erik argued. "You're using Elysians as a chip to get what you want."

"I'm not doing anything," Hunter replied, fingers running circles on Mabel's thigh. "I'm simply delivering you some unfortunate news and giving you a resolution. You'll speak to your half-breed, won't you, Grayson?"

"She has a name," I gritted out through my teeth.

"Because if you don't, I could always pay her a visit."

I opened my mouth to reply when a deep voice boomed through the house. "Hunter!"

"Archer! Stop!"

Larkin and Archer burst into the room. She had her hands pressed against his chest, trying to push him away, but he continued, brushing her aside.

"This just got very interesting," Mabel muttered gleefully.

Archer's eyes flashed as they landed on me. "How many lies did you feed her? What did you tell her to get her to accept your bond?"

"Pure charm and a dick that makes her scream," I answered him flatly.

If Quentin heard my reply, I would be celibate for the rest of my days, but I'd been on my best behaviour with Hunter and the chaos was clawing at my chest and skull, begging to be released.

"You have to do something," he said, turning to my older brother. "He's going to use her."

Hunter stood so quickly that Mabel fell from his lap. She picked herself up, pouting as she dusted herself off.

"You all need to leave," Hunter demanded. "I need to speak to Archer."

"I don't care if we have an audience," he replied. "I'm sick of only getting part of the story."

"Out!" Hunter barked.

Larkin didn't hang around, used to his temperamental ways, and I had better things to do than watch Archer have a meltdown because his plans had gone awry.

Erik shot me a look before wrapping himself in red, and I left seconds after him, landing back in the hallway of Quentin's home.

A small body barrelled into me as she came off the bottom step. My arms wrapped around her frame to keep her in place.

"Where are you going in such a rush?" I asked.

Quentin had pulled her hair up into a bun and had her bag slung over her shoulder. Her access card hung from a lanyard that sported the colours of the rainbow.

"You're back," she noted. "Is everything okay?"

"Answer my question first."

"I'm going to the lab."

"Why?"

Her cheeks flushed. "We've wasted enough time with this project."

"Archer told you what's going on in Elysia when he visited?"

"How did you know he was here?"

"He went straight to Hunter after I assume you told him you had no plans to break our bond." I pressed a kiss to her forehead. "You should have told him about your plans to become my wife to really drive home the point." She gave me a shove, and I released her from my hold. "Why did he come to visit?"

Quentin stepped around me, walking into the living room and grabbing some papers from the bookshelf. "No reason."

"Honesty works both ways, golden girl."

She froze, and I could almost hear the way her brain was trying to find a loophole that would allow her to find a way out of answering me.

"I'm waiting, Quen," I pressed.

Slipping her bag from her shoulder, she unzipped it and pushed the papers inside, taking her time with the motion. "He stopped by with a gift."

A few steps were all it took until I was behind her. "That does not fill me with confidence. What kind of gift?"

"The kind of gift that comes in the form of friendship."

"Quentin." Her name came out as a bite. "Did he proposition you?"

"No!" She whirled around to face me. "I worded that wrong. He brought a few minor Gods with him."

My eyes widened. "Has everyone lost their minds?"

"Dionne, Marcel, Tobias. Andreas was the one who told me about the Gods disappearing."

"Andreas? Do they know how much trouble you would have been in if they were caught here with you?" I grabbed my hair and Quen wrapped her hands around my forearms, tugging at them to bring them back down.

"They didn't stay long. No one knows."

"Archer knows, and he's livid right now."

"He won't be able to tell Hunter about this without landing himself in it," she replied, finally pulling my arms down to my side. "Let him waste his energy complaining about us. There are bigger issues. What did Hunter want?"

Ice-cold logic. Quentin was finding her stride again. Getting comfortable in her situation. Although she was under pressure, she was seeing threads she could use to her advantage and that offered me some calm.

"He wants you to fix the issue of the Gods."

"I assumed as much, which is why I'm heading into the lab. Once Hunter explains the situation to Gareth—"

"No, Quentin. He expects *you* to fix it. For you to take the lead and explain to Gareth what's happening."

"Gareth's going to wonder how I became the mouthpiece for the Gods. He was the chosen vessel."

I stared at her and watched her face fall as the pieces fell into place.

"No." She stepped around me and zipped up her bag. "I'm not telling him. I'm not telling any of them."

"What do you plan to do, Quen? You can't do this entire project on your own. Not in the timeframe he's probably expecting you to."

"Want to bet?"

TWENTY-EIGHT

GRAYSON

"Where's Scott?" I asked, walking into the lab.

James shrugged his lab coat off as he answered. "She's in the patient room."

"Thanks."

It was close to midnight, and the lab was empty aside from the two of them. And it looked like James was poised to leave.

Quentin spent ungodly hours in this place. I understood her need for control and although she was part Goddess, I worried about her burning out. Her mind was constantly ticking, turning over everything that was happening, and there was little I could do to calm it. The lab had become her base and home was a distant memory.

Knocking on the patient room door, Quen's voice carried through clearly. "Come in!"

I pushed it open and stared at the space before finding my obsession. She was standing on the worktop, reaching for a box on top of the cabinets.

"What are you doing?"

Quentin twisted her body to look down at me. "I need some

pipette tips. Are you okay?"

She turned away again, getting up on her toes to reach for the box. Lazily, a tendril of my aura grabbed it from the cabinet and set it down on the floor. Quentin looked at me, biting her plump bottom lip. She either didn't trust herself with that level of control or she had forgotten that her aura could be useful to her.

When I stepped in front of Quen, she placed her hands on my shoulders to steady herself as she came down from the counter. I didn't let her feet hit the floor, keeping an arm wrapped around her thighs, just under her ass, and pulled her body flush against mine.

"Gray, I'm working," she said, splaying her hands across my chest and trying to get some space.

"All you do is work," I replied. "Give me five minutes of your time."

"You have five minutes," she said sternly.

I moved to sit on the bed in the patient room with Quentin straddling my lap. She reached up and pushed the hair out of my face, thumbs stroking along my cheekbones.

Small gestures.

These small gestures were enough to consume me. I loved hearing her speak. Listening to the three little words that grounded my chaos. But her touch would always mean more. Each brush of skin and gentle caress was a constant reminder that I'd found someone who could treat me with such tenderness.

"I'm missing you at home," I muttered with a sigh.

"Bubba," Quen whispered, leaning her forehead against mine. "I need to work. I'm trying to prove it's worth keeping me around. Five more Gods."

Hunter had left us in limbo and while I kept my ear to the ground trying to understand what the Gods were debating, Quentin worked. Five more Gods had ceased to exist, and the pressure mounted until she was buried beneath data and glassware. Sometimes it felt like she carried it alone and that thought unsettled me.

"I will not lose you," I told her, gritting my teeth together. The concern over my kin was always outweighed by my concern over her.

"Unfortunately, that decision isn't ours," she reminded me.

"You have to understand, darling, that I've never had something worth losing before. I've never had someone that loves me in the way you do and I didn't expect it either. I'm a stubborn bastard. No matter what the council decides, I will not lose you."

She brushed her lips against mine and my hands slid down her waist until they cupped her ass.

"Gray," she muttered.

"I'm behaving." But I gave a firm squeeze.

"This is my workplace."

"Fine. I'll behave," I told her, keeping my hands in position.

"I'm doing what I can so that I'm still here with you. With everything, I can promise you that."

Her brown eyes looked straight into mine, and the chaos that flared in my chest eased. As people continually pointed out, bonds could break, so there was no guarantee that she might not change her mind and leave me once she had the promise of her life.

"I won't ever leave you," I told her. Even if she broke us, I'd never release her from my hold. She would only ever belong to me. "I'd have had to have lost my mind for that to happen."

"I know."

The tip of her nose touched mine, and the words flew from my mouth again. "Marry me, Quentin."

She sighed, running her hands up my arms. "Not this again."

I kissed her softly. "You would have married a mortal."

"I was a different person then. I don't feel the need to prove my love through marriage anymore."

"I'm not trying to prove anything to anyone. I want you as my wife. I wish to possess you in every way imaginable."

She slapped my chest, and I rolled my eyes at the feeble attack.

"If you wish to possess me," Quentin said, narrowing her eyes. "You'll have to ask me in the most traditional sense possible, and maybe then I'll consider it. Until then, we are bound, and that is enough."

"That would require you to tell your brother about the fact you're a demigoddess."

"I can't."

"You can. Quen, don't you think he deserves to know? You have never hidden things from him and I think it'll do you good to share this with someone. Then you can tell Gareth and stop working as if there is nothing else in your life."

"I'll think about it."

Liar. She was brushing me off, but I decided against pushing her tonight.

"I need to get back to work," she said. "Let me go."

"Come home."

"I need to finish setting up for tomorrow and then I will come home."

"Promise?"

She held out her pinky finger to me, and I scoffed.

"What am I? Five?" I asked.

She snorted. "You wish. You're ancient."

In a matter of moments, I had her pinned beneath me on the bed. "I'm sorry," I said, staring down at her. "What was that?"

I dipped down, kissing her deeply, and when we broke apart, Quen was grinning.

"I said you're an old man."

"And yet I have all this energy." I rolled my hips so that she could feel the growing erection brush against her, and that was all it took for her eyes to switch from brown to gold.

"Oh, golden girl," I breathed. "What are we going to do with you?" I rolled my hips again, and she whimpered. "You just can't help yourself."

"Gray, we can't."

"Who cares if it's your workplace?" I had no qualms about taking her wherever I could, whenever I could. As I pressed kisses along the column of her throat, Quen tipped her head back.

"No," she objected weakly. "We really can't. I need to sort out my birth control."

"You don't need it."

"I'd feel more comfortable if I was protected."

There were certain things Quentin was yet to shake. Mortal normalities were ingrained into her and she refused to let them go. If it made her feel comfortable, I'd indulge her. I'd rather she used birth control so that we could still have raw sex. I'd never used a condom and didn't intend to start now.

I stole a glance at my sweet girl. "You'll need to see Aria."

"Aria? Why?"

"Quentin, you can't stroll in and see the average doctor. Your blood…"

The realisation dawned on her face. Red flecked with golden ichor—it was bound to raise questions.

"You'll come with me?" Quen asked.

"She's not my biggest fan."

I shifted myself and pushed her shirt up before kissing along her soft stomach. There were other forms of sex that we could partake in. She hummed contently as I sucked at her skin, bruising it, and she glowed beneath my touch. I rubbed between her legs, jeans stopping me from my goal. But I got no further as the patient room door burst open.

"Scott," James said, looking up from his phone. His eyes grew wide, and the colour drained from his face. "Oh! Oh, shit!"

James floundered at the door, and I pulled back from Quen while she bolted upright, closing her legs. Her aura continued to pulse around her, and I used mine to slam the door shut, so James couldn't leave.

"Look at me," I said, turning around to Quentin. The panic was written all over her face and while her emotions ran rampant, so did her aura. Taking her face in my hands, I said, "You'll have to tell him."

"I can't."

"He's seen too much. You're glowing."

"I won't say a word," James said, shielding his eyes. "I didn't see anything."

Quen nodded slowly, and I let go of her face and stepped aside. James' gaze slid from me to his colleague, and the look on his face was one of pure awe. Jealousy bubbled through my veins at seeing another man stare at her in such a way. The adoration that poured from him in waves made my aura appear around me, ready to shield her from view.

Quentin hopped off the bed, straightening out her shirt, but didn't approach him.

"What have you done?" James whispered, dropping his hand. "Self-experimentation is highly unethical."

"What do you think I've been doing on my late nights? Getting spiders to bite me?"

"If Grayson can shape-shift into a spider, then yes."

"You're an idiot, and I can't believe I made you my second in this lab."

"I'm an idiot, I agree. But what are you, Scott?"

His fingers reached out and played with the wisps of her aura that surrounded us. I wanted to snap every single digit for doing it, without her permission. For thinking he was worthy of touching anything that belonged to her. He should have been on his knees.

"I'm a…" She stopped, faltering with the admission. "I'm a demigoddess."

"No fucking way," he breathed, dropping his hand and looking at her again.

My aura wrapped around his throat, walking him back until he hit the wall. I was done with being patient.

"Gray," Quentin called. "Stop."

"She is a demigoddess," I confirmed. "And that knowledge needs to remain a secret, otherwise there will be dire consequences."

"Let him go!" she yelled, striding over to him. I did as she asked, and James heaved in a deep breath. "I'm so sorry," Quen said, helping him stand straight. "Are you okay?"

"No one else knows?" James rasped.

"It's a little complicated. I didn't find out until recently."

James rubbed his throat as his brows furrowed. "This was why the project stopped."

"Proving why I picked you as my second," she muttered under her breath.

"Gareth doesn't know?"

"No one does apart from the Gods," I chimed, joining her side. "And it stays that way if you value your life."

Hunter was already trying to force her hand and, although I was gently coaxing her towards the idea, I wouldn't make her do it before she was ready.

James shrunk away, less comfortable around my form than Quen's.

"Please, James," she said.

"I won't breathe a word. I'm not going to risk getting my ass kicked by the Lord of chaos."

"He's a softie, really."

"Quentin," I warned, but she moved to James.

"You're beautiful," he whispered, playing with her aura again. "Not that you weren't before. You were."

My aura went from wisps to solid black that filled the small space around us.

"I mean—" he stuttered, unsure of himself.

"Thank you," Quen said, stepping back towards me.

My arm snaked around her waist, drawing her into my side. The feel of her body acted like a balm that soothed the jealousy.

James blew out a breath. "What are you? Do you have a gift?"

"Yes."

"Can I know what it is?"

She looked at me and I saw the way her mind worked behind her eyes. Quentin had latched on to an idea.

"I trust him," she said to me.

"I don't," I replied.

"I'm making this call." Her focus went back to James. "My gift is success."

He let out a low whistle. "No shit. High achiever in everything you do. Including your private life." James tipped his chin in my direction.

Quentin rolled her eyes, which were slowly fading back to brown. "Don't feed his ego."

"I'm trying to avoid him killing me," James retorted.

"He won't."

"You can't guarantee that."

Her hand ran up my chest, landing above my heart. "He's just trying to protect me, James. Gray won't do anything as long as you keep your word and keep this to yourself."

I dropped a kiss on top of her head. There was a sense of understanding between us. I could and would listen to Quentin and her logic as long as it didn't involve her being put in the firing line.

"This is so fucking strange. I don't understand what the fuck is happening here," James muttered.

Quentin stepped away from me and I felt the irritation as I anticipated what was about to leave her mouth.

"What if we tried to understand it?"

"What?" James asked.

"We're here late enough as it is. Why don't we add my samples to the study?"

I grabbed her arm and forced her to look at me. "Absolutely not. Hunter hasn't sanctioned it. If he finds out—"

"How is he going to find out? I won't say anything and neither will you. James?"

"I'm an idiot, but I'm not stupid," he chimed from behind her.

Quentin grinned, looking back at him. "You and me. A little side project. It won't take much. We're running the experiments, anyway. We would just add this in and make sure we're the ones to run them and do the analysis."

"It's not robust," he argued, earning points from me. "You have a sample size of one. It's not like anything we do would have any statistical significance."

"Listen to the man," I urged her. "He's speaking sense."

"Consider it a proof of concept," Quen said, rocking on her heels. "We add it to the paper. Aim for a higher impact factor journal." She glanced back at me. "It would help us. Allow those losing faith to understand that there isn't this cosmic chasm between them and the Gods."

James piped up. "You think *Nature* won't accept our work on Gods."

"I think we'll probably need to sacrifice our firstborn to get in there," she joked. "We'll have an edge on the rest of the facility. Better than the others."

James considered her words, and I bit the inside of my cheeks, watching the madness unfold in front of me. How was she still chasing after her mortal desires when she had divinity? None of this would matter.

"I want first author," he said eventually.

Quentin scoffed. "No way."

"You're a demigoddess. What the fuck do you need a first author paper for?"

James was rising in my estimation.

"He has a point, Quen. You don't need any of that," I added.

"Pride and ego," she admitted. "I worked my entire life and you expect me to stop because I'm part God. This is my lab."

James shook his head. "Then I'm not doing it."

I released a breath, thankful that her ego had stopped the stupid speck of an idea that would commit her to the lab for more hours than she was currently being truthful about.

"Joint first author," Quen blurted out as he turned away. "And you'll be the corresponding author. I'll have enough to deal with. Emails from the rest of the community are about as appealing as an afternoon with Hunter."

I calculated how pissed she might be if I smashed James' skull against the wall and killed him. We'd need to clean up the body and there would be some trauma for her to deal with, but I was pretty certain I could convince her to forgive me.

He turned back to face her and nodded. "You've got yourself a deal, Scott."

James held his hand out to her and Quentin went to reach for it before I pulled her away.

"No cuff," I barked, and she blushed. "I hope you both know I don't approve of this plan."

"I know you don't," she said, looking up at me with a smirk. "But I also know you're going to do everything you can to make sure no one finds out that we're working on this."

I sucked in a breath. "It's a lie when I tell people you are no trouble."

TWENTY-NINE

QUENTIN

In the haze of work and the ever-looming prospect of being called up in front of the council, I'd abandoned most other things. I refused to stop at the pub and returned home to sleep every few days. Five more minor Gods had ceased to exist, and the pressure was crushing me. It was hard to imagine anything existed outside my sphere, but it did, and I was being faced with it tonight.

Elva's host, Professor Bruna Conti, had graciously given up her home as a venue for tonight's celebrations. I gripped Gray's hand as we materialised in her living room that was decorated in purple and orange. The colour scheme reminded me of Halloween.

"If you hold on any tighter, I may lose my fingers," Gray muttered. "We're here to celebrate an engagement. Nothing sinister."

"Nothing sinister," I repeated sceptically.

There were a few faces I didn't recognise who must have been granted clearance to join us on Earth. Gray marched past them, making a beeline for Ignacio and Elva. They were dressed in their respective colours, and Ig kept an arm wrapped around her waist, beaming proudly at anyone who approached.

"Took your time," Gray said as we reached them. They shook hands, but Gray pulled him into a hug, clapping his back. "Congratulations."

"I'm so happy for you both," I said, echoing the sentiment and kissing both of Elva's cheeks.

"We have to thank the both of you," Elva said. "Hunter couldn't argue his usual points when he knows Gray was made for someone else. Made the entire conversation a lot easier."

"Glad to be of some use."

"It's exciting to think the family is growing." Elva tucked some of my hair behind my ear. "We'll have more members than we know what to do with soon."

"You, me, and Ignacio are hardly a crowd."

"Cassidy and Sophie."

I was still finding it difficult to merge both sides of my life together. My brain didn't compute that we were all a family.

"Grayson," Elva continued, dropping her voice. "Which means we have Erik and Sloan and their children. Not to mention Larkin and, unfortunately, Hunter. Gray's parents. Quentin, we'll have so many people around us."

The reality settled around me quickly. I'd gone from having Cassidy and Sophie to having an entire room full of people that could be considered family.

"Isn't it wonderful?" Elva asked me, grinning.

A traitorous part of me swelled with happiness and kicked my heart into double time. It happened more often. I gave in to the possibility of having it all. Why shouldn't I be able to enjoy having a large family around me? A sense of belonging and contentment that I'd craved my entire life?

Because it felt like I was abandoning Cass. My brother had always looked out for me and while I was enveloping myself in a large family, he only had Sophie. What was wrong with me?

Gray's hand ran along my back and pulled my attention to him. There was a crease in his brow as he tried to decipher my thoughts. We were in tune with the other's feelings, but it was a guessing game to understand what brought on the emotions. I offered him a smile, burying my internal battle. There was no need to ruin the night with my overthinking.

"Grayson." Malachi had made his way across the room to the group. "Would it be possible to take Quentin for a few moments? Some of the Gods would like to meet her properly."

He motioned towards one side of the room where a God and Goddess had their eyes trained on me. My gaze quickly flicked back up to Malachi, searching for any threat or deception.

"I'll be happy to make the introductions," Gray said tightly.

Placing a hand on his arm, I shook my head. "I can do this alone."

"I don't think so."

"Gray, I'll be on the other side of the room. You can watch me the entire time."

His hands cupped my face. "If they try anything, I will not be held responsible for my actions."

I tensed momentarily as he brought his face close to mine. For months, we'd kept ourselves a secret, but there was no need to do so amongst the Gods. They knew of our bond, but it still felt strange to be openly affectionate in front of the entire council.

When Gray's lips met mine, the familiar liquid warmth flooded my veins and pooled in my stomach, melting me into his touch. He broke away and whispered, "Go and dazzle them, golden girl."

He straightened, stepping away from me, and it took all my strength not to pull him back. Even when I was with Ethan, I rarely relied on him for a supportive role. We were two lines that ran in parallel through life, heading in the same direction but never overlapping. With Gray, we intersected so much that I found it almost impossible to untangle our threads.

Pushing down on the sensation, I turned to Malachi and smiled. "Lead the way."

Malachi nodded his head before crossing the room. I walked behind him, letting his large frame shield me temporarily. Music and laughter flowed around us, but the most prominent noise was the thumping of my heart in my ears.

"Flynn. Waverly," Malachi said, stepping aside, so I was in sight. "This is Quentin Scott. Quentin, let me introduce you to Flynn, God of travels; and Waverly, Goddess of rest."

"It's nice to meet you both." The fact any words left my mouth was a small miracle considering how dry it suddenly became.

Flynn leaned forward, grabbing a hand I didn't offer him, and shook it enthusiastically. "You've made things a lot more interesting in the heavens." His dirty blonde hair danced around his shoulders while he drank me in.

"Interesting isn't always a good thing," I muttered in return, taking my hand back.

"It's not a good thing if you plan on revolting and murdering us in cold blood."

"Flynn," Malachi groaned. "You promised to ease her in."

"Why waste the time?" Waverly asked. "It's the most precious commodity, even to us if things continue the way they have been."

Waverly looked younger than the rest of the Gods. She had plump cheeks that were rosy pink and large brown eyes that reminded me of a doe. Her hair was cut short, but it did little to mature her.

"Grayson's been singing your praises to anyone who'll listen," she said. "Says you've been working tirelessly on the project."

"I'm doing my job," I told her as she gave me a glimpse into what Gray was doing behind the scenes.

"Even after we destroyed your kin, you're trying to save us," Flynn said.

"Flynn," Malachi hissed.

"Oh, please. She's probably heard worse from Grayson."

Flynn looked past me, and I quickly peeked over my shoulder to see Gray leaning against the wall with a little cloud of black surrounding him. When I looked back to Flynn, he was blowing Gray a kiss and wiggling his fingers in a wave.

"He hates me," Flynn pointed out cheerily.

"It's a long list. You aren't special," I replied.

He tipped his head back and laughed. "Very true." Flynn shuffled across the sofa and slapped the space next to him and I sank into it. "Don't take it personally," he said, knocking his shoulder into mine. "The whole *wanting to kill you* thing. It's survival of the fittest. We're all looking out for ourselves."

"Except for you," Waverly pointed out. "Why help us? And don't tell us it's your job."

My gaze flicked over to Malachi, who stood over us, arms folded across his chest. They were all waiting for my answer.

What would be the harm in being honest? It was the first time

I sat with elite Gods who were willing to listen to me, so I took my chance to appeal to them the best way I knew how. By presenting them with facts.

"I never believed in you because I felt like none of you listened to me. I took this job because I wanted the glory that would come with it when we finished," I admitted, looking down at my hands.

When I glanced up again, my eyes fell on Gray. Ignacio and Erik flanked him as they spoke, gesturing wildly, and Gray tried to pry them apart. Elva and Sloan hovered nearby, looking amused at the scene that was unfolding before them.

"I didn't expect to fall in love with one of you," I said, still watching Gray. "I didn't expect to find family when I was certain I had none."

Elva tucked herself into Ig's side, scrunching her nose when he kissed the top of her head. It was the same reaction I had with Gray.

"I don't want to get rid of any of you," I said, tearing my eyes away. "I don't want to cause trouble." The admission was on the tip of my tongue, the one that I had tried running from, but it was becoming more and more difficult to escape it. "I want to have the chance to come home and learn about a piece of me that's been missing for as long as I can remember."

"Way to make me feel like an asshole," Flynn muttered, and I pulled my attention back to them. "I had you down as a murderous wench."

"He really doesn't know when to stop talking," Malachi said as a way of an apology.

"You should try to spend more time with us," Waverly pointed out. "Step out of your lab from time to time. It would be a good place to start learning about yourself."

"I didn't know if anyone would want me around. You're not the most welcoming bunch."

She shrugged. "Well, the offer is there now. I'd be happy to get to know you better."

The tension around us eased, and the conversation flowed away from my mortality and into gossip. I sat quietly, listening as Flynn explained Erik would want to run the wedding ceremony, but Ig would rather eat his hat.

It was strange to think that Gods and Goddesses did such menial things like share whispers when they were in charge of the fates of so many mortals. It was all a balancing act they'd grown comfortable with.

As Waverly launched into explaining her latest fight with Aria, I caught sight of Larkin. Her expression was stony and miserable as she weaved gracefully through the guests and out of the room. Anxiety pitted in my stomach, making my fingers twitch, and I waited a few moments to see if anyone followed her. When none of the guests left the room, my chance to put my plan into action materialised into reality.

"Would you excuse me for a second?" I asked, getting up from the seat. "I'll be right back."

Shuffling out of the room, I watched Larkin climb the stairs at the end of the hallway and counted to five before following her. She disappeared through a doorway and I took a deep breath, pushing the door open and joining her in the space. She whirled around as I shut the door.

"What do you want?" she snapped, voice echoing in the bathroom. "You're spending too much time with Grayson because this borders on creepy."

"Larkin—"

"I see you didn't bother listening to my warning."

"I heard what you said, but Gray is different."

"Because you're bound?"

"Even before that. He wouldn't hurt me."

"You have no guarantee of that."

"I trust him."

"Well, good luck. Don't say I didn't warn you."

Larkin pushed past me to exit the bathroom. I reached out, grabbing her wrist, and felt her tense beneath my palm. I quickly let go, not wanting to make her feel uncomfortable.

"Please, listen to me," I said. "I've been thinking of how to help you."

"I never asked for your help."

"I know, but that doesn't mean I don't want to offer it."

Larkin shook her head and turned away, hand on the door. I couldn't preface this because she wasn't giving me a chance.

"Use my gift," I blurted out. She froze, and I continued in a hurry. "I'm not sure if it'll work because I'm only a demigoddess, but if there's a chance, then it's worth a shot."

The silence crowded in around us and I felt like I'd made a horrible mistake offering my gift to her. I had one shot at helping her and it panned out disastrously.

"This won't change my mind," Larkin said, blue eyes narrowing. "I won't change my vote. I can't be bought, Quentin."

"I'm not trying to bribe you," I replied incredulously, trying not to take offence. "I don't care if you vote against me."

A small lie. I cared very much about trying to keep myself alive, but I wasn't trying to bribe Larkin into changing her mind. This offer came without an agenda. I'd never factored my life into the equation when the rogue thought took root and flourished that night.

"If you want me to not exist, that's your decision. I'm asking you to use my gift because I don't want you trapped in a marriage with a…" I couldn't even finish the sentence.

"How did you get Gray to approve of this?" she asked quietly. "Because I swear, if you told him—"

"Do you really think I'd be standing here with you if Gray knew anything about this? He would have kept us at home to make sure I couldn't find you."

Larkin snorted, her hard facade crumbling at the truth I'd spoken. "Why would you do this?"

"Because no one deserves to go through what you've been through."

"I've been cruel to you from the moment we met. I voted for your death."

"And if that's something you can live with, then that's fine. I won't—and I don't—hold it against you."

She stared at me for a few moments. "You're a peculiar being, Quentin. How you were designed for Grayson? I'll never understand."

"He's very blessed," I explained with false modesty.

Nervous laughter trickled from her, and she took a step closer to me.

"You asked Sloan for help," I pointed out.

"Sloan is family. I can trust her."

"You can trust me."

Larkin hesitated, indecision colouring her eyes.

"Quen?" Gray's voice sounded down the hall, and I straightened.

"Now or never, Larkin," I prompted.

She sucked in a breath and whispered in a rush, "Quentin, Goddess of success, I ask you directly for your gift. Aid me in leaving my husband and dissolving my marriage. Bless me with your success."

The sentence was simple. No bells and whistles. Nothing beyond what she truly desired, but the effect it had on me was dire.

I'd grown used to the warmth of my aura. It was a gentle hum when I called on it myself and a rush of heat when my emotions got the better of me before it was released.

This was different. It was a fire that lit up every nerve with excruciating pain. It prickled like a million hot needles driven into my skin. There wasn't an inch of my flesh that didn't feel like it was on fire. I doubled over, gasping as something deep inside was ripped from my body. It left a gaping hole inside of me and a deep sadness hit in my chest before it morphed to emptiness, making my eyes wet with unshed tears.

"Quen?" Gray's voice was closer.

My knees hit the floor, pain shooting through the joints, and I held myself up with my palms. From the periphery of my vision, I saw wisps of silver before the door opened.

"Quentin!" Gray's worried voice sounded before I was lifted from the ground. He sat me on the bathroom counter and I dropped my head against his chest, too weak to support myself. "What's happened?" he asked, trying to move my head back so he could look at me, but I refused. The steady thrum of his heart, a fraction faster than what I was used to hearing, calmed me down. "Did someone do something?"

"No," I mumbled, clutching his shirt. "I don't feel very well."

That was an understatement. It felt like the grief I'd packed away had unfurled itself so furiously that I couldn't breathe. Something was missing, and I didn't know how to get it back. Even though I'd given her permission, my body mourned the loss of something sacred.

Large palms rubbed along my spine and I took in the comfort Gray offered. Carefully, I tipped my head back to be greeted by his worried face and the guilt solidified in my chest at the small white lie I told him.

"This happens when you work every hour of the day," he grumbled. "I'm taking you home. I don't want to hear any argument."

THIRTY

GRAYSON

When Quentin looked at me with tired eyes from her lab stool and called me "bubba", how was I meant to refuse doing the coffee run for her?

If the rest of her colleagues in the lab thought it was a strange sight for me to march out of the room after talking to her, none of them made a comment. The Gods may have known of our relationship, but the mortals remained steeped in gossip with no confirmation.

Despite my protests, Quentin returned to the lab the morning after the engagement party and continued with her long hours. She batted away all my concerns and, to make matters worse, she'd visited some of the other council members.

She relaxed around Malachi, feet curled up beneath her as he talked to her about politics. Waverly was still cautious about where Quentin stood with us, but they found common ground to discuss more trivial matters. The most irritating of the visits was Flynn. He always sat a little too close, placed his hand casually on her body, gossiped about all the people at the facility and in Elysia, and encouraged her to let her aura loose. Quentin left every visit with him with a grin on

her face, and I left wondering how to snap his neck while making it appear as an accident.

As I stepped onto the ground floor and headed towards the break room, I bumped into Holden. The oaf had requested to work on a different floor and I thanked my kin for getting rid of the man from my direct line of vision every day.

"Grayson," he said, nodding curtly and drawing himself up straight.

I couldn't suppress the urge to roll my eyes. "Holden."

"What are you doing on this floor?"

"Last time I checked, you aren't responsible for me in any form, but if you must know, Quentin requested coffee."

His expression soured. "Still seeing each other?"

"Yes, and it's progressing beautifully," I said, smirking. "I've been thinking of taking things down a more serious route."

His lip curled into a snarl, and he pushed past me. "I don't know what she sees in you."

A deep, hearty laugh rumbled in my chest and echoed around me as I entered the break room. It died on my lips at the sight of white blonde hair on the sofa. Erik was sprawled across the piece of furniture, hugging a cushion to his chest and sobbing. My beautiful little brother looked ethereal even amidst tragedy.

"What the fuck happened?" I asked, clearing the room in three steps.

I sat him up straight, but he clung to the pillow and sobbed harder. Dropping to my knees in front of him, I tried to get Erik to look at me.

"What's happened, Erik? Is it Sloan? The kids?" The chaos

bubbled in my chest as a myriad of scenarios ran through my mind, each more violent and devastating than the last. "Do we need to go back to Elysia?"

Erik shook his head, hair swinging with the motion. "No. It's nothing like that."

He sniffed—a disgusting, snotty sound—before heaving in a deep breath and palming his chest with the heel of his hand.

"Tell me what's happened and we can deal with it," I demanded.

The chaos I thrived off was seeping into the lives of the ones I loved, and it was beyond me to rein it in. Without a way to stop it, all I could offer was to find solutions to ease the burden.

Another deep breath that caused fat tears to roll down his cheeks. Erik's lip wobbled as he delivered the news. "Hunter and Larkin have divorced."

It took all my strength not to slap my brother for instilling panic in me over something so trivial. It was only the knowledge that Quentin would never forgive me for it that stopped me.

"My heart bleeds," I drawled, getting up from the ground and dusting myself off.

"Gray." Erik looked up at me with large, tearful eyes. "This is awful."

"You never wanted them to get married in the first place."

"Even so. Divorce… it rattles me."

With a sigh, I landed on the sofa beside him and noticed the trembling of his body.

"Will you be okay?" I asked, more concerned for him than the dissolution of marriage.

"I assume so. I just need time to recover."

"I'm surprised Hunter granted Larkin's request."

"From what I understand, it was Hunter who wanted the divorce." He sniffed again and wiped his face with his sleeve.

"You are disgusting," I said, getting up and grabbing some tissues for him.

Erik had always been the messy younger brother that I cleaned up after. Nothing had changed. Not even with millennia of history and a marriage with children. His vulnerability wasn't a weakness, but it could hamper how he functioned, and that was when I stepped in.

He took the tissue and dabbed at his face.

"I'm surprised Hunter chose now to divorce her. He's been talking about showing a united front."

"I haven't had the strength to find him and ask why," Erik admitted.

"Perhaps he's ready to upgrade Mabel from mistress to wife." A truly horrifying thought, but I wouldn't put it past Hunter.

"That isn't funny," Erik snapped.

"Who said I was joking? Hunter has been wanting an army of children and Larkin refuses. Even I thought she would have relented by now."

All it took was the Gods' will for a pregnancy to occur in Elysia. The simple act of desire aligned with both parties. Larkin had always been resistant to the idea, but I thought in a moment of weakness, in the tenderness of marriage and intimacy of sex, she may have relented long enough for a child to take root.

"Mabel's shown willing by pledging her loyalty to him. Feeding him information from the heavens, and he's given her clearance to come down here," I continued. "Although with a gift like vanity, I'm not sure she'll be eager to lose her figure for a child."

"I won't bless the marriage if he asks," Erik told me firmly. "I should have done more to stop the last union. I won't make the same mistake again."

The fear was that Erik wouldn't have a choice in the matter.

"Where's Sloan?" I asked, knowing that his wife was the only one who'd be able to pull him out from under the current.

"At home."

"Then go home, Erik."

"But I'm needed—"

"They can manage a day without you here. You're a God. It's your prerogative to make them work to your schedule."

A weak smile graced his face. "You're terrible."

"I know, and I'm so good at it."

We rose from the sofa and Erik pulled me into a hug.

"You have always had a good heart beneath it all," he whispered. Letting me go, Erik disappeared from in front of me.

Forgetting the reason I came into the break room, I walked out and took the lift to the ninth floor.

A good heart? I wasn't sure I could agree with Erik on that part. It was a corrupted organ that sat inside my chest, infested with chaos that it pumped through my veins. It cared in its own way about a select few, but good might have been a stretch.

I lurked outside the lab on Larkin's floor, drawing a few cautious glances, but couldn't see her inside.

"Why am I not surprised that you're stalking my lab?" Larkin's reflection appeared in the glass and I turned to greet her.

"Erik tells me often that I like to revel in the misery of others," I shot back.

"He told you."

"I found him sobbing."

Larkin's stony expression softened, and she hung her head. "He never wanted us to get married in the first place. I should have listened to him."

"Why would you? You had a shot at the top and you took it. Never regret ambition."

"Look at how it ended."

"I hear it was Hunter who requested it."

"You really are the most awful being I have the misfortune of knowing," she spat. "What did you expect to find? Did you think I'd be crying my eyes out at being tossed aside for the likes of Mabel?" She said her name with such distaste that I laughed.

"So, he is replacing you?"

"Probably. Not that I give a fuck. If she's stupid enough to take up with Hunter, that's on her. I've done my best to warn her against the beast, but the deluded fantasist thinks I'm jealous. Jealous? He was my husband."

"You've wanted out for a while," I said, realising that the glimmer of unhappiness we all saw ran deeper.

"Longer than any of you know," she said, running a hand through her hair. "I'm finally free and I have Quentin to thank for that."

My mood darkened instantly. "Quentin? What does she have to do with this?"

Larkin tensed. "Because of her, Hunter is losing the plot, and it's obviously forced his hand with certain decisions."

It was a plausible explanation, but it didn't sit right with me.

Larkin rarely thanked anyone. She'd been vile towards her since we'd stepped foot on Earth.

"Have you spoken to her?" I asked, unable to curb my suspicions.

Quen had mentioned nothing. From what I could recall, there wasn't a time where they were alone together. Not that it meant anything. Keeping tabs on Quen would be easier if she had a collar and a bell sometimes.

"Why would I?" Larkin snapped, but she couldn't meet my eye.

"You took her gift." The words came out quiet, but there was a dangerous edge to them. "She was in a state when I found her at Ig and Elva's party. She wouldn't let go of me."

"If you didn't want someone clingy—"

"You took her gift from her," I hissed through my teeth.

Larkin finally looked me in the eye. "She offered it to me and, as you just said, I won't regret ambition. I wanted out, and she gave me a way."

"You had no right! Quentin doesn't understand everything properly. You voted to kill her, but you still took what you could from her."

"She offered!"

"You should have said no!"

Familiar laughter echoed through the building, pulling me away from the argument. I pushed past Larkin and held onto the rail, staring down the gap that ran through the rectangular floors and gave a view of the foyer below. Quentin held a coffee cup in her hand and walked in step with James.

The metal beneath my palms gave way, warping under my touch with a muted screech.

"You're riled up over a mortal," Larkin said, leaning over the rail and watching the pair disappear into the lift.

"I can't stand the interest people take in her. *She's mine.*"

"She doesn't argue that. Does she?"

"No."

"Then I'd get used to it. If she survives this mess, she'll be popular. Look at what her gift is capable of. Who wouldn't want to brush shoulders with success?"

"I won't allow it."

"How do you plan to stop it?"

"She'll be my wife, Larkin. I am her priority, like she will be mine."

Larkin pushed herself away from the rail, brow furrowing. "You're engaged?"

"Not yet. She hasn't agreed."

The laughter was unkind and rang across the floor. "Smart girl."

"Fuck you." I prepared to leave, not willing to have this conversation with her.

"Why do you want to marry her, Grayson? To trap her? Make her do your bidding?"

"Make her do my bidding? Have you met Quentin? That woman won't do anything unless she comes up with the idea. You would know that if you're speaking the truth." I was livid, but deep down I knew Quen had extended the offer, but I didn't understand why. I wasn't sure I cared. "As far as trapping her is concerned—yes, I intend to trap her by my side for the rest of eternity. If she asked, I'd tell her the same thing. I'm not ashamed of it."

"How is it possible for her to love someone like you?" Larkin muttered under her breath.

"I ask myself the same question every day."

"She is too good for you."

"Are you trying to say you'll change your vote?"

"I still think death is a kinder fate than spending her days with us, even if you are bound to her. Eternity can be cruel, Grayson. Not all of us are comfortable living with our mistakes."

"You think she'd be making a mistake?"

"I think she's a mortal who had her head turned by a God. Ask yourself, do you truly think she'd be happy in Elysia? Away from the friends and the family she has here? You're asking her to live an eternity knowing the people she loves will die, leaving her alone. What kind of life is that?"

"Whether she chooses to be in Elysia or not, that will happen. She's a demigoddess, Larkin. Immortality runs through her."

"Not if the council decides against her. Think carefully, Gray. Everything you're offering her—Elysia, marriage—comes at a cost."

I was done with this conversation. Larkin didn't even warrant a farewell as I took off down the corridor to head back to the lab where Quentin would be back at work with a coffee I failed to deliver.

"Don't trap her in a life because it's what you want, Grayson," Larkin called after me. "If you care that much about her, then let her go. There's a reason you refused to tell her and the rest of us, Gray!"

The rest of her rant was cut off as the doors of the lift closed, taking me up to the floor where Quentin would be working.

Larkin had no idea what she was talking about. I had no intention of letting Quen go.

She was my bound and I would hold on with everything I had.

THIRTY-ONE

QUENTIN

"He's a prick who works too late in the lab," I grumbled. James didn't bother to look up from the laptop as he hammered on the backspace key. "People say the same thing about you."

"Who? I want names."

"Why? Are you going to get your boyfriend to destroy them?"

"Like I'd need Gray's help."

That comment made James glance up at me. "Too brilliant for that."

"Obviously."

"What do you plan on doing?"

"No clue."

I sighed at the latest problem that plagued my life. Dr Emmanuel Teixeira, residing on the fifth floor of the facility, was working alongside Archer. While I spent the break worried about if I would live to see another day, that fucker had continued to work all the hours he could and gloated about results he refused to divulge until the next facility wide meeting.

Success accompanied me through life and while it ensured that my cells survived in incubations and that western blots took less time to optimise, it hadn't culminated in finding the results that would allow us to wrap up this project.

At least it had proven useful in helping Larkin out of her situation. Gray delivered news of the divorce, along with a flurry of probing questions. He knew, but he wanted the admission from me. When I finally plucked up the courage to tell him I offered Larkin my gift, he asked why, and I lied. If Larkin still refused to tell him, then I had no right to share that part of her life. I hid behind my curiosity, and Gray lectured me about learning things with him instead of turning to whoever was available.

My lack of charm didn't help my current cause, as I tried all day to get Teixeira to spill information. I'd lap up the tiniest crumb just so I could hit the ground running again. But the man had an iron will that rivalled mine. His lack of scientific camaraderie stung, but what put the cherry on the cake was the patronising tone he used while telling me to work harder and not to expect success so early in my career. I should have known it wouldn't have ended well after our last meeting in his lab, where Archer and Gray had their little spat.

James checked the watch on his wrist that read eleven-fifteen and lowered the lid of his laptop. "How open are you to breaking and entering with the intent of theft?"

"As opposed to breaking and entering just for fun? Why are you asking me this question?"

There was a soft click as he shut the laptop properly. "We could raid his lab."

"You want us to spy on him?"

"We need answers, Scott. You want the work done, I want the paper, and that guy is a colossal dickhead. We wouldn't be the first people in scientific history to steal a few answers, and we won't be the last."

"Where was this a few months ago? I thought you were happy to coast."

"I was, but things have changed." He leaned back in his chair and looked at me. "I know you don't believe in the Gods. Wait. Has that changed now?"

"I still don't believe in them."

I wasn't about to get into the intricate details, but I trusted in a single God, and that was because he possessed half of my soul and I possessed half of his. We were the same.

James cocked his head. "But you are one of them."

"It's a complicated relationship," I said, scratching my eyebrow with an index finger. "I can't get into it."

He raised his hands in understanding. "I'll take your word for it. Like I said, you don't or didn't believe in them, but I do."

James opened his laptop and swivelled it so I could see the screen. The desktop wallpaper was a girl with her arm slung around his shoulders, beaming at the camera. She possessed the same sloping nose and dark hair that James had but was a few years younger.

"My baby sister," he explained. "She had cancer when she was a kid and we didn't think she was going to make it. I prayed to every God and Goddess I could think of. If I wasn't at school or the hospital, I was in the temple."

I bit my tongue from responding about skilled doctors and drugs and probability and chance. All the avenues that I would have taken if someone I loved was given that diagnosis. James' faith kept him from falling apart, and it felt wrong to impart my cynicism on him.

The Gods didn't lie. Their gifts were something they heralded, and they were cautious about who to share them with. I thought about it more often with my success. Helping Larkin was an obvious choice. But plenty of people prayed for success. If I handed it out so easily, would people value it? Would they turn to me? The Gods balanced granting prayers with rejection, testing the faith of their followers.

"And your way of repaying them is to steal?" I asked quietly, after I swallowed all the other arguments.

"No, Scott. I'm devoted to them. If they asked, I would obey. That's why I took up this post when Gareth found me. They wanted a project done, and I agreed."

That would describe half the facility. The other half were just too curious for their own good.

"I'm not following," I said.

James huffed a laugh and stood up from his chair. "You're one of them and you need me to do something, so I'll do whatever I can to help. I am devoted to you."

The blood rushed to my cheeks, and I swallowed hard. "Don't let Gray hear you say that."

"It's not like that."

"I know." Awkward silence stretched between us until I couldn't stand it. "If we get caught, I'm putting all the blame on you."

I turned on my heel, grabbing my bag and leaving the room. There were no pit stops as I walked to the lift and jabbed the button. James stumbled down the hallway after me, slipping inside before the doors closed.

"I don't want to be treated any differently," I said, staring ahead.

"But you are different."

"James, I'm just Scott. I work in a lab and I have an unhealthy addiction to coffee. Please. Or I might lose my mind."

"I'll try."

We stepped onto the fifth floor and I crept along the corridor with James at my heels.

"I doubt he's still here," he whispered from behind me. "Only complete psychopaths work this late."

I flung my elbow backwards but didn't connect with anything. The lights in the lab were off, and through the glass, I couldn't see anyone in the space. "How are we meant to get inside?"

"No clue."

"How did you float the idea of a heist without a true plan?"

"I really expected you to say no because you might have an unwavering moral compass now."

I ran my hands down my face. "Have you seen the God I spend most of my time with? I can try something, but I need you to look away."

He looked at me like I was crazy.

"I'm going to see if my aura can help but—"

"You have performance anxiety? You didn't seem to have an issue the other day in the patient room."

"It starts with theft but it's going to end in murder," I gritted out, but he did as I asked.

My body trembled as I called to my aura, the gentle hum of warmth filling me until there were gold wisps surrounding my body. I placed my hand on the door and jiggled the handle, but it didn't move.

I concentrated, moving the tendrils of aura towards the handle and the electronic access pad, but nothing.

"I think this plan is dead in the water. We're going to need to swipe an access card if we want to succeed," I explained. Sighing, I leaned against the door and let out a yelp as it swung open and I landed on the floor.

"She is beauty. She is grace," James chanted as he stepped over the threshold and helped me to my feet, avoiding touching my skin.

"Find his lab book," I said, rubbing my ass to soothe the pain. It wouldn't last long.

James went ahead as I dusted myself off. I glanced around the lab and was unsurprisingly uninspired. It was identical to ours, although the benches were a little tidier. A thought blossomed in my mind, making me wonder how different my life would be now if they had assigned me to any other God. I probably would never have found out my heritage and lived a quiet life in some university lab until it was time to shuffle off the mortal coil. It sounded so dull compared to the promises of eternity that divinity brought with it. It sounded unbearable without Gray.

As I walked down the aisle, towards the freezers at the back of the room, a window box with a small light caught my attention, and I changed my course, navigating between the benches towards it.

"James," I called, walking over to the windowsill where blooms grew in the boxes. "Do you know what these flowers are?"

The same flowers were growing in Archer's manor on his bedroom windowsill. These looked much healthier, but they weren't common. At least, not that I knew of. The pink petals were bright and inviting under the lamp that offered them light and warmth.

"I'm not a botanist, Scott," he mumbled, flipping through a lab book he found. "That's Imran's field. I thought you might have an idea, considering you helped with the cuffs."

"I wasn't involved in making them. They handed me a rack of different liquids and left it at that. They just needed me to check the biological effect. Fascinating what happens when you look at it all down the microscope."

Hunter was the test subject for those experiments. I watched keenly down the microscope as the blue flecks in his golden blood dimmed when the liquid was nearby. Enclosing it in the cuffs had a similar effect.

"They must be looking for something stronger for the cuffs," I muttered to myself.

But if these were flowers to help design restraints, why was Archer growing them in his home?

It further irked me that Emmanuel probably had access to the flowers and extra information because he belonged to whatever boys' club had banded together in the facility.

"Nerd," James called in his low timbre, and I would have thrown something if I had it to hand.

"You should show me some respect. I'm a deity."

"Partially."

"Still better than you."

"Ladies and gentlemen of the jury, she says she doesn't want to be treated differently."

Away from the rest of the Gods, away from the man who wanted me to spend eternity by his side, it was easier to pretend that nothing was wrong. James had no idea how violent Elysia was or how corrupt the Gods were. He knew what he'd been taught and what he'd been taught was to fall to his knees in his time of need and pray to them.

"Oh, Quentin," James muttered as he took photos of the pages that he thought were useful. "Goddess of success, hear my plea. I ask of you to bestow on me—"

"Stop it," I hissed.

The unearthly warmth ran through me and no matter how hard I tried to push it away, James' utterings were putting power behind it. The heat wasn't gentle like when I called on it. It scorched through me, burning me from the inside and reminding me of when Gray was on his knees in front of me in the rain.

"James, I mean it. Stop!" I rushed over to him.

He laughed, turning around, but the smile dropped when he saw me. The glow of my aura pulsed around me and I would bet money that my eyes had changed.

"You remind me of a glow stick," he mused, clearly biting back on a grin.

"I'm going to get Gray to snap you like a glow stick."

"Does he like to be called Daddy when that happens?"

My jaw dropped open. "Get out. You're causing more trouble than I thought."

James laughed, closing the lab book and pocketing his phone. "I think we've got everything we could from here."

Another idea flourished in my mind. "Have you prayed to me?"

He shook his head. "No. I haven't really needed to."

"Would you?"

"I thought you didn't want me to."

"Not now. Not here," I said, untangling my thoughts. "Pray to me for this project. For us to find success before the rest of them."

"You want to cheat?" he asked, raising his eyebrows.

"James! You just made us break into someone else's lab. You don't have the right to suddenly have a moral compass now."

"Whatever you say, Scott," he replied with a shit-eating grin.

Somehow, I'd been able to help Larkin, and as embarrassing as it was to ask James to do this, I felt it might be the only viable option. Gray couldn't ask because Hunter would figure it out easily, but if James prayed, and I found a way to answer, this could be over quicker than expected.

"I feel like we've risked enough for the night," I said, excitement bubbling in my stomach at the prospect of finishing this project and getting an answer on my life. "We'll look at them in the morning. See what he's done and what we can emulate."

"Can I start at ten tomorrow?"

"You just tried to kink shame me and now you want a late start?" I replied.

"I did not kink shame you. I would never. I just wanted to know if you called him Daddy."

I shoved James and shook my head. "I do not."

"I would. Any Gods or Goddesses looking for a mere mortal as a partner?"

"Even if they were, you would get in so much trouble."

"You didn't."

"I'm an anomaly." It was meant to come off as light-hearted but sadness weaved its way into the sentence.

James wrapped his arms around me and pulled me into a hug. "Some of the best discoveries come from anomalous results."

"Bullshit. They fuck up data sets and drive us mad."

"I never said they didn't."

My laughter was cut off when my intuition grew, pressing against my ribcage. Turning my head, I looked outside the lab to see wisps of electric blue.

"Get under the bench," I hissed at James. "Now."

When he didn't move immediately, I grabbed his wrist and pulled hard. The skin-to-skin contact was a mistake. Images flashed quickly through my mind. James lifting a trophy, being awarded a head boy pin, closing on a flat. His successes in life were displayed before me without any hesitation.

As they cleared away, James stared at me curiously, but I took us to the floor, crawling under the table. Squashed together under the desk, I listened as footsteps walked across the lab. I didn't trust myself to get us out of the room without alerting attention. The one time I'd used my aura to transport myself anywhere had been out of sheer anger.

James' hand landed on my knee and squeezed. Turning my head towards him, I pressed a finger to my lips. He gave a curt nod in return, and my breathing became shallow.

"I thought the news of my divorce might make you smile." Hunter's voice was patronising. "And yet, you are still in my ear about things. Will anything get you off my back?"

It didn't take long to figure out who he was talking to.

"Getting what I want," Archer replied.

"We have that in common."

"It seems like I'm holding up my end of the deal and you're doing everything you can to get out of your commitment."

"Watch your tone," Hunter hissed. "I'm doing this in a way that won't raise too many questions."

"You're taking your time."

"We have plenty of it. You should be grateful. She's still here, isn't she? In the comfort of the world, she knows."

"With him."

"I won't be rushed by the likes of you. I'm not going to risk making a mistake because you're growing impatient."

"I'm growing suspicious, Hunter," Archer snapped. "You won't tell me the full story, and I can sense you're hiding something. What is it you want out of this? Because it's something more than we agreed on."

"Did you ever think your gift gives you an unhealthy dose of paranoia? Just do what you came here for."

More footsteps came before they stopped nearby. My heart thundered so raucously that I worried everyone else in the room could hear it. I clamped a hand over my mouth, concerned about my breathing, and James gently took my free hand, squeezing it tight.

"They aren't ready," Archer said.

Hunter sucked in a breath. "Take the clippings up to Tobias. You've found a way to grow them, right?"

"Why should I do anything for you when I can't get the truth from you?"

"You want my word that she'll survive?" Hunter asked.

"That isn't the truth I'm after, but would you give me that?"

"She needs to work for it. If she can't convince them, then there's nothing more I can do."

His tone was so blasé. Like discussing my existence was boring to him. I would have liked to swing for him, but that wasn't currently an option.

"You need to be careful, Hunter. You're underestimating her. Lower Elysians can't wait to welcome her home properly. You lose her and you're going to fall out of favour quickly. Can't hide behind the rest of the council when you're the one who's leading the vote—"

"Don't threaten me," Hunter hissed. "Do what you've been told to or maybe I'll just let slip to the rest of the heavens how closely you've been working with me. I'm sure the council is bound to favour me over you."

Silence fell over the lab, but I didn't move. My intuition told me we still weren't alone.

Measured footsteps grew closer until they stopped by the end of the bench, and I swallowed the lump that formed in my throat. When my gaze dropped to the floor, I saw the tips of Archer's shoes peeking around the side of the bench.

"Don't worry, angel. He's too wrapped up in his own world to notice anyone else here. All it took was a little help from my gift to disguise your presence," he said, and my heart froze in my chest. "And I won't say a word, but you shouldn't sneak about. You'll get yourself in more trouble than you're already in." There was a beat of silence. "But I'm doing what I can to get you out of it."

His toes disappeared in his signature forest green, and I dropped my hand from my mouth and let out a shuddering breath. A gentle tug from James had me release his hand. He rubbed his fingers to help with the circulation.

"They were talking about you," he said, crawling out from under the bench.

I followed him and walked around the worktop, trying to figure out what they were doing here.

"They were talking about me," I confirmed. "Not everyone is as happy as you are about my existence."

His face was pale. "Scott, they were talking about your survival…"

"I know," I whispered. "James, for your sake, I don't want to discuss this any further."

"Are you in trouble?"

I looked back at him and chewed on my bottom lip. "Be careful which Gods you trust."

Turning around again, my fingers trailed along the bench until I noticed the window box. The flowers had been snipped from their stems and one head laid on the windowsill. I picked it up and turned it over in my hand. Without a chance to doubt myself, I stuffed it into my jacket pocket, making a note to look into it once I got home.

THIRTY-TWO

GRAYSON

The car rolled to a stop in the middle of the road, and Quentin got out. She bent at the waist, displaying her plump ass to the world, and I took in a deep breath through my nose.

"I'll see you at ten-thirty tomorrow," she said.

"You're my favourite Goddess," James replied before she slammed the door shut and watched him disappear down the street.

As she faced the house, a sense of relief and calm washed through me. It was a feeling I'd grown accustomed to, and a single being made me feel this way whenever she was close. It was as if my soul breathed a sigh and grew lighter and impatient, waiting to be close to its other half.

"Do you feel it too?" she whispered.

I stepped out of the shadows of the house and met her on the path that led to the front door. "The way my soul tells me you've been away for too long?" I replied, cupping her face. "If I was a jealous being, I'd be pissed at all the time you're spending with James."

"You are a jealous being."

A sinister grin came to my face before I pressed a possessive kiss

against her lips. "I am," I agreed, pulling away. "James will be later than ten-thirty tomorrow."

"What have you done?"

"He's going to suffer a puncture on his way to the lab."

"Gray, we're already starting late."

"So there's no harm. You can stay in bed with me until you need to go."

Quen flushed at the suggestion. "I'm not encouraging this."

"I don't need any encouragement," I said, kissing her again.

"We're not going to make it inside if you start here," she mumbled against my lips.

"Ah." I straightened up. "We have to put a slight pause on those plans. I have a surprise for you."

"That sounds ominous."

"I promise you'll love this one."

Her fingers laced with mine, body leaning against my arm as I guided her back into the house. The fatigue was evident in the way Quen dragged her feet along the floor, barely picking them up.

"I hope the surprise is food or coffee because I have some things I want to look into," she said, looking up at me with a hopeful expression.

"Better, darling."

She scoffed. "There is nothing better than those two things."

"I'm going to try not to take offence at that," I muttered, pushing open the living room door and gesturing her inside. The gasp that came from her made me laugh.

"Cassidy?" she said, looking straight at her brother. "Cass?"

He stood up from the sofa and Quentin launched herself across the room.

"Quen! Wait!" I called.

Of course, my soulbound didn't listen to me. Why the fuck would she? She collided with her brother and I was behind her in seconds as she read him. They stood frozen for a few moments before Quentin pushed away from him.

"I'm sorry," she whispered, eyes wide.

Cass stared at her. "What just happened?"

"Oh, Gods," she squeaked.

"Breathe," I warned her, but the panic of her brother finding out had taken hold and gentle gold wisps fluttered around her fingertips.

I wrapped my arms around her so that she didn't bolt. When Quentin was caught off guard without a plan, she defaulted to running. It happened when Gareth found out about us and I was sure she would do it again if given the chance.

"You just read, Cassidy," I explained softly.

Cassidy's questions could wait. Calming Quentin was my priority. Making her feel comfortable in her own skin had become my job, and I took pride in it since I was the only one who could successfully handle the task.

"You saw his successes," I continued. "My money would be on the fact that Cassidy is so successful comes down to having you in his life."

"He's had a lot of success, Gray."

"It's your responsibility, golden girl." I kissed her hairline. "It won't happen again unless you ask."

"Can someone explain what is going on?" Cass asked, looking at us warily.

Quen's body jerked as she tried to free herself from my hold. This wasn't what she wanted to do tonight, and it wasn't how she imagined delivering the news, but we found ourselves in yet another impossible situation.

"Tell him," I coaxed her. "Trust him."

"Duck," Cass said, tentatively taking a step towards us.

"What if I wasn't mortal?" she blurted out.

"But you are," he replied matter-of-factly.

It fascinated me how not a single drop of common blood ran through their veins and yet they were the same person. A Scott would accept only pure facts.

"Duck, what are you saying? No riddles," Cass demanded.

Utter silence filled the room and Quentin's frame shook against mine. Her steel spine softened in front of the man she called her brother. Her fear of rejection rose to the surface and pulled her under until her knees buckled, but I kept her standing.

"I'm a demigoddess," she whispered, words sounding thick as she fought against her anxiety.

"How?" Cass asked.

They were raised in a house of logic. Her family might have believed in the Gods, but they worked every day in fact and that was what Cassidy was chasing after. Observation and understanding.

"My mother—my biological mother—she was a Goddess. She fell in love and got pregnant by a mortal. They both died, and I ended up in the care system." Cassidy opened his mouth to respond, but she rattled on. "I had no idea and then I went to Elysia and there's this pool and it gifts you. Gray basically saved my life using the pool, but it realised it hadn't gifted me and now—"

Slowly, her aura drifted into view and reached out towards her brother. Cassidy shot backwards, tripping over his feet and landing in the chair. Quen's aura retracted quickly, floating around us.

"I won't hurt you," she whispered, voice breaking. "I'd never hurt you."

"I think you need to leave," I said, pushing a dark tendril out towards him.

"Gray, don't." Quentin wiggled out of my grip. "Cass, please don't hate me. I'm still me. I'm still Quentin."

He looked up slowly, the crease in his brow softening. "My duck. I always knew there was something special about you."

The relief was palpable and a half-laugh, half-sob came out of Quentin. I watched Cassidy cautiously as his fingers cut through her aura.

"What are you in charge of?" he asked.

I pulled her back against me and kissed the back of her head before answering him. "Success, if you'd believe it."

Cassidy laughed loudly. "In which case I won those games of monopoly for years because you're a cheater."

"I didn't know!" she protested.

"It's still cheating."

"It doesn't count!"

Cass got up from the chair, looking like he could burst with pride. "My little sister is a demigoddess."

"I haven't told anyone. James at work knows, but that was an accident. And the Gods, of course, but please, this can't go any further. It'd be dangerous for both of us."

"I won't tell anyone."

He opened his arms, and I released her so she could hug him.

It was lucky for Cass that he was accepting because if it had gone any other way, I would have stripped his innards from his body and decorated the house.

"Why don't you shower and I'll order food for us?" Cass suggested. "You can tell me everything about Elysia and your family."

"You're my family," she said fiercely.

"You know what I mean."

"You haven't even told me why you're here," Quentin replied, wiping her face. I shared a look with Cass, and Quen tensed again. "What's happened?" she asked.

"I wanted to keep it as a surprise, so Gray helped. Sophie and I decided to move home. I'm here to sign off on the last bits. Start getting the house in shape."

"Are you being serious?"

"As a critical medical condition."

"You sound like Dad." She laughed.

"Go and I'll tell you everything once you're comfortable."

Quen broke free again and kissed her brother's cheek before turning on me. "We need words about this. I feel you love him more than me."

I shrugged, and she kissed me before leaving the room.

"She's always been destined for great things. Everyone said it when we were growing up," Cass said, collapsing in his chair.

"And now she gets to fulfil that destiny."

He took in a deep breath and shook his head. "If Mum and Dad could see her now, they wouldn't believe it."

The mention of her parents spurred an idea in me. In record time, the seed flourished into a full picture and there was no stopping it.

"Cassidy, if I could have a moment of your time." I crossed the room and closed the door with a soft click, trapping us both in the space. "I'd like to discuss something with you."

"Sure. And thanks again for helping with everything. Not just the move, but everything that has been going on with Quen. She clearly trusts you."

"I'd do anything to see her happy."

A smile tugged at his lips. "What can I do for you?"

For a moment, it was easy to see how Cassidy Scott grew up in a home with a loving father. How often had Alexander Scott sat in that chair and waited patiently for his children to finish their stories?

If Quentin wanted me to ask for her hand properly, then fine. I'd do what she wanted in hopes she'd agree to marry me.

"I—" This suddenly felt more difficult. Clearing my throat, I said, "I love your sister, Cass."

"I know you do."

"I'd like to ask her to marry me." There was no need to tell him I'd asked her multiple times already. Not with the way his eyebrows disappeared into his hair. "And I would have asked her father, but given the circumstances, I thought you were the next person to ask."

Cassidy stood there, looking at me with narrowed eyes. "You want to marry her?"

"Yes. I would like to make Quentin my wife."

Fuck me. I'd never felt this nervous in front of a mortal, but I suddenly wasn't sure if this was a great idea.

"How would it work?" he asked curiously. "If she agreed, would you both live in the heavens?"

It was a question I asked myself a lot—what would life be like when this project was complete? How would Quentin and I live our lives when they weren't plagued by stress and threats?

I'd been alive for millennia, and Elysia was my home. Her home. But Quentin had been raised on Earth and, most importantly, had a family she loved here. Cassidy and Sophie did not have an eternity like we did. There would be a time when Quentin no longer had the family she'd grown up with, and that was what cemented my decision. I would sacrifice the comfort of Elysia for her to spend as much time as she could with the people she adored.

"You've just moved, Cassidy," I replied. "I have no intention of taking your sister away from you. I'd reside with her here."

"You know she's been down this road before, Gray. She's been messed about. If you want my blessing, you better be damn sure you want her for life."

I almost laughed. Life was never ending for us. "I give you my word as a God, Cassidy, that I have every intention of staying with your sister for the rest of our days."

Cass regarded me for a moment and, for the second time in my life, I felt my heart in my throat. The first was when I saw Quentin lying on the road that night.

Why should I be so nervous? No matter what his response, I would continue to ask her.

"After Ethan, I really thought she would close herself off to falling in love again. It pulled her apart in a way I didn't think was possible." He glanced at the floor before looking back up at me. "She took time putting herself back together. If she gave you the chance to get to know her, to love her, then I trust you are the right person for her."

"It means a lot to hear it from you."

"You have my blessing to ask her to marry you. She… well, I mean, she wouldn't be able to do any better, would she? You're a God, for fuck's sake."

I laughed because, under normal circumstances, he was right. But Quentin was a demigoddess who had the entirety of Elysia to court her if she wished. She sparked enough interest in her short stint in the heavens.

"Let's pray she says yes," I muttered, leaving out the words 'this time.'

THIRTY-THREE

QUENTIN

I crossed another item off the notepad on the office desk as the clock ticked towards five. Lists helped me to feel organised and like I wasn't completely wasting my time.

After the shock of Cass coming home last night, I didn't touch a thing. We sat up talking until the early hours of the morning, picking through Chinese takeout until he couldn't keep his eyes open. While he went to bed, I returned to the lab with a spring in my step. There were no secrets between us and no ocean either.

James and I had started to decode Emmanuel's work, devising a new plan for the experiments we'd need to run. I'd already drafted the outline for the paper so we could slot the information straight in as we received results. Gray reluctantly agreed to help me find James' prayers in the flurry of other voices and the optimism hit me hard. I could actually do this.

At the bottom of the page sat the letters 'BC' for birth control. I tapped my pen beside it a few times before getting out of my chair and taking myself down to the sixth floor. The ripple from my intuition notified me that this wasn't a wasted trip. Knocking on the lab door, I

waited for someone to let me in.

"I just wanted a quick conversation with Sloan," I said, but she'd already seen me and made her way over.

"Is everything okay, Quen?"

"Yes. Can we talk somewhere private?" I asked. "Maybe step outside the lab."

"Of course."

We walked into the hallway and I waited for the door to click shut.

"What can I help you with?" Sloan asked.

My face flushed slightly. It was one thing talking to my doctor, but it was another thing coming to Gray's sister-in-law and asking her for help with this matter.

"I need to replace my birth control," I explained. My hand went to the opposite arm where my implant sat beneath the skin.

The pill was never an option. I was too forgetful and I couldn't trust myself to take it as I should, meaning it wouldn't be effective. The implant had always been my choice and had served me well.

I shuffled my feet. "Could you?"

"Oh, Quentin, I can't. I can," she corrected herself, "but it's not really what my gift was designed for."

"I thought your gift was fertility."

"Exactly. I answer to those who want to have children. I rarely prevent it."

Biting my bottom lip, I said, "I know you've helped Larkin."

Sloan blanched, rosiness giving way to pale white. "Her situation was different. There was no other option and it was painful to go against my nature. She mentioned you helped her as well. Thank you."

"I didn't really do anything."

"We both know that isn't true." Sloan offered me a soft smile. "You'll need to ask Aria for help with your birth control," she explained patiently, but the smile had dropped from her face. "It's your body and your choice, but I can't help you with this. Aria is the person you need." She looked like she wanted to say more, but kept her lips pressed together.

"I told her that." Gray's voice sounded from behind me, and I looked over my shoulder. "Why do I never find you in the places I expect you to be?"

"I like to keep you on your toes. Keep your mind sharp in your old age."

Sloan laughed, and I grinned at her. My smile dropped when I felt his imposing figure behind me. Gray had a talent for making me feel like I was much smaller than I was.

"You should listen to this old man," he said. "You'll end up offending someone, asking them to do the opposite of what they were designed for."

"I didn't mean to cause any offence. I'm sorry, Sloan."

"It's fine. Aria's not at the facility, so I assume she'll be at her host's home. Why don't you stop by and ask her? If I can do anything else, just let me know."

Sloan pressed a kiss to my cheek and then reached up to repeat the motion with Gray before disappearing back into her lab.

Gray placed his hands on my hips and turned me around to face him. "Will you ever listen to anything I say?"

"I'm very selective," I replied, stepping away from his touch. He frowned and my gaze flicked towards the lab, where a few curious stares came in our direction. "People are watching."

He sighed and threw up a wall of his aura that blocked the glass front of the lab. Gray's possessive grip returned, and he pulled me flush against his body.

"Stop it," I muttered, but he cut me off with a kiss, squeezing my ass and I clung to his shirt.

"Let's see Aria, so I can finally take you home and fuck you." The words made heat pool between my thighs. "And Quentin," Gray said, running his nose along my jaw. "There'll be no quitting tonight."

His aura wrapped around us and when it dissipated, we were in a living room that I didn't recognise. Aria stood up instantly from the table she was sitting at and bobbed—almost a curtsey.

"I don't need formalities, Aria," Grayson brushed her off.

"Good, because that's the most you'll get from me."

"I'm not here to pick a fight. I need your skills."

She quirked an eyebrow, and I stepped forward.

"Hi," I said. Aria was an elite Goddess that I'd yet to speak to personally. "I would really appreciate your help. My birth control—"

"You want me to waste my precious time—"

Gray cut across her. "I'll remind you who you're talking to, Aria."

She stopped and folded her arms across her chest, looking pissed.

"If you can't help me, just say the word and I'll find someone else," I said, sharpness rounding out what should have been a simple request.

A smirk settled on Gray's face, but Aria narrowed her eyes. "I can help, but I'm not being watched like a hawk," she replied.

"Tough." Gray sniffed. "I'm not leaving."

"Waverly mentioned you followed her around like a dog."

Surprisingly, Gray didn't rise to the bait. "She needs an incision. I'm not leaving."

"Then you can both leave."

I turned towards him. "I'll be fine. Wait outside for me."

He held my gaze before standing down, brushing his lips against mine. "I'll see you out there."

Once Gray had left, I faced Aria to find her dark eyes trained on me. "Take a seat," she said, gesturing to a chair. I sat down as she continued, "I don't know anyone who can tell him what to do. It's not in his nature."

"As a God. Yes, I know."

"Not just as a God. As a King. His heritage puts him above the rest of us."

"Sorry?" I choked on the word.

"You know his title. Lord of chaos. King of destruction."

"I thought that was just…"

"Words?" She let out an unkind laugh. "Not quite. Even amongst Gods, there is a hierarchy that runs deeper than the council. Kieran was the one who appointed the council and got rid of the line of royalty. He believed a democracy would be better for the heavens."

My head spun with this piece of knowledge.

"Lift your arm and rest it here," Aria instructed, and I followed. "It makes sense now that he wanted to save you. All because he has an interest in you."

"It's a little more than a fleeting fancy."

"I bet Hunter isn't happy about it."

I didn't bother to respond. What was the point? Clearly, Hunter wasn't impressed by anything linked to me, otherwise I wouldn't be trying to get everyone on my side.

"You're dangerous, Scott." Aria felt around my upper arm, pressing against the implant. "Not just because of what you are, but because of your gift."

"I don't plan to use it." Small white lies. I used it, but not in the way they thought I would. Not against them in some lone crusade.

"Do you think that matters? We all have a gift and it works in our favour even when we don't call on it. Grayson, for example, will continuously welcome chaotic situations into his life. People love Erik with ease. Waverly never tires. And you, Quentin Scott, have the gift of success so we can expect there will be situations that turn in your favour without even trying."

I wished that was the case. If it was that simple, I wouldn't be breaking my back in the lab, trying to get results and convincing the council I was worth keeping alive. Apparently, being a demigoddess didn't come with the full complimentary package of perks that the rest of the Gods enjoyed. Not even a damn muffin basket as a welcome.

"What do you think I'll do, exactly?" I asked.

"I'm not sure, but the last time we had demigods, they tried to rebel. Who's saying you won't?"

"Who's saying I will? Aria, why would I want to rebel against you? I barely know any of you."

Not the right thing to say. The pale peach of her aura made a point and sliced into my arm without warning. I hissed as she fished out the implant.

"All done," she said brightly.

"You aren't going to patch me up? Replace it?"

"You'll heal. And why would you want to replace your birth

control? It's useless, and surely, that's part of the plan, right?"

"Plan?"

"You got Grayson. You went not only for an elite God, but a King and now if you fall pregnant, you'll have more demigods at your whim. Or are you more of a consort type? Maybe he won't care if you sleep with other mortals and have more children that way. Weren't you seeing one of them not so long ago?"

I stood up, aura blazing into life, and Aria brought hers around her body. She had no right to reduce my relationship with Gray into something seedy and meaningless. He was my soulbound, and she knew it. Before I had the chance to move or say anything, Gray appeared by my side.

"I suggest you don't do anything stupid," he warned her.

"She needs to learn her place."

"And you need to learn yours!"

"She isn't your Queen, Grayson! By our standards, she isn't even a God. She hasn't ascended."

"I'm sorry, but remind me who placed you in charge of the council? She may not be a Queen, but I am a King and you will remember that."

They looked ready to fight, but Aria whisked her aura away and the room was left in shades of black and gold.

"Of course, *sire*." The sarcasm dipped from the words and she bobbed a courtesy again. "If you wouldn't mind, I have work to do."

Gray didn't say another word as he grabbed me, pulling me against his body and cocooning us in black. When the light appeared again, we were in the hallway of my home.

"Let me see," he demanded.

"She said it would heal."

"You will, but it'll take some time."

Gray lifted my arm, the sleeve of my t-shirt stained with blood. He pushed back the fabric, revealing the cut along the soft flesh of my arm. A mixture of red and gold smeared across the skin and clotted slowly. Gray's palm covered the incision, fingers wrapping around my bicep, and a rush of warmth flowed through my arm. When he removed his hand, the cut had healed itself.

"She thinks she's better than everyone," he grumbled.

Shaking my head, I said, "It's going to be a lot harder to convince them than I thought."

"What did she say to you?"

"That I'm going to rebel against you all. That I'm with you as part of a grand master plan to have children so I can have an army of demigods. Or I could just sleep around with mortals and do it that way—"

"I'm going back there."

"Don't!" I grabbed his arm before he could move. "Don't. We always knew this wouldn't be easy. We can't convince them through fighting. Maybe my gift will help when I get more comfortable with it."

Gray's lips twitched into a small smile. "Your gift is beautiful, but I'm jealous you'll get to work so closely with Ignacio."

"Just like you work with Elva. There's no need to be jealous, Gray."

"I always will be when it comes to anyone taking you away from me."

I slipped my arms around his waist and hugged him. He was possessive, bordering on obsessive, but I wouldn't change him. He squeezed me back before lifting me off my feet and putting me over his shoulder.

"Gray! No!" I said as he walked up the stairs. "I can't."

There was a crack as his palm landed against my ass. "Guess we'll just need to be creative."

THIRTY-FOUR

QUENTIN

"We're going to be late," James said.

He sat on the desk in my office, nursing the biggest takeaway coffee cup they offered and swinging his legs. The late nights were taking their toll, but the prayers were working. With Gray's guidance, I found James' voice, and the results trickled in. Stats were analysed, graphs and figures produced. It made me delirious to think that the finish line was within touching distance. A few more days to pull things together and we would have the first draft of a paper.

The first step would be sharing the findings with our colleagues. Gareth had set up the facility-wide update meeting for seven-thirty. Most of us weren't functional in the early hours, but we had a lot to get through and an earlier start meant getting back into the lab quicker, and that was all that mattered to me.

"I'm aware," I replied, watching the progress bar race towards the end.

James was saved from my growing irritation, thanks to the matching coffee cup that had my name incorrectly scrawled across it.

"But Gareth will have to wait. I swear he thinks we're lab rats he can train."

James cocked his head to the side. "Did you just call me a rat?"

"Lab rat," Grayson corrected him as he lounged in my office chair. "She's afforded you some purpose. I'd rank you as a sewer rat. Pure vermin, basking in filth."

I would have loved to genetically analyse James because, with skin so thick, he had to be related to a hippo. Nothing Gray said bothered him.

"Scott, have I ever told you you're my favourite Goddess?" James asked in a singsong tone.

"Yes, but I'd like to hear it again."

As I pulled the USB stick out of the port, the room behind me darkened. A thin tendril crept up my leg before wrapping around my waist.

"If you open your mouth," Grayson said to James, "I will only be too happy to make your life a nightmare."

"No," I replied. "We don't have time for that, bubba. We're going to be late. You'll have to address your murderous tendencies towards him later."

"Promise?" Gray asked as he got up from the chair.

"It's between you two and I'm not playing referee," I said, swiping the coffee cup and making my way out of the room.

"I take back that you're my favourite," James muttered under his breath, following me.

I jabbed the button for the lift and we stepped into it. Gray wrapped an arm around my waist and pulled me into him. The way he looked at me made my knees weak and my mouth run dry. His lips brushed against mine gently, and when he pulled away, he rested his head against mine.

"I am so proud of you," he whispered, making my heart swell. "Good luck with the presentation."

James mumbled from my left, "Do I get a good luck kiss?"

Gray straightened up, narrowing his eyes. "What?"

"Nothing." And then he added under his breath, "Daddy."

I choked on my laughter and bit on my bottom lip to save myself. "Stop," I hissed, but the smile made my cheeks ache.

Moments like this made it seem like I had everything in hand. The control was mine again, and I was mastering the new facets of my life while balancing them with what I'd grown up with.

Thankfully, we reached the ground floor, and James and I fell into step with each other as Gray walked behind us. I checked my watch to see it was closer to quarter to eight, but I was sure Gareth wouldn't be too pissed at our lack of punctuality.

James pushed open the door to the large lecture theatre at the back of the institute that was built for these purposes. Several floors of colleagues gathered to see what we'd come up with so far. I rubbed my palms against my jeans, pushing the nerves aside. I'd presented in front of more people than this. As we walked into the theatre, the din fell away to nothing. Dozens of eyes shifted towards us.

Not us.

Me.

The weight of the stares transferred and transformed into a block of lead that settled in my stomach and forced my feet to stick to the ground.

Gray's palm was flat against the small of my back and for the first time since we'd descended from Elysia, I couldn't keep my emotions under control. Pure panic flooded my system and as Gareth pushed himself out of his seat and down the aisle, my aura appeared around me. Gasps sounded from the room and my tastebuds turned sour. Every muscle in my body was paralysed.

"Breathe, Quen," Gray said through gritted teeth.

"They know," I choked out. Every whisper was magnified, transmitting the fresh piece of gossip across the space.

Gareth's steps were tentative, but my gaze flicked away from my boss and searched the crowd before finding Hunter. He sat with the rest of his research team, features pinched and arms folded across his chest.

"Quentin," Gareth said, stopping in front of me and bowing his head. The way he said my name had lost the fatherly, caring nature it once held. Instead, he breathed my name like a prayer filled with reverie and awe.

"Don't do that," I snapped.

Gareth's head whipped up, and his face crumpled. "Sorry."

My nails dug into the soft flesh of my palm as I realised he thought he'd upset me. Gareth was a devout believer in the Gods. That was why he was chosen to lead this project. Snapping at him made him metaphorically drop to his knees for repentance.

"I wish you'd have told us sooner," he said. "We could have—"

"What?" I asked. "You hired me to do a job and I've been doing it. How did you find out?"

Gareth looked uncertain.

"Who told you?" Gray asked darkly from next to me.

Gareth sighed and admitted, "Aria let it slip this morning."

"Everyone knows?" I asked.

"Most of the facility was here," Gareth confirmed. "And you know how fast gossip spreads."

"Can I address everyone?"

"Whatever you need."

Gareth returned to his seat, and James looked at me.

"Are you going to be okay?" he asked.

"I kind of have to be."

He gave me a curt nod, prying my coffee from my hands before climbing the stairs towards the rest of our research group.

"What are you doing?" Gray asked, gripping my wrist as I tried to walk past him.

"Having my say on this. I'm not having another God think they can run my life," I said, pulling my wrist free.

I walked up to the lectern at the far side of the room, and Gray followed. I didn't know if I was thankful for his presence or if this all would have been easier if he went to sit down so I could look at him when I needed some strength.

"Morning, everyone." My voice reverberated around the room as the microphone attached to the lectern picked it up. "You've all heard what Aria told you this morning."

My colleagues stared back at me with a mixture of expressions. Most of them looked on in amazement or fear, but there were a few, Emmanuel Teixeira included, that looked at me with fury seizing their muscles and tinting their irises.

Without hesitation, my gaze slid back to Hunter, whose face remained impassive. If I made the wrong move, the entire council was here to witness the disaster. I would seal my fate and undo all the hard work in a matter of sentences.

As I took in a deep breath, I felt the world swayed, but I held on to the lectern with a deathly grip. "What Aria told you is true. Obviously." My aura still fluttered around me as I navigated through a whirlwind of emotions. "I chose not to tell any of you because it's been difficult to process."

"You didn't think we deserved to know who we were working with?" Emmanuel piped up from his seat. "Didn't classify yourself as a danger to the others around you? We had a right to know."

"You're still in one piece, Emmanuel," I bit back. "I didn't realise you had such a sensitive disposition when working with the Gods. If my partial divinity is such a concern, how do you manage daily in your lab?"

His cheeks flushed red and his bottom lip trembled as if he was about to say more, but Archer placed a hand on his shoulder and pushed him back against his seat.

I ran a hand through my hair, composing myself again. "The Gods have helped me to familiarise myself with my powers." I stuttered on the last word, feeling uncomfortable. "They've been gracious and accommodating while I work to understand what exactly I am."

Hunter raised an eyebrow at my words. It was a complete lie, but he wanted mortals to believe in them. If I spilled the truth, that my life hung in the balance, there would be several mortals in this room who would refuse to work alongside them, let alone believe that they were the kind and merciful deities we were led to believe they were.

"I'd ask the same courtesy from you all, please. This project is important to all of us and we still have a goal to meet."

"Some of them have been more accommodating than others, right, Scott?" Matthew called out from towards the back of the room. He sat with the rest of Larkin's team—where he had been reassigned after our issues came to a head.

My face flushed at his comment, and I ignored him. "If you have any concerns, please come and talk to me. Or—"

"Or Grayson," Matthew continued, raising his voice for the room. "Since your boyfriend's probably known about this from the start."

There was a split second before the room erupted into fresh whispers and the urge to run gripped hold of me. The chance would have been a fine thing when Grayson stood behind me, pinning me to the lectern.

"My brother's private life has little to do with this situation," Hunter said clearly, silencing the room again. "If you have an issue with Quentin, I suggest you have that conversation in private rather than airing it in a public forum to make yourself feel better about your inadequacies as a man."

I was shocked to hear Hunter defend us, but he wasn't prepared for a mortal to embarrass the Gods. Even a demigoddess was better than someone who lacked any divinity running through their veins.

Gray's fingers squeezing my hip brought me back to my senses, and I spoke up again. "I think it would be better for us to start this meeting or we'll never get back into the lab."

Stepping away from the lectern, I backed into Gray. He moved to the side and held a hand out to me. I regarded it for a long moment before slipping my hand into it and letting him guide me across the room and up the stairs. My cheeks felt like they might burst into flames at any moment.

Gray tried to nudge me into the aisle first, but I shook my head. He frowned, walking, taking the lead and sitting next to James. I sat in the seat right at the end, away from everyone else. When I tried to pull my hand away, he kept it in a tight grip and I sank further into my chair as if I could disappear.

Gareth took his post at the front of the room and immediately launched into a discussion about contracts and NDAs. My existence was a bureaucratic nightmare. It should have been no surprise. I zoned out, completely exhausted by the way the morning unfolded.

Gray squeezed my hand, and I turned my head to look at him. In his other hand was the coffee cup James had taken from me earlier, and I took it from him.

"He said to give him the stick and he'll present," Gray whispered, kissing my temple.

Usually, I would have fought James for the chance to stand in front of everyone and show our results, especially when I knew they were so promising, but the last thing I wanted to do was be put on the spot with them all staring at me again. There were enough glances being thrown over shoulders.

Shifting in my seat, I fished the USB stick out of my pocket and handed it to Gray, who passed it over to James. The *thanks* got stuck in my throat as I clutched Gray's hand again and tried not to sink into the sadness that ripped a gaping hole in my chest.

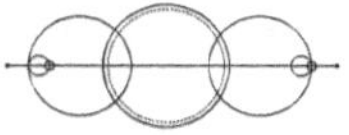

The lab had always been my refuge, and I was ashamed to admit that if Grayson was with me, I might have been brave enough to step into my domain after the meeting. But Hunter had asked to see all the Gods, minus me, so I sloped back to the floor and straight into my office, avoiding the rest of my colleagues the best I could.

The coffee James had gifted me was stone cold, but I sipped from the cup anyway, willing some normality back into my life as I opened my inbox and started drafting out an email to Gareth.

As I hit send, there was a knock on the office door that made me still. My breathing became shallow before I realised how ridiculous I was being. I couldn't hide away until this project was done. I'd need to face everyone at some point.

"Come in," I yelled with more confidence than I felt.

The door pushed open and Charlie stepped into my office, closing it behind her. I pushed myself up in the chair and swallowed hard.

"Can I take a seat?" she asked, still hovering by the door.

"You've never asked me before."

"Things are a little different now."

I bit the insides of my cheeks, tasting blood as she settled into the chair at the other side of my desk.

"You're not glowing anymore," she pointed out. "That makes you a little less terrifying."

"Good, because I'm not aiming to be the terrifying type of Goddess."

My joke fell flat. Silence stretched like a chasm between us and Charlie bowed her head, staring at the hands in her lap. "You could have told me. I thought you would have trusted me."

"I didn't tell anyone."

"Really?" Her chin tipped up as she met my eye. "Because James didn't look too surprised at the news."

I closed my eyes for a moment. "He found out by accident and I told him to keep it a secret."

"Right."

"Don't be mad at me over this. Please. Everything in my life got flipped upside down in one night, Charlie. I went from being a scientist doing my job to a demigoddess with no idea how to control anything."

She sighed, shoulders slumping, and reached a hand out across my desk. I shook my head and raised my hands close to my body.

"No cuffs," I explained. "It wouldn't be smart of me to do that."

"I understand." She retracted her arm. "It's easy for me to say, but don't worry about the rest of them. Teixeira and Matthew. It's always been a boys' club. They're just pissed that they weren't the chosen one."

"I'm not Harry Potter," I mumbled.

Charlie smiled at me kindly and something in my chest caved with relief, welcoming soft wisps of gold into the room.

"Sorry," I said, trying to rein in my emotions.

"Don't apologise, Quentin," Charlie told me, eyeing my aura warily. "I'll understand if this means you can't make it to the wedding"

"No, I'm still going to be at your wedding, Charlie."

She nodded, looking unconvinced.

I expected things to be different when people found out, but I was surprised that Gareth and Charlie were the ones who seemed so wary. They were two of the people I was closest to and I'd hoped they could take it in their stride, but I shouldn't have made that assumption.

"Okay." Charlie rose from her seat. "I'll let you get back to work. Maybe you can stop by Murphy's soon and we can have a proper catch up."

I wanted to say something, anything, that would make her stay for a little longer, but she needed time to process, and I needed to accept that maybe I wasn't in control of every little thing in my life.

THIRTY-FIVE

QUENTIN

"This is the last thing I feel like doing," I muttered as Gray tugged me over the threshold of the bar. "Can't we pretend I'm ill?"

"No," Gray said bluntly, and I was a second away from stomping my foot. "You need to embody a pageant queen tonight because I don't know why they asked for drinks."

"Maybe they're going to put me out of my misery and kill me."

Gray stopped abruptly, and I bumped into his colossal frame. When I tipped my chin to look up at him, my blood turned to ice in my veins. Unimpressed didn't even scrape the surface of what Gray was portraying.

I placed a palm over his heart and gave him a sheepish grin. "Just a joke, bubba."

"Do not quit your day job," he replied darkly; but paired with the kiss he pressed to my forehead, I knew he wouldn't hold a grudge.

Grabbing his hand again, I smoothed my skirt as Gray led us to the back of the bar. It was a small blessing they hadn't picked Murphy's or I would have been less inclined to tag along. Things remained strained

between me and Charlie.

Flynn's raucous laughter could be heard before we saw the Gods tucked away in a booth at the back. "There she is!" Flynn announced, holding up a beer bottle. "Guest of honour!"

"Sit down!" Malachi hissed, pulling him back down into his seat properly. "You're drawing attention."

Gray slipped into the booth beside Waverly and I was about to join him when Flynn patted the empty spot next to him.

Pageant queen.

Fixing a smile in place, I shuffled in beside Flynn, who scooted up, squishing Malachi to the wall so that I had space.

"I asked Aria to join us, but she refused," Waverly said.

Gray's eyes narrowed. "What made you think she'd be welcome after the stunt she pulled?"

I resisted the urge to kick him under the table. If I had to be on my best behaviour, then so did he.

"I thought if she spent some time with Quentin, then she might be convinced to change her mind." Waverly shifted in her seat. "I don't agree with what she did, and I told her as much. It felt like overkill to request an apology."

"I thought Hunter was going to rip her in two," Flynn added, knocking back the bottle and throat bobbing as he drank.

"What happened?" I asked.

Gray had been reluctant to tell me about the meeting when he came back to the lab. His mood was dismal, and when I tried to pry, he snapped. The pressure of the situation got to the both of us and I didn't help with the macabre sense of humour that I'd developed since my secret was revealed.

Flynn leaned against me, pressing his shoulder into mine, and whispered conspiratorially, "Hunter went off. Told Aria that if she tried to behave like head of the council again, he'd make sure she was removed from her position and wouldn't even have a space in lower Elysia."

"It's all about control." Waverly ran a finger around the rim of her margarita glass, scattering salt onto the table. "He's head of the council and he wants it to stay that way. Can't have someone else treading on his toes. He didn't even afford Larkin that luxury, and she is his wife."

"Was," Flynn corrected her. "*Was* his wife. Now we're probably going to deal with Mabel."

I snorted a laugh when Flynn mimed vomiting over the table. Gray hummed and the attention of the crowd turned to him. The ease that they lounged with disappeared and was replaced by tension, and I cocked my head to the side.

"We mean no disrespect," Malachi said calmly.

"As if I care." Gray waved him off and took a sip of his beer. "You can disrespect him all you want in front of me."

Flynn cracked his neck. "In which case—"

"Don't," Malachi warned him.

Waverly sniffed. "It's difficult to tell where you all stand at times. He came to your defence when that mortal attacked your relationship."

"He was defending his pride, not me," Gray explained. "Can't let a mortal have the last word and show up the Gods."

"Do you think he'll deal better with Gods showing him up?" Flynn mused, nudging me and winking.

My eyes widened. "I'm not trying to show anyone up."

"Not everything's about you, sweet cheeks." Flynn pinched my cheek, and I swatted his hand away. "Sometimes it's about the rest of us."

Gray became uncomfortably tense before leaning across the table. "If this is your idea of a sick joke—"

"I pride myself on having a better sense of humour than that. Quentin can attest."

"We wouldn't joke about something like this, Grayson. It isn't worth your eternal wrath," Waverly pointed out.

"Can you stop speaking in riddles, please?" I asked.

Malachi leaned forward, looking past Flynn to me. "The reason we asked you to come and join us for a drink was because we wanted to tell you—"

"We want you to live," Flynn cut across him, grinning wildly, while Malachi shot him a withering look. He wrapped an arm around my shoulders and pulled me into a crushing hug. "We're going to change our vote when Hunter calls the council meeting."

"All of us," Waverly added. "Which will push you over the threshold you need to ensure you can keep your life even if someone else changes their mind."

"This isn't a cruel joke?" I asked, not daring to believe them.

"I wouldn't let them do something like that," Malachi assured me.

The lump in my throat grew so fast that I couldn't swallow it and a tear spilled over. After the nightmare at work, I was losing hope again. Hunter's mood was difficult to decipher, and I couldn't tell if he would hold Aria's mistake against me. Fighting, although necessary, was exhausting, and every setback made me question why I should bother. Winning felt like an impossibility.

"Don't cry, tiny demi. An eternity with Grayson isn't as bad as it sounds," Flynn assured me.

I laughed through my tears and saw Gray's blurry pissed off face. My boyfriend reached across the table, and I wiggled out of Flynn's grasp to change seats so that I was between Gray's legs. He stroked my arm and kissed the top of my head.

"Why did you change your minds?" I asked, hiccupping midway through the sentence.

"You need to calm down before you end up showing this bar what you are," Gray mumbled against my temple.

I shook in his hold, trying to control my breathing. The pad of Gray's thumb swiped away the stray tears and stroked my cheekbone comfortingly.

"Good girl," he whispered as I let my body relax against his.

"What happened to make you change your minds?" I asked them again.

"We've spent time with you, Quentin," Waverly said, shrugging. "You've indulged us in conversation, and you're bound to Grayson. We don't believe you're a threat. Please don't prove us wrong in that assumption."

"You could have told the entire facility the truth about where we stood with you, but you lied to them. If you'd told them the truth, it would have aided in our demise. Plenty of people to spread the word about how barbaric we are," Malachi mused.

"You took one for Team Divine," Flynn said, offering me his fist. I bumped it gently with my own. "You're one of us. It would be a dick move not to welcome you home when you've given us the loyalty we were looking for."

"Shall we toast?" Malachi asked.

"I think that would be appropriate," Gray said, squeezing back against him. He lifted his beer bottle and said, "To Quentin."

"To eternity," Malachi added.

"Yes, baby!" Flynn called as we knocked our glasses together. "Means you can enjoy your birthday party."

"Flynn!" Waverly hissed.

He slapped a hand over his mouth and ran it down, revealing a sheepish grin. "Oops."

"What birthday party?" Gray demanded. When no one answered, he slammed his bottle on the table. "What birthday party?"

I should have scolded him for being so aggressive, but my body didn't feel like it was my own. I felt like I was floating. The last time I'd been this relieved was after my viva when they told me I'd passed my PhD.

Malachi sighed. "Erik is planning to throw her a party. It was meant to be a surprise."

"He thought it would be something to enjoy and give everyone the chance to spend time with her," Waverly explained.

"Who would have thought our teeny tiny demi was going to cause so much chaos?" Flynn asked, but then he let out a bark of laughter and pointed his bottle towards Gray. "You did, right?"

"I'm going to kill him," Gray gritted out through his teeth. He looked down at me. "Are you okay with this? I can put a stop to it."

"Whatever Erik wants," I replied. "I don't care."

"Quen, he won't be subtle."

"I really don't mind."

"You're delirious."

The evening sunk into conversation and drinks. To think I was going to miss out on all of this, to sit in the lab and stare at my samples for a few more hours.

Alcohol heated me from the inside until my laughter spilled without hesitation and my limbs were loose at the thought of impending freedom. When Gray tried to persuade me to eat, I pushed him away and opted to frequent the bar with Flynn instead. Drinking amplified the feel-good attitude that had awoken deep in my belly since they delivered the news of changing their vote.

"All right, darling," Gray said, hoisting me into his arms. "I think it's time we go home."

"Boo!" Flynn called before laughing.

"You can stay away from her from now on. Look at the state she's in."

"We need to build up her tolerance."

"I'll help her with that."

I dropped my head against the side of Gray's face so hard that there was a dull ache in my forehead.

"Quentin, be careful," he scolded, shifting me in his arms.

I wrapped my arms around his neck and smiled. "You're always looking after me."

"It's an honour to do so," he muttered in response. "Say goodbye to everyone."

"Bye!" I twiddled my fingers at the rest of the booth. "I really, really love you all."

Waverly giggled in her corner and shook her head as Gray strode out of the bar. I continued to wave at anyone who looked in our direction and blew the bartender a kiss. That marvellous man had served some of the best drinks I'd tasted. Maybe that was the alcohol talking. I laughed to myself and Gray sighed as we stepped out onto the streets.

"Are you going to carry me the entire way home?" I slurred, clinging to him.

"No, I'm going to take the shortcut."

"Shh!" I hushed him loudly. "Home!"

The world went black, and when Gray's aura disappeared, we were back in my bedroom. He set me down on the bed and kneeled on the floor in front of me, slipping my shoes off.

"Are you going to get naked, too?" I asked, wiggling my eyebrows.

"Usually I wouldn't decline the offer, but I'm not about to have sex with you when you can barely stand."

I pouted. "But you give me the best dicking."

His shoulders shook with laughter. "I promise the minute you're sober, I won't deprive you of my dick."

"I'm sober as a judge."

"I'm sure you are, golden girl."

Gray helped me out of my shirt and skirt before untangling himself from me. I flopped back on the bed, still pouting.

"I'm going to get you some water," he told me.

Rolling over onto my stomach, I cocked my head to the side. "Gray, should we get married? I think there's a place somewhere by Sal's that does it."

"Not yet, golden girl. One day, but not yet."

THIRTY-SIX

GRAYSON

My fingers brushed the stray strands of hair away from her face. Quentin was nestled against me, legs and arms tangled with mine and breathing shallow. A slice of peaceful perfection that belonged to me.

Selfish.

I was utterly selfish.

After finishing late in the lab, she stumbled over the threshold, announcing that they'd sent the first draft of the paper to Gareth. The results arrived thick and fast, filling her template until she and James finally rid themselves of it.

She panicked when I brought her back up to our home last night. An unsanctioned trip into Elysia was sure to change minds. But this was all down to me and if anyone found out, which they wouldn't, I would take the blame.

I wanted Quentin to wake up on her birthday in our home, in our bed, without the need to rush into the lab on a weekend. Every second she had to spare should be with me, where I could spoil her until I was forced to share her with everyone else tonight. We'd been separated

for too many years. Even if I didn't know her then, my soul still craved her, and I'd claw every spare moment that she'd allow me.

Carefully, and reluctantly, I slipped out of bed so I didn't disturb Quen, and went down to the kitchen. The mixture of gold and black around our home lifted my heart. There had never been colour within these walls until she appeared. Her gold lit up all of my darkness and made it bearable. She made existence bearable.

The coffee was freshly brewed, and I loaded the tray with pastries that Poppy brought last night when Quentin went to bed. I trusted Poppy to keep her mouth shut about our little trip, like she had with everything I'd asked for help with so far. Picking up the tray, I felt the ripple run through my chest and smiled to myself.

"Gray?" Quen's sleepy voice came from behind me.

When I turned around, she stood in the doorway of the kitchen, drowning in one of my shirts. The sleeves were pushed up to her elbows, top buttons undone to reveal the curve of her breasts and her legs on display.

Quentin rubbed her eye. "You weren't in bed. I thought something happened."

Balancing the tray in one hand, I cleared the kitchen and lifted her up with the other. Her arms went around my neck, holding on tightly.

"Happy birthday, golden girl," I said, nudging her face out from the crook of my neck so I could kiss her.

Quentin smiled against my lips. "Thank you. Is that for me?"

She eyed the tray in my hand as I took us back to the bedroom. Keeping one arm around my neck, she reached out for the coffee mug.

"Quentin," I warned her. "Wait."

She batted her eyelashes at me. "But it's my birthday and I get what I want."

I blew out a sigh and moved the tray towards her so she could safely pick up the mug. A sleepy smile graced her face, and she kissed my cheek before trailing them along my jaw.

If you met Quentin, you might not like her straight away. She was cold and abrasive when she wanted to be. Work took precedence over all other matters. She often drifted away from conversations that bored her. But in reality, she craved simple things like stimulating conversation and people who didn't run from her when she exhibited difficult moments.

Fresh coffee.

Deep kisses.

An appreciation of the woman she was.

"Hold it tight," I instructed and deposited her back on the bed.

She nestled back against the pillows, and I placed the tray in front of her. Quentin crossed her legs, pretzel style, and sipped from the mug, looking content. Sitting down next to her, my hand cupped the side of her face and she looked at me.

This obsession I had with her was infuriating at times. I was powerless against it. Quentin Scott was my first thought from the moment I woke until I finally needed to close my eyes. The smallest things reminded me of her, and I sought her out regularly.

"It won't be long before this will be our life," I whispered. "A life you deserve."

There was a glimmer of excitement in her eyes. Quentin lowered her mug and leaned into my palm, biting down on the flesh.

"Tiny feral beast," I muttered affectionately, kissing her forehead.

She released my hand from her teeth. "I can't believe I'm excited about the vote."

"You seem more settled with your divinity."

"I don't think I'll ever fully comprehend it, but I guess it's not so bad."

"Oh?" I asked, raising an eyebrow.

She placed her mug on the tray and picked up a sticky pastry. "It feels like home. It feels like somewhere I belong, even when I know not everyone is happy."

"Fuck everyone else. Are you happy?"

Moving the pastry from one hand to the other, she raised her sticky fingers towards her mouth. I caught her wrist and pulled them to mine, sucking away the sugary residue while she flushed red and her aura pushed itself out around us.

"Are you happy?" I repeated, moving to the next digit.

"Happier than I have been in a long time," she admitted in a whisper.

That was what I needed to hear to cement my decision.

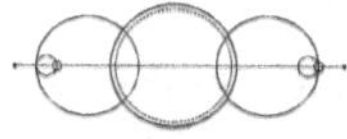

The day had not gone according to plan. She was meant to be mine and yet Poppy had let slip to a very specific crowd that Quentin was back home. We'd barely finished breakfast before Dionne, Marcel, Poppy, and Andreas invaded the house. While the three attacked her with birthday wishes and last-minute gifts, Erik's father-in-law hung back. He had never been the type to openly offer affection to anyone that wasn't his wife or daughter.

No matter how much I tried to usher them away, and I wasn't subtle in my attempts, they settled into the house as if they were long-time friends and showered her with attention. A job that should have been left to me.

By the time they finally left, we were due back on Earth for her party, courtesy of Erik.

There was a good reason I hated people.

I pulled on my suit, debating whether I would need to change my plans once again. Sometimes I didn't appreciate the pure chaos that ruled my life. A moment of organisation would have been admired, but that was too much to ask.

I adjusted the cuffs on my suit, staring in the mirror. Full black attire for the evening, apart from the gold cufflinks at my wrist.

"Darling, are you nearly ready?" I called, aware that Erik wouldn't be impressed if we were late.

Keeping her hostage here was a tempting idea…

Quentin opened the bathroom door and stepped into the bedroom again, smoothing the fabric around her stomach. The glittering gold jumpsuit left her back bare and hugged her curves.

"Fuck me," I breathed.

Her head shot up, large curls bouncing around her shoulders. "Grayson."

She walked over to me and I took her hand, turning her so I could take in every inch of the woman who drove me wild. Once she completed a full circle, I pulled her in for a gentle kiss. Her lips were painted black and matched the dark smoky eye makeup. I wondered if she noticed the way she was drawn to my colour.

I couldn't wait. If we were late, so be it, but I couldn't spend another second in limbo.

"You look beautiful," I told her.

"You don't look too bad yourself."

"I'd like to take you somewhere before we join the party."

"Where?"

"Do you trust me?"

Her features softened as she held the lapels of my jacket. "With all I have."

Her response drew a smile on my face, and I wrapped my aura around us, whisking us away from the bedroom and onto the clifftop at the back of our property.

"You brought me out to the grounds?" Quen asked, looking confused.

"I come here when I need some quiet."

She left my side and wandered towards the edge of the cliff, looking up at the vast, dark sky.

"Do you like it here?" I asked, watching as she gazed into the night.

"I don't think I'll ever get used to how beautiful it is. There's always something that takes my breath away."

Suddenly, the nerves flooded my body, but I forced myself down on one knee behind her.

"Quentin," I called.

She turned to face me. "Yes, Gr— What are you doing?"

Her eyes were wide as she stared down at me.

"Quentin, there is no one else for me. For some reason, your stubborn, infuriating, and amazing self was made for me. You consume my thoughts, and I am thankful that I will never have to imagine a single day without you. My soulbound. How lucky am I to have found you.

"We are bound by soul, darling, but I desire more than that. I want you to become my wife, Quen. I wish to spend every moment of our immortality bound to you in every way possible. So I did as you asked. I spoke to Cassidy, and he gave us his blessing."

A tear rolled down her cheek and Quentin trembled as she stood in front of me.

"I am a God, down on my knee, asking if you'll be my wife for the rest of eternity. Would you do me that honour, Quentin? Would you marry me? Be my Queen and I will give you the stars."

Quen stared at me, silence consuming us, and a knot formed in my chest. This could go either way, and I wasn't filled with confidence.

"Quentin?" I prompted. When she continued to stay quiet, I rose from the ground and walked towards her. "Golden girl?"

When I took her face in my hands, she broke out of her trance and whispered, "Yes."

"I'm sorry?"

"Yes, I'll marry you."

THIRTY-SEVEN

QUENTIN

I hadn't expected Gray to be on one knee when I turned around. He hadn't asked me to marry him for a while and I thought he might have given up on the notion.

The thought of how much love flowed between us terrified me. The intensity of it was something I didn't believe was possible. Soulmates were nothing more than a fairy-tale that people deluded themselves with, and yet I faced a man who was created for me. No other being for the rest of eternity would be able to evoke a love so deeply satisfying from me in the way Gray could.

All this time I put off saying yes to him because I was worried he might hurt me. But Gray proved to me repeatedly that he would stand by my side through anything. I didn't want to push him away anymore.

Gray was on one knee. He'd spoken to Cass—a fact that made me cry. This idiot God in front of me took me so seriously when I said he might stand a chance if he asked me traditionally. So traditional that he went and asked my older brother's permission for my hand. I wasn't a possession, and I didn't need his permission, but it was cute,

and I knew it must have taken a lot for Gray to swallow his pride and do that.

"Yes, I'll marry you," I said, but Gray stared back at me blankly. "Gray?"

My feet came off the ground as he lifted me up, spinning me around. Laughter bubbled up my throat and spilled out of my lips as I gripped his shoulders.

"Are you serious?" he asked, placing me back on the ground.

"I give you my word as a demigoddess."

There was nothing to run from. No plausible excuse to turn him away. Malachi, Flynn, and Waverly had given us their word. All that was left to do was wait until Hunter called the meeting. With my life no longer hanging in the balance, I could see a future again, and I didn't want to let any fears hold me back. After everything Gray had done in the last few weeks, how was it fair to judge him on my past experiences?

He grabbed my face, kissing me hard, and I melted against him. The golden glow lit up the cliffs and I didn't try to restrain it, letting it join in with the celebrations.

When we pulled apart, Gray reached into the inner pocket of his jacket and pulled out a black velvet ring box. He opened it slowly and nestled inside was a stunning ring. A black hexagonal stone sat in the centre of a gold band and on either side of it was a cluster of three small diamonds.

"Gray," I whispered before biting my bottom lip.

He plucked the ring from its resting place and took my left hand. "Do you like it?"

"It's perfect."

The metal was cold against my skin as he slid it onto my finger. I flexed my digits, taking it in, and my brow furrowed, seeing the stone shining even in the darkness.

Gray tipped my chin up with his fingers so I looked back into pitch-black eyes. "I had this ring made for you. Something as unique as the person who will wear it for the rest of her life, but it still wasn't perfect, so I called in a favour. I asked Marcel to help me with it. It will always shine like that. He created the smallest stars and placed them in that stone."

"There are stars in this ring?" The question came out high-pitched. "Actual stars?"

Yet another moment where my scientific mortal life and my life as a demigoddess refused to work in harmony together.

"Yes, Quentin. I know it isn't a traditional diamond—"

A diamond paled in comparison. Anyone could have picked out a rock from behind a glass display. Gray went through the trouble of making sure a part of him was with me wherever I went. The black centrepiece did not go unappreciated.

When he said he would give me the stars, it wasn't a joke. It wasn't just words.

"I couldn't ask for anything better." Hugging him close, I laughed into his chest. "We're going to get married."

"You'll be mine for the rest of our lives."

"What have I done?"

"Given up any hope of peace," he answered honestly. "But I will give you everything that I can within my power."

"Do we have to leave?" I asked.

"Not yet. There's one more place we need to go."

THIRTY-EIGHT

GRAYSON

"I don't know about this," Quentin said.

"They'll love you."

"You don't know that."

As if I didn't know my parents well enough to know they'd be ecstatic that someone decided to anchor themselves to me for life.

Originally, I'd wanted to wait until Quentin had the council's official stamp of approval, but Mum and Dad deserved to meet the woman I would marry.

I raised my hand to knock on the door, but Quen grabbed it before I could. The panic was written across her face, and I pulled her in, hugging her tight.

"I'll be with you the entire time," I assured her, placing her back on the ground.

"How do I look?" she asked, straightening out her clothes.

"Beautiful as ever," I replied.

"Biased."

On so many counts, and I always would be where she was concerned.

"Are you ready now?" I asked.

"Not in the slightest."

"Tough shit."

"Love you too, dickhead."

I chuckled as I knocked on the door, and a few moments later, my mother answered.

"Mum."

"Hello, sweetheart." She reached up to kiss my cheek. "Your brother and Sloan are already here."

Quentin had disappeared and hid behind my back. I grabbed her hand and tugged her back into view.

"Quentin," Mum breathed. "We've heard so much about you. Come in." She moved out of the way so we could step inside. "I should have started by saying congratulations to you both. And happy birthday."

If I thought my mother would favour me, I was mistaken. She dived for Quentin, embracing her as if they'd known each other for years. Mum let go of her and moved to me, grabbing my face in her hands.

"I never thought I'd see the day," she whispered, tearing up.

"Mother. Let's not."

"Come through to the living room." She walked in that direction before looking back at Quen. "Kieran, Gray's dad, has been eager to meet you. We wanted to stop by when we first heard about you, but you've proven to be quite popular and we didn't want to add any pressure. I'm Evadine, but you're more than welcome to call me Mum."

It was easy to see where Erik got his talkative nature from.

"I… Thank you. I appreciate that," Quentin said, still pink in the cheeks from the hug.

"Plenty more," Sloan said as we walked into the living room. "What else keeps you busy in your old age?"

Dad chuckled in his seat. "I'm sure I can find other things to preoccupy my time rather than looking after a swarm of grandchildren." The way he said it told the room he was teasing.

"Get used to it, Kieran," Larkin said, jerking her chin in our direction. "These two haven't even started yet."

Quentin radiated heat as the pink transformed to red, and I shot Larkin the middle finger, but there was a ghost of a smile that graced my face.

Dad got up from his seat, pulling me into a hug and clapping my back. "I believe congratulations are in order. After you found out you were soulbound, I wondered how long it would take."

"I've been asking her for a while," I muttered.

"Looks like you know how to make my son work for things," Dad commented, pressing a kiss to Quen's cheek.

"Nothing worth having comes easy," she replied, making Dad laugh. Quen looked at the others. "I thought you were all going to be getting ready for the party."

Erik arched an eyebrow. "I know Flynn told you."

"In his defence," I said, "he was tipsy."

Quen looked at them. "You knew Gray was going to ask me tonight?"

"We know he's asked you for weeks," Larkin pointed out. "I still think you should have said no."

"She knows a good thing when she sees it," I pointed out.

Sloan beamed. "She knows she'll have eternity with us."

I watched as Quentin lit up, the smile on her face brightening her features. No stress. No worries.

"Can you produce your flower yet?" Mum asked curiously. Quen shook her head. "When you can, please give us one. I'd love to add it to the garden."

Larkin answered Quen's questioning look. "Eva likes to put all the family flowers in the garden so they can grow together."

"It's a little concerning," Dad commented, eyeing Quentin. "It's been a long time since Gods were disappearing at this rate. Hunter's initiative isn't working in the way he hoped."

I gritted my teeth together. He had always been like this. Casually putting forward arguments in order to get information.

"It was never his initiative to begin with," Larkin muttered.

I raised an eyebrow, surprised by her comment. "Do tell."

She breathed in deeply. "Do you really think he had the thought of coming up with all that on his own?" Larkin's gaze flicked to my parents. "No offence."

"None taken," Dad replied. "He was always quick to act. Less likely to think of a long-term plan if he can get a quicker solution."

"No wonder you took such joy in telling me," I grumbled, looking at Larkin.

"It did the soul good to know that my plan unsettled you so much. If you think about it, I'm the reason you have Quentin."

"Hey!" Erik piped up. "I'm the matchmaker in this family."

"Didn't you try to keep them apart?" Larkin pointed out.

I cocked my head. "She's right. You weren't too keen on us being together."

"I was trying to keep you alive," he countered.

The conversation picked up around us, but Quen sank into herself, gazing at the floor.

Leaning in, I whispered to Quen, "Is everything okay?"

She had taken a lot on her shoulders in the lab and talking about the success of the project was bound to put a dip in her mood.

"May I be excused? I just need two seconds." She didn't wait for a reply. Quentin made the quickest exit I'd seen.

Erik looked alarmed. "Is she okay?"

I shook my head. Something wasn't right. The pain radiated through our bond.

"I'm going to check on her," I muttered, walking out of the room.

My intuition led me to the back garden. Quentin was sitting on the stone steps that led down into the grounds. I closed the door behind me and joined her quietly.

"Do you want to tell me what's going on?" The ache resonated deeply, but I didn't understand what had upset her.

"I feel out of place. Like I don't belong," she said, staring ahead.

"They're our family, Quentin. Of course you belong."

"They're your family, Gray."

She turned her head to look at me and the sadness ran through her features. This was not what I wanted for the day.

"Come here," I demanded, holding out an arm. She scooted closer, tucking herself into my side. "I set this up after what you brought up in bed the other night."

"What?"

"You got me to promise you I would always be there."

"What does that have to do with your family?"

"*Our* family, Quen," I stressed. "I wanted to show you it won't only be me who will be there for you. You have so many others."

She let out a shuddering breath, and I rubbed her arm, offering her a small token of comfort.

"I know no one could ever replace your parents or Cassidy."

"Ever."

"I know."

"My brother is one of a kind."

"You're both a pain in the ass."

She shoved me gently and bit her bottom lip to stop herself from smiling.

"But," I continued, "you will always have family here and they will love you like their own. You see how crazy Erik has been about you since day one?"

"I think he likes me better than you."

It was always a competition with Quentin, but I wasn't about to admit that she might be right in this case.

"You're missing them?" I guessed tentatively.

"I'm always curious what they would have thought of you. I wonder if we would have had traditions. Gray, I wish they were still here."

I hugged her close to me, unsure of what to say. When I'd lost people, it hadn't impacted my life in the way it had with Quentin. If our binding was letting me feel even an ounce of how she felt, then I'd do everything in my power to never lose people I cared deeply about because even this small fraction was immensely painful.

"The closest we can get is reliving your memories of them if you share them with me. Remember when I shared my memories of Mallory?"

She nodded.

Sharing memories made them vivid. Almost like you were standing in them as they happened. I wished I could do more, but even as a God, death was final.

"I think I'd like to try that when we're alone," she said.

"Whenever you want."

Quentin gave me a squeeze, and I brushed my lips against her forehead gently. I could and would give her nearly everything in the world, but this was where I felt powerless.

"Let's go back inside," she said.

"Are you sure you're okay?"

"I've got you, haven't I?"

I rose from the step, taking her with me until she was on her feet. As she turned to enter the house, I slapped her ass, earning me a stern look over her shoulder.

We walked back inside and headed towards the living room, but Hunter's voice drifted down the hallway before we reached it.

"I'm just trying to figure out how the invite wasn't extended to your son but was passed on to Larkin, who isn't considered family anymore," he said.

Dad sighed. "If you're planning to stay, Hunter, I expect no trouble."

"That's usually more Gray's avenue."

"And here you are trying to steal my thunder," I said, gripping Quen's hand tight as we entered the room. He was nowhere near her and that was how I preferred it to stay.

"Mabel said she saw you both down here," he commented. "I expected both of you, but I didn't realise the entire family was coming together. What are we celebrating?"

"It's my birthday," Quentin answered.

Erik stepped towards Hunter. "And this was my idea."

Hunter's eyes narrowed as he took in Quen. "That's a beautiful ring you have on your finger."

She moved her hand behind her back quickly.

"Grayson." Hunter clucked his tongue. "You know you require permission from the head of the council for marriage."

"You'd deny me my bound?" I asked in return.

His face pinched with frustration. "Is no one going to make a toast?"

I ground my teeth together. "There's no need."

"Now, now, Grayson. Surely, you want to celebrate?"

"That's enough, Hunter," Dad warned.

"I'll make the toast." Erik swirled the liquid in his glass. "Grayson. Quentin. I don't think there could be anyone in the room more pleased for you both than I am."

Larkin rolled her eyes, and Sloan leaned back, trying to hide her laughter. Erik would monopolise on this and I didn't blame him.

"I am ecstatic to see another bound pair find each other and now that you're making it official, I couldn't be happier for you both.

"Gray, I think we had all come to terms with the fact that you were content with your own company and that you weren't interested in finding someone to spend eternity with. Quentin, thank you for opening his eyes and his heart." Erik sighed wistfully. "You're family now."

Hunter cut across him with a scoff. "Not yet."

"Well, she will be."

"If she survives the council vote."

"I suggest you stop talking about her death as if it's imminent," I hissed. "You've witnessed the way she's interacted with all of us. The way she's integrated herself between both worlds."

Hunter cocked his head to the side. "But that doesn't mean anything has changed in the eyes of the others. We love to play games. Toy with gormless mortals."

I opened my mouth, but Quentin stood beside me and cut me off. "I've knocked you on your ass once already. Do you want to make it a second time?"

Hunter was quicker than Quentin and the electric blue of his aura struck her directly in the chest, throwing her back into the wall.

Larkin and Sloan jumped to their feet, rushing to her, and I turned to my brother, but Dad and Erik got there first. Bouts of copper and red fighting with blue. I threw my aura into the mix.

Hunter disappeared from view before appearing next to Quentin.

"Stay away from her!" I roared.

Rather than attack him, I placed a thin wall of my aura between them. Quentin's golden tendrils cradled her. A slender trickle of blood ran leisurely from a cut in her hairline.

"I just want to talk," he crooned. "You were much more pliable when you had an audience in front of you at the facility."

"What do you want, Hunter?" she snapped.

"What would you do for my brother?"

The question caught us all off guard. It was a strange way to phrase it. When I was younger, I might have believed that Hunter was looking out for me. Now, I was suspicious why he wanted to know her intentions.

"Sorry?" Quentin asked, propping herself up properly.

"You heard me, Quentin Scott. What would you do for Grayson?"

"What game are you playing now?" I asked, trying to understand his reasoning.

Hunter looked at me, feigning innocence. "You think I can't have your best interests at heart? Protection is my responsibility, little brother."

Erik put a hand on my arm, keeping me back.

"Are you going to answer my question?" Hunter asked, turning back to Quentin.

Her gaze flicked to me before returning to him. "Anything," she answered confidently. "I would do anything for Gray."

"Such devotion is admirable. I hope you understand that marriage sometimes wears that away to nothing," he replied, throwing a glance at Larkin. "Mabel sends her love, Larkin."

"Mabel can choke. How she still exists when others are leaving us is beyond me," she bit back.

"I really should get back to her. I'm grateful she told me of this little get together."

Mabel was going to face my chaos soon. If Hunter even thought about trying to bring her into this family, he would be met with resistance.

"But next time, an invitation for us both would be appreciated," he continued.

Once he'd left, I strode over to Quentin, ushering Sloan and Larkin out of the way. Pulling my bound into my arms, I brushed my finger across her cut, and she winced and pulled away. Superficial wound that would heal in a few minutes.

"That was a strange turn of events," Erik muttered. "He's losing the vote, and he knows it, but I thought he was coming around to the idea."

"Archer has probably been whispering in his ear again," Quen said. "He's not happy about this arrangement."

"If he doesn't learn to keep his nose—"

"I'll speak to him," Larkin said. "Try to figure out what he's up to." She sat on her knees, staring at the space where her ex-husband had occupied moments ago and voiced what we were all thinking. "I don't trust Hunter, so the more we know, the better chance we have to stop whatever he's planning."

THIRTY-NINE

QUENTIN

Skipping lunch, I slumped back in my office chair and read Gareth's email for the third time. Spotify blared a collection of rock music as I skimmed through the simpering words and swapped the screen for the document. Gareth was afraid to correct the work we'd done for the paper, but some polite suggestions still littered the page, and I was grateful that he tried.

Researchers from the other floors had been copied into the email, but I'd only received data from three of them. Resentment was rife, and I tried to brush it off, but it bothered me. I didn't ask for divinity. I didn't expect to fall in love with one of the elite. And yet, I didn't blame them because I would have been furious if our positions were swapped.

When my intuition twisted in my stomach, I didn't bother to look up. I didn't sense a threat and assumed Gray or Flynn were stopping in to see me.

"Scott?"

The voice surprised me, and when I looked up, Larkin glided into my office before taking a seat opposite me.

"Hey. What's up?" I asked, turning the music down so it was barely audible.

"I thought we could chat."

The last conversation we had one-on-one was about her using my gift. We weren't a pair who usually sought each other out but were thrown together, thanks to circumstances.

"I was about to revise the paper, but I can talk," I said, curious why she searched for me.

The tension that resided between us from the first time we met had eased. Her sour mood, I realised, was more an influence of Hunter and years of abuse than a facet of her personality. She was a strong woman who protected herself in the best way she knew how, when no one else would.

"I wanted to check that you're sure about all this," she said as I turned away from the screen to give her my attention.

"About being a God?"

She let out a small laugh. "Not that bit. Unfortunately, you don't have a choice about that."

"So I've learned."

There were a few moments of silence before she said, "I meant about marrying Grayson."

I stared across at her. My engagement ring sat on my left ring finger. In quiet moments, I found myself admiring the piece of jewellery and wondering how Gray had created something so perfect. "I'm sure," I replied. "Why are you asking? What did you learn from Archer?"

"Nothing much," she said, brow furrowing. "Our relationship is a little strained and he wouldn't let me in the house."

Twisting the ring, I mulled her words before I replied. "What's the worst he could do?"

"Archer? Or Hunter?"

"You know them both better than I do."

"Unfortunately." Larkin sighed. "Archer is vengeful. He's been wronged a lot over his existence. His gift made him think he could figure out who was lying to him, but as you've seen, gifts can be fickle. They can work with us when they want, and at other times, they offer no advantage. He's fixated on getting revenge and somehow he's aligned himself with Hunter, though I can't understand how."

"It's a recent development?"

"Archer wanted to be part of the project and caused a fuss in the lower heavens. We had to clean it up. Hunter extended the invitation in order to keep some peace. Archer can cause issues if he wanted to, but Hunter is the dangerous one," she continued. "It was difficult to understand what he was planning when I was with him. Now we're not under the same roof, it's impossible."

That didn't help my predicament, but I would much rather know that Larkin was away from him than have them still married so she could gather intel. We would find another way.

"I'm glad we finally divorced. That I'm free." Larkin's gaze slowly lifted. "I never said thank you for what you did. You helped me get out when no one else could. I'll never be able to repay you for that."

"You don't need to. I didn't do it to gain any favours."

She nodded her head. "I took marriage seriously. I thought he would be my eternity."

It was a strange sight every time I saw her so vulnerable and honest.

"How does dating even work as a God?" I asked. I knew she wasn't ready to jump into that pool yet, but I didn't want her to dwell on Hunter.

"Ugh." Larkin's beautiful features warped into disgust. "It's a nightmare. You know everyone or everyone knows you and so you've seen them in their awkward phase."

"Sounds awful."

"It is."

"Would you ever consider a mortal? Because James…" I trailed off.

"If Hunter doesn't want to murder me now, he definitely would if I dated a mortal."

"Forget Hunter. Would you?"

"It's complicated, Scott. Gray took a tremendous risk. Mortals die. We can live forever. Imagine getting attached to someone that deeply to know that one day they would leave you."

I chewed on my lip. "I guess that would get complicated."

A bouquet of yellow tulips materialised on the desk between us, and I sighed. Larkin picked one up, twirling the stem in her fingers.

"Did something happen between you and Archer?" she asked curiously.

"Nothing. He likes to mess with Gray, and I'm worried Gray will actually murder him one day if he doesn't stop, but Archer won't listen."

"He's a handful," she said fondly. "Always has been. Even Elara struggled to get him to listen."

"Did you know her?" I asked, ignoring the email notification that came up on the monitor.

"Yes. Elara worked with Gray, so I knew her. Soft soul. Quiet woman. Archer's opposite until you got under her skin. She asked for my permission to date Archer."

"Because you were with him before Hunter."

"Exactly. And she didn't want to upset any of the elite."

"Did they have any children?"

"No. I think that was the plan, but then…" Larkin trailed off.

Things changed and their children would have been in the firing line for not being pure-blooded deities.

"I feel for him," I admitted. "He hasn't had it easy, and I wish I could help, but he's an idiot."

"He'll heal. Archer talks a lot, but I've never seen him do anything truly vicious. Gray, on the other hand… Just remember what your darling fiancé is capable of."

If I thought Gray was becoming soft, I was sorely mistaken. Some tulips appeared in the house and Gray lost his control, threatening to rip Archer in two.

"Hard to forget when he's such a hothead."

Larkin snorted. "At least you won't have to deal with Archer at the wedding."

Elva and Ignacio decided not to wait. They'd kept their relationship hidden for so long that they were happy to finally make it official.

"That's probably for the best," I mumbled.

"You'll see how we do things."

"Should I be worried?"

"Not at all. We love a good party."

"I've seen that. The gifting balls have been pure extravagance."

"Oh, if you thought that was bad, what do you think Erik is like with a wedding? That's his forte. Not that he's getting the chance this weekend."

"Dear Gods."

The laughter erupted from the both of us, echoing around the room.

"What's so funny?"

I raised my head to see my fiancé walking through the door towards us.

"Just enlightening Scott about what Erik will be like at this wedding," Larkin answered, tossing her hair over her shoulder.

Gray let out a groan and nudged me out of my seat, taking it himself and pulling me between his legs. My ass perched on his thigh as I leaned my body against his.

"Think of a kid in a candy store," Gray told me, "but ten times worse."

"That's why they refused to have him run the service."

"I'm not surprised."

"I don't understand," I said, feeling left out of the secret.

Gray's fingers brushed along my side. "Any Gods that have a responsibility for love can sanction a marriage. Erik is known for not being able to keep his shit together when he starts."

Larkin rolled her eyes. "It's like a drug to him, so his aura is out of control, and at the last one—"

"The last one." Gray picked up the story. "He couldn't stop giggling."

"Has he asked you yet?"

Another groan from Gray that reverberated in his chest. "Of course he has," Gray answered. He dropped his head against mine and pressed his lips to my hair. "Please don't give in to him."

Rearing back, I said, "He wants to conduct our ceremony, doesn't he?"

"Yes. And I said no, but then said the decision is yours, so let me plead my case." Gray cupped one side of my face, turning my head until I looked him in the eye. "Erik, my little brother, has been a pain in the ass for our entire relationship. Before our relationship even started. I've never met someone so invested in something that technically has nothing to do with him. Please tell him no so we can have a peaceful day."

I covered his hand with my own. "You can't be serious."

"I am deadly serious."

Turning my head away, I looked at Larkin, who was stifling her laughter. "Larkin?"

"Erik never approved of my marriage, so he didn't offer to conduct the wedding," she explained.

"He's never done it for family? Grayson, we can't say no to him."

"Fuck you, Larkin," Gray spat, but it didn't seem as harsh as usual. "Why couldn't you just lie?"

"Because I like to see you suffer."

My hand slipped around his neck, playing with the hairs on the nape, and he relaxed.

"Fine," Gray muttered. "But you have no idea what you're unleashing."

"Have you set a date?" Larkin asked curiously.

"We haven't been engaged for very long," I answered.

"Gods don't hang around, Scott."

Gray rubbed my side, warming the skin beneath my shirt. "I

think we'll wait until Quentin gets her acceptance."

"He's dragging his feet," Larkin said, getting onto hers and brushing her skirt down. "He knows the vote will swing in your favour. Just be patient. There's only so long he can hold off calling the council meeting when everyone is waiting to welcome you home."

Her words brought a comfort that eased the constant knot in my stomach. I'd discussed it with Gray, the way I fit in amongst the elite and lower Elysians. How Elysia was beginning to feel like home away from home. The waiting made me antsy, as if we might tip back towards uncertainty again, but I continued to spend time with the elite when I could and steered clear of the likes of Aria, deciding not to make things worse.

"Scott," Larkin said as she walked away from us, towards the office door. "You can count on my vote."

FORTY

GRAYSON

The rabble moved across the heavens and was so loud it wouldn't have surprised me if the mortals we resided over could hear us. It had been years since we had a wedding and even those who weren't invited had taken the celebrations into the streets.

"You know, it really should have been me who conducted the ceremony," Erik huffed, eyeing the minor God who'd taken his role for the afternoon.

We were at Elva and Ignacio's reception, held at Ig's estate. His minimalist home was crowded with guests, flowers, and warmth. The party spilled out onto the grounds of his estate where drinks were being passed around while Gods mingled and celebrated. After all the deaths we'd suffered, a wedding was a welcome distraction.

Sloan raised an eyebrow at her husband's comment and Quen tugged on my hand. I looked down at her with a tight jaw and sighed.

This conversation had gone on for days. In every available moment, Quen bothered me with it. At first, I dismissed her easily as she raised the topic in bed. But when she broached it while in the lab and elbow

deep in tissue culture, I knew this was something she wanted, and I was powerless to deny her.

"Go ahead," I grumbled.

She beamed up at me before looking at Erik. "We'd love for you to conduct ours when we finally decide to get married."

His blue eyes grew wide, and he shifted his attention to me. "Are you being serious? Because you told me I had no chance in this millennium."

"Yeah, well." I sniffed indignantly. "This one has a soft spot for you."

Erik grinned and pulled her into a hug. "I promise to be on my best behaviour."

"So many blatant lies being told."

Quen swatted at me, and I pulled her body back into mine. The place was swarming with Gods and I almost decided not to attend after the dinner with my parents, but Quentin gave me a look that said my existence wouldn't be worth it if I forced her to miss Elva's wedding.

I wrapped my arms around her waist so that her back pressed against my chest. My chin rested on her shoulder and Quen let out a quiet laugh as my beard tickled her skin. Elva and Ig took to the centre of the grounds for their first dance and we stood off to the side, watching them with the rest of the Elysians.

"You're glowing," I whispered into Quentin's ear.

"You look handsome too, bubba," she replied.

"No, darling. You're glowing."

She looked down and then snapped her head back towards me.

"Many people are wishing them success in their marriage," I

explained. I jerked my head towards Erik, next to us, emitting his own red glow, and she relaxed against me again.

"This is going to take a lot of getting used to."

"You'll get there. You have time."

Leaning down, I pressed a kiss against the warm skin of her cheek and swayed us to the music as we watched husband and wife twirl around in the grass. Elva's tinkling laugh rang out loud, and before long, others were invading, stepping into the space to join them. Quen stayed glued to me until Sloan left to check on the children.

"May I steal Quentin for a dance?" Erik asked me brightly.

I was reluctant to let her go. Unwilling for anyone else to take up her time, but she turned around and gave me a quick kiss.

"Promise we won't cause too much trouble," she said to me.

I narrowed my eyes. "The pair of you don't know how to behave." My gaze fell on my brother, who was bouncing on the balls of his feet. "Look after her, Erik."

He grinned and pulled Quen away from me, both still glowing as they danced together.

I went back inside to grab myself a drink rather than finding another dance partner. Glass in hand, I leaned against the exterior of the house and watched them. She always drew my eye. In a crowd of a million people, I would fixate on Quentin.

In truth, Erik was the only person I truly trusted with her. I knew he would keep her safe if I wasn't around. It pained me to admit it, but Quentin was right when she said Erik liked her more than me. The last person he'd been this taken with was his wife.

The pair of them giggled as they danced, completely out of sync with each other, and a smile tugged at my lips. Without a doubt, this was where she belonged and I was glad to see her so relaxed in the presence of Gods.

Let them see her for how she truly was.

Perfection.

Unfortunately, my peace didn't last for long. Hunter tread across the patio and joined me. When I made to move away, he grabbed my arm. I refused to make a scene, but I couldn't stand to be around him, unable to forgive him for hurting Quentin again.

"What would you do for her, Grayson?"

This fucking weird question again. He asked this when he appeared at dinner.

"What would you do for her?" Hunter repeated.

"Anything," I bit back without hesitation.

My answer was the same as Quen's. I glanced over at her again, still carefree with Erik. With my golden girl, I had seen it all. I'd seen her so fucking angry, crying and broken, and overjoyed. Over the past few months, I'd come to terms with the fact that this woman was my everything and I would do anything she asked me to if it meant keeping her safe and happy. It was why I asked—begged—her to become my wife.

"Why?" Hunter asked.

When I looked at him, he watched her, and I suppressed the urge to rip his eyes out.

"She's my soulbound, Hunter." I could have sworn that the share of the brains was split between me and Erik.

"So, if you weren't bound, would she mean nothing to you?"

"She would still mean everything to me."

Long before I knew of what she was or what existed between us,

I was drawn to Quentin. Her fire and chaos reflected my own. She did not fear me. She longed to bury herself in my darkness in order to relinquish her own.

"That is a very big claim, little brother," Hunter commented, refusing to take his eyes off her.

"What do you want?"

"She draws people in. She's become quite popular."

He jerked his chin in her direction and I saw what he meant. It wasn't just Erik with her, but Bexley had joined. Dionne. Andreas. Flynn. Quentin tipped her head back, long dark locks cascading down her back as she laughed, and for a moment, I was lost in how beautiful she was, surrounded by the golden hue of her aura.

My golden girl.

"You sound surprised," I said, voice thick with emotion.

"I am."

I wasn't. She could be charming when she wasn't trying to rip your head off about something or other.

"Her existence may not pose as much of a threat as I originally thought," Hunter said, continuing to watch her.

There was no spark of hope. I couldn't guarantee that Hunter wasn't trying to lull me into a false sense of security. "I told you she belongs with us up here."

"So you did."

"The council is growing restless, as is lower Elysia. How much longer do you intend to keep us waiting?"

"I will call the council when the time is right, Grayson. From my understanding, you have little to be concerned about. She's exceeded my expectations with the project and with integrating."

I narrowed my eyes as he walked away, joining the thick of the crowd and pasting on the fake smile that so many fell for. I downed the rest of my drink, ready to join my fiancée and her friends, when Malachi stepped in front of me.

"Mal." It was almost a growl. "Can I help you?"

"I wanted to talk to you."

"Then get talking because, and it may come as no surprise, I would rather spend my night with Quentin and not you."

"I saw Hunter."

"And?"

"Before the wedding. He was talking to Archer. They were in an argument over something."

"What did you hear?"

"Nothing, really. I couldn't risk hanging around, but Hunter said something about making good on their deal."

I knew he was up to something from the moment Quen was passed over to Archer, but I didn't know exactly what it was. What could benefit them both? They weren't even fighting on the same side when it came to Quentin.

"Why are you telling me this?" I asked Mal. "You'll probably be removed from your position if Hunter finds out."

"Because I like Quentin and she deserves to come home and be with the rest of us. If Hunter's trying to manipulate the vote—"

Hunter was right, and I'd always known it. People liked her. People wouldn't do things for me because of me. But they would do things for me because of my association with Quentin. It hadn't escaped my notice how much more welcome I'd been around my kin when Quen was by my side. We'd secure her life and then work on making the council ours.

"With Archer?" I questioned. "That wouldn't make any sense. Archer isn't part of the council and Hunter seems to be coming around to our way of thinking."

I couldn't guarantee that, but our conversation had been the smallest step in the right direction.

"I don't understand it either, but you have to admit it's unusual."

"Whatever they're planning, whatever deal they have, I doubt it has anything to do with Quentin's existence. I've no doubt he's been trying to get Hunter to stop the impending wedding."

Archer had continued to send her flowers and his outbursts concerned my bond with Quentin. He wanted to pull us apart and he would try everything, including running to Hunter but it was impossible. There was nothing they could do to break what fate had gifted us.

"Do you think he will?"

"He can try." I laughed. "But it won't work. I'm going to marry that woman even if it's the last thing I do."

Malachi relaxed. "I expect an invitation."

"She wouldn't let me miss you off the list," I explained. "Let's join the madness."

We walked back onto the grounds where our kin danced wildly and without care of what they looked like. My presence cut a course through the small group and the smile that lit up Quentin's face when she saw me set my chest on fire.

"Enjoying yourself?" I asked, taking her into my arms.

She hummed. "Are you going to dance?"

"You all seem to have that part under control."

There were some curious eyes from people who'd heard her comment. I wasn't known for being the most social God. While I attended events, I was happy to stick to the wall and observe from a safe distance.

"Please." Quentin reached up and kissed me. "Or I'll be stuck with Flynn all night." I frowned, and she laughed. "Is that a yes?" she asked.

"Yes, trouble. I'll stay and dance with you."

Things would change soon enough. My reputation as a sulking God with minimal patience would fractionally soften because, with Quentin permanently by my side, it would be difficult to keep every sharp edge I'd accumulated over millennia. But as I joined her, watching her sway to the music and laugh with Erik, minor Gods backed away, giving us space.

Quentin was safety and warmth. She was a symbol of what so many people had lost and thought they would never have again. And I was the symbol of what led them to that belief.

They left a core group of us together, and I accepted the fact, again, that Quen would forever be the reason anyone ever gave me a chance. Then we could build on our future together. Quentin was the priority, but I hadn't given up on my ambition. My brother wouldn't maintain his position for long.

FORTY-ONE

GRAYSON

"I look forward to the day you ascend and can leave this forsaken job behind," I grumbled.

Quentin sat in between my legs, laptop open in front of her as she corrected the paper on the screen. The sun streamed weakly through the window of our estate as she satisfied her mind by working.

"The reason I work is so that I can ascend," she said in return, squinting at the screen.

I growled in her ear, "Take a break."

My lips skated across her neck and she swallowed hard, getting distracted. The skin on her bare thighs transformed with goosebumps as I ran my palms along them. Her fingers froze over the keys as I inched the shirt further up her legs.

"Are you wearing my favourite pair?" I whispered, biting the shell of her ear. "You look devastating in black lace."

My favourite view was of my bound in my colour. Lace along her hips and breasts, like a gift being presented to me, awaiting my favourite form of destruction. There was so much satisfaction

in ripping away the delicate threads of her underwear and savagely claiming her as mine.

She relaxed back against my chest as I bunched the shirt around her hips and a hand dipped to the apex of her legs, expecting to be met with material. Instead, I found the warmth of her bare pussy. Dropping my head against the nape of her neck, I hummed my approval. My tongue dragged along the smooth skin, and she whimpered. My fingers left her pussy, licking them before returning them to their previous position. She jerked slightly, but the work had truly been abandoned.

"Were you expecting me?" I questioned.

"You always get your way," she breathed as my other hand slid up the shirt to play with her nipple. It had already hardened in anticipation. Glorious was the only way to describe the way her body reacted to mine.

My thumb brushed against her clit, pressing down and circling the bundle of nerves. "And this is all about me, isn't it?"

Her head dropped back against my chest. For someone so wilful, my girl gave up so easily when I put my hands on her.

She hummed in response.

"Let's get you out of this." I took my hands off her and tugged the shirt over her head, leaving her naked in front of me. "Much better."

"I'm meant to be working," she argued weakly.

"Mandatory masturbatory break."

"With a helpful aid."

Her laughter turned into a moan when I pinched her nipple, rolling it between my thumb and index finger. She arched her back, letting her hands drop between her legs.

"Don't you dare," I warned her, but let my aura out to move them away. Two black tendrils pinned her hands to the bed. "You're my toy, Quentin. I get to play with you how I want, when I want."

"Please don't tease," she whined.

I kissed along the back of her shoulders as she shifted on the bed, trying to get some sort of relief.

"But if I don't tease you, I don't get to hear that delicious sound you make," I explained.

My fingers ghosted along her inner thighs, barely grazing her pussy as they moved upwards.

"Gray, please," she begged.

"You really are impatient this morning. See how all work and no play makes Quentin a frustrated girl?"

She nodded her head obediently.

"Tell me why I shouldn't keep you waiting like you do me."

"I always give in," she answered quickly.

She did. There wasn't a single morning or night where Quentin didn't wrap herself around my body, screaming my name to Elysia. She gave me everything until she was spent and still allowed me to use her, trying to keep up with my pace and needs.

"I'll need more than that, golden girl," I said, moving my hand away from her breast so it could wrap around her throat. I felt her pulse thundering under my fingertips, reminding me she was alive and well in my care.

"What do you want?"

My fingers dragged along her clit, and she whimpered. I played that sound on repeat in silent moments and drove myself mad. The pure dependency her body had on me to help reach her high. The unadulterated need that such a small sound conveyed.

"I want you to tell me I'll be your priority when this project is officially closed," I said. "You'll take time off and we'll travel the world together. You have been testing me and I am not patient."

"I promise," she whispered.

I let a finger dip lower through her wet folds and push inside her. A satisfactory moan escaped her.

"You're a liar," I said, squeezing the sides of her throat gently. "You say whatever you need to in order to get what you want."

I added another finger inside her, thumb stroking against her clit. Quen's hips bucked as she ground against my hand.

"You're the same," she breathed.

Tipping her head back, she looked at me with golden eyes. Her aura slowly came out to play, marbling with my own. Light and shadows danced across her perfect body. For a Goddess, Quentin was utterly sinful.

"I'm worse," I reminded her, leaning down for a kiss.

It was hungry and messy. A true sign she let go of control. Whenever she submitted to me, stopped fighting, it was a reminder of her trust. No matter what had happened in my past, Quentin trusted me with everything she was.

Her mind.

Her body.

Her soul.

She rode my hand; the wet sounds of her arousal filling our bedroom. I pressed harder at her throat, bruising the skin beneath it before her walls clenched around my digits and my name spilled from her lips as a quiet prayer. As her body relaxed against mine, I pulled my fingers from her pussy and released her from my grip.

That beautiful post-sex haze hung around her and her mouth popped open, waiting to clean my fingers. Who would believe this fierce woman could become so docile?

I placed my fingers into my mouth and groaned when the sweet taste of her spread over my tongue. She turned around, sitting up on her knees and wrapping her arms around my neck. Taking my fingers out of my mouth, I pushed them past her lips and let her taste the remnants of herself mixed with my saliva.

"You always have to have it your way," I muttered, enjoying the feeling of her tongue swirling around my digits. "Go clean up and get back to work."

"What about you?" she asked when I removed my fingers from her mouth.

"I can wait."

"You said you weren't patient."

"I didn't say how long I would wait. You better work quickly."

She grinned, making a grab for my shirt I'd discarded earlier, but I got there first.

"You don't need this," I told her.

"You're going to have me work naked?"

"Perhaps I still want to play."

She bit her bottom lip before moving away and walking into her bathroom. I laid back on the bed and closed my eyes.

There would be a time when this was life without the impending dread that followed. These moments wouldn't be sparks of light and joy to escape darkness. One day, she wouldn't need to chase away the panic with a high, because ecstasy would constitute her entire life. I would make sure of it.

Quentin's weight joined me on the bed and her lips brushed against mine softly.

"I love you," she said, crawling back to her laptop.

Sitting up, we resumed our position again. My fingers traced the numbers, one, four, three, down the length of her spine.

"I need my USB. Can you grab it from my jacket, please?" she asked, pointing over to the black jacket that hung over the back of a chair in the room.

"Whatever you wish, Goddess," I replied, getting out from behind her. It gave my dick a chance to calm down before completely ruining her morning work schedule.

Quentin rolled her eyes as I fished through one pocket to find nothing. I stuck my hand into the other pocket and winced at the burning sensation that spread across my fingertips, retracting and looking at the skin.

"What the fuck do you have in your pocket?" I asked, diving back in and grabbing something small and dry.

This time when I pulled my hand out, I found wilted flower heads that made my stomach drop to my feet. I hissed, dropping them on the ground and rubbing my hand against my sweatpants.

"Why do you have those?" I asked sharply.

Quentin pushed herself off the bed and joined me. She stooped down to pick them up, but I pulled her away before she had the chance.

"Don't!" I barked.

"It's fine. They're just flowers."

"Oleander. Where did you get this? Don't make me ask again."

Quen pushed herself out of my grip. "Emmanuel Teixeira had

them in his lab."

"Quentin." I was losing my patience with her and she could tell.

"James and I broke into his lab. I have no idea why he had them in there. He must have some sort of side project in the works with Imran because he doesn't need them."

"Neither do you!" I ran my hands down my face and then instantly pulled them away. "You stay away from this stuff. It's dangerous for us. It hampers our divinity. My guess is they've managed to enclose it in the cuffs somehow."

"If it's so dangerous, why do you have it in Elysia?"

"You brought it up here."

"That's not what I meant. You have it in greenhouses in Elysia."

"We don't. Hunter had to harvest it from Earth before we destroyed the demigods." Her face paled, and I towered over her. "Oleander struggles to grow in Elysia. What have you seen and where?"

"Archer has it in his home," she told me. "I thought he took it from the greenhouse."

"It can't grow."

Quentin shook her head. "You can't touch it?"

"No. It burns, but it's only lethal if ingested or enters the bloodstream."

"Tobias," she said, closing her eyes. "He was at Archer's place and they wouldn't let me hear the conversation. Archer has them in his bedroom. It has to be Oleander. When I was at the casino, Tobias' hand was burnt. I couldn't understand how he could be injured, but he was quick to move it out of view."

Tendrils of my aura shot out, punching straight through the walls and the floor of the room. Quentin gasped and stumbled backwards from me, holding onto the desk, and I tried to rein in my temper.

"Why didn't you say something sooner?" I asked, gritting my teeth together.

"I forgot. I didn't know they were dangerous." She was inching back towards her laptop.

"You're not going to find the answers on Google or Wikipedia, Quentin."

She froze, and I regretted the words. Quentin coped with all situations by gaining as much knowledge as possible and I'd made fun of it.

"You share the same heavens and are so obsessed with yourselves, you didn't realise someone was hiding a lethal plant up there?" she said, biting back. "Don't talk to me like I'm stupid."

"I'm not." I crossed the space towards her.

"Fix our home."

Muttering under my breath, I repaired the wall and floor before Quentin let me hold her again.

"I'm sorry." Apologies were becoming a speciality. "Archer took them from his lab and back to Elysia."

"Why?" she asked. "He can't take care of them himself. He's getting Tobias to help him, and Tobias knows exactly what he's dealing with. Do you think the other minor Gods know?"

If Quentin wasn't in my arms, staring up at me with inquisitive eyes as she tried to piece together the puzzle, I would have brought the house down to its foundations.

"He's planning a war," I said firmly. "There's no doubt the others would know. If they don't, they will soon. How much did he have?"

"One little planter and the plants didn't look healthy, Gray. He can't start a war with that." She chewed her bottom lip. "But Archer and Hunter were in the lab that night. Hunter knows he's taking them. He was instructing Archer. Hunter's the one who's pulling the strings."

"Malachi heard them talking about a deal. What the fuck are they playing at?"

"I don't know, but this can't be good, right? It could just be preparation for when he calls the vote?" The colour had drained from her face.

Hunter and Archer had never seen eye to eye, but suddenly they were inseparable. The pair of them were having secret conversations and whereas I'd been brushing it off as nothing more than trivial matters, a deep churning started in my gut that told me I was missing a piece of the puzzle.

I hoped my misstep wouldn't cost us everything we worked towards.

FORTY-TWO

GRAYSON

Erik ran his hands through his hair and pulled violently at the pale blonde strands.

If I had it my way, I would have gone straight to lower Elysia and dragged Archer back here, but Quen stopped me. Her logic won out over my rage and I pulled in the only other person I trusted.

Quen abandoned her work to join us. I wasn't sure if it was her drive to find answers or if she didn't trust that I would stick to the plan instead of going rogue.

"It might be nothing," Erik mumbled into his hands as he ran them down his face.

"Do you really believe that?" I asked him. "I might have thought the same if Hunter hadn't been there with Archer, picking flowers like they were on a date. Oleander, Erik."

"Oleander is needed for the cuffs. He might be working on a project. He had them produce the collar."

"The collar was created down on Earth! Hunter made the mortals do that dirty work!"

Larkin's brow furrowed. Her presence was thanks to Quen. She

was the best bet at an answer. Hunter might have been our brother, but we'd spent little time with him. She had been his wife. His confidant.

"Stop pacing," I said, my eyes following Quentin as she walked up and down the room.

"It helps."

Erik suddenly shot up from the seat and grabbed a pen and notepad. "The minor Gods who've passed recently, do you remember them all?"

"Phillipe," Larkin started.

We worked through the list while Quen hovered nervously. There was little she was able to contribute to this discussion, and I would have preferred for her to busy herself with work or visit Sloan. Answers would not come easily here, which meant peace would not settle in her soul.

When we pulled apart, the sheet was filled with names.

"What are you trying to figure out?" Quen asked. "Do you think there are more people involved in this than Hunter and Archer?"

Erik waved her off, staring at his list, and she clamped her mouth shut.

"Does it strike you as a coincidence that these minor Gods were in favour of cleansing Elysia of the demigods?" Erik said eventually, straightening up and turning back to us.

I snatched the paper out of his hand and looked at the names. "Are you sure?"

Memories grew hazy when years stretched out behind us.

"Most of them, if not all of them, helped to round them up," Larkin confirmed, staring over my shoulder at the list.

My brain connected the dots quickly. "You don't think it's an accident that they've ceased to exist?"

"Oleander is being brought up to Elysia. Archer's attempting to grow it up here and minor Gods who fell on the other side of the argument suddenly start disappearing *en masse*."

"You think Archer's picking them off one by one?" I asked.

"And there's a chance that Hunter might already know about it?" Quen added.

"I don't think Hunter would be involved," I pointed out. "I'm the last person to jump to his defence, but he seemed genuinely concerned when he realised what was going on."

"Archer's doing all this behind his back?" Quen asked.

"*If* Archer is doing anything at all," Larkin pointed out. "You're going to both get in trouble if you keep going down this line without evidence. You're so close to freedom, Quentin. Do not throw it away over a wild goose chase."

"What if we found proof?"

"How do you expect to do that?"

"Archer had the planter in his room. If we showed people he's been growing it." Quen glanced at me. "Do you think we could convince Tobias to admit what they've been up to? He's involved in it even if it's just to help grow the oleander."

I shrugged as the chaos rolled through me in violent waves. "We can make him talk."

"Can't you both hold off until after the vote?" Larkin asked, looking uncomfortable. "Hunter won't have anything to hold against you after that."

Erik shook his head. "There's oleander in the heavens again. Who's to say who or how it's being misused? Who's to say one of us won't be next?"

"This is all down to me," Quen told him, digging her nails into my palm as she balled her fist. "You don't have to worry about Sloan or the children, Erik. I won't mention you. Or Larkin."

"And you must be mad if you think I'd let you take the fall if anything goes wrong here," I said viciously, staring down at her. "This will be on my shoulders."

"You need to come up with a plan. You can't exactly knock on Archer's door," Quentin said.

"Do you have a better idea?" I asked.

Even as I said it, a plan already formed. Quentin was right. If I turned up on Archer's doorstep, a fight would ensue. I'd draw negative attention, and Archer, the slippery snake that he was, would twist it into his favour and paint me as the detriment to the heavens again.

"You need to find him," I said, turning to Quen.

"Why me?"

"You're the object of his fascination at the moment."

No part of me was comfortable putting her up as bait, but it was the quickest way to find the root of the problem. If Archer was occupied with Quentin, then it gave us a clear shot to search his home and grounds without distraction. I'd pull in Dionne and Marcel to help before going after Tobias.

"But I never seek him out, Gray. It's going to look strange if I suddenly try to find him and engage in conversation. What would I even talk to him about?"

"Tell him you see his point. That you're reconsidering the engagement."

"No!" Quen's voiced was echoed with Erik's.

I shook my head. "It would keep him preoccupied."

"He'd see through the lie straight away," she hissed.

"What's your suggestion?"

Silence engulfed the room, and the anxiety washed over her in waves until the shaking started at the centre of her chest. Pure chaos. While I revelled in it, there was only a certain amount that Quentin could handle. We'd pushed her limits over the last few months and this was yet another unexpected twist.

My hands held onto her upper arms, offering her some stability.

"You're okay," I said softly. "We don't need to figure this out tonight, but we just need to come up with a plan."

"I can go again," Larkin said. "He wouldn't let me into his house the last time I tried to talk to him, but now I'm wondering if there was something more behind that. If he has cultivated those flowers in Elysia. On his grounds."

"Could you imagine what Elara would say?" Erik whispered, shaking his head. "It would devastate her."

I gritted my teeth together, trying not to imagine what my old friend might say if she knew her husband had corrupted their grounds with a deathly flower so he could carry out his murderous rampage in her name.

"Can't you get in touch with Dionne?" Quen suggested. "If Archer's down here, she could check the house?"

"I'm not sure Bexley would be pleased if we pulled her girlfriend into this mess," Larkin argued.

Quentin's shoulders slumped. She understood the bond between siblings and the difficulty of wanting to breach boundaries. I'd have sold Hunter for a stick of gum whereas I would lay my life on the line for Erik.

"We can wait," Erik said.

I narrowed my eyes. "Erik."

"We can wait," he said, more forcefully this time. "The project is almost done. Hunter won't be able to delay the vote forever. If we rush into all this straight away, it'll raise suspicion and we could ruin Quentin's chances of survival."

"We're not burying the issue," Larkin agreed. "But we've always put our own first." She shared a look with Quen. Whatever had transpired between the two and led to Larkin's divorce had left my ex-sister-in-law grateful to Quen. "We can keep an eye on the situation and gather evidence to bring to the council once she's safe."

Holding Quen against me, I pressed a kiss to the top of her head. Everything I'd done over the past few months was to keep her alive. I'd lied, my ambition took a backseat, and I made myself somewhat palatable so I could talk to others about her.

Pushing past the darkness that pulsed inside me, I took in a deep breath. As Erik said, we had time. The vote would happen soon and Quentin would be safe. Once that happened, I would tuck her away in a far corner on Earth before we rattled the heavens with our revelations.

"You are my priority," I reminded Quen. "I don't want you to worry about this. Nothing has changed."

"Everything is changing."

"We'll get to the bottom of it," Larkin said, stepping towards us. "Don't give them the satisfaction of ruining your chances now."

Quentin nodded her head slowly, fist gripping tighter on my shirt. We were asking her to walk beside murderers and act as if nothing was wrong. It was a task we were versed in, but Quen was being thrown into the thick of it.

"Why don't you come back to mine?" Larkin suggested.

"No." I wasn't letting her leave my side.

Larkin fixed me with a stare. "It'll be good for her to be seen with people other than you. We'll laze by the pool and unwind from this mess."

"I think I'd like that," Quentin said before I could stamp out the ridiculous idea.

"We'll all go."

"No." She rubbed my arm gently. "I'm going to spend some time with Larkin. You are going to see your niece and nephews. We don't have to be attached at the hip."

My eye twitched. "We're not attached at the hip," I gritted out. "We're bound by souls."

She pressed a chaste kiss to my cheek, and I tried to catch her lips, but she pulled away.

"Spend time with your family," Quentin told me, still looking uncertain. "I'll be safe with Larkin."

Pulling away from me, she joined Larkin's side. The chaos still poured from Quen's form, but starting a fight now wouldn't help the situation. We'd discuss it when we were back on Earth.

"I'm trusting you, Larkin," I said, still staring down at Quentin.

She snorted. "First time for everything."

FORTY-THREE

QUENTIN

"I'm still decorating," Larkin said as she led me through her home. It was more modest than any of the others I'd walked through, but still put my family home to shame.

The walls were bare, and the rooms held little furniture. I couldn't help but peer through doors as she led us out to the garden.

"You haven't been here much to get started on decorating," I commented.

"It won't be long. I have lots of ideas for how I want the place to look. Hunter had the final say when we were married. I'd have burnt the place to the ground given half the chance."

I nodded, squinting as we stepped out into her garden. Larkin's grounds were unlike the rest. No stone statues or intricate topiary. Her gardens reminded me of the glossy images of LA mansions. A large pool took up the centre of the space and there were tennis courts and neat rose bushes.

"They're your flowers," I said, brushing my fingers against the petals.

"Yes, they are."

I sank onto a sun lounger, pulling my knees up to my chest, and Larkin perched on the edge.

"I hoped bringing you here might cheer you up. It's a little brighter than Gray's place."

"Sorry," I mumbled. "I appreciate you bringing me to your home."

"I can always take you back to him. But Gray can be a little intense and you looked like you needed some space."

"I love him."

"I'm not arguing that."

"He's doing the best he can, but he's not in my shoes, and sometimes I don't want to admit everything I'm thinking to him."

"Do you want to talk to me about it?" Larkin asked.

I chewed on my bottom lip, trying to untangle the mess of thoughts that had caught me in knots. "Everyone thinks I'm going to cause trouble and I've tried everything to show them I won't, but this is my fault."

"What is?"

"All these deaths."

"No, they—"

"They weren't happening at this rate before, Larkin." I rested my forehead against my knees and steadied my breathing. "If anyone else makes the connection that the Gods who are disappearing were against the demigods, it won't take long for people to point a finger at me."

"You don't know that."

Slowly, I raised my head. "Tell me it's not what you would have done a few weeks ago."

"I would have," she admitted.

I appreciated Larkin wouldn't bullshit me. There was no point hiding the truth, and I didn't hold it against her. If our roles were reversed, I would have been highly suspicious of her.

"It's not just that," I whispered. "I don't want anyone else getting in trouble because of me. Erik and Sloan have the kids to think about. Gray shouldn't have called him."

When I first landed back at Gray's place, I held a small grudge towards Erik for the lack of contact. But I understood he wanted to protect his wife and his children. They were the most important people in his life. I didn't want to cause tension between us by continuously being at the heart of fatal issues.

"This isn't your fault," Larkin said firmly. "I never imagined Archer would be capable of something like this. He's very skilled at lying, but murder isn't his style."

"Yeah, well, he's been glued to Hunter's hip recently. It's probably rubbed off on him."

"Hunter won't be content until he has everyone dancing to his tune, or he's destroyed them for defying him."

I opened my mouth to reply, but a bell rang through the house. Larkin's brow furrowed at the noise.

"Strange," she muttered, pushing herself from the lounger. "I wasn't expecting anyone. Are you okay if I answer the door?"

"Yeah. Go ahead."

She squeezed my shoulder with her slender fingers before walking back into the house.

I stretched my legs out and leaned back against the seat, trying to find some comfort. Anxiety was chaos. If this was what Grayson was attuned to, it was a miracle he functioned because the constant madness made it hard to breathe.

Closing my eyes, I focused on the feeling of the sun on my skin. The warmth was inviting, and I thought about the way we would resolve the issues as soon as the council meeting was done. We would hold all the cards if we could just make it to the vote.

"Quentin," Larkin called.

My eyes snapped open, and I twisted to look over my shoulder. Following Larkin from the bottom of the stairs and moving towards me was Mabel. She wiggled her fingers at me and flashed a fake smile.

"Hunter—" Larkin started.

"Oh, Larkin," Mabel trilled. "It's hardly your place to convey his messages. He sent me for a reason. He trusts me."

"He's using you."

"Green really isn't your colour, babe," Mabel said as I got to my feet. She looked at me. "Hunter's requested to see you."

"What for?" I asked.

"You'll see."

"I need to get Gray."

There was no way I was about to step in front of Hunter without Gray by my side. He could read the room better than I could and make sure I didn't mess up any further.

"Don't worry about Grayson. Hunter already went to see him. He'll be waiting for you."

I glanced at Larkin. "Will you come with me?"

Mabel huffed. "I don't think that's a good idea."

"Did he say she couldn't come?" I asked, seeking a loophole. "You don't have to," I said, turning to Larkin and realising my mistake. "I'll be fine."

I had no right to ask her to step foot back into a house that held awful memories for her and stand before a coward who'd created that situation.

"She can't," Mabel said, placing her hands on her hips. "You'll receive instructions soon, Larkin."

"Gray will be there," Larkin told me. "I'll see you as soon as you're done with him."

Nodding my head, I let Mabel wrap her fingers around my wrist before the neon pink clouded my vision. When it cleared away, we were standing in an office.

"You have some interesting choices for who you keep as company," Hunter said.

Mabel abandoned her post and joined his side behind the desk. But I wasn't concerned with either of them.

"What the fuck?" I asked, eyes landing on Gray.

He was sitting in a chair, looking suitably pissed off with a copper collar around his neck and wrists bound.

"Gray?" I walked over to him.

"He's fine," Hunter assured me. "He'll be freed as soon as we conclude matters."

"That's ridiculous. This isn't necessary."

"I don't trust either of you to keep your tempers in check if the vote goes against you."

A heavy weight settled in my stomach and I looked over my shoulder at Hunter. "You're calling the vote."

Fingers brushed against my hands and my attention was drawn back to Gray. "It's just until after the vote. He wouldn't agree to hold it without us being in the restraints. We'll be released from them before you know it, but you need to do this for now."

He didn't look happy with the arrangement and I wasn't convinced, either. After figuring out what Archer was up to and that Hunter was encouraging it, my distrust had grown to paramount proportions. But if we caused a scene before the vote, there was every possibility of people changing their minds. We'd worked too hard to watch it crumble now.

Hunter moved to me after Mabel handed him rings of copper. My jaw was locked as I raised my hands and let him lock the cuffs into place. When he opened the collar, I reared back, and he tutted. "You've been well-behaved so far. Don't ruin it now," he coaxed patronisingly.

The collar was something I hated. Out of Gray's hands it became a demeaning symbol, but I didn't move when Hunter approached me a second time and secured it around my neck.

Hunter moved a lock of stray hair away from my head. "That was easy. Wasn't it?"

The cuffs were heavy on my wrists, and instantly, something was missing. I reached for my aura and there was no response, leaving me with a deep, aching emptiness. No wonder Gray screamed the first time he came through the institute. I was utterly powerless. For all the times I cursed my divinity and the chaos it welcomed into my life, for all the times I wished I could go back to a dull mortal life, it was a part of who I was and being stripped of it left me lost.

"It's only temporary," Gray reminded me again, struggling to his feet.

"Have you let the others know?" Mabel asked, leaning back against the desk.

"You realise you don't have a seat on the council," Gray pointed out, lip curling in disgust. "Playing personal assistant to him might be cute, but don't expect a seat to the show."

"She'll be there," Hunter said, walking to the door of the office.

We fell into a procession. Hunter leading us from the house, Gray behind him and me and Mabel taking up the rear.

There were so many loose ends. This felt like another thread that had frayed, but it would be knotted and secured soon. I clung to that hope, that by the end of the night I would be surrounded by familiar faces who would welcome me home and fuck the rest of them.

Fuck everything, because I deserved a small amount of relief.

I waited for Hunter to stop us and transport us straight to the council chambers, but he continued walking through the streets.

"Where are we going?" I asked.

Elysia may not have been my home, but I knew we weren't headed in the right direction.

"To your vote."

"But the chambers are that way," I said, jerking my head backwards.

Mabel laughed, a chilling and tinkling sound. "We're not going to the council chambers."

Gray stopped, and I bumped into his back. He turned around and gestured me to his side. I wished Hunter had just left us in the collars because I wanted to grip Gray's hand and have him absorb all the chaos.

"I suggest you keep walking or you'll make it worse for yourselves," Hunter said, glancing over his shoulder. "You have people waiting for you. Weren't you both eager to get this over with?"

Gray didn't move. "Where are we going?"

"The park." Hunter sounded irritated. "This concerns the whole of Elysia, so I thought it would be better to have the vote in the open. No one can twist the truth then."

My heart beat so dangerously in my chest that it caused a thundering in my ears. In theory, Hunter's move made sense for us. If anything went badly, we were out in the open where nothing could be swept away under lies. But I didn't trust him and wish I could figure out how he benefitted from this.

"I appreciate being punctual, so we should move," he ordered.

Glancing up at Gray, I gave a slight nod. We could hardly stand in the street all afternoon and even if we tried to dig our heels in, Hunter could force us to wherever he'd chosen to hold the vote.

My feet hit the cobbled streets as we started walking again, marching towards the park. The trees rustled in the gentle breeze, but it wasn't the peaceful picture it usually was. The streets were lined with minor Gods and they focused on us. Dozens of eyes tracking every movement without relief.

Hunter strode ahead, and we followed behind him with no other choice.

The hairs on my arms stood on end, but I couldn't figure out what was happening. The vote should have happened in the chambers just like the first time. I wasn't naïve enough to believe Hunter had rolled out the welcome committee for the moment they reached their decision.

He stepped up onto a small dais that was erected in the park and when he spoke, his voice rang out clearly.

"My fellow Gods," he began, and a hush fell over the crowd. No more whispers. "I thank you for gathering here today at such short notice."

Did he expect to make a spectacle of the vote? There was no need to hide me now. The heavens knew all about me.

"As you are all aware, the relationship between the elite and minor Gods has been strained for several years."

The crowd grumbled around us, tension thickening the air. It hung like static electricity, waiting for the moment that something would spark it into a full fire.

"Many of you felt as if there has been no justice for the suffering you endured when the demigods were taken from us and I am inclined to agree."

Hunter looked in my direction. His eyes gave nothing away, but he would have to possess a soul to show any emotions.

"Recently, I've had the pleasure of speaking to many of you, including Archer."

To the left of the dais, Archer stood and quirked an eyebrow. He caught my eye and mouthed the word, *Sorry*. My heart sank and bile rose in my stomach.

This was it.

He'd got me to meet my end.

Hunter continued, but his words sounded muffled in my ears. "What happened so long ago with the demigods may have been unfair and unjust, and that cannot be the case if we wish to progress and keep our existence. After all, the more unity we have here, the more likely mortals are to pray. Harmony in Elysia equates to harmony on Earth."

There was a hum of approval.

"And I understand now that for unity to occur, it means justice must be served." Hunter once again rested his gaze on me. "Therefore, in penance for what occurred, I offer he who killed with wild abandon and continues to show little remorse for all he does. I offer to sacrifice my brother to make amends for the great injustice that was had."

The world around me swayed, and I struggled to breathe. What had he just said?

This was a meeting about my fate, but what Hunter had announced centred on Gray.

My head turned towards my soulbound, who stood next to me looking livid.

"Hunter," Erik said, stepping forward. "You can't be serious." He was wide-eyed, looking up at his eldest brother.

His voice had broken the spell. The minor Gods around us began to clap and cheer. They were getting what they wanted. An eye for an eye, but I couldn't let it happen.

I pulled at the cuffs, needing them off.

"Gray," I said, trying to get his attention.

He didn't look at me, laser focused on Hunter. Two Gods I didn't recognise marched towards us.

"Grayson." The panic coloured my voice.

Gray looked down at me. "I love you."

"No, Gray. Gray, we have to do something."

The Gods reached us and grabbed him by the shoulder. I couldn't fight back. I was powerless in the cuffs.

"Erik! Look after her!" Gray called.

They pushed him through the crowd towards Hunter.

"I won't go down without a fight, brother," Gray said when he reached Hunter.

Hunter grinned. "I wouldn't be so sure of that, Grayson."

"A well-played ambush. I'll give you that. Possibly the smartest thing you've done other than get us all to do your dirty work."

"I hope you've said your goodbyes."

"Gray!" I yelled, trying to get his attention.

He didn't look at me. Why wouldn't he look at me?

Hunter wrapped his aura around Gray, and the full weight of panic hit me.

"Grayson!" I ran towards the dais, but a red tendril caught me, dragging me backwards. "Erik, let me go! Grayson!"

The screams were so loud that my throat grew raw with the effort, and just as Hunter's aura enveloped them, Gray turned to look at me, his fingers moving through the familiar sequence.

One. Four. Three.

EPILOGUE

GRAYSON

The holding cells beneath the council chambers hadn't seen life in eras. After cleansing the heavens of demigods, the space became useless. The council dealt with matters in a less aggressive manner.

Of everything Hunter was capable of, I hadn't expected this. That was my fault. I should have known nothing was beneath him. While I would never regret making Quentin my priority, I should have kept a closer eye on what he was doing. Figured out a way to get close enough that I wouldn't fall prey to an ambush.

"So, are we prolonging this or?" I asked, sounding bored.

"Always to the point, Grayson."

Of course, I was straight to the point. I'd never been so furious in my life and it wasn't just my situation. If this was how things would end for me, then so be it, but I was furious because of Quentin.

I could still hear her screaming my name and see the look on her face as we left the streets. My golden girl, who carried herself with so much strength, looked like everything had been torn away from her. I would never forget that look seared into my brain for however long

I had left.

I wished I could have said more to her before we left, but I needed to make sure that I could keep her safe. Erik would do that for me.

"Well," I said. "If you're intending to kill me, I'd rather you not draw it out."

"Is there ever a point where you'd show some humility?"

"Never in front of you."

Footsteps sounded down the stone steps, hitting the ground before growing louder. Archer emerged from the shadows of the hallway and my rage intensified.

"Happy now? Is this justice for Elara or are you just bitter that Larkin left you and Quentin never wanted you?"

He smirked. "You've been a thorn in my side ever since that day, Grayson. I watch you strutting around like nothing bothers you. It doesn't even faze you that you murdered her. At least this way I don't have to see your face again and Quentin can be safe."

"You are delusional."

Archer's aura struck out at me and I went to call mine before realising I was still bound in copper. The impact of the blow sent me off my feet and across the room. He hit me again, and I endured the pain without being able to defend myself.

"Enough!" Hunter barked.

Archer stopped when he blocked me with his aura. The gold blood that belonged to me seeped from fresh cuts, and I wouldn't heal like normal while under the influence of the cuffs.

"Oh, no," I spat, watching saliva and ichor hit the cobbled floor. "Please continue! Because these actions will bring back your wife, won't they?"

Archer tried to strike out again, but Hunter kept his aura before me as a shield, offering respite from the attack.

"Go home, Archer," he ordered.

"I want to see him pay."

"I said, go home!" Hunter's voice boomed and echoed around the stone cells.

Archer's face fell before wrapping himself in green and leaving us alone once more.

"Do you expect me to thank you?" I asked as Hunter withdrew his aura.

"No. I expect you to cooperate with me."

That response piqued my interest.

Hunter helped me to my feet before pushing me into a cell. He closed the door, and the bars separated us. No longer brothers. Captor and captive.

The bars that were once steel had been replaced, and I shook my head. Copper. The same material that was wrapped around my wrists and neck enclosed me in this space. Hunter was taking no risks. He'd been busy while we ran around trying to gain the favour of the others.

"I don't want to kill you, Grayson," Hunter mused, staring at me.

"I can't say the feeling is mutual."

He snorted a laugh. "However, there is something I want."

"What?"

Hunter cocked his head to the side, looking thoughtful. For a few moments, I thought he was bluffing, wracking his brains for an answer, but when he spoke, it wasn't difficult to see that he had been piecing this plot together for some time.

"I want Quentin."

"What?"

"I want Quentin," he repeated.

The anger boiled in the pit in my stomach, and if I had control of my aura now, Hunter wouldn't have been spared pain. He'd put me behind bars and was telling me he *wanted Quentin*.

"Let me make it clear to you," Hunter said, taking a step back and clasping his hands behind his back. "Quentin Scott holds more value than I originally thought. She represents success. It won't be long before mortals swamp her under the weight of their desires. She already won around most of the Gods. She's completed my project in record time and I am not stupid enough to believe that was without help from her gift. With someone like her at my side, I tick all the boxes. A demigoddess—check. Liked by the Gods—check. Feisty but still breakable—check and check."

I pushed my face against the bar. "You stay the fuck away from her, Hunter."

"But I don't intend to, Grayson."

"She wouldn't look at you twice. She won't do anything you say."

"Oh, she will," he said, a twisted grin stretching across his face. "Because I'm going to offer her something she can't refuse. I'm going to offer her your life."

ACKNOWLEDGMENTS

Alhumdulillah

To the friends and family who gave me so much of their time during this project – it wouldn't have been done without you. I spent months talking and you spent months listening to make sure this project was finished.

For my gorgeous cover and formatting, I am always grateful to work with Books and Moods. The fuzzy images in my head always become something beautiful at your fingertips.

Hi, Zainab! You're not quitting no matter what you said in your notes. Who else could edit my madness the way you do? But I need to thank you for more than the edits this time. In the moments where I've had a crisis of confidence, you picked me up and kept me going. Thanks for putting up with me through the panic, cliffhangers and grammatical errors.

Kendall and Sarah, thank you for taking the time to beta read this book. Your input is invaluable, and I am grateful to have your honesty. I was terrified to let anyone read this book and your kindness helped to eliminate those fears and shape it into its best version.

The more I read over this story the less I wanted anything to do with it, so I have no idea how you managed it, Ellie. From alpha reader to proofreading and everything in between, you saw so many versions of this over the months. For your own sake it might be better to just yeet me into the skip now because how many more times are we going to do this?

My street team! It's safe to say I didn't expect to meet such a wonderful group of people who were so willing to champion my writing. Thank you for all the help you gave in promoting this book. Thank you for the belief in me and my writing.

The last and biggest thanks go out to every single person who read Of Gods & Monsters. The original idea was spawned in the lab during the long hours of my PhD. It evolved over time until I finally had the courage to write it. It surprised me just how many people enjoyed the story and I'm grateful for every message I've received about it. You were the biggest driving force behind Of Truths & Bonds and for that, there aren't enough words of thanks.

Keep in Touch

If you want to keep up to date with all the news on my writing and releases you can follow me on:

Instagram
Facebook Group
Website

www.ingramcontent.com/pod-product-compliance
Lightning Source LLC
Chambersburg PA
CBHW030951190726
48285CB00004BB/1299